DOGGERLAND

HEIDE GOODY

IAIN GRANT

1

"It's trite but true that distance gives you a whole new perspective on things."

It was night. From six miles out at sea, Skegness was a long and blurred strip of light — white, orange, red and blue. A bulge in the strip might have been the fairground, might have been the pier. Slightly nearer, an uneven line of giant wind turbines loomed from the black North Sea, warning lights winking at their bases.

The sports cruiser rocked freely on the rolling waves. The pilot of the boat had to hold the rear rail to stay upright, whereas Bob Ackroyd was more securely seated in a wheelchair, parking brake on, a thick seatbelt holding him in. His eyes darted between the view and the pilot but he didn't speak, on account of the carpet tape across his mouth. He could only listen as the pilot kept up a one-sided conversation.

"Eventually, you get to a point in life — I'm sure you have,

Bob — where you look back at all the things you thought were important in your youth, and you regard them with utter bafflement. The little pleasures you denied yourself, the acts you wouldn't permit. What only seemed right and proper back then seems mad in hindsight. Hmmm?"

The pilot sat down and fitted a pressurised gas tank nozzle into the neck of a weather balloon. The hiss of helium was just audible above the noise of the waves and the low thrum of the nearest turbines.

"When Pat bought a share in this boat, I thought it a ludicrous extravagance. Who'd want a power boat, a cruiser? Very indulgent. And worse still, a power boat round here? It's not exactly Monte Carlo or Cannes." A mist of freezing sea spray washed over them, as though in agreement. "No marina round here to moor up and sip champagne while the sun goes down. I saw it as a foolish dream. Now —" A heavy sigh. "Maybe Pat had it right, enjoying life while one could, making hay while the sun shines. It was mostly for fishing or just messing about on the water. There's a parasailing chute in that box there. Parasailing. Flying above the waves." A laugh. "Can you image Pat doing that? Or me?"

A length of cord secured the neck of the weather balloon. It rose a dozen feet, tugging itself out of the pilot's hand. The line tied to the harness around Bob's chest went taut. He grunted at the sudden pull.

"Of course, you'll be going much higher."

There were four balloons up there now, pulled back and forth by the wind and the boat's movement. The tension around Bob's chest harness was strong now. It occurred to the pilot that it would not do for Bob to be

asphyxiated before he took his maiden flight. The pilot leaned forward and ripped the tape from Bob's lips. Bob gasped.

"You all right?" said the pilot. "Hanging in there?"

"Stop this, please. It's madness."

The pilot gave this due thought. "I'm not really a boat person, it's true. That was always Pat's thing, not mine. I would have sold the boat after Pat died, but it's jointly owned and it seemed more trouble than it was worth. But I got us out here okay, didn't I?"

Bob stared. Frightened, yes, but gobsmacked, unable to believe the situation. "This is crazy."

The pilot looked at the weather balloons above and started to fill a fifth one. "Of course it's crazy. As methods of murder go—"

Bob began to cry, producing a weak keening sound, like a creaky door that would not stop.

The pilot put a hand on his knee to comfort him, to stop him. Bob flinched and flailed with his hands, but they were also bound together with several feet of carpet tape. It was a decidedly pathetic gesture, but at least the noise stopped.

"As methods of murder go, it's ridiculous," continued the pilot and gestured upwards. "Do you know how much that quantity of helium costs? It is not cheap."

"You'll be seen!" blurted Bob.

"And there's that. Even at night, someone might spot half a dozen weather balloons shooting up into the sky. Do the RAF watch the coast round here? I've no idea. But it's that thing about distance and perspective. I hope you were listening. It's not something I care about anymore."

The fifth balloon was attached to the harness. Bob gasped at the additional pull.

"Last one now," said the pilot and crouched to fill the balloon. The sound of the gas was a thought-erasing, thought-freeing white noise. "Joint ownership. Joint enterprise. You do know why you have to die, don't you, Bob?"

"You don't have to do this," he sobbed. "A good joke. It was a good joke. I get it. I'll go. I'll leave Otterside."

"At quite a rate of knots," the pilot agreed. "You didn't keep up your end of the bargain, Bob. We did yours for you and then you refused to carry out your duty. You got cold feet."

"I didn't know..."

"What? You thought it was all a big game of make-believe? No. You owed a debt and refused to pay. You owed us a life, and when you threatened to go to the police. Well."

The sixth balloon was tied to Bob. If the pilot's calculations were right, that was a hundred and eighty pounds of lifting power around his chest. Bob was a man in his late seventies and had lost a lot of weight in recent years. Lifting Bob in his younger years might have required a seventh or even eighth balloon.

The pilot checked the knots. "There. All secured."

Tears and snot were running freely down Bob's face.

"These balloons can reach heights of twenty-four miles," the pilot explained conversationally. "From about six miles up, there really isn't enough oxygen. It will be jolly cold up there too."

"Please. Please, please, please." With the plosive 'p' of

each sobbed "Please", flecks of snot were cast out into the sea.

"Have you ever seen the film *Up*?" asked the pilot.

"What?" said Bob.

"It's really quite heart-warming. A man is widowed in later life and ties hundreds of balloons to his house and flies it away to ... South America I think." The pilot held up a finger to test the wind. "It's northern Europe for you, I reckon. Might get as far as Sweden."

The pilot reached for the seatbelt clip at Bob's waist. Bob fought with his bound hands, pushing away, managing a shove that sent the pilot up against the rear rail.

"Bob!" The pilot's tone was disapproving rather than angry. "None of that silliness!"

"I won't let you," Bob whimpered. He would have been slumped in the chair but for the half dozen balloons hauling him up.

"This is not the way to behave! Now move your hands!" The boat rocked in a swell; the wheelchair slid sideways a foot. The pilot crouched beside the wheelchair. "Lift your hands away." It was said more gently this time.

"I don't want to."

"You're going to. There's nothing else to be done."

Bob didn't move, but the hesitation was evident.

"Anyway, the house sails away," said the pilot.

"What house?"

"In the film. *Up*. It sails away. Quite serenely. Through the blue. And when it comes down, it's in paradise." The pilot gently raised Bob's hands. He didn't resist. "It'll be like that."

"No, it won't," whispered Bob.

The pilot released the seatbelt clip. "No," the pilot agreed, "it won't."

Bob rose, not at speed but with an unarguable certainty, hoisted by the forces of physics. A gasp of shock stole his initial scream. By the time he'd found his breath he was only visible as a series of grey orbs against the night, and an indistinctly wriggling figure. His screams were little more than whispers on the wind.

The pilot continued to watch even when Bob had vanished into the night. Eventually the pilot drove the boat back to shore.

THREE MONTHS LATER...

Polly Gilpin arrived at Otterside Retirement Village in the back of Erin's car. Erin's husband, Cesar, stepped out to open the rear door for Polly, making her feel a bit like the queen, but not enough.

Otterside Retirement Village, a mile to the north of Skegness and on the seaward side of the coast road, was centred around a three storey horseshoe of apartments that dropped to a flat-roofed single storey at the southern end. It was expensive as retirement villages went. Erin had been very clear on that point.

"There should be someone here to meet us," said Erin, taking the opportunity to puff on her e-cig vaping thing. Polly's niece wore a terse, put-out look on her face. Erin was a doctor, a very busy woman – she generally looked terse and put-out. Vaping didn't seem to help her mood, just making her look like a terse and put-out dragon, ready to flame.

Erin walked into reception in search of the expected

reception party while Cesar went to unload the luggage from the boot. When Polly tried to assist him, he waved her away with his soft pudgy hands.

"It's fine, it's fine. I can manage these." He was right. There were only two cases.

Erin came back out, dragging a somewhat bewildered individual with her. He turned out to be the duty manager, a man with the air of someone definitely on their way somewhere else before being roped into being part of the big show of welcoming Polly to her new home.

With Cesar bringing up the rear with the luggage, the manager, Chesney, did a brisk and cheery tour of the facility. The reception area was at the bottom of the horseshoe, with dining hall, various lounges and function rooms branching off from it.

"We have a daily programme of entertainments laid on by management," said Chesney. "And a very active residents social committee."

"My aunt is looking for a bit of peace and quiet," Erin said to Chesney. "She gets confused easily."

Easily confused. It was a point of burning irritation and shame for Polly. Things had taken a turn for the worse over recent months. There had been moments of confusion, unforgiveable slips of memory. She had shouted at that poor boy at the supermarket and alienated some of the neighbours with what she now recognised as abruptly out of character behaviour. Erin had prescribed her some pills and things had calmed down a little, but the shadows of that confusion and shame remained.

"Dementia-like symptoms," Erin said to Chesney.

"Ah." The manager gave her a look of demeaning pity, a look she had seen more and more of late. As though she was some feeble old dear who had lost her marbles. She was only seventy-five – no age at all! – and not deserving of that level of condescension. Not yet, not while she had the eyes and the brain to recognise it for what it was.

However, Otterside itself offered a less patronising attitude. Yes, there were older people everywhere, but it was not the dozing-in-front-of-the-TV brigade she had feared. In the lounge they passed a group of women sitting round a table, talking animatedly as they painted on small canvasses. On the lawn, a dozen people were taking tai chi instructions from a young bald man. In the conservatory area there was loud chatter and raucous laughter from a mixed group.

"There's a bar," she noted.

"We have two," said Chesney cheerily. "Two restaurants also. They're open to the public, but very popular with residents."

"You're not a drinker, Polly," Erin told her.

"I need a new hobby," Polly replied.

"And it's up the wooden hill to Bedfordshire," said Chesney, gesturing for them to follow him up the stairs. "Although we do have a lift." He looked back at Cesar. "You okay there, sir?"

"He's fine," said Erin without pause for input from Cesar.

"You're on the second floor," Chesney explained as they came to the top floor. "It's quieter and the views are better."

"You said this room had only become free in the last week," said Erin.

"That's right."

"Had to do a deep clean, yes?"

Chesney gave her a sideways glance.

"When someone dies here," said Erin, lowering her voice as though people might be listening. "Polly would be pleased to know that you thoroughly cleaned out the—"

"Oh, oh, I see," said Chesney, grinning. "No, Mr Ackroyd. Bob. He didn't die. He left."

"Oh."

"Several weeks ago. We held onto the room in case he returned."

"From hospital?"

Chesney gave her an elevated jiggle of the head; a 'who knows?' gesture. "A bit of a mystery in all honesty. But it's all been put in good order for you, Polly. Here we are."

He unlocked an apartment door and ceremoniously passed Polly the keys.

The apartment was certainly clean, and neatly furnished too. A two-seater sofa in a square fifties style. A small, circular table by the kitchenette. A pendulum cat clock on the kitchenette wall with eyes that ticked from side to side. A modest single bed in the bedroom. The colour scene was bold primary colours against simple white walls, like a holiday villa. Neat, small, modest, simple.

She had lived in a three bedroom house for the last thirty years of her life. To have it suddenly reduced to this was an abrupt shock. It wasn't a holiday villa – it was her new home. This was it.

Cesar put the suitcases down. "You've got a lot in there, Polly," he said with a merry puff of his cheeks.

"Not really," she said, almost to herself. Where were her

bookshelves? Where were her plants? Where was her garden? "I had a big house—" she began.

"We'll leave you to settle in," said Erin. She was already turning to the door.

"You're going? Already?"

Erin blinked at her. "Is there something you need? Do you want us to help unpack?"

"No..."

Erin's mouth twitched, a suggestion of a smile, if only she had time to smile. "We need to get to the bakers in town. Talk about Iris's birthday cake."

Big cake! mouthed Cesar with an idiot grin.

"Yes," said Polly. "I wanted to get her something for the big day."

"Don't worry yourself about that."

"She's seven," Polly said to Chesney.

"Let's not bother the nice man," said Erin. "We'll leave you in peace."

Cesar gave her a wave. As they left, Chesney told her someone would come and do the admin and arrange an induction. And then the three of them were gone. It was her, alone, in the simple and modest apartment.

"Induction," she muttered. "Like I've just joined some sodding cult."

She stood in the little lounge but didn't know what to do there, so she stood in the little bedroom. The shelf beside the window was empty but for an ornamental snow globe. Inside it was a little scene. A frozen lake with a bare tree leaning over it. On the ice, two skating figures executed in poorly detailed plastic. A boy and a girl.

Polly gave it a shake. Snow swirled round the silent scene.

She looked at her new home.

"This is it then," she said and, because that didn't seem to quite encapsulate it, added an emphatic "Shit!" for good measure.

2

_____

"**R**egional support and dispersement."

Sam Applewhite sat up, nearly tipping herself from her office chair in the process. She had been on hold to DefCon4's head office for fifteen minutes before her call was picked up. This was possibly a new record for speed.

"Hi, this is Sam Applewhite, Skegness," she said. "I need some help with the tasks on my app."

"*This is regional support and dispersement,*" came a woman's voice. "*You need technical support.*"

"Wait, wait, don't hang up," she said, sensing the woman's hand drifting to the disconnect button. "I don't think there's a problem. I just have a problem with this task."

DefCon4, an amorphous national corporation that had started out as a security cash transportation firm before branching out into 'we'll do anything as long as you pay us' territory, directed its staff through its own bespoke phone app. Sam's day was controlled by a series of messages dropped onto her calendar by mysterious agents at some other office.

"It says I need to collect a mammoth."

"Pardon?"

Sam looked at her phone and read out the task in full. "Twenty-fourth of November. Pick up mammoth specimen from Professor Springer at Humber College of Sciences and transport to LRPC research centre. Specimen is not permitted to defrost. Consult training course C11B43 for temperature-controlled transport, blah, blah, blah."

"Mammoth?"

"Well, yes, that was my thought. Mammoth?"

"And it definitely says mammoth?"

"I maybe wonder if the admin at head office who entered the details had..."

"Had what?"

"I don't know. Succumbed to a medical emergency and fallen face-first on their keyboard." There was no other logical explanation.

She'd already used the keyboard of the desktop computer to test her theory. Falling on the keys to spell *mammoth* wasn't easy to picture when she looked at where the keys were placed.

"I also tried it on my phone to see if it was an autocorrect thing."

"And?"

"It's fine. It even suggests a jaunty elephant emoji to accompany it."

The kettle in the corner of the office clicked off and Sam

went to pour herself a hot chocolate. Crappy autumn days called for hot chocolate.

"*Mutton specimen?*" suggested the woman.

"Mammary specimen?" Sam countered, stirring the cup.

"*Mammal specimen?*"

"It doesn't sound much better."

The woman made a thoughtful noise. "*Maybe you should ask your office administrator. They could look into it.*"

"Yes," said Sam. "However, Niamh our administrator isn't here."

"*Well, when she gets back...*"

"I think she's off ill. That's what I was told."

"*And are you expecting her back soon?*"

Sam shrugged. "I don't know. Never met her."

"Oh, you're new?"

"Eight months into the job."

"*Long term sick, I see. Your regional manager should be able to deal with it.*"

"Bob Newitt. Yeah, he's not here either. Not a hundred percent sure if he ever started."

"*The previous manager?*"

"Left before I arrived. I think."

"*Perhaps one of your colleagues knows who's covering in their absence.*"

Sam looked round the room. Four desks, all empty apart from hers. Well, one of the desks had a little name plaque on it for a Doug Fredericks. There had also been a cactus on the desk, which she had called Doug. Doug had been the closest thing she'd had to a colleague. His nameplate remained, but the cactus standing in for an actual human had met an unfortunate (and unlikely) end when it was rammed down the throat of a violent intruder. Sam liked to think Doug had sacrificed himself to save her, but she missed their chats. She would get another plant one day. She was sure Doug would understand.

"*Well, I suppose you will have to go to this—*"

"Humber College of Sciences."

"*—and collect whatever it is. Do you have something to collect it in?*"

"Well, that brings me to another matter," said Sam. "We've had a parcel arrive."

"*We?*"

"I. I had a parcel arrive."

She looked at the big delivery box resting on one of the empty desks. Next to it, surrounded by polystyrene packing chips, was the box's contents. Another box.

"I've got a box here, one of those oversized picnic box things. It says 'Human organs in transit' on the side."

"*Oh,*" said the woman, interested. "*What've you got that for?*"

"Well," said Sam. "I have two theories. One is that it's empty, and that at some point I'm going to be asked to do transplant organ delivery for DefCon4. Or mammoth specimens. Whatever. I hope it's not actual organs. I should tell you that's not something I plan to get into. For one, I don't have anywhere to store organs here."

"*I'd be surprised if you did.*"

"My second theory is that the box does indeed contain human organs in transit."

"*Have you looked?*"

"No, and I don't want to. I am not going to be held responsible for the state of whatever's inside."

"I could try and find out for you," said the woman.

"That's lovely," said Sam. "But it doesn't help me understand what this actual task is—" She stopped. The woman had already put her on hold.

"Damn it all," she said to herself. She would have said it louder if there was anyone to hear. She missed Doug.

Her phone buzzed. Another call coming through. It was her friend, Delia.

"Morning," said Sam.

"He's been murdered," said Delia.

"What?"

"Definitely murdered."

As conversation openers went, it was a unique one. Maybe it was a morning for odd conversations. "Murdered?" said Sam.

"I know it sounds silly, but it's true."

"Sorry," said Sam. "Who?"

"Drumstick!" said Delia, as though it was the most self-evident thing in the world.

Sam tried to process this.

"I need you to come over with your stuff and, you know, solve it," said Delia.

Sam tried to process this as well. She could just about make the leaps of logic to make sense of her friend's words. Delia ran a junk shop in the town and, against all odds, was the most recent winner of Skegness and District Businessperson of the Year. She was also one of the few friends Sam had made since returning to the town.

"I've got to go to this college in the next hour but I..." She stopped herself. "Of course, I'll come over." There was little else a friend could say. She hung up and prepared to leave.

"Right, mammoth transportation," she said. With no better container to use, she opened the 'Human organs in transit' box. It was deep, with a weighty lid and a solid plastic carrying handle. It was – thankfully, naturally – empty. Assuming she had to move something frozen, and hoping it wasn't a whole mammoth, this would probably do.

She recalled images of whole mammoth carcasses being dug up from the Siberian tundra or some such place. A dead mammoth, even one crushed and squished by centuries in the ice, would not be going in the back of her tiny Italian work van.

"And I'm not even going to bother trying to download the frozen goods training," she told Doug's nameplate. "I'll just end up spending an hour fighting the logon system and the company network."

The decision to completely ignore the frozen goods training was a pragmatic one, based on her knowledge of DefCon4's labyrinthine IT systems and nonsensical documentation. Besides, if the training suggested more advanced equipment was needed than this box, she would not be able to requisition it either. The requisition of equipment was a workflow process requiring sign-off by the most senior local person. That she was the most senior local person (and therefore not permitted to authorise her own requests) had proven to be an immovable blocker that she'd never found a way past.

With an empty box, a pick-up address and more wishful thinking than confidence, she set out for the day.

DELIA'S HOUSE was a ten minute drive through town and out the other side. Skegness: the jewel in the crown of the flat and featureless Lincolnshire coastline. The largest seaside resort for a hundred miles in either direction. A lurid kaleidoscope of amusement arcades, fairgrounds, deckchairs, donkeys, and fish and chips. Even on a cold morning, people were already out on the promenade, wrapped up snugly. To an individual, they were either in search of a morning fix of caffeine, sugar or alcohol, or taking a bracing walk along the front to justify one.

Delia's house was a small semi-detached on the outskirts of town, with a crop of abandoned toys in the front garden and the world's smallest poultry farm in the back. Sam parked her three-wheeler Piaggio on the driveway and rang the doorbell.

When Delia answered the door, Sam could see she had been crying. Not a lot, but she'd been crying.

"Hey," said Sam and hugged her.

From inside came the sound of playfully squabbling children's voices trying to compete in volume with a television turned up loud.

"Come see the crime scene." Delia smiled briefly and with difficulty, to show she was joking, or at least trying to.

Sam picked her way through a hallway littered with shoes, dropped coats, bags of partially emptied shopping and the other detritus of a young family struggling to get its act together. The back garden was long and narrow. Halfway down, a run had been constructed from old pallets and wire fencing, and a tall turkey padded about inside. It cocked a beady eye at Sam as they approached.

"Twizzler's okay?"

Delia nodded and wiped her nose with a tissue. "He's down. He knows something is up."

"Christmas," said Sam to herself because she couldn't help it.

"Twizzler was always the quiet one. Never up to greet the dawn. I think Drumstick thought he was meant to be a cockerel."

"And where is Drumstick?"

Delia gestured to the other side of the garden path. A black bin liner had been laid over a mound on the earth. Sam crouched and flicked it aside. The turkey was laid on its back, its eyes half-lidded. There was dried blood in the creases of its knobbly head.

"You found him like this?"

"No, he was in the run. But I couldn't leave him there. Have I contaminated the crime scene?"

Sam looked up at Delia and said, as kindly as possible, "I don't actually tend to do turkey murders, Delia."

Delia tucked a strand of her untidy hair behind her ear. "But you can, can't you? You've got equipment and stuff."

"I'm hardly *CSI: Poultry Division*."

"You think this is funny?"

Sam tutted, at herself. "No. I don't. It's just ... animals die, don't they? It could have been a fox, or a stoat, or even a cat." She looked at the size of the bird. "Okay, maybe not a cat."

Delia was shaking her head. She lifted a length of wood from the borders. It had a dark red mark on it and an obvious splatter pattern. "A fox? With a plank?"

"Maybe it fell over accidentally. Was it windy last night?"

"It was leaning by the back door."

The back door was twenty feet from the turkey run. That would have to be some wind.

Sam glanced around at the house, the side gate, the trees of the neighbour's garden visible over one fence, the second and third floor apartments of the retirement village visible over the other. "Not a fox. Not an accident."

"No," agreed Delia firmly.

"But who would want to murder a turkey?"

s she unpacked her things, Polly Gilpin intermittently watched the women from her bedroom window. It gave her a clear view of the garden. It was the principal view from her apartment. The garden was littered with toys, muddied and abandoned things. She could imagine the kinds of children who lived there – delightful wild tearaways with uncombed hair and jam-smeared mouths. Children as children should be.

She looked at the photos of Jack and Iris, her great nephew and great niece, which she'd placed on the dressing table. School photos; rigid, formal.

There was something energetic and urgent about the women's manner. The one with untidy blonde hair seemed fraught, on edge. The other one – younger, more measured – was striding about keenly observing this and that. Maybe she was looking for something lost. Dropped keys perhaps.

Polly was tempted to open the window to try to hear

them, but she suspected the distance was too great, and the autumn wind would whip away the sound and blow unpleasantly into the apartment. The lives of people outside Otterside retirement village were distant things now, inaccessible.

Deciding she would inevitably have to go and explore this new world of hers, Polly put on a vibrant pink cardigan (chosen to dispel her mood and the gloom of the season) and, with the one book she had brought with her under her arm, went out.

"A little bird tells me that you're Polly Gilpin," said a voice beside her as she walked down the stairs. A man had fallen into step with her, roughly her age, a square-jawed man in a hat.

"Why would a bird tell you that?" she said, stiffly. "Seems a rather boring thing for a bird to tell you."

He laughed. It was a rough, throaty laugh, like at some point he'd had a heavy smoking habit. "Birds are bloody stupid, ain't they?" he said. "Tweet bloody tweet." He had a southern accent, estuary English maybe, *Tweet bladdy tweet.*

They'd reached the bottom floor. He turned to face her with such confidence she felt compelled to mirror him. His hat was a black trilby with a striped band round it. He was handsome in a rough sort of way, although any facial symmetry was countered by a fading strawberry birthmark on his upper cheek. Polly didn't care about birthmarks, but she wasn't sure how she felt about men who wore hats indoors.

"Course I know you're Polly Gilpin," he said. "What I'm trying to do, in my humble way is introduce myself and ask if you'd like to take a walk around the gardens with me this morning."

She frowned. "But I hardly know you," she said honestly.

"Hence the introductions and the walk around the gardens." He smiled with a set of nice white teeth that were quite possibly his own.

"But why?" she said.

He nodded at the book she carried. "Cos the alternative is just sitting and reading."

"I like books."

"As do I, as do I. More of a papers man meself. But even lady bookworms might like a bit of variety. Besides, the doctor says I got to do ten thousand steps a day, and I don't like doing them alone."

She was still doubtful.

"Don't worry, princess," he said. "I'm not one of them sexual predators or nothing. Chance'd be a fine thing. They've got me on so many prostate tablets, Little Strawb's been knocked into a permanent coma."

"Strawb?" she said.

He grinned again. A seventy-something with teeth as good as his would take every opportunity to show them. He held out his hand. "Mike Fisher, but my friends call me Strawb."

She took his hand and shook. "Strawb because...?" she said without meaning to.

He poked the large birthmark. "That's right. Funny. Most people never notice."

4

Sam considered the possibilities in the death of Drumstick.

DefCon4, despite what Delia or her dad might say, did not do murder investigations. DefCon4 had contracts with various police forces for crime scene evidence management, appropriate adult and medical services for people in custody, prisoner transportation and post-release offender management, but it generally left the crime-solving to actual police officers. However, Sam had watched enough detective shows to pick up some basics.

"Means. Motive. Opportunity."

"I think the means is fairly obvious," said Delia, gesturing to the plank.

"The murder weapon, yes," Sam replied. "But there was also the means of getting in."

She paced the garden and inspected the fence. Despite the general air of chaos about Delia's home, the garden was secure and the fences high. An athletic individual could haul themselves over, although the slatted garden fences would potentially break under the weight of an adult. The only other ways into the garden were through the house or the garden gate.

Sam inspected the gate. There was a bolt on the inside, with a latch handle of hooped iron. It was currently unlocked. "You bolt this gate?"

"It should always be bolted," said Delia. There was sufficient doubt in her voice.

"Bolted or not?"

"Bolted. I'm a certain percent certain."

"And it happened in the night?"

"Between me putting them to bed and this morning when..." Delia looked to the sky and clutched her chest to forestall more tears.

Sam looked at the top of the gate and imagined an unfolded coat hanger being slipped over the top and hooked through the bolt or some other burglar's trick. "And that's definitely your plank?"

Delia blinked at the blood-stained board. "Why wouldn't it be?"

Sam shrugged. "I don't know, I'm just wondering — if they intended to kill the turkey, why didn't they bring their own murder weapon?"

"Crime of passion? Heat of the moment?"

"Why would anyone want to kill a turkey anyway? Someone with objections to you raising them for Christmas? An angry vegan? No, that doesn't work."

"We never said that these were going to be anyone's

Christmas dinner," said Delia firmly. "After this upset, young Twizzler is going nowhere."

Sam shook her head. "The motive is just not there. The means and the opportunity. It seems straightforward, but it doesn't add up. If only there was a witness."

Delia stepped aside and gestured plainly at Twizzler. The turkey made a 'blobble-obble' noise and pecked at an orange bucket of feed.

"A witness who can talk, perhaps," Sam suggested kindly.

Delia hmphed.

Sam looked at the windows of the Otterside retirement village. At least two of the second floor apartments had a view of the garden unobstructed by trees. And was that a CCTV camera on the side of the building? If she was supremely lucky, it might even be a DefCon4 camera.

"Right, I've got work this afternoon. A mammoth to collect."

"A what?"

"Exactly. But this investigation will continue. And..." Sam gestured to the covered corpse of Drumstick. "I'll take the body away."

"For forensic analysis," nodded Delia.

"Sure. Yeah."

"Thanks. That means a lot," Delia sniffed and her expression suddenly brightened. "Hey, I've got something for you."

"Oh?"

"An early Christmas present."

She nipped into the kitchen for a moment and came out

with a dinky plant pot, holding a small but perky powder puff cactus.

"A replacement for Doug," she said.

"A Doug Junior."

"No one should work alone. You need a colleague."

Sam took the young cactus. "More of an apprentice," she said. "That's lovely."

It was a touching gesture. It made Sam feel guilty that when Delia had mentioned forensic analysis of the turkey, her mind had already gone to cranberry sauce and stuffing and all the trimmings of Christmas dinner.

5

P olly and Strawb walked a route that roughly followed the perimeter of the Otterside property. He pointed out the main features of the retirement village: the swimming pool, the outbuildings, the path to the gate that led to the beach, the pitch and putt course.

"Pitch and putt?" she said, staring at the overgrown lawn of weeds. "At a care home?"

"Retirement village, not care home," said Strawb. "Big distinction. And yes, there used to be a pitch and putt out there. Lost in the mists of facking time." His accent seemed to bloom when he swore. "Like everything here. Otterside, out of mind."

It was a weak pun, but she smiled anyway.

To her surprise she found Strawb to be exceedingly good company. He had an obvious charm, a working class lad happy with his place in the world. As they continued their walk, he rolled his shoulders, filled with a restless energy, as though merely walking was too little for him. He was an outgoing man, yet he didn't dominate the conversation. He guided it, he nudged, but let her do all the talking.

She was saying something about her late sister (though she couldn't remember how they'd gotten onto the topic) when Strawb pointed at the trees ahead. "Look. A robin."

She peered at the undergrowth and saw a flash of brown and orange.

"I bladdy love robins," said Strawb. "Cheeky buggers they are."

"They're used to human company."

"Scavengers."

"Our mum used to say they were Father Christmas's spies, checking if we've been good."

"Like I say, cheeky buggers. And have you been good this year, Polly?"

"I was never a good girl," she said with feeling.

Strawb laughed. "You know what," he said, gesturing at the little-used lawn around them. "We should have something out here. Games and stuff."

"I don't think I was ever a fan of pitch and putt," she said.

"What about some crazy golf, eh?" He grinned. "Everyone loves a bit of crazy golf."

Polly would have disagreed except, reflecting on the matter, she had always found the game whimsically diverting.

"I know a bloke who could sort us out. Fact, I saw Ragnar's van up at the car park. Shall we do that, Poll? Bit of crazy golf to put a smile on your face?"

She stopped and gave him a somewhat stern look. "Is this

what you do, Mr Fisher? Whisk women away from the comfort of the day room and bedazzle then with promises of crazy golf?"

He thought on it. "That'd be a bladdy weird thing to do, wouldn't it? Nah, I'm on the social committee. Me and Margaret and Jacob. It's our job to think up ways of staving off the endless boredom. Got to keep the new blood entertained or they'll just up sticks and leave, like Bob who used to have your apartment."

"Oh, he actually left of his own accord?" she said.

"Yes. Why? What did you—?"

"My niece and the manager—"

"Chesney."

"Yes. They were talking about it. I just assumed it was code for him having died."

Strawb barked with laughter. Polly was less amused.

"People seem to talk in code a lot these days," she said. "Like if they're a little vague and give little secret winks, I won't know what they're talking about. My niece seems to think just because I have symptoms of dementia, I've gone completely do-lally."

"And do you?"

"Have dementia?" She stared blankly for a moment. "I've behaved oddly. I swore horribly at the poor young man in the supermarket. I gave him the 'V's as well."

"Did he deserve it?" asked Strawb.

"I honestly don't recall."

"Well, you don't look in the least bit do-lally to me, Polly."

"Oh, your medical opinion is clearly one I should listen to. My niece gave me some tablets."

He pointed ahead. "Here, let's ask Jacob what he thinks about your crazy golf idea." He strode over to where a small man in round glasses was apparently inspecting the quality of the perimeter fence. "Oi, Jacob," called Strawb. "What do you reckon, eh?"

"What's that?" said Jacob. He had his shirt done up to the top button though he wore no tie. He had a shiny well-pressed air about him. He looked like a mint-in-the-box little old man toy.

"Crazy golf over 'ere," said Strawb. "We could get Ragnar to build it."

"Golf causes more sporting injuries than rugby," said Jacob.

"But this is just crazy golf."

"Forty thousand people are hospitalised each year by flying golf balls."

"I'm not hearing a no," said Strawb. He turned to draw Polly into the discussion. "Polly thinks it's a marvellous idea."

"Oh, do I?" she said.

6

Back in her Piaggio Ape 50 van, poor dead Drumstick was temporarily stored in the organ box with two packs of frozen peas from Delia's freezer on top. She would use these to keep the mammoth specimen cool. Sam re-checked her task list on the company app. The mammoth task hadn't magically disappeared. Well, the only thing to do was to go to the Humber College address and collect the package from this Professor Springer.

She placed her new cactus on the dashboard and pinned him in place with a lump of Blu-Tack that was stuck to the dash for just such situations. "Welcome to the team, Doug," she said.

Doug Junior was a quiet sort and didn't actually respond, but she sensed a silent optimism in him that spoke of his intentions to make the best of his new role.

Her app's suggested travel time from Skegness to the Humber College of Sciences was another example of

DefCon4's loose grasp of reality. The college was in Hessle, just outside of Hull, sixty miles north and on the other side of the Humber estuary. Her app gave her an hour and a half to make the journey, which would have been perfectly reasonable if the company had provided her with an ordinary vehicle. However, the Piaggio Ape 50, a beautiful piece of low-cost, three-wheeled Italian engineering, was a tiny van with a top speed of little more than thirty miles an hour.

She pootled unhurriedly north, out from the flat coast, through the rolling hills and scattered villages of the Lincolnshire Wolds – Wold Newton, Ashby cum Fenby, Riby, Swallow – before reaching the wide Humber. The one and half mile suspension bridge linking Lincolnshire with East Yorkshire had toll booths at the northern end. The man in the booth looked out at Sam and scowled.

"What?" she said.

"Is it a car or a motorbike?" he said.

"It's a van," she said, with a high-pitched defensiveness she didn't necessarily feel.

"Van's cost even more."

"It's a motorbike," she said.

"Right-o," he said. He nodded at the 'organs in transit box' beside her on the passenger seat. "You got organs in there?"

"Huh? No. It's empty. I'm on my way to make a collection."

"High pressure job."

She shrugged. "As long as I get it back to Skegness before it defrosts, it's fine."

The man might have engaged her further but she'd handed over her coins. The barrier was up and she drove on.

As she followed the sat-nav round a looping road that circled beneath the bridge, Sam's phone rang. It was her dad, Marvin. "You okay, dad?"

"What kind of way is that to start a conversation?" he said amiably.

"Just asking if you were okay."

"What you were doing," said Marvin, *"was assuming I couldn't be left alone for a day without doing myself some mischief. A heart attack while watching* Loose Women."

"Why? Does *Loose Women* cause your heart to race?"

"Or a fall down the stairs."

"You live in a bungalow."

"May the gods of light entertainment save us from facetious children. There are stairs in this house."

He was right. *Duncastin'*, the bungalow home he currently shared with Sam, was a sprawling centipede of a house and probably had more individual steps than a normal house.

"Also, the implication – which wounds me deeply – is that I would only phone you if I was in trouble or needed help."

"Sorry, dad," she said. "What is it?"

"I wondered if you could pop to the shops for me."

"So you do need my help."

"Hush now. Just to pick something up for dinner. Something light. Chicken. Fish."

"I'm on my way to Hull."

"You don't have to go to the docks to get it. Just a little something. We've got a guest for dinner."

"Who?"

"Tez."

"Who's Tez?"

"A lovely chap. Thought you should meet him."

The fear that her dad was trying to fix her up with a man gripped her. This wasn't normal behaviour from any parent, but he had been suggesting she might be lonely in their little seaside home, and that she hadn't had a boyfriend since she'd split up with Rich.

"Just a little chance to meet him before we have a chat man to man."

"Er..."

"Fish then?"

"I'm busy at the moment," she said and hung up.

She gave Doug Junior a look. "That wasn't what I think it was, was it?" she said, adding, "Careful. He might try to set me up with you next."

Humber College of Sciences was on a side road, down a turning beside a large supermarket. The college was a square modern building in open parkland. She went to reception, but they had some difficulty locating her contact, Professor Springer. A few minutes after Sam rang the phone number she had been given, a breathless young man appeared in reception and smiled at her.

"Hi, you phoned me?" He waved her over to a seating area.

"Professor Springer?" Sam asked.

"Ah, yes. Very nearly."

"Nearly how?"

"Professor Springer is more of a concept than an actual

person. The figurehead we use for some of our project work. I'm sure you know how it is."

"Not really sure I do," said Sam.

"Don't worry about it. If it makes it easier for you to call me Professor Springer, then please do." He mimed air quotes around Professor Springer.

"Are you engaged in something illegal?" asked Sam. DefCon4 had policies for Insider Trading and Modern Slavery, but she was certain there had to be something covering 'generally dodgy stuff' if she looked.

"No, not at all," said Springer, looking shocked. "There's a world of difference between what might pass as legal and what is acceptable in academic circles, though."

Sam waited for him to expand on this.

He sighed. "Sometimes our research grants don't cover all of the costs that we incur. So we are obliged to get creative in terms of sourcing alternative revenue streams."

"What is the research you've been doing?" Sam asked.

"Microbial evolution in Northern Canada between prehistory and the present day," said Springer. "It doesn't attract big grants."

"You surprise me."

"It's gone way over budget, but there's a lot of interest in our findings, so we're keen to see it through to the end. If we need to monetise some of our assets, then who can blame us?"

"So, to be clear," said Sam. "The asset that you plan to monetise is...?"

"A frozen sample of mammoth tissue," said Springer.

"And to doubly clarify. That's mammoth as in..." She did a little mime meant to represent tusks and a trunk.

He nodded enthusiastically. "*Mammuthus primigenius.* Haven't you been briefed? It needs specialised transportation."

She raised the organ transit box she carried. "Yeah, I assumed the mammoth part was a typo. I should be fine with the equipment that I have – as long as it's not the whole mammoth."

"No, you're fine. Just a chunk of ol' Ethel." He mimed an approximate size with his hands, something like a shoebox. "Shall we go and make the transfer?"

Sam followed him out to the car park. He led the way to an aged Volvo and opened the boot. He had a cooler in there that looked a little bit like Sam's, except this one had a power cord snaking away to somewhere in the car. He opened the lid and indicated a pinkish, shrink-wrapped lump.

"It just looks like meat," said Sam. "How is that even possible? Mammoths died out, like, ten thousand years ago."

"Ethel here was trapped in the permafrost, so it is exactly like a piece of frozen meat, yes."

Sam had mixed feelings. On the one hand, this highly specialised transport job was essentially on the same level as a supermarket trip; but on the other, she was tasked with the care of something that was ten thousand years old but looked like it had been prepared for a Sunday roast.

"Can I ask you a question?" asked Sam, as she opened up the back of her van. "Why didn't we do this in your office?"

Springer looked suddenly shifty. "If you recall, there are some elements of this that I would like to remain confidential. If the establishment where I work were to see me doing this, they might—"

"Wait. This isn't even your college?" Sam asked, incredulous.

"Well ... no. This is a sixth form college. A levels and such. I work ... elsewhere."

After a moment she shrugged. Whatever ethical dilemmas faced Springer, they were not hers to worry about. She had a simple transportation job. She transferred the mammoth chunk into her organ box. The bags of frozen peas were cool to the touch but no longer frozen.

"Is that your temperature controlled transport system?" said Springer.

"Yes," she said neutrally.

"Why have you got a dead – I'm gonna say turkey – in there?"

"It's been a busy day," she said. "Do you care?"

"Not really," said Springer and wandered off.

He was right though. Two packs of semi-frozen peas and a dead turkey were not going to keep the sample solidly frozen.

There had been a supermarket on the road back to the bridge. She put the lid on the organ box and drove.

She parked and went into the shop. There was a large frozen food section in the back corner. There were lots of frozen goods. but appeared to be no actual ice. Maybe it was a seasonal thing. Sam had to decide which of the frozen items would be a good substitute. She had several factors to take into account. One was cost, as she would be paying for this herself. The second was whether she could eat it later in the day: it would need to be something both she and her father would enjoy. The third was the vague concern some things might somehow be better at retaining the cold than others. It was obvious that a frozen chicken was a massive block of coldness that would stay that way for many hours, whereas ice cream would melt quickly. Why was that? There must be a scientific scale she could apply, but she wasn't sure what it was. Did the cold from the ice cream move into its surroundings? If so, it might be better at keeping the mammoth cold. Sam suspected that wasn't the answer.

"You wanna close that door. You're letting all the cold out," said a nosey shopper as she trundled by.

Sam closed the door and stared through the glass. Sausage rolls seemed like a strong possibility. The pack was flexible, so she could wrap the mammoth up in chunks of coldness, then she could cook them all when she got home. She would probably need two packets of thirty six mini sausage rolls. That was a lot of sausage rolls to eat over the coming days. She could invite Delia round and make an event of it. She wasn't sure what sort of event would involve eating a ludicrous number of sausage rolls, but if she threw in some cocktails it might seem like an actual thing.

She grabbed two bags from the freezer.

"Those are three for two," said the nosey shopper. "You need another one."

"No, I'm fine," said Sam. Her phone rang. It was her dad again. "Yes."

"You don't know the question yet," said Marvin.

"I'm in the middle of something."

"Look, you've got to have three," said the shopper. "Third one's free."

"It's about that fish... I just needed to check whether you could or you couldn't."

"Busy, dad."

"Sorry. Still in Hull?"

She nodded. "In a supermarket. In Hull."

"Oh, well, if you're already in the supermarket..."

The shopper had opened the cabinet and presented Sam with a third bag of sausage rolls.

"I don't want three," said Sam.

"But it's free. It only makes sense."

"I only need two."

"What's that?" said Marvin.

"Someone wants me to get three for two sausage rolls."

"I'm not thinking a finger buffet. More a light, cultured supper. Some white fish, some greens."

"Don't you want them?" said the shopper.

"I'm happy with two," said Sam.

"I mean if you're buying the sausage rolls and they're three for two..." said Marvin.

"If you don't want them, I'll come to the till with you and you can give them to me," said the shopper.

"I'm not buying you sausage rolls!" said Sam.

"You might as well get them," said Marvin. *"Makes economic sense."*

"They're not costing you nothing," said the shopper.

Sam growled and snatched the bag from the interfering woman.

"*Got to be money smart these days,*" said Marvin. "*Tez is good with money. We need to make a good impression.*"

"Do we?"

"*So get the sausage rolls, and maybe some monkfish or pollock. Oh and some asparagus.*"

"I'm not buying asparagus! I haven't got time."

Sam stalked towards the tills, searching savagely in the freezer compartments for something to satisfy her dad's demands en route.

"Am I getting those free sausage rolls or not?" the shopper called after her.

Sam paid, ran towards the van and jumped into the driver's seat.

"Right!" she declared angrily and set about creating a cold space for the mammoth sample. She hoiked the mammoth chunk and turkey out, put in a layer of sausage rolls, placed the mammoth on it, surrounded and layered it with yet more sausage rolls, then crowned it with several white fish fillets from the chiller cabinet.

There was no longer any room for Drumstick, who had to be placed with very little ceremony in a bag in the back.

"There's sixty miles to Skegness," she said to Doug Junior. "We've got a chunk of frozen mammoth, a hundred and eight sausage rolls, it's starting to rain and my hands smell of fish. Let's hit it."

Doug Junior wobbled on his dashboard pedestal as she drove.

At the Humber Bridge there were three toll booths open, but a man leaned out of one to wave her forward. It was the toll collector she'd seen coming over. "Is that it?" he said, nodding with evident excitement at the box.

"Er, yes."

"I mentioned it to Humberside Police boys."

"You what?"

"Bit of a hurry, yes?"

"Well, yes, but…"

He leaned further out of his booth, resting one hand on the roof of her van and waved again. "This is her, lads!"

"What's going on?" Sam said.

"Police escort."

"What?"

"Skegness, yes?"

"What?"

"No charge either," he grinned.

Sam really didn't know what to say. She really, really didn't.

The barrier went up. She drove through onto the four-lane bridge. Seconds later, a police pursuit car slipped in front of her and a second slotted in behind her. Their blue lights flashed although there were no sirens.

She considered it was probably the most ostentatious escort ever given to a lump of meat, a ton of sausage rolls and some cold fish. It was surreally pleasant, but she had no idea what she was going to say to them when they got to their final destination.

The delivery address was along Drummond Road in Skegness. The app said it was the LRPC Research Centre. Skegness was the centre for many exciting things, but not for any kind of research. Unless it was along the lines of 'How much money can one kid feed into a slot machine in an hour?' or 'How many vodka shots does it take to get a hen party from Worksop paralytic?'

Drummond Road, one street back from the sea front, featured a mix of second-rate pubs and shops, suburban family homes, and small hotels shoehorned into spare plots of land. Every once in a while (especially on the corners) there might be a surprisingly grandiose building, with turrets and balconies. Sam's precise delivery address was one of these grander buildings, a seemingly abandoned hotel. There were ornate gateposts, a driveway car park looping around a defunct fountain covered in coppery rust, and a cracked white façade that looked one winter storm away from crumbling entirely.

The old hotel's name, a rather unimaginative *Hotel Splendid*, was just about legible as a series of faded marks across the crenelated roof top. A much smaller plastic sign had been placed immediately above the door: *LRPC RESEARCH CENTRE – MAKING TOMORROW'S FUTURE NOW – TODAY!*

"Okay, Doug," said Sam, pulling up. "Skegness is the centre of scientific research. Who knew?"

Two police cars pulled in beside her. A chunky cop poked his head out of one. "I thought this was a transplant thingy. Aren't we going to a hospital?"

Sam lifted the box as she got out. "Research samples," she said, deciding not to mention the sausage rolls and fish.

"It isn't an emergency?"

"Maybe it's the cure for a disease."

"Like polio," he nodded.

"Or one they haven't cured yet," she suggested.

While he talked to his colleague and reported back to base on the radio, Sam climbed the steps and went inside.

The foyer belonged in a magazine, or a Christmas movie. It had a mosaic tiled floor (missing a few tiles), a high ceiling, and a staircase with an ornamental balustrade that wound around the sides. A huge dusty chandelier hung down in the centre of the space.

There was no one at the reception desk.

"Hello!" Sam called. "Anyone here? Someone order a frozen mammoth?"

A man appeared at the curve of the stairs and paused for

a moment, surprised, before approaching. He was short, and from his firm jaw and brown skin appeared to have some Polynesian ancestry. He wore a thin pencil moustache and a black double-breasted suit with shiny buttons. He looked suspiciously like a butler.

"I think I'm meant to be delivering this?" Sam said.

"DefCon4?" he said.

"That's us. Me. That's me."

He nodded in understanding and gestured for her to follow. They went up the impressive sweeping staircase and then up a far less grand set of uncarpeted stairs to the second floor, where the man flung open a set of double doors to what might be the only furnished apartments in the otherwise neglected building.

The main lounge was richly furnished, with a balcony view over the beach and the North Sea. Even though it was a grey and dreary November day, the balcony doors were opened wide to let in the sea air. A man stood at the balcony, cocktail glass in hand.

"Rich?" said Sam.

Rich Raynor turned. "Sam! How lovely to see you!"

Was he surprised to see her? He didn't look surprised.

"What the hell are you doing here?" she said.

"I own it," he said, taking in everything with a wave of his hand.

"Skegness?"

"This hotel!"

"And LRPC?"

"Is me!"

Richard Raynor could loosely be described as Sam's ex,

although it had been a long time since they were together. He could also be described as a millionaire businessman, but Sam rejected that label because Rich was so much more than that. And so much less. Yes, millionaire. Yes, inventor of some silly dog poo gizmo that had sold millions. Also international playboy, 24/7 party creature, non-stop man-child. At this moment he was annoying, definitely annoying.

"What the hell's going on?"

He gestured at the organ box and made a face of childlike wonder. "Is that for me?"

"You ordered a lump of frozen mammoth flesh?"

"I certainly did. Peninsula, please."

The butler stepped forward to take the container from her. Sam was too surprised by Rich's presence to pay any attention as the box was whisked away.

"I'm just using this place as my base of operations for a few weeks," said Rich. "I've got somewhere much more fun that I plan to move into shortly."

"Where's that?" asked Sam.

"I'll show you as soon as it's fit to make a visit," he said, with an exaggerated wink.

"Sir!" came a shout from somewhere in the apartment.

Rich sighed. "He's meant to come when I call, not the other way round," he said blithely. "Come take a look."

She followed him through several rooms to one of stainless steel work surfaces and cabinets: half restaurant kitchen, half laboratory. On a worktop, the butler had opened the cooler box.

"What is it, Peninsula?" said Rich. Then he saw and looked at Sam. "Sausage rolls?"

"Underneath," said Sam. "That's my fish too. Yeah, I had an issue with the cooling. I'll be eating a great many sausage rolls in the near future."

"We can cook some now if you like?" said Rich and nodded to his butler.

The butler lifted out the sausage rolls, tenderly but speedily excavating the mammoth chunk.

Rich gasped in delight as the lump of mammoth emerged, although it looked no more exciting than a joint of beef. The butler transferred it with some reverence to a tall freezer unit with an external thermometer and a secure locking handle.

There were trays, samples and sealed boxes on all the freezer shelves. Sam couldn't be sure what any of them were, but one box was definitely labelled *Siberian Cave Lion*. A laboratory then, she decided.

"Would you like me to put madam's fish in the chiller too?" asked the butler.

"It's okay. I'm not staying," said Sam.

"But the sausage rolls..." said Rich. He gestured to Peninsula. The butler swiftly turned on a nearby oven, as though that somehow decided the matter and the laboratory or kitchen conundrum was still to be solved.

"I've got to get home to my dad," said Sam. "He's trying to fix me up with someone over dinner, I think."

"A date?" Rich looked momentarily shocked. They'd never been the most startling couple. It had been a relationship they'd fallen into rather than worked on, more an extended holiday fling than anything else, but Rich had definitely taken the split harder than she had. Sometimes he even forgot they were no longer an item.

"I don't know," she said with a weariness she truly felt.

"Sausage rolls," said Rich and twirled his cocktail glass. "A small Manhattan. And I'll show you my plans."

The butler coughed politely.

"What?" said Rich.

"Non-disclosure agreement, sir."

Rich waved him away. "That's for ordinary people, Peninsula, not Sam. I can trust her."

The little man made a grumbling noise but argued no further and set about laying defrosting sausage rolls on an oven tray.

Rich led her back through to the lounge. "There are lots of things that I'm going to need help with over the coming weeks," he said.

"Me?"

"DefCon4. They're ideally placed to provide that help."

"You do know that DefCon4 in Skegness is just me, don't you?" Sam said. "Unless you're doing something in Manchester or Glasgow or whatever. There are loads of people working there. At least I think there are. I've never met any of them."

"What, never?"

"Nope," she said. "Apart from Doug Junior. He's just started with us."

"Wow. Anyway, this is very much a local thing. It's your help I particularly need."

"I see," said Sam, even though she didn't. Was it possible to get a sense of impending déjà vu? She had a feeling she was at risk of re-entering a pattern of behaviour she'd escaped once before. Rich tended to have such a clear view of how things should be, of bright, golden and fun-filled futures, that he would overlook the possibility other people might have a different view. Or even want a choice. It was probably that same single-minded vision which accounted for his vast wealth, but it could be disastrously bad for those in his orbit. Rich was generous and loving, but he assumed control at all levels.

"It will be interesting to see what you have in mind," she said. "Although does this work have to be here? In Skegness?"

He stepped closer to the balcony. "Skegness today. But what was here before?"

"Fens and miserable farmers?" she suggested.

"Before that."

"Vikings?"

"Before that."

She shrugged.

"Doggerland!" he declared in a loud whisper of amazement.

"Er, what?"

"Doggerland!" he said in exactly the same tone.

"Um." Sam had heard the word before, but she didn't know what it applied to. She knew there was a region called Dogger on the BBC Shipping Forecast, between Tyne and Fisher if she recalled correctly. But Dogger*land*? If asked to guess she might suggest it was a theme park for people who enjoyed having sex in public.

"Doggerland!" he declared a third time.

"Nope," she said.

"A prehistoric landscape. Where our ancestors hunted mammoth and woolly rhino across the ice and snow. It's real. Utterly littered with amazing archaeological finds."

He pulled her over to a display table which appeared to have been stolen right out of the British Museum. Flint arrowheads, crude tools and yellow-brown teeth sat on plinths, each with its own tiny label. He talked her through each, though she was perfectly capable of reading labels.

"And you want to – what—?" she said.

"Bring this historical wonder to a twenty-first century audience."

"A museum."

"A visitor attraction in Doggerland. Actually *in* Doggerland."

"A sort of Doggerland-land."

"If you must."

"Sounds..." She wasn't sure what word she was going for. 'Fanciful?' 'Stupid?' 'Crazy?' All seemed apt, but Rich, while being a naïve fool of a man, also seemed to be blessed with an astonishing amount of good luck, and words like fanciful, stupid and crazy would be no barrier to him. "Interesting," she said.

"I've been various places over recent months," he said. "Mostly I've been tracking down some specialised help which I'm going to need for the new project."

"Your sausage rolls, sir." The butler, Peninsula, appeared at the door with a shiny platter of steaming nibbles. Their smell filled the room and Sam's tummy rumbled.

"Someone told me that you'd gone back to France or somewhere," she said to Rich.

"France. Siberia. Pacific Islands. That's where I picked up Peninsula here. Jurang Peninsula. Finest butler this side of the international date line."

"You are too kind, sir," said Peninsula, drily.

"But, no, I'll be here in the Skegness area for the foreseeable future, among my own people."

France, Siberia, the Pacific, Skeg – hardly a natural progression, thought Sam. Rich had been photographed with supermodels, Formula One stars, actors and business moguls. The idea that he would prefer to rub shoulders with the oddball cross-section of society living in the east coast outpost of Skegness was almost laughable. Yet he clearly meant it.

"Doggerland is waiting to be reclaimed," Rich continued, "and I expect you to play a big part."

"Sure," said Sam. "As long as you know I am very used to using my initiative and working unsupervised."

"Understood!" said Rich with a smile. "You don't like to be micromanaged. I'm sure DefCon4 have a very hands off approach to management."

"That's one way of putting it," she said, taking a sausage roll from the tray.

8

There was a black saloon parked outside her dad's house on Albert Road. Few visitors realised that there was a rambling bungalow of giant proportions behind those hedges until they were almost upon it. As Sam pulled up onto the drive, she wondered if the car belonged to the man her dad had invited to dinner.

Sam left the 'organs in transit' box in the Piaggio Ape, taking the chilled fish and remaining sausage rolls inside.

Marvin Applewhite sat at the kitchen table across from a fresh-faced Asian man. He wore a suit that made her think of religious evangelists or double-glazing salesmen.

"Evening," she said and slid the food onto the counter.

"About time too," said Marvin.

"This would be..." She brushed her hands on her jeans to wipe off the frosty damp, then considered they were probably still a bit fishy. "I won't shake. Been handling unsavoury things. Tel, isn't it?"

"Tez actually," he said. He was more fresh-faced than she'd initially perceived. Positively schoolboy-ish.

He was so youthful, she considered the possibility of the young man being an aspiring magician, come to prostrate himself at the feet of Mr Marvellous, the master stage conjurer. Such things were possible, maybe even expected when having a former stage and TV magician for a dad.

"Sorry. Tez," she said.

"I'm terrible with names," said Marvin. "I've a great memory for faces. Rubbish with names. Isn't that so, Saffronella?"

Sam rolled her eyes. Even after several years of retirement, the old stage tomfoolery wasn't far from the surface. Or maybe that was dads everywhere. Sam didn't know, she didn't have an ordinary dad for comparison purposes. Maybe all dads told bad jokes and did substandard dancing at the most embarrassing moments.

"Pour yourself a cup," said Marvin. "Pot's freshly made."

"Just got to get something else from the van," she said.

"More food?"

"Murder victim."

Tez looked from Sam to Marvin and back again.

"Search me," said Marvin. "This a work thing, Saskatoon?"

"A sort of off-duty favour to a friend. A private investigation."

"Are you a private investigator?" said Tez.

"Young man, no one knows what she does for a living," said Marvin, which was by-and-large the truth of the matter.

Sam went out to the van and collected the bag

containing the sadly departed Drumstick. She brought it back to the kitchen, along with the definitely defrosted peas.

"Small corpse," said Tez.

"I met a pygmy while doing a tour to entertain the troops in the Falklands," said Marvin.

Sam held up the bag. "Turkey."

"Fairly certain it was the Falklands."

Sam put turkey and peas in the freezer, sat down, remembered her hands, got up to wash them, and sat down again. She looked levelly at Tez. Had her dad really invited a young man over to set her up with? If so, her dad had a worryingly high opinion of her attractiveness. This man, Tez, was at least five years younger than her and had a physique that, whilst more willowy than hunky, was definitely on the attractive side of slender.

"So, dad invited you over?" she said.

"That's right," said Tez.

"And you'll stay for dinner," said Marvin.

"Oh, I don't want to intrude."

"Fish for tea. Sam went all the way to Hull to get it."

"I didn't go to Hull to get it," she said. "I was in Hull."

"Fresh fish from Hull."

"Seriously, a cup of tea is more than enough," said Tez and smiled. "Your dad just wanted me to come over and discuss some matters."

"How very formal of you," said Sam.

"It's a serious business and I think he was keen that you were present."

"You think?" she said.

"I think Marvin thought you might be home sooner and we didn't want to delay but..."

"I was chatting to Rich. He wants to open a theme park in Doggerland."

"Rich is her ex," said Marvin.

"A theme park in Doggerland?" said Tez.

"They've been split up a long while now."

"Thank you, dad."

"Well, it's true."

Tez was frowning deeply as though he was considering something unpalatable. Had her dad not mentioned her past love life to this stranger he'd wheeled in to marry her, or whatever?

"Something about that bother you?" Sam asked him tartly.

Tez's frown only deepened. "Sorry. Just trying to get my head round the concept."

She nearly snorted at that.

"Thing is," said Marvin "Way I see it, I'm not going to be around forever."

"You're not dying, dad," said Sam and reached for the teapot.

"No," he conceded. "But I need to think of your future. And this whole complicated business is not something I want you to have to face alone once I'm gone."

"Again, not dying. Not any time soon."

"No, your father is right to think about such things. If he hadn't approached me, I'd probably be asking to talk to him. I was—" he grinned "—I was relieved when he got in touch.

If you let time tick by, your options are reduced. You'd be much better to come to an arrangement—"

"With someone like you."

"If you like."

"We should listen to what Tez has to offer," said Marvin.

"Oh, there's an offer?" said Sam.

"I'd need some guarantees," said Tez. "Beyond the house, I mean."

"What the hell?" said Sam.

"I'm sorry. That's the way of things. Age is a factor here."

"Hey, don't try to sugar-coat things, huh?"

He pulled an apologetic face. "I'm just saying that, however accommodating I try to be, some things are not negotiable."

"I've not even said I'm interested yet."

"This is ultimately my decision," said Marvin.

Sam pushed herself away from the table and stood. "Have I literally just fallen through a hole in time? Do I get any say in this?"

Tez frowned. "Not legally."

"What?"

"Unless you wish to act as your father's guarantor."

Sam froze. Sam thought. Sam rewound as much of the conversation as she could recall. "Tez…"

"Yes," he said.

She looked at the young man's suit in a new light. She saw the briefcase on the floor beside him.

"From the bank…?" she hazarded.

"Eastshires," he said and produced a card from his top pocket.

Tez Malik
Eastshires Bank, Lumley Road, Skegness

"I THOUGHT you'd be pleased I'd shown some initiative," Marvin said to her. He looked to Tez. "She's been banging on about my money woes for months. Thinks the family estate is under threat."

"Um," said Sam.

"Practically forced me to sell the old Jag," said Marvin.

"Not quite true," she said, keen for something to say, keen to cover up her utter misunderstanding.

"It's great that you want to sort things out, Marvin," said Tez.

"I indeedly do."

"And we could definitely look at extending your loan with us, or helping to consolidate other loans you have."

"Do you have funds to do that?" asked Sam.

"Well, I'm going back to work again," said Marvin.

"Are you?" said Tez.

"Are you?" said Sam.

"I'm looking into a few potential bookings."

Tez grinned. "Ah, the old magic routine."

"Well, maybe not so old," said Marvin reproachfully. "I'm working on a new illusion in which I chop off a volunteer's hand with a rusty saw."

"And reattach it?"

Marvin gave him a steady look. "Wouldn't be much of a magic trick if I didn't. Would you like to see it?"

"For sure."

"Wait there."

As Marvin got to his feet, Tez said, "It's great that you're looking to work again, but we're not necessarily going to be able to extend your existing borrowing without proof of income or a medical report."

"And you'll need a medical for public liability if you're going to perform again," Sam added.

"Not a problem," said Marvin breezily, going into the other room to get his props.

Alone in the kitchen with Tez, Sam found herself in possession of several conflicted feelings.

It was true her dad did have money woes, debts that savings from a lifetime of stage magic were failing to cover. He had sold the prized Jag – although in truth he had secretly done that months before Sam had even suggested it. And the house was indeed under threat. Sam had already earmarked some estate agents she'd need to call if the situation could not be resolved. The man was broke, turning a blind eye to it for too long. Calling in the bank for a chat was actually a mature and sensible thing for him to do. However, she felt a bizarre annoyance that he had done it without her. She had mentally put herself in charge of resolving his mounting problems; now she felt oddly wounded that he was trying to do something about it himself.

On top of that, now she had grasped the fact that Tez had not been wheeled in as a potential beau, she also felt mildly cheated. Yes, he was younger than her. Yes, he was a slim and handsome fellow who clearly took care of himself (Look at his neat nails! Look at his polished shoes!). But that didn't necessarily mean he was out of her league; that she was somehow left on the shelf, distanced from all the young and sexy people. She didn't want a new boyfriend, but she couldn't help but feel something akin to jealousy.

"So," she said. "Could I possibly tempt you to stay for dinner?"

"Oh, really..." said Tez, a gentle 'no' with a wave of his hands.

"I bought more fish than my dad and I could possibly eat."

He hesitated. "Do you really investigate murders?"

Sam shrugged. "It's not in my actual job description. Mostly it's security cameras and health and safety checks. Tomorrow I'm supervising a community payback team."

"Payback? As in community service?"

"That. Think we're going to do some weeding at the Otterside Retirement Village. I need to have a chat with the manager there anyway."

"But murders?"

"I've encountered a couple."

"I'd love to hear more." He pulled an apologetic face. "If that doesn't sound too ghoulish of me."

She smiled. "I'll take that as a yes to dinner then."

"And your ex..."

"He's not coming to dinner."

Tez's brow beetled in confusion. "Is he really planning to build a theme park in Doggerland?"

Sam retrieved the fish from the freezer and pierced the film packet with a knife. "He said so."

"You do know where that is?"

"Somewhere local?"

"Doggerland is underwater."

"Flooded?" The local area was prone to flooding. Storm surges and heavy rains often put the villages south of Skegness under several feet of water.

"I mean it's at the bottom of the North Sea," said Tez.

She put the knife down. "As in...?"

"A hundred miles out to sea. Has been since the last Ice Age. Like, ten thousand years or whatever."

Marvin returned with a some felt bags, a chopping block and a hacksaw. "Right. Who wants their hand chopping off?"

9

"This is stupid," declared Greg Mandyke, shaking his refuse sack and litter-picker.

"Are you about to complain about something, Greg?" said Sam, neutrally. "That is so unlike you."

This drew a few sniggers from others in the community payback team who, over the last few weeks, had come to know Greg and Sam well.

They were outside the Otterside Retirement Village. The agreed programme of work created by DefCon4 and the courts said this session should be the weeding and tidying of green spaces. Sam had selected the verges, pathways and grounds around Otterside.

"What could possibly be stupid about this?" said Sam, gesturing at the open lawns and gardens about them. "We're out among the greenery on a delightful sunny—"

"It's grey and horrible."

"—on this grey and horrible day. We're getting some exercise and ticking off our community payback hours."

"We're meant to be weeding!" said the silver-haired semi-retired builder.

"Which we are."

"It's late November! There's nothing to weed. Nothing's growing!"

Sam gave him a deliberately puzzled look. "But surely that just makes it easier." She glanced back along the grass. "It's looking lovely."

"But it's pointless. It's madness."

"Gosh," she said, deadpan. "If only there was something you could have done to avoid it."

"Got myself a better solicitor," he muttered and carried on.

"Okay," said Sam to the team. "We'll work our way up to the fence, then round to the other side. Not long now, folks."

She maintained a forcibly upbeat tone in her voice. Overseeing community service work was a chore. The individuals who'd been given community service by the local magistrates court obviously didn't want to be there. Sam didn't want to be there. Furthermore, the tasks the group were set (generated by some Kafkaesque DefCon4 system) were rarely vital community projects, mostly seeming to exist only to give the offenders something to do. Unwilling workers led by unwilling management in a task that no one wanted doing. Even though this description could be broadly applied to much of Sam's job, community payback just seemed to rub it in.

All Sam could do was present a positive attitude and let

her inner self switch off, sleepwalking through until it was done. She reckoned most of the dozen offenders here did the same. Stacey, the hairdresser with a penchant for pub car park fights, looked like she had perfected the trick. The lights were on but no one was home as she mechanically moved from point to point, picking up miniscule fragments of rubbish, or pulling up any little shoot that didn't look like grass.

By comparison, Hilde Odinson, working through her allotted punishment for theft (even though she argued that she thought the telephone engineers didn't want the telegraph pole any more, since they had just left it lying there), seemed to take continued interest in every little thing she came across.

"What have you got there?" Sam asked her.

Hilde touched the rusted hoops hooked over her arm. "I'm not rightly sure. Reckon these'd be pegs from some giant tent."

"Or the remains of a forgotten croquet set?"

"Croquet?"

Hilde was an Odinson, part of the amorphous clan of ne'er-do-wells which lived in their own hellish corner of the most dilapidated caravan park in the local area. The Odinsons were, for the most part, insular creatures, generally regarded as lacking in personal hygiene, education and respect for the laws of the land. However, Hilde was possessed of an unusual intelligence and an untameable creative streak, and although her education might not have encompassed something as mundane as lawn croquet, Sam imagined she'd have those hoops put to some use in her workshop before the day was done.

"It's a game," said Sam. "With mallets."

"Like hammers?"

Sam nodded.

"Maybe me grandpa would like it."

Ragnar Odinson, patriarch of the clan, had long ago decided that his family were of Viking stock and chose to live his life accordingly. Beards, fighting, and the occasional raiding party, were all part and parcel of the Odinson way. Most of the men wore stylised versions of Thor's hammer as religious amulets.

Sam tried to picture an Odinson version of croquet. She couldn't see them strolling across manicured lawns in white slacks and straw boaters, sipping on Pimms with mint and cucumber between shots. It was easier to picture them with tankards of mead in hand, staggering through mud to whack whatever poor object they'd decided to use as a ball.

"Maybe," said Sam. "I think this whole area has been used for various games. Stacey found a cricket wicket. There's a golf flag over there."

"Oh. Would anyone be bothered if I took it?" Hilde looked hopeful. "Don't want to be stealing or owt."

"We can only ask," said Sam.

They caught up with the rest of the group. Greg had taken another pause and was looking back at the retirement village.

"Picking out an apartment for yourself?" Sam asked.

He scoffed. "Rather be dead than in one of these places. No, I was just thinking. I know someone who moved here."

"Family or friend?"

"A whinger, I recall," he said, moving on. "Bet she's looking down on me and laughing."

"Cheer up," said Sam. "Soon, it will all be over."

He looked at the distance left to go in their weeding efforts. "Until the next time."

"I meant after today, your time owed will be down to single figures."

"Hooray for that," he said with a small amount of cheer. "And it's taught me something."

"Oh?" said Sam. There were little evidence of rehabilitation among the offenders.

"Footwear," he said.

"What?"

He rocked on his heels, showing off his pale green wellingtons. "Le Chameau. The original sixty-five design. A mere hundred and fifty quid."

"For wellies?" she said, considering her six quid pair of squeaky boots.

"Always the right shoe for the job. You can't compromise on luxury."

The first time they'd met, he'd attempted a beach-cleaning task in expensive espadrilles which had been stolen by opportunist thieves. If the only thing weeks of community payback had taught him was the value of protective footwear, then...

Sam sighed. The whys and wherefores of justice were none of her business. She was just the woman who made sure it happened.

Once the team had returned to the retirement village car

park, Sam gathered the bags of weeds and litter and signed off the timesheets for the offenders. Greg sat on the lip of the open boot of his Lexus and carefully swapped over-priced wellies – he had a special carry case for them, Sam noted – for a pair of moccasin shoes.

"Can I then?" said Hilde, hovering at Sam's shoulder.

"Huh?" Sam looked down at the collected scrap and oddments the young woman had in her hands. Seeing no sign of retirement village staff, Sam said, "Sure, why not?"

Hilde practically skipped up the driveway to the main road where a dirt-grey van waited. A non-specific bearded Odinson was leaning out, chatting to a trio of older people – a woman and two men, one in glasses, the other in a wide-brimmed hat. Seeing her looking, the Odinson gave Sam a devil's horn salute of greeting.

Sam gave a vague wave in reply, dumped the rubbish in the site bins and went inside to talk to the manager, Chesney Trout. As she crossed the car park, a dark Lexus swung out in front of her and fishtailed towards the road, spraying gravel as it went.

10

The Lexus might be a large car, but it responded to Greg's touch like the hot young thing it was. It was childish to be sure, but he smiled at the woman's surprised face as he swung past her. Doing community service was demeaning enough, but having it overseen by some unqualified clipboard-warrior from a nameless corporation made it infinitely worse. As punishments went he'd take his chances with prison next time.

It had been a travesty of justice anyway. He, a respected businessman, dragged up before the courts for simply seeking what had been owed to him. That stupid woman not understanding the difference between VAT inclusive and VAT exclusive building quotes; not understanding that building work sometimes hit snags and costs went up; not having the foresight to put enough money aside to cover the increased cost of the build. And the prosecution somehow managing to dress his behaviour as 'demanding money with menaces'.

That reminded him. Time to make a house call.

He cut inland along Church Lane and through the back roads of Ashington End and Orby to get to the sleepy nowhere village of Welton le Marsh. In the last few months, he'd snatched up a number of new-build properties which the owner had been forced to offload in a hurry. The occupants were already in, but there was money to be made from the final fix ups and finishing touches – gutters, fascias, driveways and paths. One of the new homeowners had called him with a query, the kind of query that needed nipping in the bud.

Past the church, he turned into the wide access road he'd had built across land he already owned, and round to the first house in brand new Stickney Close. He stepped out, rang the doorbell and stepped back. A good clear ten feet between him and the door. Let no prying eyes accuse him of being demanding or of using menaces.

Mr de Winter answered the door. He was an odd-looking character from his droopy moustache to his obvious penchant for silk shirts. Greg had initially been unsure if the man was a retired porn star or a bargain basement stage magician. It turned out the man was a jobbing psychic. Apparently there was a market for such things. Greg was surprised a bloody psychic could afford the mortgage on a two bedroom property.

"Oh," he said as greeting.

"You rang, I came," said Greg.

"You didn't say you were coming." He seemed surprised.

"Couldn't you read it in the stars?" said Greg. "I've come about concerns regarding the last schedule of works and payment?" He had a copy in his hand. "I can go through them if you'd like me to."

De Winter adjusted his silk shirt. It was too darn nippy for such things. "I wasn't expecting any additional payments. I paid for the house, the bill was settled with Frost and Sons. Bank transfer."

"Yes, it was." Greg looked up at the shoebox house. "And you must be very proud of your new home. But it needed signing off with building regulations and there were additional works that needed doing, weren't there? Drain covers. Timber supports. We talked about that."

"And I assumed that was included in the price. We paid the agreed price for the finished house. Miss Frost said—"

"Jacinda Frost is on remand in Peterborough Jail, if I recall correctly. My company took over the properties. We don't do extra work for free, Mr Winter."

"De Winter."

"Mr de Winter," he said and smiled. No one could accuse you of demanding money with menaces if you smiled. "There were costs on the document I gave you."

"I thought they were for information only."

Greg raised a genial eyebrow at his naiveté.

"It was eight thousand pounds," de Winter said, as though the size of the number mattered.

"Quality work costs," Greg replied.

"We didn't sign a contract." De Winter said it with a finality of someone who thought they had won.

"We did not," Greg agreed. "And I haven't submitted your

house for final approval with building regs at the council planning department. Currently – if we want to be picky about things – you're living in an illegal building. The council could ask for it to be knocked down. At your expense, mind."

"But you've done the additional work." De Winter's brief bubble of victory evaporated.

"And we could remove what we've put in, if you don't want to pay for it."

De Winter blinked and Greg judged he'd said enough. He backed away, pleasant-like, to his car. "Just let us know what you'd like to do," he said cheerily, and departed.

As he drove back down to the main road and Skegness, *Queen's Greatest Hits II* turned up high on the stereo, he couldn't help but feel a warm glow. He'd put a customer straight, greased the wheels of business with a personal visit, and there had been no need for raised voices or conflict. The ridiculous Mr de Winter, who perhaps needed a few lessons in the realities of this world, would stew upon his situation for a day or two, then pay up. Everyone would be happy. He might have to make a number of similar visits to the other occupants of the new houses or, if he was lucky, word would travel and there would be no more truculent silliness from his new customers.

11

"What exactly is it you're looking for?" asked Chesney for the third time.

Chesney Trout was a man who always acted as if he wanted to be somewhere else. Sam knew him, although not specifically as the duty manager of the Otterside Retirement Village. She'd seen him up on stage at the Sand Castle pub venue, doing a stage performance of Tony Christie and Gene Pitney numbers. She'd also heard rumours that he worked as a taxi driver on his days off. Cabbie, singer, manager – he was always on his way to something else and seemed to have little enthusiasm for the here and now (unless the here and now involved wearing outdated clothes and belting out *Twenty Four Hours from Tulsa* to lacklustre pub audiences).

Sam clicked back along the timeline and tried a different array of cameras.

She sat in the little security room to the side of the

manager's office, scrolling through the security footage for the past day or so. Otterside didn't use DefCon4 as their security contractors, but the offer of some free weeding, plus a little corporate gobbledegook about professional courtesy between security contractors was enough to blag her way in.

However, the CCTV was of next to no use. The camera nearest to Delia's fence, which might have presented some revealing footage of what happened in that back garden the night before last, was angled squarely down at the footpath running around the outside of the main Otterside building. It encompassed the main building, the path, and a row of retirement village outbuildings squeezed along that section. The bottom edge of Delia's fence appeared as a shadow in the corner, but there was nothing more.

Sam scooted along the timeline for the night in question. It would have been helpful if the camera had caught a masked figure in a stripy burglar shirt or a vengeful animal-killer in an 'I hate Turkeys' T-shirt, but no such luck.

"Is this going to take long?" said Chesney.

"Just trying to keep the residents safe and secure," said Sam, which was a piece of empty nonsense.

"I need to get off and pick up my dry cleaning."

"Performing tonight?" said Sam.

"Maybe."

"I can do this without you," she said. "I'll lock up afterwards."

"If you like," said Chesney.

The CCTV revealed nothing. Sam clicked out of the archive and the screen flicked back to the live feed. One of the outbuilding doors was open and two figures were stepping inside carrying bundles of she-couldn't-see-what between them.

"That's Ragnar and Hilde Odinson," said Sam.

Chesney glanced at the screen as he slid on his coat. "Yeah. Ragnar does some odd jobs for us around the place. The residents' social committee get him to help out sometimes."

"What strange company people keep," she mused.

Chesney grunted, disinterested, and left.

The CCTV had been no use. The other option was to ask the people who had rooms overlooking Delia's garden.

12

P olly Gilpin heard the knock at her door and almost leapt to her feet in her excitement to answer it. She immediately felt sad and foolish.

She recalled how, as a child, she would rush to the front door when the postman called, sometimes racing against her sister to get there first. Post had been an exciting thing, a letter addressed to her doubly so, a parcel triply so. Then she had grown up and post became something that was functional at best, though more often boring or worrying – junk mail, brown envelopes with little windows, red bills.

And here she was, one day into her sentence at Otterside, and she was leaping up to get to the door because any visitor was better than no visitor at all.

It was a young woman with sensible shoes and grass stains on her trousers.

"Yes?"

The woman stood on tiptoes to look past her, seemingly at Polly's window. "Can I ask you an odd question?"

"Isn't that an odd question in itself?"

"Point."

Polly realised she recognised the woman. She had been talking to the homeowner in the garden of the house next door: odd gesticulations and earnest searching in the grass.

"Do you, by any chance, want to take a look at the garden?" said Polly.

The woman looked surprised.

"I saw you talking to the other woman," said Polly. "You seemed to have lost something."

"Oh, you're observant," said the woman. "I like that. I'm Sam. I work for DefCon4. I have a card here somewhere." The woman patted herself down.

"You can come in," said Polly.

"Really? Letting strangers into your home, even in this place…"

"Well, you can't steal my family silver because I have none. I'm Polly Gilpin. I moved in yesterday."

"Yesterday? *Yesterday* yesterday?"

"I think there's only one yesterday," said Polly. "The day before today."

"Damn it, that's a shame."

"Oh, it's not too bad," said Polly, following her to the window. "This place seems nice enough. Lots of activities. Very active social committee. Walking groups. Sports tournaments. I think there's a trip planned to Candlebroke Hall in a week or so."

Sam from DefCon4 pressed her face right up against the

window to look down on the garden next door. "I was interested in what happened here the night before last."

"Before I arrived," said Polly.

"Exactly," said Sam.

"And what did happen?"

"Someone killed a turkey."

"Is that a euphemism?"

"Pardon?"

"It sounds like urban slang."

"For what?"

"I don't know. I'm not familiar with urban slang. I struggle with my memory enough as it is apparently, without learning jive talk."

Sam turned away from the window. "Was there perhaps a person in here the night before?"

"I don't think so," said Polly. "The last occupant was a man called Bob. Ackroyd, I think. He didn't die." She smiled at Sam's frown. "It's all I know about him. Upped sticks and left."

Sam considered the window again. "Do you know the occupant next door?"

"Occupant? Rabbits in cages are we now?"

Sam had the decency to look sheepish. "Poor choice of words."

"I was a little tart. Mood swings. Bernard."

"Bernard?"

"Next door. I think I've seen him the once. He's more of a smoky presence. We're not meant to smoke in the building, but I'm sure he does." She went to the door and out into the corridor.

"You're coming with me?" said Sam.

"If anyone's got juicy information on a turkey murder then I'd like to hear it."

Polly went so far as to knock on her next door neighbour's door for Sam. The man who opened the door was wearing flip flops, a white dressing gown hanging open, and what Polly charitably decided were swimming trunks. Bernard's large belly was as brown and shiny as a basted roast. Was that a smear of tobacco ash on the upper slopes of his belly? There was undoubtedly the stink of a dedicated smoker coming from his apartment.

"Oh, sorry," said Sam. "We didn't mean to disturb you while you were..."

Her sentence trailed off with nowhere decent to go. Bernard's attire would have been appropriate on a tropical beach but possibly nowhere else.

"You weren't disturbing me," he said. "Who are you?"

"This is Sam from DefCon4," said Polly.

"Who are they when they're at home?"

"That's what I thought," said Polly. "Never heard of them. Sam's investigating a murder."

"Someone killed a bird in the garden next door," Sam interjected quickly.

"Don't know nothing about it," said Bernard.

"Well, I was wondering if you might have heard something—"

"I was in bed all night. Deep sleeper me. Twenty years in the army taught me to get shut eye whenever I could. Didn't hear a thing."

"I didn't actually say when—"

"In bed all night," he insisted. "Didn't leave once. You can check the cameras." He gestured along the corridor at the CCTV camera pointing their way.

Sam was perplexed. "I ... I can. I was only asking. It was the night before last and—"

"I do have things to do, you know," he said and shut the door.

Both women stared at the door. Sam looked to Polly.

"That was a really odd conversation, wasn't it?" she said.

"I'm glad you thought so too," said Polly.

13

G reg Mandyke resided in a spacious house on Derby Avenue in the town. He rarely stayed in a single property for more than a handful of years. Houses were like shoes. You bought them when they were beautiful and pristine, wore them in for a while and then, with a bit of polish applied around the scuffed edges, passed them on and got yourself something new. Being in the trade, he had men working on various other properties which, given a year or two, he might step into while selling this one off for half a million of pocket money.

If he did, there would be one thing he'd miss about the place. He'd had a spa room and pool constructed in the garden. The garden stretched a hundred feet out to a sea view, but the sea views in this flat landscape weren't worth a damn so he'd had the spa room and pool put in instead. Its pine construction gave it a nice Nordic feel. The frosted glass in the domed roof provided all the privacy he desired.

Greg kicked off his moccasins in the hallway and went through to the kitchen.

"HomeHub, turn on kitchen lights," he said, nibbling on a biscotti from the counter jar while he rooted around in the fridge for a beer. He opened the beer and headed into the garden. Evening was drawing in quickly. He stripped as soon as he entered the heated spa room. He didn't bother with trunks. If you couldn't enjoy being naked in your own home, where could you?

The warm yellow lights of the spa room dispelled the gloom of the outside world. The underfloor heating provided a touch of summer, of carefree days. He took a long dive into the pool, all but glided its ten metre length, then hauled himself out to get into the hot tub at the far end.

Greg loved his hot tub – not just the swirling heated water but the utter indulgence of it. It had cost several thousand to buy and install but the bitch drank electricity like she just didn't care. Even more so when he pulled back the curved roof to relax beneath the open skies. Global warming be damned, a hot tub was Greg's two fingers to a world telling him to cut back and compromise.

He slid over the side and into the waters. It immediately went to work on his tensions. The indignities and dirt of that pathetic community service crap were eased from his pores. The idiocy of others that he'd had to deal with were washed away. Already Greg could feel the cares of the day pouring from him.

He sank to his neck and called out. "HomeHub, some music."

The smart speakers in the spa room should have blasted

forth with classic driving rock or cheesy and cheerful Carpenters, but nothing happened.

"HomeHub, play my music."

Still nothing.

He sat up and looked round to the utility closet where the speaker system was connected to the main, He saw the figure in the shadows.

"Jesus!" he gasped and made to stand.

"Don't move," said the figure, stepping far enough into the light for Greg to see the pistol they held in a hand.

"What the hell...?"

The intruder had white-grey hair. The hand holding the pistol was wrinkled, gnarled. Were burglars getting older these days?

"You want something?"

The intruder said nothing. Was there an element of hesitation or nervousness in the way they stepped from foot to foot? Greg suddenly doubted this was any sort of burglar. His eyes were drawn repeatedly to the dark eye of the pistol barrel.

"I have valuables in the house," he said. "Cash. Some jewellery, I think." He tried to stand again but the pistol was raised and aimed.

"Stay where you are, Mr Mandyke," said the intruder.

He remained as he was.

"Back in the water," said the intruder. "I'm not going to talk to a man while I can see his meat and two veg."

Greg lowered himself into a fearful sitting position. The bubbles of the hot tub were no comfort now. He felt more like a missionary in a cannibal's bubbling cauldron.

"Do I know you?" said Greg.

He studied the face, realising that the intruder had chosen not to wear a mask did not bode well. He wondered if he knew them from somewhere. Was it someone he had angered, bested in a career of business and financial victories? Greg realised he had a long list of names to pick from.

"Is there something I can do for you? Tell me."

"You're a crook," said the intruder. "You're a cheat, you're a swindler and a bully. You have robbed people of their homes and their livelihoods."

"Now, I don't know who you've been talking to," said Greg, "but I have been nothing but scrupulous, fair and honest."

"You have made people's lives a misery," said the intruder.

Greg opened his mouth to argue further but what would be the point of that? "I should atone?" he suggested. "We could go to the police. I could confess. Is that what you would like?" He pointed up vaguely to indicate the wall speakers. "I could record a confession on the HomeHub. We could call the police now."

"I unplugged it," said the intruder.

"So it wouldn't record this conversation," said Greg. "Always listening. Very smart."

There was a headshake from the intruder. "I needed the plug socket."

For the first time, Greg saw the intruder was holding something in the other hand. He frowned.

"Is that my NutriBullet?" he said, feeling a misplaced indignity that the intruder had been in his kitchen.

The intruder stepped forward. The NutriBullet's power cable was linked to a long orange extension cable that snaked into the utility cupboard. With acute clarity, Greg saw what the intruder intended.

"Wait!" he cried. "You can't do this. You can't murder a man in his own hot tub."

The intruder turned the little blender on. Its whir echoed coldly in the sparsely decorated space. "They'll assume it was an accident."

Greg screwed up his face. "Who in their right mind would take a NutriBullet into a hot tub?"

"Maybe you wanted a smoothie while you're in there."

"That doesn't even make sense."

There was a minimal shrug. "Catch," said the intruder, and tossed the electric blender to Greg.

He instinctively stood to catch it, saw his own dripping wet hands and pulled them aside, only to see the blender arcing into the water. He froze, he panicked, he slipped as he tried to turn away. He screamed as the blender plopped into the tub and his whole body braced for a pain he couldn't imagine.

His scream eventually faltered when he realised nothing had happened. Gasping, he looked round. The power cable and good few feet of orange extension hung in the hot tub. Nothing had happened. He hadn't been electrocuted.

A small brown sausage bobbed on the froth of the roiling water. He'd shat himself in fear at the moment of impact.

But he wasn't dead. He *wasn't* dead.

He looked at the intruder. The gun was still pointing at him.

"Is this a joke?" Greg gasped.

A headshake. "It doesn't always work. If the electricity can earth itself through the water and the tub there's no reason why you'd be electrocuted. It's about the path of least resistance."

"You gambling with my life?"

"We can try again?" suggested the intruder.

"You mad fuck!" Greg hissed. "I was properly scared there."

Greg's toe brushed against hard plastic – The NutriBullet. Damned thing. Nearly killed him.

Irritated, infuriated, Greg scooped it up and pulled it out to toss it safely away. As it cleared the water, his body snapped taut with the electric shock. His arms, his legs, his torso were suddenly no longer his own. An immense vibration – too forceful, too painful to comprehend – shook him. He was a piece of glass being fed into a belt sander. Shards of fire spat inside him. He couldn't speak. He couldn't even exhale to scream. He could only stare with rapidly blurring eyes. He saw the hairs on his arms burst into flame along his steaming skin. He saw the turd bobbing on the surface of the water.

Through the agonies of his final conscious moments, a nugget of embarrassment similarly bobbed on the surface of his thoughts before it sank into the heat and the darkness.

14

L ate evening and Hilde Odinson was still at the Otterside old folks home.

After a long, jocular conversation between her granddad and the loud man in the hat, Strawb, hands had been shaken and a space in one of the external storage buildings next to the main building was given over to them with the understanding that a 'crazy golf' course would be built.

Hilde had heard of crazy golf. She had seen it played, at a distance, by Saxon holidaymakers. She understood the basics and had earnestly set to making plans for the task she'd been given. She hadn't been given it directly, of course. Farfar Ragnar was the front man. People liked to deal with him. He had an air about him. She'd heard it said it was an air composed largely of stale tobacco, illegal hooch and body odour, but he commanded the sort of presence that was useful in business negotiations.

As she understood it, the Saxon residents of this place enjoyed the sort of lifestyle which came with active retirement in a relatively good state of health. They went on trips, organised workshops and social events, and were the main patrons for evening courses at the college in the town. In the past, Ragnar had suggested some of Uncle Bjorn's beehives might do well in the grounds of Otterside. There were beds of lavender planted by the pathways, and Bjorn had often waxed lyrical about the honey (and of course the delicious mead) that lavender helped to create. Ragnar had come up with the idea that elderly hobbyists might enjoy learning a little bit about beekeeping, but there had been some residents who were fearful about stings. Still, there were opportunities here, and the latest one was crazy golf. Strawb made it clear they wanted something much more interesting than the standard, pedestrian seaside crazy golf. This was the sort of project that Hilde enjoyed.

The challenge of simply constructing something was not enough for Hilde; it had to be something extra, something above and beyond. Creating something unique and innovative while staying within the set budget was the true challenge. Keeping costs down was something her family would definitely get on board with, but generally they acknowledged that Hilde knew what she was doing and let her get on with it in her own way.

There was a pile of old household items and assorted junk Ragnar had found about the site and which she was keen to incorporate into the finished item. She added sketches to her pad as the ideas came to her.

"What does tha reckon to this?" said Ragnar, entering

from the night with an aged vacuum cleaner in his hands, cradling it like a dying swan.

"Superb. We'll use that for sure," she said, gesturing for him to lay it down on the table.

The vacuum cleaner had components, like the ribbed hose, that would be really useful for sending a golf ball on its way. She could also harvest all of the electrical flex, knowing from past experience she could use it in a multitude of ways. She could coil it up into a bouncy mat, she could glue lengths of it to a flat surface to channel the ball, or she could use it to suspend a swinging component. The motor from the vacuum cleaner would be a different matter.

"We could take the innards home," she said. "I need a new motor for my belt sander."

"Aye," said Ragnar. "Always hold some stuff in tha back pocket."

Hilde pulled out an old toy garage from the pile of junk. It was the sort with a spiralling plastic ramp for the cars to go down, which she could definitely use. It also had a pulley lift to take the cars back up to the roof. She mulled over that for a few minutes. She'd need to examine the pulley, but she hoped she could extract the basics, extend the height to at least a couple of metres, and then add a fun way to wind it up. Motorising it would be easy, but she could do something less obvious.

There was an old and unloved exercise bike in the corner.

"Reckon the Saxons'd like to pedal their golf balls to the ceiling?" she said.

"Mebbe," said Ragnar.

"Then it could roll back down through some guttering or summat."

"I saw some rotten guttering on one of the other outbuildings we could use."

"Rotten?" she said with a sideways look for her granddad.

Ragnar gave her a look of hurtful surprise, his bearded mouth a round hairy 'O'.

"I'm still doing community service for the last trouble I was in," she said. "We're not ripping down owt just so we can use it."

"Rotten, I says. And we'll get the contract for fitting some new."

She chuckled. With a bit of luck, the Odinsons would be paid to fix the guttering and she would get to use the old and leftover pieces of guttering in this project. The Odinsons were very switched on when it came to upselling their services.

"Time for summat to eat, I reckon," he declared and reclined in a folding garden chair.

"Cheese toastie?" she suggested.

"Aye."

"And a glass of mead?"

"Sounds grand." Her farfar Ragnar was a man of simple pleasures.

Hilde poured him a glass of mead and then put the heat resistant mat on the workbench. She lit the blow torch and unwrapped the foil around the cheese sandwich she'd brought. She played the flame over the bread, careful to keep the perfect distance, so she didn't burn the bread before the cheese melted. She flipped the sandwich over and did the other side before sliding it onto an enamel plate.

"Here you go," she said. "What's that thing there?" She pointed at the pile of discarded things they'd been given.

"That's a record player. Tha's seen one o' them, surely?" Ragnar said.

She shook her head, bewildered.

"For playin' records? Vinyl?" he said.

"Music?" she asked.

"Aye, lass. I s'pose it's all CDs and suchlike nowadays?"

"I don't really remember CDs. Before my time."

"Aye, like I said."

She fetched the turntable over to the workbench. "Why's it so wide? What do all these other parts do?" she asked.

Ragnar swivelled in his chair to look. "Used to call these music centres. Proper swanky, back in the day. You could play tapes an' get the radio on 'em an' all." He rootled in a box near his feet. "Here."

He passed her a huge cardboard sleeve. She tilted the cardboard cover and an inner sleeve came out. This was protecting the record, which was a glossy black thing, attractive in its own way.

"Keep tha fingers off the surface," said Ragnar. He showed her how to hold it cupped by the edges. There was clearly a ritual to be observed. Did everyone do this or was it a Ragnar thing? Her grandad did love a ritual.

She placed it on the turntable.

"Not going to play it, are ya?" he said distastefully.

"What's wrong with this? These people look like they're having a good time," said Hilde, holding up the cover, which featured a cheerful couple holding a trumpet. "Herb Alpert's Tij-u-ana Brass."

"It's Tijuana," he said. "It's a silent 'J'. Mexican. And don't play it. You know I can't stand Saxon music."

She frowned. "I thought you said it was Mexican."

"Mexican Saxon music," he grumbled and took a bite out of his sandwich.

Hilde ignored him and plugged in the record player. Various parts of it lit up. She could see the arm that was held in place by a tiny clamp was intended to ride upon the record. She released its clamp and flipped the adjacent lever. The arm rose up and moved across to the edge of the record, then it sank gently into a groove. There was a gentle hissing sound from the speaker. After a few seconds trumpets blasted out in a cheery tune that was slightly familiar, although Hilde had no idea where she'd heard it before.

Ragnar shook his head and pretended to hate it, but Hilde noticed that his foot was tapping.

"Oi oi, Ragnar, how's it going?"

Hilde looked up from the record player and saw Strawb enter the workshop and slap her granddad on the shoulder. She turned down the volume on the record player.

"I love a bit of cheery music," said Strawb, grinning. The man was as relentlessly cheerful as Ragnar was guarded.

"You got everything you need, mate?" Strawb said, strutting round. "Nice that you're looking after young Hilde while you work. Send her in for a hand of gin rummy if she gets bored. You know she'll get spoiled by everyone."

Hilde rolled her eyes. It didn't matter if she was wielding a drill or a spot welder, the people here always assumed she was along for the ride, kept entertained by Ragnar. She was twenty two years old, but they treated her as if she was twelve.

Ragnar nodded along.

"Didn't you say that you'd need the keys to the bin store, farfar?" said Hilde.

"Aye," said Ragnar.

"And you wanted to warn everyone there would be noise between eleven and twelve tomorrow while you were drilling."

"Aye."

"And you wanted to see what golf clubs people were using so we'd know how hard they'd be hitting the balls."

"Aye."

"Not a problem," said Strawb. "Easy as. We can sort all that out for you. Any thoughts on what you're going to do with this? Everyone's keen to hear your ideas."

"Oh, granddad's got some great ideas," said Hilde. "He's thinking that we'll have themed stations. So one of them will be futuristic, with a space theme. Spinning planets and so on. One of them will be a forest theme, so it'll be decorated with trees and animals. One will be like the beach, so it will have donkeys and stuff."

"You're all over this, I see Ragnar," said Strawb, impressed. "Great ideas, I don't know where you come up with these things, I really don't."

"Well," said Hilde. "Granddad said the racehorse game in the amusement arcade was what inspired the beach idea. He really wanted to do something that's got the same visual impact as those horses moving along. He's hoping to do that with the beach donkeys."

"Clever. Always got those eyes open for inspiration. A true artist." Strawb saluted Ragnar.

The music came to an end.

Ragnar clapped his hands. "Ah, 'fore I forget, Strawb. Must have a word with that fool Chesney about the guttering on one of the buildings."

"Oh?" said Strawb.

"Aye. It's clearly rotten. Let me show thee."

15

Polly Gilpin sat in the south lounge, a half-finished cup of tea beside her. The south lounge had a large many-paned skylight but the sky above was grey, although the morning drizzle outside had stopped. A scrunched up bourbon biscuit wrapper was in her cardigan pocket, the crumbs carefully swept off the table to leave no trace.

Erin, her niece, appeared at the door, saw her and approached through the minor maze of chairs and tables. "I'm not staying long," she said.

"Jack and Iris not with you?" said Polly.

"It's a school day," said Erin. "They're at school." She pulled out a chair and inspected its seat before sitting down. "You do know it's a school day, don't you?"

Polly gave her a convinced nod. Lapses in memory might be a symptom of dementia. The thought of Polly developing dementia would upset Erin. Polly tried to look alert and bright as a button. "It's Iris's birthday tomorrow," she said.

"*I* know that."

Polly took the present from the seat next to her and placed it on the table.

"What's that?" said Erin.

The present was wrapped in silver-blue paper and decorated with cartoon unicorns.

"I was going to give it to her. If not today, then maybe tomorrow. You could—"

Erin frowned. "Bring her here? On her birthday?" She looked around. "It's her birthday. Her seventh birthday."

Polly tried to ignore the hurt. "Got big plans for the day?"

"We are having a party at the house for her classmates."

"Jelly and ice cream and cake. That's lovely."

"You sound like Cesar. It's not the nineteen eighties you know. There will be fruit segments and carrot batons."

"Carrot doesn't sound much fun."

"But batons. Batons are fun."

"If you say so."

"And there's dips and vegetable crisps."

"Humous?"

"Precisely. Humous is fun."

"That's nice," said Polly because she felt it was expected.

"And on Sunday we're going up to Seal Land."

"Seal Land. That place still open? I remember going there with you and your mum when you were just a nipper."

"I don't."

"We did. You gave a fish to one of the penguins."

Erin adjusted her posture stiffly. Mentioning her late

mum rarely drew a positive reaction. "Sounds unsanitary," she said.

Polly looked at her cautiously. "Of course, if you're passing this way up to Seal Land..."

"I said we're not coming here for her birthday."

"It would be the day after her birthday."

"And we've clearly got plans."

Polly tried her best smile. "I could come with you."

"It's a five-seater car."

"I could sit in the back."

Erin leaned sideways and took a deliberately long look at Polly's waist and hips, mentally measuring them against the back seat of her car. "How's the aquarobics going?"

Polly nodded.

"And the fitness class? You're going to that?"

She nodded again.

Erin looked away and out the window. "Don't lie to me, Polly. You've not been to either."

"I..."

"I asked. At the desk. It's not difficult. You've not been to any of them. Even the aquarobics. It's just jiggling about in water, for goodness sake."

"I don't like getting wet."

Erin sniffed. "You need to make an effort."

"I do."

"Look at you." Polly tried to follow Erin's sweeping and critical gaze. She felt a perverse need to explain that the fat folds in her cardigan were the wool, not her belly. "If you want to spend time with the children you need to be presentable."

Erin leaned over a picked a crumb of bourbon biscuit off Polly's chest. A big crumb, a corner piece.

"This," said Erin. "Unacceptable. Refined sugars. Do you know what they are doing to you?"

"It's just one," lied Polly.

"This place isn't cheap, you know."

"I pay for it."

"You think the proceeds from the sale of the house will last forever?"

"Long enough."

"Oh, that's the plan, is it? Kill yourself with sloth and gluttony?"

"It was just a packet of bourbons."

Erin was stunned. "Packet?" she whispered. She shook herself. "We're happy to pay for you to stay here."

"I pay...!"

"But you have to make an effort. You have to try to get better."

"I'm not ill."

"I'm not going to put Jack and Iris through—" The 'what I went through' went unsaid. "We need to present the best of ourselves to the children. Bright and happy, showing life lived to the full. And that doesn't mean a gin and tonic every afternoon at four." Polly opened her mouth but Erin got there first. "I've *seen* the till receipts and your room bill. Do not sully your mouth with further lies."

"I'm not an alcoholic."

"It's undignified at your age."

"I'm seventy-five, Erin. That's barely any age these days."

Erin picked up the birthday present. "What is it?"

"A present."

"Something nice? Hard to tell from a woman who'd let a child feed raw fish to a penguin."

"Just some crayons and a book."

Erin huffed. Polly could tell she wanted to criticise it in some way. If it had been a doll or make up, Erin would have accused her of being sexist or some such. If it had been chocolate, it would have been treated as poisonous.

"If you want to be part of this family, if you want to continue to live here, if— I don't want to start using terms like 'power of attorney'."

"Please, let's not fight."

"We are not fighting," Erin growled. "I say this all out of love." She took out her phone. "Time for a photo."

"What for?"

"The children will want photos."

"Not the actual me?"

Erin scrolled and fiddled on her phone. "Smile for the camera. You can hold the present if you like."

Polly did not feel like smiling but picked the small gift up all the same and smiled.

"Rein the smile in," said Erin. "You're a sweet old auntie, not a drunkard at a bus stop."

Polly let the edges of the smile drop.

"And with your eyes," said Erin. "Smize, Polly. A bit of warmth."

Polly didn't know what to do. The phone gave the tiniest of clicks. Something winked at her.

"You need to start treating your life and your body with respect," said Erin. "I'll know when you haven't attended the classes you're signed up for. I'll know what you're having at mealtimes and what you're ordering from the café or bar. Watch your weight. Watch your blood sugars. Go get some exercise. If you don't like aquarobics, go for a walk. There's a perfectly lovely pitch and putt course out there."

"Is there?" said Polly.

"I'm not letting you see the children while you're in this state," said Erin.

"What state?"

The disgust on Erin's face was evident. She wrapped the bourbon crumb in a tissue and then took out a slim pack of wet wipes to clean her hands. "Our role is to be part of the happy memories in the minds of others. And then, when our time comes – a long, long way in the future one hopes – to die like Bambi's mum."

Polly frowned. "Shot by a hunter?"

"Off screen," said Erin.

With clear reluctance, she picked up Iris's birthday present. Her other hand removed her e-cig vape thing from her pocket, a sure sign that she was going.

"I'll Instagram the photo."

"I'm not on Instagram."

Erin's displeased expression only deepened. "I do wish you could make more effort to be part of this family," she said and left.

16

The text on Sam's phone said: *COME OVER.*

She replied with a curt: *WHY?*

COME OVER. I HAVE SOMETHING TO SHOW YOU.

In her experience of men (which she thought of as distinctly average) 'I have something to show you' rarely involved a 'something' she had much interest in seeing. However, she decided to make an exception for this ambiguous invitation from Rich.

The man had, over the course of their relationship, tried to show her everything she could possibly want to see, and more besides. There were no surprises left to be had. Besides, she was in the vicinity of Rich's hotel digs, having been on an afternoon errand to update the DefCon4 *ATTACK DOGS PATROL HERE!* signs at a car compound. There had never been any DefCon4 attack dogs. If there had been, they were lost in the post. Furthermore, she had been itching to speak to Rich just to check he knew what she now knew –

that the prehistoric Doggerland was under a dozen or so metres of seawater.

She pulled into the Hotel Splendid car park.

"I love your van," Rich shouted from a balcony high above. "It's so funny."

"Hilarious," she shouted back.

"Come on up! Peninsula, show Sam the stairs!"

"I can find the stairs," she muttered as she stomped in. She met the butler coming down as she climbed.

"Ah, you found the stairs, Miss Applewhite," said Peninsula.

"Are they hard to spot?"

Peninsula produced a minimalist facial shrug. "Mr Raynor always has the good sense to make friends with intelligent people," he suggested as he led the way back up.

Rich came through to greet her as she entered his suite. "I had it finished this week. Hand-painted by a genuine craftsman."

"Right."

He gestured for her to follow, like a child dragging their parents to the tree on Christmas day, over-eager and pathetic. He led her through to a room that was too small to be a ballroom but too gaudily opulent to be anything else. A red cloth was draped over something huge and unevenly shaped on a central dining table.

"I had Peninsula cover it up," said Rich. "I just wanted you to be the first to see it."

"Apart from yourself," said Sam.

"Well, yes."

"And the master craftsman..."

"Obviously."

"And Peninsula here when he covered it up."

"I can assure you that I averted my eyes, Miss Applewhite," said Peninsula drily.

"Apart from them," said Rich. "Peninsula, if you would."

The butler gathered up the edges of the sheet, lifted it high, then flung it aside with a matador flourish.

"Gosh," said Sam, eventually.

"Isn't it?" said Rich.

"Yeah – wow – it certainly is," she agreed.

She felt a strong urge to ask what it was, even though that was pretty clear. On the table was a large scale model of … something. In scale and construction it reminded Sam of a Hornby model railway, except there was no railway or trains. No, she corrected herself, there was a monorail running around the inside wall of the scene.

"Um," she said.

"Um?" said Rich, worried.

"So you *do* know that Doggerland is underwater," she said.

"Of course I do."

The exterior of the model was taken up by the sea. It was several inches deep and, at the edges, held back by sheets of dark, semi-translucent material. There were tiny model fish visible in the model North Sea, sunken ships, and a possibly inaccurate shark. The polymer sea did not fill the entire table, but was held back by what Sam assumed were meant to be concrete walls, An oval dam revealing the now dry seabed.

"Doggerland," she said.

"Doggerland recovered for a new generation," said Rich.

The soil was a dusty yellow and dotted with sprouting greenery. An ancient landscape, brought into the sunlight once more in an age of high sea levels by brute force engineering.

"The water would be pumped out?" she said.

"Continuously," said Rich. He pointed out grey pipes and tiny industrial buildings.

"And the water wouldn't just ... crush the walls?"

"They're cantilevered. The water pressure pushing down holds them in place. This would be on Dogger Bank. It's a naturally higher area of Doggerland. The walls will only need to be forty metres high."

"Forty..." Sam shook her head. The number was meaningless. The whole thing was meaningless.

She was staring at a model of a something out of a stupid sci-fi film, a park on the seabed. There was a monorail. There was a hotel. There were cafés and stripey-roofed ice-cream stands. There were fenced off areas, compounds.

"Can I ask...?"

"Please do," said Rich eagerly.

"Those mammoths there. And those – I'm going to say bears? And that rhinoceros... Are they going to be models in your Doggerland theme park?"

He was already shaking his head. "Ice age creatures brought back to life through genetic engineering."

"You are aware that *Jurassic Park* was not a documentary?"

"The science is sound," said Rich. "We have DNA samples of all these creatures. Not fossilised, but perfectly preserved in ice. Frozen, usable."

She couldn't help but look to Peninsula for some sanity. The butler pulled back as though unwilling to be part of the conversation.

"Mr Raynor has spent considerable time and funds talking to members of the scientific community," said Peninsula.

"With proper degrees from proper universities," said Rich.

"And this will work?" said Sam. She gently tested the edge of the retaining wall between thumb and forefinger. Was she testing it or just seeing if it was real?

"The science is sound," repeated Rich. "Exciting, huh?"

"Expensive, surely," she said.

"Oh, and then some," grinned Rich. "We just have to get in there before the others."

"Others?"

"British companies planning on building windfarms in the region. The Dutch and the Germans are planning on building up an artificial island nearby to manage their windfarm network."

"So you're not the only loony out there," she said.

Rich laughed. "I'm the only one with mammoths."

Sam walked her fingers along the top of the wall to a grand observation tower that looked like an evil supervillain's lair.

"And you're going to build all of this?"

"Well, not that," he said, nodding at the tower. "That's already there."

"What?"

"That's Valhalla platform. It will be the base of operations during the construction phase."

"What?"

"It's a gas drilling platform," he said. "Decommissioned. And I own it."

Sam looked to Peninsula.

"Oh, he certainly does," said the butler, deadpan.

"And I want you and DefCon4 very much involved in this," said Rich.

She shook her head. She couldn't imagine what she or her chaotic employer could do, unless Rich wanted her to put up some ATTACK MAMMOTHS PATROL HERE! signs.

17

Strawb looked over the itemised bill. Polly watched his face, his big hands scratching and teasing at his craggy chin. "There's a lot of biscuits on here," he said eventually.

"Oh, God. You're as bad as her."

"I'm just pulling your plonker," he laughed and patted her knee. "But seriously, there's a corner shop just down the road. Family size packets of biscuits for half the price." He shrugged. "What's the problem?"

"She can see what I'm buying."

"Your niece?"

"Erin."

"Why?"

Polly tapped the page. "She gets in touch or logs on, I don't know. She does the thing and it tells her what I'm spending my money on."

Strawb frowned. When he frowned and the set of his jaw

was just so, he made a passable impression of an English bulldog, all lined and jowly. "Two questions," he said.

"Yes?"

"One. If you're the one who's paying for your rooms here—"

"I am."

"—then why does she get to see what's on it? That's a data protection thingy, isn't it?"

"I don't know."

"And, b, why do you care?"

"Sorry?"

Strawb put the bill on the lounge table between them. "Why do you give a fack what this horrible niece of yours thinks?"

Polly squirmed inside. The simple answer was that she shouldn't, that she was her own independent person. But more than that, there was the business with her great niece and nephew. She didn't know them as well as she should but they were her youngest relatives, the closest thing to a legacy. No, it wasn't even that.

"I used to have a home," she found herself saying.

"And you don't now?"

She shook her head. "It was large, detached. Wickenby Way. There was a kitchen, apple white walls, and a hob with five rings. The hallway had an Axminster patterned carpet. The living room was long with seating for at least six people, and on the display cabinet were the pictures of our mum and dad's wedding and of Lucy and me."

"Lucy?"

"My sister. And there were Laura Ashley bedspreads in

the bedrooms and cushions and silly little teddy bears and a power shower that – oh, I loved that power shower – and..." She trailed off, not sure what she was saying.

"And now you live in a little box in a building of little boxes with a bunch of other bewildered people wondering where the last fifty years went?" suggested Strawb.

She laughed. "Yes. Yes and no. Yes, it's my physical place in the world. Yes, it's stuff. But also... Families. They're complicated things, aren't they?"

"Too bleeding right," he said. "My other half's family were a nightmare."

"Your other half..."

"Gone ... eight years now." He caught her look and she could almost see him filing his emotions away. He tapped the bill with an aggressive fingertip. "We'll sort this out."

"Or I could buy my biscuits somewhere else," she suggested.

"Yeah, but not your G and Ts. Nowhere serves a G and T like the Otterside," he grinned.

18

Sam was down at the DefCon4 office early to meet Delia. Sam had promised to accompany her dad to the doctors later, and Delia had a shop to open at nine sharp. Sam wasn't sure who the key customers for Delia's specialised brand of repurposed junk were, or whether they demanded entry to *Back to Life* at the very start of the day, but she didn't want to be the reason for any loss of takings.

Sam climbed the stairs, turned on the crappy heater and put it on the desk next to Doug Junior.

"Ooh, it's colder in here than it is outside!" said Delia, following her up.

"Yep. Some days I just keep my coat on all day. I have a hot water bottle for when things get very bad."

"Don't you have heating in here?"

"There's that tiny low wattage thing over there."

"Doug looks like he's positively shivering," said Delia.

"Nothing bigger is allowed, according to facilities management. This one would probably warm the place up if it could come on at four in the morning or something, but company policy forbids the use of heating when the office is unoccupied."

Delia rolled her eyes. "Your facilities management sounds rubbish. Who is it?"

"It's me, but I can't make any actual decisions. It's all down to a website I put details into."

"Details like...?"

"Like the size of the office, and the occupancy."

"What about your absent colleagues?" Delia asked, waving a hand around at the empty desks.

"I can only add people if I have their national insurance number. Believe me I've had a go. I'm not permitted to request personal identifiable information unless I'm a hiring manager."

"Huh." Delia was stumped. Sam could see her mind whirring, and knew she'd keep coming up with ideas. She didn't want to stop her, just in case she found an angle that could work, but Sam had applied herself to this problem with the motivation of the permanently shivering, and was pretty sure she'd tried everything. "Well I probably can't fix your heating, but maybe I can take your mind off it."

"I'm all for distractions," said Sam.

Delia delved into her large tote bag and fetched out a large cafetière. "For you."

"For me?"

"A thank you for your help with Drumstick."

Sam felt a little deflated. "I've done nothing. Apart from

asking a few questions in the area." And putting the bird in the freezer ready for Christmas, she added silently.

"You were there when I needed you," said Delia. "It's appreciated. Now, I will make us some proper ground coffee. You realise this will increase your productivity as well?"

Sam caught on. "Oh! Because now I won't have to go to Cat's Café for a coffee and listen to her talk about her play or anything. I don't even know what I'll *do* with all the extra time!"

Delia gave her a triumphant fist bump. "I'll go and put the kettle on."

As Delia prepared coffee, Sam checked through her tasks for the day. It was a surprisingly sane list: checking the smoke alarms at a packaging factory, secure cash collections in the town, and the slightly cryptic *Hygiene management* at a local hostel – which basically meant checking the cleaning was getting done. The final task of the day was *Staff familiarisation with fitness support trackers and related training material*. There was a parcel on the desk linked to that one.

"You know what else you're going to need?" called Delia from the kitchen area as Sam scored along the edges of the well-sealed box.

"No, what's that?"

"You'll need a cosy to keep your coffee warm in this freezing building. At least I know what to make you for Christmas now." Delia walked through with a full pot of coffee. "Can I have a piece of paper?"

Sam handed her a piece from the scrap pile.

Delia wrapped it around the hot pot, scrunching, folding and eventually tearing it to size. "There! That's my template," she said. "You'll just need to drink it quickly before it goes cold in the meantime."

"Not a problem," said Sam. "Why have you brought me a cafetière anyway?"

"I said—"

"No, I mean what prompted that particular gift? Not that I'm ungrateful."

"I've got six of them in the shop," said Delia. "It's as if Skegness has reached saturation point with the damned things. Now that I've thought of making cosies for them I reckon I can package them up as desirable Christmas gifts though. So, thank you."

"Happy to be of service." Sam sifted through the unnecessary layer of packing chips in the parcel. "Say, what do you know about wearable devices?"

"Wearable devices? You talking about kinky strap-ons?"

Sam snorted. "That would be a step too far, even for DefCon4. No, wearable tech, like fitness trackers." She wiggled a boxed fitness tracker watch as she pulled it out from the packaging.

"Oh, *those*. Have you seen the things that count as fitness?" asked Delia, waggling her eyebrows suggestively.

Sam looked at her, really not sure where she was going. "No. I mean yes. Walking, running, cycling. The usual things."

"You missed shagging," said Delia, her face a mask of barely suppressed glee.

"What? No."

"It's true. You can use it to track your sexercise. I reckon some of these things are designed by voyeurs, just so they get to know when the rest of the population's getting it on. It's only a matter of time before they start popping up adverts for condoms or suchlike."

"Well, they'd be very disappointed with me," said Sam.

"Wow, going through a dry patch?"

Sam gave her a hard look.

"Rich came into my shop the other day," said Delia.

"Rich and my sex life. One thing's got nothing to do with the other. He's old news. He's a good friend but I like him better at arm's length."

"Arm's length is near enough." Delia poured coffee. The aroma was wonderfully powerful.

Sam pulled the fitness tracker out of its packaging. "I'm going to be delivering training on these soon."

"DefCon4 moving into hawking electronic tat to people now?"

"Health monitoring," said Sam in her most professional voice.

"And do you know how to deliver training on these?"

Sam shrugged. "The DefCon4 way. Do a combat roll out of the door and come up fighting. I'll just read the instructions."

"Can't see any instructions," said Delia, examining the minimalistic box. "Have you put them somewhere else?"

"No." They both searched and then Sam spotted a line of text on the inside of the wristband.

DOWNLOAD THE *FITMEUP* APP FOR FULL INSTRUCTIONS.

"WELL, THAT'S CHEEKY," said Delia.

Sam already had her phone out and the app was installed a few minutes later. "Yeah. Everybody thinks they've got a right to force their app onto your phone."

She put the wristband onto her wrist and followed the steps to synch the device. "Ooh check me out. I have a heartbeat!" she said.

"That's pretty much all most men look for in a woman. You should be beating them off with a stick. Move around, see if it knows," urged Delia.

Sam stood up from the desk, jumped on the spot for a few minutes and then ran across the office as quickly as she could, although the room was so small it wasn't a very challenging run.

"It knows! It knows!" shouted Delia. "It's saying you've commenced a workout."

"Cool," said Sam.

"Now fall down quickly, see if it can tell when you've died."

"What?"

"Go on! Some of them are super clever. Give it a go."

"Or we could just read the instructions."

"That is no fun at all. Besides, it might be an undocumented feature."

"You're making stuff up just to get me to throw myself on the floor."

"Basically, yes." Delia was almost jumping up and down in anticipation. "It's a skill you'll thank me for one day."

"Faking a fall?"

"Yeah, there must be loads of times it would come in handy."

"Like...?"

"Oh, I don't know. Say you need to get out of a really boring meeting, or a bad date or something. I bet there are loads of scenarios where you could use it."

"How do I do it then?" asked Sam.

"What? You just fall over."

"No, how do I do it without hurting myself?"

"Maybe you can't," said Delia. "If you really want the device to react, then half-measures won't work."

"Oh, for crying out loud," said Sam and she launched herself at a clear bit of floor. "Argh! Oh, balls! That *hurt!*"

She sat up, carpet burns on her forearms and knees. Did she have any other injuries? Possibly. She tried not to think about the tears she'd probably put in her clothes.

"You were too quick. I wasn't watching the app," said Delia. "Do it again."

"If it really thought I'd died, I'd hope it would do more than just pop up a brief message," said Sam. "I am not doing that again."

Delia stabbed at the app while Sam got to her feet.

She kept the tracker on but gathered the packaging and put it on one of the spare desks, out of the way. Next to it was a small pile of wireless security cameras. She passed one to Delia.

"Here."

"What's this?"

"A little something for you. A thank you for the coffee pot."

"The coffee pot was a thank you for helping with the turkeys."

"And this is a thank you for your thank you," said Sam. "You can stick one of these in your kitchen window and point it down the garden. Download the app – yet another app – and you'll be able to keep your eye on Twizzler the turkey when you're away from home."

Delia nodded appreciatively.

Sam's phone buzzed; a new task had appeared. She read it. "I might have to kill Rich," she said.

"I can stop insinuating you're an item," said Delia. "No need to go for such extreme measures."

Maybe Delia caught the look on Sam's face, or maybe it was time to crack on with the day's business. Regardless, she picked up the scrunched paper coffee cosy template and stood. "I've got some coffee pots to sell to the good people of Skegness."

Sam nodded at the cafetière. "A very generous present. What would I do without you?"

Delia shrugged merrily. "But if you do decide to kill Rich, don't call me to help dispose of the body, you hear?"

As Delia clomped down the stairs to the street, Sam re-read the task that had just appeared.

Sam had seen some tasks on her planning app that raised her eyebrows. She'd learned early on that the channels for querying whether something was correct were very limited. The help she could expect to get on the end of a phone line did not extend past 'it must be right, because the computer says so'. As a result, she invariably just got on with it. On this particular occasion she could phone the person who had commissioned DefCon4 to do the work.

She didn't have a phone number for the LRPC Research Centre, but she did have Rich's mobile.

"*Sam!*" he said, too happily, too loudly when picked up. "*How the devil are you?*"

"Rich, I see you've commissioned me for some work."

"*I did indeed. I know I can rely on you to do a great job.*"

Sam wondered how best to phrase this. Bluntness seemed like the only way to go. "Rich, are you mocking the work I do here?"

"*What?*"

"Just because DefCon4 gets me to do literally anyth—"

"*Mocking you?*"

"Yes, mocking me. As in—"

"*Of course not. I would never do that.*"

"Well, are you doing it to create work for me or something? I have plenty to do, you know?"

"*Sam, I don't know where this is coming from. I've asked DefCon4 to do this piece of work because I really need it to be done, and done well.*"

"Really? Because it sounds pretty unlikely." She took her phone from her ear, swiping to the DefCon4 task app so she could read it directly. "You have requested an escape drill for the animals which you'll be keeping in your Ice Age park."

"*Correct. It's a risk management exercise. You wouldn't believe how many stakeholders insist upon this sort of thing.*"

"You want me to engineer a practice drill for capturing

animals that haven't existed for thousands of years in a park that is currently at the bottom of the sea."

"It's the right thing to do, of course."

"Animals you've got scientists creating in a lab somewhere. They don't even exist yet, do they? Do I get some elephants and cover them in carpet as mammoth stand-ins?"

"Now Sam, I can't get this risk assessment a moment too soon. It's a key document. Which is why you've got the extended budget to hire other people to help with it."

Sam glanced down at the app. This was something she hadn't encountered before. Budget? "Very well, you're the client. I just wanted to check."

"Thanks Sam, looking forward to seeing the results and recommendations."

Sam ended the call and hunted around for evidence that she had money to spend. There it was!

"Doug," she whispered in awe, "we've got a budget!"

19

J ust before her official lunchtime, Sam drove back home to collect her dad and take him to the health assessment the bank had insisted upon before granting him any further loans.

"You look decidedly chipper," said Marvin as he climbed in the Piaggio. "Does the prospect of your old man getting prodded and poked by the sawbones fill you with a general glee?"

Sam realised she was grinning and had been grinning for much of the morning. "I've got a budget for a project."

"Is that a novel thing?" he asked.

"Rare as unicorn poop." Sam pulled out of Albert Avenue and headed for the Heath Road Medical Centre.

"So how do you feel about your old man getting prodded and poked?"

She gave a twitchy facial shrug. "I don't."

"Maybe the doctor has some bad news for me."

She looked across at him. "You think the doctor will have bad news for you? Are you worried?"

"Pah. No. I'm just saying. Death comes for us, doesn't it?"

"Jesus Christ," she hissed, laughing. "It's a medical. We're not getting you fitted up for a coffin."

"Oh, I've already had that done," he said.

"Stage coffin?" she said.

"For a show with Dave Allen. Remember him? It was a tight squeeze. I must remember to tell the undertaker to give me a bit more wiggle room in my next coffin."

"Doctor, dad, not undertaker. Have you not been for a medical before?"

His brow creased as he tried to see across the years of memory. "Sure. Only thing I recall is the nurse telling me to turn my head and cough. Not even sure she was a qualified nurse."

The Heath Road Medical Centre was a two mile journey from *Duncastin'*, an unpleasant walk in this cold for an older man, but only a ten minute drive up through the town and round the War Memorial playing fields in the van.

"You coming in with me?" asked Marvin as they entered the reception.

"Do you want me to?" she replied.

He pulled an indecisive expression, but not enough to be convincing. "In case the doctors try to baffle me with science lingo."

He was nervous. It was an odd thing to witness. Marvin Applewhite had treated his entire life like a stage routine and had long ago ceased to be afraid of his audience. To see him on edge was to see a weakness the man rarely showed.

"Sure," she said.

The receptionist gave him a clipboard of questions before calling him through to the consultation room. The room was decorated in soothing NHS green. The doctor's desk – dark wood and leather top – looked like it had been pilfered from a pirate captain's stateroom.

"Mr Applewhite," she said, looking to her notes, then at Sam. "And who is this?"

"I'm his daughter."

"Do you need to be here?"

"I asked her to come," said Marvin. "Just in case I don't follow all the things you're saying."

"Do you have a hearing problem?" said the doctor.

"No," he said. "But my attention has a tendency to … um…" His eyes drifted to the ceiling and his finger traced the flightpath of an entirely imaginary fly.

The doctor blinked.

The Toblerone name plate on the desk said DR ERIN HACKETT. The woman it belonged to had a profoundly serious air about her as though fun and frivolity, whilst not being entirely forbidden, were not welcome.

"Sorry. My dad is an acquired taste," said Sam.

"I'm like anchovies," he said. "Where do you want me? On the rack? These your instruments of torture?" His hand waved over the items on her desk. Sam was sure the thing between the stethoscope and otoscope was actually an e-cigarette.

"Just sit," said Dr Hackett. "This shouldn't take long." She clipped an oximeter on the end of his finger and asked him to roll up a sleeve. "This is for an insurance medical?" She looked at the form before her.

"The bank," said Marvin. "I need to re-mortgage the house. And I'm going back to work."

She nodded and slipped a blood pressure cuff on his arm.

"You're thinking of going back to work?" said Sam.

"It's good to keep busy," said Dr Hackett. "Decent honest labour. What do you do?"

"Stage magic," said Marvin.

The doctor didn't reply, but her silence made the gulf she believed existed between stage magic and 'decent honest labour' quite clear. "Blood pressure's a bit elevated," she said eventually.

"You got me thinking about my house," said Marvin.

Dr Hackett made a noise. "My family and I are currently moving house. A place on Wickenby Way. They say it's one of the most stressful things you can do."

"Avoiding having to move is pretty stressful too," he said.

"Stress is manufactured in the mind. It's something you do to yourself."

"My stress is my fault?"

The doctor nodded.

"That's a stressful thought," he said.

The blood pressure cuff was ripped away with a loud Velcro sound. "Right. Up onto the scales, Mr Applewhite. Let's see how much you've been abusing your body."

20

The Otterside Residents' Social Committee met in the north lounge on an almost daily basis. It had only three members, none of them elected. Margaret Gainsborough liked it that way. Time and experience had taught her the difference between what was nice and what was effective. Democracy was nice; dictatorships were effective. Inviting the opinions of many was nice; keeping the group to a manageable three was effective. In truth, it should have been called the Otterside Residents' Social Junta or Cabal, but neither sounded as nice as 'Committee'. Niceness had its uses.

Margaret had drawn three chairs up to a round table and sat at its head. It was hard to say that a round table could have a head but Margaret had a knack with such things.

Jacob and Strawb took their seats, Jacob shuffling and repositioning his until he was happy, Strawb dropping into his with a boneless ease, like he was the king of fools upon his throne.

Jacob opened his notebook. It was a leather bound book with an elasticated strap, filled with lists and notes and *aides memoire*. He kept the minutes of their meetings. No one asked him, but he did anyway.

"We're looking at the schedule of entertainment for December through to January," said Margaret. "The regular social events are fixed. We're just looking at the additional items. I'd really like to push the boat out."

"Sailing?" said Jacob.

"Metaphorically," she said.

"As long as it ain't more bladdy arts and crafts," said Strawb.

Margaret pursed her lips. "Nimble fingers make agile minds."

"Just cos we're old, don't mean we want to be knitting and doing macramé and – what's that one? – origami?"

"Origami," said Jacob.

"That's what I said."

"But you asked."

"If you want us to use our hands, why don't we get in that girl who teaches massage? A bit of mutual massage."

Jacob's face screwed up in disgust. "What? Touching each other?"

"I've got a right knot in this shoulder." Strawb twisted to present his back to Jacob. "Why don't you dig in, Jake? Give it a bit of a pummelling."

"For one thing, I am not trained," said Jacob, holding

tightly onto his pen and notepad. "Furthermore, I'm not entirely comfortable with the ... physical contact."

Strawb guffawed shamelessly. "You crack me up." He tapped the planner sheet Margaret had placed on the table. "Go on. Put it down. Bit of massage."

"I do fear some people might misinterpret what 'massage' entails," she said.

Strawb snorted. "Not enough 'happy endings' in this place anyway, if you ask me."

"Happy endings?" said Jacob.

Strawb raised a hand to give an explanatory hand gesture. Margaret raised her own to stop him.

"I'm just saying there's nothing wrong with enjoying ourselves a bit more," said Strawb. "Not just sitting around doing a – what was it? – jigsaw marathon."

"There will be no more jigsaw marathons," said Jacob sniffily. "There are still four pieces missing after the last one."

Margaret had seen the 'missing' posters Jacob had put up around the building. They had featured photographs of the missing pieces. The inherent implication was that Jacob had either photographed each jigsaw piece before the jigsaw marathon or had, post-marathon, sought out copies of the jigsaws and taken images. Neither option sounded plausible and yet, with Jacob, both were equally believable.

"Entertainment is indeed what we need," said Margaret.

"Something enlivening," said Strawb.

Jacob made a noise. "Oh, everyone gathering around the old Joanna for a bit of a sing song. A bit of *Knees Up Mother Brown.*"

"I'm not a bleeding Cockney," said Strawb. "How many

times do I have to tell you?"

"A few more. You're fooling no one."

"Practically racist, that is."

"I've booked some pre-Christmas entertainment," Margaret interrupted.

It was enough to stop their squabbling. Her lieutenants bickered constantly, but only as asides to the proper business she laid before them.

"I know someone who knows someone who handled the bookings for Carnage Hall back in the sixties," she continued.

"Now you're talking," grinned Strawb. "Bit of rock and roll. Who've you got? Billy Fury? I used to love him."

"I believe he's dead," said Margaret.

"Who else was there? Adam Faith?"

"Also dead," said Jacob.

"Bladdy hell. Lonnie Donegan. A bit of skiffle. Is he still touring?"

Margaret didn't have the heart or will to tell him. "I am going to get someone. We'll see. I'm sure we have enough funds in the kitty to splash out on a little Christmas concert here at Otterside."

Jacob coughed and tapped at his notebook. The words CRAZY CRAZY GOLF were written in Jacob's angular block print and underlined. Twice.

"*Crazy* crazy golf?" she said.

"Crazy *crazy* golf," said Jacob.

"Are we going ahead with that?"

Jacob looked at Strawb.

"Already bunged Ragnar a few notes," said Strawb.

"Coming on a treat." He caught her look. "Who doesn't love a bit of crazy golf, eh?"

"People who don't like crazy golf," said Jacob.

"We agreed it last time."

"We said we'd think about it," said Margaret. "Is it possible you've confused 'think about it' for approval?"

"I'd say it's entirely possible," said Jacob.

"Ah, but I was thinking that we as residents can save money in other ways." He put a sheet on the table. "This is Polly Gilpin's bill for services."

"Yes?"

"Did you know we all have to buy into this health insurance thing that covers the nurses and visiting health people? I've been shopping around. We could get it for cheaper, especially if we sign up for these health tracker things." He placed a brochure on the table next to the bill.

"The FitMeUp wearable activity tracker," Jacob read.

"It's a heart monitor?" said Margaret.

"It's a thirty percent discount on health insurance premiums," said Strawb.

"I see you've become quite pally with Polly of late."

Strawb smiled shamelessly. "I have."

"And?"

Strawb shrugged good naturedly. Margaret looked to Jacob. "And?"

"And what?" said Jacob.

"Is she a good fit? For Otterside?"

"I'm still assessing."

"Thought we'd invite her on a little jolly," said Strawb. "After hours. Sound her out."

21

After dropping her dad back home and in between the other eclectic tasks which rounded out her day, Sam spent time watching escaped animal drills on YouTube. They were actually a thing. They were very much a thing. Particularly in Japan.

According to several of the videos, Japanese zoos needed to perform such drills as it was an earthquake-prone country, and lions, tigers and bears slipping out of damaged enclosures was a real concern. However, Sam suspected, some people just liked the opportunity of dressing up for the day in unrealistic animal outfits and running wild in zoos.

Either way, hiring folk to pretend to be animals or zookeepers in a massive game of 'tig' seemed the way to go. If there were animal costumes that needed making, then Delia was the obvious choice.

Night was falling. Sam would contact Delia another day. Then she'd just need actors to play animals and park staff, and equipment to aid in their recapture. Plus the small matter of a full-sized recreation of a prehistoric theme park at the bottom of the North Sea. Maybe she needed to recheck that budget.

She tidied the office as much as an office with one inhabitant needed tidying, said goodnight to Doug Junior, and went downstairs. The last act of departure each day was locking up and clocking out on the DefCon4 app. It constantly tracked her location, but she had to manually tell it she was done for the day after she left the office.

She turned out the lights, locked the door and clicked the button to go off shift. The app made an unhappy buzzing sound and refused to close.

There was an unfinished task.

COMMUNITY PAYBACK HOURS NOT LOGGED, declared the app.

Well, that was nonsense, she thought. She had filled in the timesheets for the offenders at Otterside and scanned them in at the office, as she always had. The offenders could then hand their sheets to their probation officers, or forward them through the court liaison system. Sam had done her bit, so maybe...

She stood on the cold pavement and tried to interrogate the unfinished task. The words, INDIVIDUAL OFFENDER FILE UPDATES NOT COMPLETED, confirmed her suspicion.

"Well, that's not my fault," she told the app and tried to log out again. Again, the unhappy buzz.

She gritted her teeth. It looked like she would have to ring round the offenders in the morning and stay clocked on in the meantime.

22

P olly woke in the night and felt a moment of panic. The lines of the rooms about her, the geometry of darkness, were strange and alien. Then she recalled she was in her room at Otterside, her new home and she would have to get used to it. She lay there, blinking at the ceiling and wondering why she had awoken when the knock came at her door again.

She sat up and looked at her clock. Finding no answers there, she got up and went to the door. Strawb stood in the corridor, fully dressed, even with that silly hat on his head.

"What time do you call this?" she said.

He consulted his watch. "Midnight. The witching hour. You want to come and see?"

"See?" she said.

He jerked his head to indicate something outside. "Margaret and Jacob and I are having a sneak look."

"But it's midnight."

"There's no point sneaking around unless you do it at a suitable sneaking time. Now, get dressed before matron does her rounds and sends us back to bed."

"Aren't we allowed out of our rooms at night?"

"Of course we bladdy are, but it's much more fun if we pretend we're not."

Bewildered but intrigued, Polly went back in and swapped her pyjama bottoms for trousers and pulled a thick fleece around her top. "You must be mad, Polly Gilpin," she told herself. She met Strawb in the corridor again. "This all very *Mallory Towers*," she said.

"What's that?" said Strawb.

"Girls' boarding school. Midnight feasts. Sneaking around after dark. Did you not read any Enid Blyton as a child?"

"Never been in a girls' boarding school. Must put it on my list."

They went downstairs to where neatly-pressed Jacob and a tall, longed-face woman with ash blonde hair waited. The woman looked past Strawb at Polly.

"Polly's here as an independent observer," said Strawb.

The woman smiled thinly and nodded to Polly. "Margaret Gainsborough," she said.

"The chair of the social committee," said Polly, recognising her. "Observer of what?"

"The new crazy golf course," said Strawb. He led the way out, into the night, skirting the dewy lawns and round to the outbuildings to the side of the main horseshoe. As he walked, Strawb gave them a personal insight into the specification he'd provided for the job. Skegness was not known for year-round good weather, so they would have an indoor crazy golf, with links to the outside part for when the weather was fine. Strawb spoke about the extensive use of papier-mâché for the interior models and weatherproof fibreglass weatherproof outside.

"Ragnar Odinson's been cracking on with it," said Strawb. "Late into the night."

He opened the outbuilding door to the temporary workshop. Strawb passed Polly a torch and turned on his own.

"Feels spooky," said Polly.

"Are you afraid?" said Margaret with a dry playfulness.

"No."

"Course she ain't," said Strawb. "What's there to be afraid of here?"

"Rusty nails. Tetanus," said Jacob, giving the workshop a critical look.

The garage was empty, the workers gone, but there was much evidence of industry. Large shapes, cut from sheet metal, hung from wires suspended from the ceiling. They'd been sprayed with undercoat, presumably as the last task of the day, so the fumes would disperse by morning. Right now the solvent smell was very strong. Polly wrinkled her nose.

Jacob peered down at the music centre. "I would not have imagined Ragnar Odinson to be a fan of Herb Alpert."

"Each to his own," said Margaret simply.

"He seems to spend all of his time sitting around," said

Strawb. "I wonder if he gets that granddaughter of his to do the donkey work while he dreams up the next part."

"A minor wouldn't be covered by liability insurance if he does," said Jacob.

"I don't think she's a minor," said Strawb.

"It's highly likely her presence merely energises Ragnar," said Jacob.

"Energises?" asked Margaret.

"Yes. It is a recognised phenomenon. Perhaps simply the human urge to remain relevant to the up and coming generation. Whatever it is, many people perform more effectively and creatively when they co-exist with younger people."

"I wonder what they plan for this," said Polly having peeked under the corner of a protective sheet. "It's a leaf blower, isn't it? With some wood thing around it."

They crowded round the puzzling construction.

"Be a surprise, I suppose," said Strawb.

"I do not like surprises," said Jacob.

"Lighten up, Jacob," said Margaret.

"It's a crazy golf course, not a space programme," said Polly.

In this place of strange constructions and behaviour which, although not quite wrong, was definitely *outré*, Polly could not resist pressing the *On* button.

It set up with a loud noise that made her give an 'Oh my!' of surprise.

"What the bladdy hell are you doing?" shouted Strawb.

"I just..." She could hardly raise her voice over the racket. The protective sheet dropped down onto the floor as the leaf blower, its nozzle embedded in a hole in a large sheet of wood, rose up by several inches. The air had inflated a large, previously unseen bag beneath the wood.

"God in heaven, it's a hovercraft!" shouted Jacob.

Margaret stepped onto the wooden platform, clearly with the intention of squishing it back into place. The hovercraft stayed inflated, starting to drift sideways across the garage. Strawb leapt forward to help, but the air bag was still mostly inflated. He reached for the leaf blower, in order to turn it off, but the whole thing tilted with their weight, skidding to a halt when it hit the wall on the other side. Strawb and Margaret staggered off. He scrambled for the controls of the leaf blower and turned it off.

"What on earth were you thinking, Miss Gilpin?" said Margaret, once everyone had ascertained they were uninjured.

"I'm sorry," said Polly, who realised she was not sorry at all. Those seconds of silliness had been the most fun she'd had in weeks.

"I do not like surprises," pouted Jacob. "And hovercrafts are dangerous."

"Really?"

"Four people died in a hovercraft crash in Dover in eighty five."

"Well, we're nowhere near Dover so we should be perfectly fine," said Margaret. She had the air of a headmistress about her, or perhaps a hospital doctor: imperious and judgemental. "It was probably wrong of us to come here. We should leave Ragnar to his own devices. We'll have to tell him that one of the dementia patients got in here and did this."

"We don't have no patients," said Strawb. "Dementia ones or otherwise."

"He doesn't know that," she said.

23

olly was reading in the south lounge. To an outside observer she might not have appeared to be reading, as she was reclined in the armchair, her arms folded on her book and her eyes closed. The outside observer might even have concluded that, with the surprisingly piercing winter sun shining down through the skylight, she had taken the opportunity for a nap, perhaps pretending to sun herself in warmer climes.

"I think she's asleep," she heard Strawb whisper.

"I'm not asleep," she said. "I'm reading."

"With your eyes shut?"

"I'm digesting the words."

"Is Rosamund Pilcher particularly hard to digest?"

"Can't consume it all in one sitting."

"One might be led to believe you had something of a late night."

There was a giggle.

Polly opened one eye and saw there was a woman next to Strawb. He had his arm lightly around the woman's waist, and Polly surprised herself by feeling a small but definite touch of jealousy. Strawb, so easy to talk to, so very engaging, had shown more interest in her than any man had in ... she couldn't think how many years. To see him sharing any level of intimacy with another woman sparked feelings Polly had genuinely thought gone forever.

"This is Alison," said Strawb.

The woman, wearing large glasses, and a heavy bob that made her round face look even rounder, gave Polly a smile and a finger-wiggling wave. "You settling in all right?"

"Like I've never had another home," said Polly.

Strawb gestured for Alison to sit, putting himself in the armchair directly opposite Polly. There was something formal in the act, like this was a meeting or an intervention. He produced some papers. Polly recognised her itemised bill.

"I've been working on your problem," said Strawb. "Your niece having a sneaky butcher's at your bill."

"I don't want to cause a fuss," said Polly.

"It's a challenge," said Strawb. "It's like the wossname, the HMRC. A bit of cat and mouse. Here's your bill. I showed it to Jacob cos he's got a mind for such things. There's stuff on here I don't think you should be paying for. Health insurance and liability cover and such, but we're gonna take a look at that together. But you, you don't want your niece finding out you've been spending your time sinking glasses of gin instead of attending the yoga or whatever."

"It's not that much gin," Polly said to Alison, embarrassed. "Just a normal amount."

"I don't drink, myself," said Alison. "I do like the yoga, though. I love it."

Polly thought yoga had clearly given Alison the figure of a Buddha, the Buddha in his later, jollier phase, but of course said nothing of the sort.

"Now, we want to make sure that those items Erin doesn't approve of don't appear on your bill," said Strawb.

"Right," said Polly.

"But every time you pay for something here, or book onto something, you have to give them your resident's card like..." He gestured open-handed to Alison. "Give us your card, love."

Alison produced her apartment key. There was a credit-card attached to the ring, with a hole punched in the corner. Polly had one just like it.

"You go to the bar," said Strawb. "You go 'a double gin and tonic please, Suzie'."

"I never had a double," Polly told Alison.

"She swipes, till goes bip, and there's a double G and T on your files."

"Never a double."

"Point is, from card to till it goes straight on the bill."

"Yes. I know," said Polly. "Can you fix it?"

Strawb shrugged like a lazy swell in the tide. "I thought I could use my computer skills."

"Do you have any?"

"I thought I did," he said. "I thought what I'd do is go into Chesney's office, open the Word file, and do one of them search and replace things. Swap gin for salad or something."

"And?"

"There isn't a Word file. It's some clever accounting software I don't understand. So I have a chat with Jacob. He starts talking about some hacker people he knows, or someone who knows someone. Started going on about the dark web and encrypted packets or something." He rolled his eyes. "And then I thought, all we're trying to do is make sure that your bill looks a little, um, health conscious."

"Yes?"

"Make you appear to be a bit more like our Alison here."

Alison smiled.

"Yes?" said Polly.

Strawb unthreaded Alison's resident's card from the key ring and offered it to Polly. "Swapsies?"

Polly stared, and then grinned. "You don't mind?" she said to Alison.

"Happy to help," said Alison. "That's what we're all about here at Otterside."

Strawb spread his hands wide. "There might be some settling up to do at the end of the month, but..."

"It'll work," said Polly. "Will we get into trouble?"

"Does that bother you?"

Polly shook her head serenely and found herself touched by memories. "I was always the naughty one. Out of Lucy and me. That's my sister. I was the eldest. I was always pushing the boundaries. Drawing on my mum's curtains, getting into fights at school, staying out late with boys."

"Oh, this one was a wild child," Strawb grinned.

"And when we got into trouble together—" she frowned in thought "—playing a game of 'pigs', I think we called it. Rolling in mud in the school playground. I'd get the blame because I was the oldest. Eventually, even when my sister did things just by herself. I remember her trying to kill a wasp with a ladle and breaking a window. I happily took the blame because it—" Polly shook her head. "I guess we had found our roles in life."

"Well, I'm happy to take the blame for you in this case," said Alison.

24

D elia's shop, *Back to Life*, stood on the corner of Scarborough Avenue, on the opposite side of the road to Skegness pier. Opening the door set off a clanking sound from a new set of do-it-yourself chimes. Sam looked up and saw it was made from old cutlery suspended from a lampshade frame. Delia's efforts at upcycling and selling the unsellable knew no bounds.

"Morning!" Delia shouted. "I'm in the workshop if you need anything."

"It's me, Sam."

"Putting the kettle on!"

Delia came through a moment later.

"Oh, have you had highlights put in your hair?" asked Sam.

Delia brushed a hand through her fringe. "Er, no. I've just been using the gold spray paint to make some Christmas decorations. I might have got caught in the drift."

"Cool. What kind of decorations?" Sam asked.

"Angel tree toppers mostly," said Delia. "Although frankly, I'm spraying anything that I think might shift more easily in the festive period."

Sam wandered over to look at the tree toppers. "Ah, I recognise those dolls!"

"Yes, the good old Capitalist Whores."

Delia had collected many hundreds of washed-up dolls from the beach throughout the year. This was clearly her latest attempt at making them into something people might want to buy.

"Listen, I know you must be really busy in the run-up to Christmas..." said Sam.

"Rushed off my feet," said Delia solemnly, indicating the empty shop.

Sam grinned. "Would you be interested in a paid commission for some costume making?"

"Paid work? As in actual money? Bring it on!"

"You haven't heard what it is yet."

"Why? Is it horrifically dull? Do you need two thousand Santa hats? Who am I kidding, I'll still do it."

"No. No, it's definitely not dull," said Sam. "Quite the opposite in fact. I will attempt to explain. Have you ever heard of Doggerland?"

Delia went over to the kettle and clattered around making them a drink. "Doggerland, Doggerland. Is that in Norway somewhere?"

"No. Turns out it's not very far from here. In the old days, like the *really* old days, it's what you would have walked across to get to Europe. It's under the sea now."

"Oh. I see. Carry on."

"Well, this is the mad part. No, actually it's the *first* mad part. Rich has a project in mind where he wants to reclaim some or all of Doggerland."

"Won't the sea get in the way?" Delia asked.

"Yes, but he's got engineers looking into it. We don't need to worry about that part. Anyway, once he's got it reclaimed, he plans to build a theme park on it, with real creatures from the Ice Age."

"Righto," said Delia.

She was taking this very much in her stride. Why wasn't she querying the insanity of it? Sam concluded that Delia's appetite for insanity exceeded her own. Which was probably good.

"So, Rich needs to do a risk assessment. He needs DefCon4 to carry out an escape drill for the theme park. I need to hire some people to dress up as the animals, hire some others to be the zookeepers. Then we practise what would happen if the animals escaped."

"Like the Japanese zoos?"

"Like the Japanese zoos." Sam wasn't surprised that Delia had heard of them.

"That sounds brilliant," said Delia. "So the costumes you want ... what are they?"

"I have a list," said Sam. She consulted the app. "Here we are. Apparently, it's not everything that will be in the park, just the riskier ones. We need a woolly mammoth, a sabre-toothed tiger, a bison, a grey wolf, and a caribou."

"A caribou is the, er," Delia made antlers with her fingers.

"Like a reindeer? Yeah, I think so. What do you reckon?"

Delia grinned and jumped up and down on the spot. "It sounds like the best job ever! Seriously I would do that for *no money*."

"Yeah, I wouldn't necessarily repeat that in front of anybody else. You need to invoice for your time and Rich will pay."

"I'll start now. Christmas can wait," Delia rushed around, plucking things off shelves.

"I'm not sure Christmas is necessarily going to wait," said Sam, "but I admire your enthusiasm. What are you doing with that banana stand?"

Delia stopped and turned. "It's a banana stand? Get out of here!" She held up the metal shape, and peered critically at it. "You're so right. If I hang some bananas off it, it'll sell in a jiffy! I was just assessing its potential for keeping a tail erect, but I can solve that problem in a different way. Bananas! Who knew?"

"Well, let me see about some of the other logistics and I'll get back to you with a date when I'll need the costumes," said Sam.

"Yup. Have you or your dad got any old newspapers?"

"Maybe," Sam said. "Shall I drop some off?"

"Papier-mâché heads are probably the way to go," Delia said with a nod. Sam got the feeling she was talking to herself, as much as anyone else. "Oh, a thought. Some of those animals are probably quite big. I'll look it up, but do you want the bigger costumes to have two people inside? Like a pantomime horse?"

Sam gave it some thought. She tried to picture what a pantomime sabre-toothed tiger would look like, but was unable to conjure a sensible image. "No, let's assume each animal must be able to react to the rules of engagement, whatever they are. A one-person costume will give the actor more freedom to behave like the real deal."

The FitMeUp exercise tracker on Sam's wrist buzzed.

"Done your ten thousand steps already?" said Delia.

"It's telling me I shouldn't stop moving." Sam shook her head. "Between sorting out this ridiculous drill and tracking down which of my community service offenders hasn't turned in their forms yet, I've now got to deliver training on these trackers tomorrow."

"Oh? Popular."

"I need to train a bunch of people down at Otterside."

"Residents or staff?"

"Residents."

"Do old people need to track their fitness?"

"I've no idea."

The tracker buzzed again.

"Gotta do what the spooky watch tells you," said Delia.

25

"Morning Polly," said Strawb, waving her over. "Margaret and Jacob are just setting up." The two other members of the social committee were bent over an old music centre. "This time, we're going to *officially* test out the facilities." He gave an exaggerated wink.

Polly wasn't sure how the music centre related to a game of crazy golf. It had been a while since she'd seen one. She didn't really listen to music any more. Why was that? At some point before the move she'd been persuaded to get rid of her little music system, on the basis that most music was streamed now. She didn't have the first idea about streaming, and the digital radio she'd been encouraged to buy had far too many stations for her to comprehend. Her small music collection of light classical and easy listening had been reduced to a mish-mash of everything and nothing.

She stepped forward and gazed in admiration at the array of controls on the music centre.

"I used to think such things look futuristic," said Strawb. "Back in the eighties. But now…"

"It looks clunky and outdated," said Polly. "A bit like me."

Strawb gave her a saucy bump, hip to hip. "Don't believe a word of it. Choose your weapon." He gestured to the rack of putting clubs.

"So, what are we supposed to do with this?" Margaret asked of the music centre.

"Play the record," said Jacob. He pressed the power button and pulled a spring-loaded switch. The needle arm swung across the turntable.

Jacob turned to face Polly. She gave him a brief, nervous smile. Then the music blasted out from the speakers. "Wow, I haven't heard this for a long time!" she grinned.

Jacob frowned.

"Spanish Flea," she said.

"Watch out, it's doing something," said Strawb, pointing.

There was a belt looped around the turntable and it turned a spiked wheel mounted on a table behind. The wheel rotated a mechanism attached to a small toy garage.

"Lift's going up," said Polly. It was quite charming. When it reached the top, something tilted within it and a golf ball rolled neatly out, went down the road that looped around the garage, before disappearing into a large ribbed hose. They heard it clattering along, and moments later it appeared near to their feet.

"Total distance travelled: six feet," said Jacob.

"But it did it with charm and style," said Margaret.

The ball was marked with coloured paint, so its player would be able to recognise it.

"Well, I guess the game is underway." said Strawb. "I'll take this one. It's lining up the next already."

Sure enough, there was another ball making the same journey. Strawb took aim at the first obstacle: a Tom and Jerry style mousehole in the skirting board.

"Is this normal for crazy golf?" said Polly. "I thought they were mostly just obstacles with ornaments on top."

"That's why this is Crazy, Crazy Golf," said Strawb.

"I don't know if it's appropriate to call things crazy these days," said Margaret. "Not the done thing."

"Mentally ill golf perhaps," said Jacob.

Strawb tutted. "It's madness gone politically correct."

Polly was last to tee off. She took a club and gave it a tentative swing. She'd always found it pleasing that a golf club had that unexpected weight, given its skinny appearance. Her first shot was too weak and it dribbled partway towards the hole.

"Does it feel silly playing without children?" she said.

"Ignore that feeling," said Strawb. "It'll pass."

"We're beyond the age of being embarrassed by what society expects of us," said Margaret.

"Do you have children?" asked Jacob. "Grandchildren?"

"No," said Polly. She did not elaborate. Why would she? She could speak of her pride in her great nephew and niece, but she would almost certainly betray the pain that she felt at how rarely she saw them.

"I've seen that woman visit you?" Jacob asked. "Your niece."

"Erin," said Polly. The way he'd asked, it was like he already knew. Jacob with his pressed shirt and buttons done up to the top. A perfectly tidy exterior. She could imagine he had an interior to match, a mind like a library file card system.

"It's your go again," said Margaret.

She looked for her ball. "Are we keeping score? How does scoring even work?"

"We're merely testing it today, so there's no scoring," said Margaret.

"No," agreed Jacob in the manner of someone who was definitely keeping a mental score.

"There should be extra points for flamboyant play," said Strawb.

"Flamboyant?"

"Yeah. A bit of oomph. Some zhuzh. A spot of razzamatazz."

"I will put a scoring sheet together for later on," said Jacob.

Polly wondered what flamboyant play might look like. "Am I here as an independent observer again?" she asked.

"An honoured guest," said Strawb.

She grunted. Polly settled into place and relaxed her stance. The angle looked right. She swung the club and sent the ball straight through the tiny archway.

"Good shot! Are you a golfer?" Jacob asked.

"No," said Polly.

"Maybe you should be. You've still got a lot to offer, whatever Erin says."

Polly stared at him. "What? Has she been saying something?"

Jacob shook his head. "Not to me no, but I'd guess from your body language after her visits that they don't cheer you up."

"Bit nosy there, Jacob," said Margaret.

Polly shrugged.

"Listen to me, I'm prying," said Jacob, "when we came out to have fun. I'll stop it immediately. Sorry to go on."

Jacob got his ball through the archway and, with them all done, Strawb practically sprinted through the door to the next section. "We can move on now, gang. Let's see what's next!"

Speakers on the ceiling carried the music through from the other room, Herb Alpert replaced by Holst's *The Planets*. The rest of the room was very dark, just illuminated by glowing orbs floating up high. It was like a planetarium. The music made sense now. Polly hummed under her breath to the rousing *Mars, The Bringer of War*.

"Only one place to hit the ball," said Strawb. He pointed.

There was a small hole up a ramp. It did not look spectacular. Strawb hit his ball and it went in on the first try. He crowed with delight, but went quiet as something unsighted whirred into life. There was a flash across the wall: Strawb's golf ball rushing through an illuminated tube. It dashed across the skyscape, looking like a comet, fell to earth and disappeared from sight.

"Bloody hell," said Strawb approvingly, moments before the ball appeared again in another comet arc, over on the other side of the wall. It dropped down out of sight, but moments later appeared at the far end of the room, near to another of the little mouseholes. Strawb went over and tapped it on its way.

"Well that's rather spectacular!" he said. "You know what? We can get Ragnar to decorate this one for Christmas as well. It just needs Santa and his reindeer up in the sky there. Good job."

"I wonder how it works?" Polly said as she watched her own ball shoot off on its stellar journey.

"Ragnar's a bit of a genius at stuff like this," said Strawb. "As long as NASA don't get hold of him and whisk him off to design spaceships or something, he's the best guy for maintenance we could wish for."

Margaret made a doubtful noise. "Although the man is a little..."

"Weird?" suggested Jacob. "Disgusting?"

"Light-fingered," said Margaret judiciously.

"He steals things?" said Polly.

"It's not that straightforward," said Margaret. "It's more like he's a collector or something. If there's something he likes the look of, like a door or a sink unit, he'll swap it for a different one."

"What? Why would he do that?" Polly asked, confused.

"Never asked. No idea. It's harmless, unless there's someone in residence. It gets a bit awkward when you need to explain why their kitchen's been re-configured. Mostly it's older pieces that go, so it looks like an upgrade."

"That's still criminal behaviour, isn't it?"

Margaret looked at her with a curious expression. "Do we

need to worry about what's technically criminal or not? Can't we just judge things on their moral worth?"

"There are laws for a reason," said Polly automatically.

"For other people. I was given the wrong change at the supermarket the other day. Too much change. Given their prices, I didn't feel inclined to tell them. Was I wrong?"

Polly considered it.

"I used to get all my stationery from work," said Strawb. "Never bought a pen between nineteen sixty-three and ninety ninety-eight."

"That's a given," said Polly. "I think most people do that."

"I always used to save up my poos for work," said Jacob. They others turned to look at him.

"Better toilets on the third floor," he said. "Company time, company toilet paper. I worked it out once. I was being paid two pound seventeen every day to evacuate my bowels."

"Delightful," said Margaret.

Polly couldn't quite imagine a man like Jacob having a poo. In her mind's eye, his waste would appear in pre-wrapped cuboid packages.

"I had a friend who was gluten-intolerant," said Polly, hearing the words before she even thought about them.

"Yes?" said Strawb.

"Whenever she came round for tea and asked me if this cake or that biscuit was gluten-free, I'd just lie and say yes."

Margaret held back a smile.

"And when you say you *had* a friend...?" said Jacob.

"I didn't murder her with gluten, if that's what you mean," said Polly.

"Is gluten even a thing?" said Strawb. "We didn't have it in our day."

"Of course it's a real thing," said Margaret. "Although people believe in a lot of nonsense nowadays. You heard there are people who think the world is flat again."

"It was never flat," said Jacob.

"You know what I mean."

"We should send them to Australia," said Polly.

"To prove it to them?"

"No. To just get rid of them."

"Who would you get rid of?" said Strawb.

"Hmmm?"

Strawb gave her an honest look. "If you could..." He clicked his fingers. "Just like that. Who would you get rid of?"

"Hypothetically?" said Polly.

"Of course."

The final brassy blart of *Mars* faded away, followed by gentle pastoral opening notes of *Venus*.

"I think," said Polly, "that I learned long ago there's no point in imagining things that are never going to happen in real life."

"It's just a game," said Margaret.

"Life?" said Polly.

"You betcha," said Strawb and led the way through to the next room where they found a sign. "Oh, what's this?"

YOU MAY PUT YOUR GOLF CLUB DOWN
AND PICK UP YOUR BALL.
PUT IT ON THE TABLE AND FIRE THE MECHANISM.

There was a raised table, tilted slightly on its end.

"It's pinball!" declared Strawb in recognition.

He put his ball into the corner and pulled back a knob that was attached with a spring. The ball shot up the table and bounced off numerous plywood dividers before it settled into a cup with fifty written on it.

"Fifty points," he growled victoriously. "Get in!"

"I thought we were just testing?" Polly said with a wry smile.

"Fifty's not even the top score," said Margaret, thrusting forward with her ball. "There's one that's worth a hundred."

She leaned backwards, trying to get the spring stretched as far as it would go. There was a stopper to prevent it going too far, and she huffed as she reached it. She released the knob. The ball rocketed up, bouncing sharply as it reached the top and leaping over the edges of the game. It cracked into the wall and trickled towards them on the floor.

"Well, that's just not safe," said Margaret. "We need to get Ragnar to do something about that."

"Maybe you pulled it too far back?" suggested Strawb.

"Nonsense. If I can do it then someone else can, and give themselves a black eye. That's why we're testing it."

Strawb shrugged. "Maybe if they get a black eye they'll learn not to do it again."

Margaret nodded "We want something that is idiot-proof for when suspected idiots come and play it, but we want to be able to play it without protection if we feel like it. Just because we have a duty of care, doesn't mean we can't live dangerously."

"Amen" said Strawb. They'd all finished their turn

without beating his score, so Polly wasn't sure if he was celebrating that, or agreeing they liked to live dangerously.

They knocked the balls through the wall and strolled through the door. The air was cold and crisp. There was another sign.

THIS MUST BE USED WITH CARE.
PUT IN THE BALL, APPLY NO MORE THAN TEN PUMPS
AND PUSH THE PEDAL.

The device mounted on a board reminded Polly of a weed-sprayer she'd had in the past. One pumped it up to get more pressure. This had the pump handle connected up to something that looked like a drainpipe and pointed at a fixed angle towards a small lawn area about twenty yards away.

"Would I be right in thinking that this is a golf ball cannon?" asked Polly.

They all nodded. Nobody looked worried that such a thing existed, which was a little strange.

"I'm going to make my ten pumps count!" said Strawb. He plunged the handle up and down with gusto. Whether his enthusiasm made the pumping any more effective was debatable, but he seemed to enjoy it. "Right. Wait for it! Here we go!"

He stomped on the pedal. The golf ball whooshed out of the pipe and over towards the lawn. It dropped onto the grass, feet away from the hole.

"Margaret next," said Strawb, "who will no doubt put fifty pumps in to do a test."

"Haven't you read the footnote?" asked Jacob. They all looked back at the sign.

> EXTRA PUMPS WILL NOT IMPROVE PERFORMANCE.
> THEY MIGHT DAMAGE THE MECHANISM,
> AND THEY WILL MAKE YOU LOOK AS IF YOU'RE TRYING TOO HARD.

Strawb laughed. "Nice one, Ragnar."

26

L ooking out of her office window, Sam hoped the weather would be kind for the training course. She was supposed to take the attendees through the basics of the FitMeUp wristband, then lead them in some sort of group activity that would demonstrate how the device worked during a workout. She was hoping a brisk walk would be possible, as she had no real idea how to run circuit training or a step class, which were the other suggestions given.

There was a lot of paperwork that went with the course. Sam was obliged to print out a form for every participant, then scan and file a signed confirmation they had received the training. It was a challenge for the aged printer in the DefCon4 office, which found itself suddenly required to print twenty five copies of a document.

"Come on, you can do it," said Sam, wiping dust off the

little lights along the front of the printer. There were three next to the LCD display, but she couldn't remember what they all indicated. Two were green and one was amber. Either the wi-fi was fine, the power was fine and the toner was low, or the power was fine, the toner was fine and the wi-fi wasn't working. She was fairly sure if the power wasn't working all of the lights would be out.

"Just do these ones and I'll get some more toner. We'll need to do it all again next week, you know that don't you?" She looked at Doug Junior. "Times must be desperate when I start talking to the printer, eh?"

She searched for an online printer manual. Just as she found it and opened the PDF document, the printer lurched into life and started on the forms.

"Typical."

The forms were faint, but just about readable.

The amber one flashed an erratic Morse code. Sam looked it up in the manual.

"Cyan? *Cyan?* What on earth are you on about? I don't even want cyan. Well, I don't think I do. It's a stupid made-up colour that doesn't exist in the real world. All I want is black."

She didn't relish trying to order a fresh toner cartridge. If ordering printer ink from DefCon4 had been one of the labours given to Hercules, he would have given up and gone home.

Her phone buzzed. She thought it might be her task manager telling her to get to the fitness app training, but it was yet another warning message saying her current overtime wouldn't be authorised. The damned app wouldn't let her sign out until she had cleared the community payback records from the system. She'd called several people over the past day or so, to no avail. Greg Mandyke wasn't answering his phone and Hilde Odinson didn't have one.

She checked the time. Yes, maybe she had a few minutes spare to go visit one of those in person.

27

H ilde Odinson believed that everyone had a stronghold. Even in this modern age, people had a place they could retreat to – to curl up, to relax, to be themselves, to find a haven from the rest of the world.

For the Odinson clan as a whole it was their compound of caravans and rough-built huts in the furthest corner of the Elysian Fields caravan park. Protected by a wall of derelict caravans and chicken-wire fencing, the compound was home, hearth, mead hall and final point of retreat from a world that did not want them. Within it each person had their own personal stronghold. For Hilde's dad it was his bed, where he would collapse in deep sleep after a hard day's work, or a light day's work, or a day of no work at all. For Uncle Yngve, it was his truck's driver's seat: Nordic talismans ranged along the dashboard and a gel-filled lumber support on the chair.

For Hilde herself it was her workshop. It was the second

largest building in the compound after Ragnar's mead hall, but it was exclusively hers. A long shed with decent lighting, a dependable power supply and every tool money could buy or hands could steal. When the Saxon world outside didn't make sense, when the east winds howled (as they often did) and the rains rattled the roof, Hilde was snug inside, making her own sense of the world, one cog at a time. She even had a hammock strung up in one corner for when leaving her bolt-hole seemed too much effort.

The workshop was Hilde's stronghold, but others were allowed in. There was the occasional need for someone else to enter. In fact she encouraged some of the younger family members to dismantle and repair things. It was the only way to learn. What was sacrosanct, however, was her whiteboard. It served partly as a memo board and partly as an ad-hoc design space. Nobody was to mess with her whiteboard.

She was looking at said board and frowning. She shifted her welding goggles onto her forehead and looked again. *Nobody* would dare mess with her whiteboard except Ragnar Odinson.

"Farfar!" she yelled. He wouldn't be far away and his hearing was good.

When a shadow appeared in the doorway, she turned, prepared to give him the sternest ticking-off a granddaughter could give her farfar, except it wasn't just Ragnar. With him was the community service woman, Sam.

"Miss Applewhite."

"Hi Hilde," said Sam, watching her feet as she stepped inside. The Odinson compound was frequently several inches deep in mud. Hilde made an effort to keep the mud out of her workshop but it was a pointless battle. "I'm on my way to the retirement village and I needed to pop in. I didn't mean to interrupt."

"You weren't interrupting," said Hilde, glancing round to check there was nothing obviously stolen on display.

"Miss Applewhite says tha haven't finished tha community service work," rumbled Ragnar.

"It's not that," said Sam hurriedly, almost nervously. "It's just maybe you haven't cleared your latest hours with the court liaison."

Hilde shook her head, not understanding.

Sam stepped closer. "It's just that after the previous scheduled session, not everyone was ticked off by our system."

"I handed my form in. I really did."

Sam shrugged. "Fine. It's probably not you. My stupid computer system would only tell me someone hadn't completed, but not who. I phoned round everyone, except there's a couple I couldn't get in touch with and— Do you even have a phone?"

"Not sure who I would phone with it."

"Oh, I thought you'd be all over social media. You've got a really interesting hobby here." She waved at the part-repaired and part-deconstructed items around her, pieces that Hilde had fashioned for the crazy golf project but ended up not using. Devices and components that would soon be put to use around the compound. "Passion," said Sam. "You've got a real skillset. I thought you'd be watching or recording 'how to' videos, or selling things on e-Bay."

"Sell them?" said Ragnar, affronted.

"You should really have a word with my friend, Delia. She's got a shop dedicated to giving old things new life."

"We don't need to mess with Saxon shops," said Ragnar.

"And what's this here?" said Sam.

Hilde's workshop had to be big as it served as the repair garage for the Odinson's small fleet of commercial vehicles. However, the space where trucks, vans and earth-movers would be parked to have their oil changed or brakes refitted was currently taken up with the beginnings of a wooden construction: a skeleton of wooden planks, curved up at each end.

"Farfar's longboat," said Hilde. "He plans to sail it and go a-raiding."

"She don't need to know owt about that," said Ragnar.

Sam's smile was one of embarrassment. "I'm sure I don't. I've taken up enough of your time."

"I'll walk thee to tha car," said Ragnar which was plain code for 'I'll make sure tha leaves our land.'

"And then I want a word with you, farfar," said Hilde.

When he wandered back in a few minutes later, Ragnar's face was a picture of innocence. "Nice sketch," he said, indicating the whiteboard.

"Did you think I wouldn't notice that you changed it?" asked Hilde, pointing.

Ragnar pretended to study the diagram, looking for changes. "Looks right good to me, lass, what's up?"

Hilde sighed. "It's a longboat, right? Based on designs from our forefathers, who lived a thousand years ago. Wasn't that what we agreed?"

"Aye, tha's right!" said Ragnar. "We're Odinsons, mind, so we'd want it to go a bit faster."

Hilde nodded patiently. "I understand what you're saying, granddad. We can discuss some options. What definitely won't work – and when I say definitely, I *really* mean it – is to put an outboard motor on the end of each oar. It would be a health and safety nightmare. And quite honestly there are more problems than that. It's—"

"Not to worry lass, it were just an idea." Ragnar ambled across the workshop space and inspected the stacked planks. "How much more wood will tha need?"

Hilde waved an arm. "We could make a start with what we've got. It all depends on how big we—"

"—as long as it's the biggest," said Ragnar.

Hilde sighed. Ever since Ragnar had heard of the *Draken Harald Hårfagre*, a replica ship built by a Norwegian, he had been obsessed with having one that was bigger and faster. Much to his annoyance, the *Draken Harald Hårfagre* had crossed the Atlantic and toured round the coast of the United States.

"It would be much more practical to build a *snekkja* for round here," she tried. "A small raiding vessel we could carry down to the beach."

"No!" snapped Ragnar, more like an angry toddler than a powerful patriarch.

"Fine. Well you'll need more wood then. You might need to use pine or something cheaper—"

"No! It must be oak. The sacred tree of Odin!"

Hilde rolled her eyes. "You're going to need several trees'

worth of oak. It's really expensive stuff. I have no idea where you're going to get it from."

"Leave it wi' me lass," said Ragnar, tapping the side of his nose. "Mek what tha can from this lot and I'll get t' rest."

Hilde made a doubtful noise.

"Oh, and Strawb told me to tell thee that tha crazy golf was right impressive," said Ragnar. "Smashing, it were."

"Course, he did," said Hilde.

Sam was having trouble with some of the logistics. "Mrs Gainsborough—"

"Margaret, please."

"Margaret. I'm supposed to have twenty-five attendees for this training. The contract is very clear. If I don't get twenty-five forms with signatures then I haven't done what's required."

"That won't be a problem," said Margaret.

Sam looked at the individuals arrayed before her in the Otterside lounge. She counted them again. She really didn't need to. "But I only see six of you."

"That's right."

"I'm booked to deliver this to twenty-five people. I've printed off twenty-five forms." She didn't want to reveal the printer-based anguish those twenty-five forms had caused, but some of it must have come out in her tone of voice.

"I'm sure we can all manage several forms each," said Margaret smoothly.

Sam found Margaret's steely calm unnerving. Somehow she was left with the feeling that she was making unreasonable demands of a sweet old lady. Albeit a sweet old lady who wasn't budging an inch.

"Perhaps I've misunderstood this contract," said Sam. "It sounded to me as though the Otterside residents were getting favourable terms on their insurance cover, with the understanding that twenty-five residents would receive training in, *and would continue to wear,* these fitness trackers."

"No, you understood perfectly well," said Margaret.

"And yet you have only six people here. How does that meet the terms you agreed to?"

"How old are you, love?" asked the man in the black trilby, Strawb.

Sam was taken aback by the question. "Why do you ask?"

"Older people are our field of expertise, and you can't be expected to understand how things can sometimes be challenging for them."

"That is literally why I am here. So I can help them to understand these devices." Sam bridled at the assumption she didn't know what she was doing. "I am a patient and kind person. I can assure you I won't patronise your residents or leave them confused."

"No. No you won't, love."

"We know this because you're going to deliver the training to this small group," said Margaret, indicating the people sat around her. "Then we will make sure the other residents are brought up to speed. We will make sure you have all the signed forms you need, and all will be well. We organise and disseminate. Organisation and dissemination is our role. Is that clear?"

"Well, I suppose that will have to do," said Sam.

"It will," said Margaret. "Frankly, there were only going to be five of us, but Janine insisted on joining."

"I'm mad about my exercise," said the leathery-faced West Country woman on the end seat. She wore a black tracksuit with red piping that wouldn't have looked out of place on an Olympic hopeful.

Sam could see she was never going to persuade them to let her carry out the training as she wanted. "Very well, if you think it will be more effective the way you suggest, then I will bow to your expertise."

The residents nodded sagely to each other. Sam sighed.

"What I will need to do is make sure all the fitness trackers are operating correctly afterwards. I will check that all the feeds are being outputted. How would that be?"

Margaret nodded. "Not a problem."

Sam regarded the group. Margaret was clearly some sort of self-appointed leader. Sam had chatted with Polly and the rotund ex-army gent, Bernard, when she'd been in Otterside before, trying and failing to investigate the death of Drumstick. The two men, Strawb and Jacob, plus the West Country woman, Janine, were new to her.

"We can do the first part here if you like. Then we'll move around so you can see the devices in action." Sam unpacked one of the boxes. "I'll give you all a tracker now, then Margaret, you can take the others and make sure they're all on residents' wrists by the end of the week."

She held one up as everyone took their own and examined them. "You will see it looks and fits like a wristwatch. In fact, it tells the time as well. There are some special components inside each one that measure your activity, and help you to reach your own personal fitness goals."

Polly put her hand up. "What if you haven't got any fitness goals and you're happy as you are?"

"Well, that is fine. It will simply report on what you're doing. Many people start off without specific goals in mind. But once they start to see what's possible, they might decide to set themselves some challenges. You can compete in groups as well."

Sam smiled broadly. She hoped some of this was hitting home, although it seemed like a tough crowd. They stared back at her, mostly unresponsive. She'd expected only a moderate amount of curiosity, but she had the strongest feeling they were just going through the motions. Nevertheless, the material she'd been sent was quite insistent that the benefits were legion, and she should mention them multiple times.

"So, who here has got a smart phone or a tablet?" asked Sam brightly.

There were some murmurs of acknowledgement.

"Lovely! Well, you can download the app to get the most out of your fitness tracker. Why don't you all take a moment to do that?"

There was an unhurried shuffling as glasses were put on, chargers were found and the wi-fi password queried numerous times, in spite of it being clearly displayed on a laminated card on the wall.

Sam spent the next thirty minutes providing ad-hoc support. Janine kept calling her tablet Facebook, as if it was the only word she was able to associate with it. Polly's phone had a large crack down the front of it that she claimed was a problem with the app. Bernard kept trying to tell Sam she should get a phone like his, because it was clearly superior in every single way imaginable, even though Sam hadn't revealed what kind of phone she had. Only Jacob seemed to have a truly competent grasp of technological terms. He was up and running, waiting patiently for everyone else, in no time.

Eventually, everyone in the group had the app installed, opened and synched to their devices.

"Has everyone seen the heart rate monitor?" Sam asked. "You can view the graphs on the app. Once you've been wearing your devices for a few days you'll start to see patterns. You'll find it really interesting to see how your heart rate changes between different activities. When you're resting or sleeping it will be different again."

"Can we wear these in bed?" Bernard asked.

"Yes, you can."

"But will they be able to see me naked? It's always connected, you said."

"No, Bernard."

"Not even Bill Gates? Is he not going to track where I am and see when I'm naked?"

"There's no camera. Nobody will see you naked."

"But will he know if I'm naked?"

"No. The device won't know."

Bernard looked troubled. Sam wasn't sure if he was disappointed that his nakedness wouldn't be on display to the faceless Silicon Valley overlords.

"And will it know if ... someone has a crafty fag when the doctor told them to give up smoking?"

"It's only monitoring movement," said Sam.

Bernard raised his arm up and down as though repeatedly putting a cigarette to his lips.

"No," she assured him.

"But if my heart stops in the night, will it tell me," he said.

"Pardon?"

"If I die in my sleep will it wake me up to tell me?"

"You'll be dead, mate," said Strawb.

"But I'm a light sleeper," said Bernard. "Infantryman's reflexes. I'm sure if it buzzes to tell me, I'll wake up."

Sam was perplexed, and not just for the obvious reasons. "You told me you were a deep sleeper."

"Did I?" said Bernard.

"Can we wear them in the shower?" asked Janine loudly.

"Yes, these devices are waterproof to fifteen feet."

"Very good," said Janine. "How deep is the swimming pool, Margaret?"

"Hm, that is a good question," said Margaret. "The deep end is three metres, so what's that in feet?" She stood up. "I'll just go and get a calculator."

"I think you'll probably be fine," said Sam. "We should press on with the training."

"But I need to check," said Margaret. "We don't want to break them, do we?"

Sam waited patiently while the issue of the swimming

pool was cleared up. Eventually Margaret announced that the pool was in fact only two metres deep, so the devices would be safe. Sam wondered how many of the residents routinely dived to the bottom of the pool.

"Why isn't my heart working?" Bernard asked. "Should I be worried?"

"You've got it over your jumper," said Sam. "You need to have it next to your skin."

"So, I do need to be naked."

Jacob was studying the app on his tablet while taking his pulse manually. "Just checking to see if it's accurate," he said.

"Now, let's see what we can do with this. I bet I can make my heart rate go up if I think about Barbara Windsor in Carry on Camping," said Strawb with an appropriate if unlovely Sid James cackle.

"Strawb!" said Polly and gave him a playful slap on the arm.

"Can I suggest something different?" Sam said. "We can all go for a walk, then we will really start to see some interesting details. If you're all happy with the heart monitor, we'll familiarise ourselves with the step counter and take a short walk. We can discuss the results when we get back."

There were more delays as footwear was swapped and coats were sorted. Sam led them on a walk around the grounds. She thought the group looked fairly fit and active, but they tottered along paths as if they were taking part in some sort of bizarre dallying competition, where the one who could hold them up the most won a prize. Shoelaces needed to be retied, plants by the path were identified (after much discussion), and the relative grippiness of rubber or leather soles was discussed, tested and continued to be the subject of heated disagreement when they eventually returned to the lounge. The course notes recommended a brisk walk of between half a mile and a mile. Sam wasn't sure they'd done much more than a couple of hundred yards with all the messing about.

"So, who wants to share the number of steps they've done?" she asked.

"I'm so sorry, Sam, do you have much more training material?" Margaret asked. "Maybe you could leave it for us to read later? It's time for our handicrafting session."

Sam looked around the lounge. There was no sign of anybody else. "Well, perhaps we can just finish things off in the corner while—"

"—I'm afraid that won't be possible. I need to facilitate the activities. We have a very busy schedule. Activities here. Trips out. I can't afford to spread myself too thinly. And I'm sure the others are ready for a break now we have completed the allotted two hours training."

Sam felt as if she'd been expertly played, but there was nothing she could actually complain about. "Fine," she said. "I will be needing all of the forms. Everybody must connect their device up as well."

"I will make sure that happens," said Margaret smoothly, ushering Sam out.

29

Polly went to make tea while Margaret saw Sam out. Strawb, Jacob and Bernard lounged back in their seats.

"Tea, excellent!" said Margaret when she returned.

Polly poured for everyone. It was nice to make a whole pot and pour it out for others. She enjoyed a frisson of belonging, as if she was part of the gang. "That was fun," she said, testing the water.

"I do like learning about new technology," said Jacob.

"I think she meant the part where we deliberately messed up the training, Jakey," said Strawb.

"Is it bad to say I enjoyed making a mess of things?" said Polly.

"Young 'uns could all do with taking down a peg or two," said Janine. "It's good for them."

"We can't rest on our laurels," said Margaret. "There's more work to do."

"Is there?" asked Strawb. "Surely we're done?"

"We need to find ways to get these things to send a convincing data feed," said Margaret. "If we're to get our insurance costs down we need to actually use them."

"We could just get people to wear them while they're walking around," said Jacob, with his eyebrows raised.

"If anyone wants to, they are very welcome," said Margaret. "What I won't stand for is them being imposed on our community because they think we're all too simple to realise we're giving away our personal data."

"I'm happy for people to see my personal data," said Bernard. "It'd be nice to think Bill Gates is interested in me."

"You're happy for everyone to see every last bit of you," said Strawb. "No facking shame."

"I simply do not like the dystopian notion of us being forced into changing our behaviour to suit the whim of our insurers," said Margaret.

Polly saw the glint of anger behind Margaret's cool facade and realised this was not only Margaret's way of keeping the community's insurance premiums down. There were more complex reasons behind this scheme: emotional, philosophical.

"We will spend an hour or so researching the best ways to increase the step count on these things," said Margaret. "I will buy a drink for whoever finds the most effective one. Although we probably need a range of options, to make the spread of data look more realistic."

"A drink?" said Strawb. "A slap up supper for the best one, I say."

30

S am hovered in the reception area of Otterside. The fitness app training was complete, waste of time that it was. As long as she got the signed forms from Margaret Gainsborough, she could strike it from her list. She had plenty of other things to do. There was a fake Ice Age zoo escape drill to organise. She needed to check that Greg Mandyke had handed in his final community payback chits. Yet something nagged at her and would not let her leave.

The manager's door was open.

"Just come to check your CCTV again," Sam said, walking through.

"Which one do you reckon?" Chesney was holding up two shirts against his chest. Both were shiny and synthetic, with huge ruffles down the front. One was a lurid turquoise, the other a violent pink. "For my show," he said.

"I didn't think they were for a court appearance," said Sam. "Are you trying to blind the audience?"

"Trying to grab their attention."

"That one's attention grabbing, definitely," she said. "That one's a cry for help."

"Excellent." Apparently, a cry for help was precisely what he was looking for.

Sam went into the security office and sat down at the desk.

Bernard had just said he was a light sleeper. Yet previously, when Sam had come asking questions about turkey deaths, Bernard had been weird and blunt about the whole thing, saying he had witnessed nothing the whole night.

"*Deep sleeper me,*" said Sam, remembering his words. "*You can check the cameras.* Thanks – I will."

It took a while to locate the night of Drumstick's death, then find the cameras which covered the curving length of Otterside's corridors. The images filled the screen in a nine-by-nine grid. Sam ran it through at high speed, pausing and playing back whenever there was a blip of activity on the camera. There were comings and goings of a general sort up until close to midnight, when things quietened down. With self-contained apartment units, there was little need to be out and about once the bar and café were closed. A few people rolling in from a night out in town maybe, a couple coming out of their flats to shuffle about and check the world was still there before going back into their rooms. Little else.

On the length of corridor where Bernard's room was: nothing. He didn't emerge all night. Had she honestly expected him to? There had just been something in his hurried denial of knowing anything about the incident that made him seem – well, to be blunt – guilty.

"Light sleeper. Deep sleeper," Sam muttered. Was it even conceivable he would want Drumstick dead because he was waking him up with his 'gobble-gobble' dawn chorus?

The door to Bernard's flat remained resolutely closed.

A flicker of activity on one of the screens made Sam pause as she fast-forwarded through. She rewound and played. There was a creeping figure on the ground floor corridor. Actually creeping. People didn't often creep in real life. People walked, people jogged. People might move quietly or economically or timidly, but no one ever really crept, arms spread as though trying to embody the spirit of a silent spider. It was a pantomime act of a burglar. The figure even had on a dark woollen hat, the collar of a black tracksuit top drawn up around the mouth, almost entirely concealing the face.

Sam would have been unable to identify the person at all, except she had seen that black tracksuit with coloured piping only minutes earlier.

"Janine," she whispered, "what the hell are you up to?"

31

Polly timed each of her fitness app experiments. It was pretty easy for the first one, given that it involved an actual clock. There was the owl pendulum clock on her kitchenette wall, and she'd attached the device loosely around the pendulum. She would give it ten minutes, but she could already see it was working well. The steps were piling up on the app.

While she waited out the ten minutes, she pondered what to try next. She walked around her flat, scanning everything, in case it might be useful. If she'd still been in her old house, there would be a shed full of tools. She daydreamed for a moment about putting the device on the end of a spinning drill and wondered what it would make of that. Of course, she'd brought nothing like that with her to Otterside. She would have no need of tools in a place where all of the maintenance was taken care of by others. There was a creeping sense of her being subtly stripped of all the things that would pose a nuisance to others when she died. If her flat could be cleared out in less than an hour, she could hardly be the burden that Erin hinted at, could she? If it was a game of wits, she was definitely losing.

The ten minutes was up, and Polly had come across her next idea while going through some drawers. She grabbed a pair of socks and a pillow case and went down to the laundry room. She was pleased to see it was empty, as she had wondered if anyone else had come up with the same idea. She popped the fitness tracker into a sock, then put it inside the other one for extra padding, and put both into the pillow case for good measure. She placed it into the tumble dryer and set the temperature to low. She switched it on and watched the app. Oh, this was good! She sat and watched smugly while the programme completed. She could almost taste that gin and tonic.

Polly found the others back in the lounge later. Bernard came in practically wreathed in tobacco smoke. He was fooling no one.

"So, what ideas have we come up with?" said Margaret.

Jacob raised a hand. He had a laptop on his knee. "I have a spreadsheet to score our ideas. We can also use it to keep track of what we're doing with the devices afterwards."

"Good," said Margaret. "Are we scoring on anything other than the number of steps achieved in a time period?"

"We are awarding points out of ten for a solution that can be scaled up for multiple devices," said Jacob. "And an extra five points can be awarded for a solution that is thought to be particularly stylish."

"Very well," said Margaret. "Who's first?"

Bernard raised a hand and held up his app. "You know Esther, with the wheelchair? Well I fastened my device onto the spokes, so every time she wheels along it will move."

They all looked at his app.

"It hasn't registered any steps," said Polly.

"Well it wouldn't. She's asleep in the conservatory," said Bernard. "The idea's sound though. You could do loads at a time as well. She's got two wheels."

"Fine. You can have five out of ten for scaling," said Jacob with a small shake of his head.

"Polly?" Margaret asked. Everyone looked at her. This felt like a test, but Polly shook the thought away.

"I had two ideas," she said, pointing at the graph on her app. "You can see the first one here where I clocked up five hundred steps in ten minutes by attaching the tracker onto the pendulum of my clock."

They all nodded in appreciation.

"Impressive, Polly," said Margaret. "Did it slow the clock down at all?"

"Not sure. It was a very short test."

"Worth us looking at how many residents have a such clocks. Very inventive."

"Although scaling is limited," said Jacob, tapping into his spreadsheet.

"Second idea, Polly?" asked Margaret.

"I put the tracker inside a pair of socks and put it into the tumble dryer." Polly pointed at the second part of the graph. "A single cycle on cool lasted for fifteen minutes and clocked up nine hundred and fifty steps."

"Oh now, that is interesting!" said Margaret. "We could

put all of them into a cycle every day and say we're doing a mass exercise class. I like it!"

Jacob nodded. "Full marks for results and scaling," he said. "I think we might have our winner!"

"Not so fast," said Strawb, rising to his feet and putting his hands to his hips with a dramatic flourish. "I also had an idea."

Jacob rolled his eyes.

"What was your idea, Strawb?" asked Margaret.

"I will show you a photo." Strawb walked around with his phone and showed them all a picture.

"Danny the donkey," said Polly, with a smile. She recognised his colourful bridle. He was one of the donkeys giving rides to children on Skegness beach.

"Yes indeed. Six donkeys, walking up and down the beach all day. If we slip Trevor a fiver, he'll make sure those devices get a bladdy good workout whenever we want."

"Even in wintertime?" said Bernard doubtfully.

"Donkeys needed exercise," said Strawb.

"That's another potential winner we've got there." He put the details into the spreadsheet. "It's between you and Polly."

"What about Janine?" said Margaret.

Janine had not returned.

"She's probably gone for a five mile run," said Strawb. "Mad that one."

Janine appeared at the doorway. She was red in the face but she didn't look like she'd been for a run of any sort. Polly thought she looked set to burst into tears.

"Margaret," she said tremulously. "Can I have word?"

Margaret's eyes narrowed.

"It's that Sam woman," said Janine.

"Did she complain about us?" said Strawb, voicing rising in nascent annoyance.

"She's been looking at the CCTV!" Janine hiss-whispered.

Polly could not help noticing Janine's eyes flicking repeatedly in her direction, as though she in particular was not meant to hear this.

"She asked me what I was *doing*," said Janine. "I told her I was going for a run but I don't think..."

Margaret sighed and turned her gaze to Bernard. "*I'm a light sleeper*," she said witheringly.

Bernard didn't seem to have any clearer idea what was going on than Polly.

32

S taging an escaped animal drill sort of demanded a zoo, or similar, for them to escape from. Skegness was short on actual zoos. There was the aquarium in town, the exotic animal sanctuary out Stickney way, the falconry centre up towards Manby, and Seal Land in Anderby Creek. DefCon4 was the security contractor for Seal Land and Sam had spent more than her fair share of time up there after accidentally kidnapping a seal. Sealnapping was an unlikely crime, but it had been a very naughty seal and Sam considered the animal to be at least fifty percent responsible.

She drove the few miles to the isolated village of Anderby Creek, armed with questions, and spoke to Guy. Guy was the guy to speak to about animal control. Guy wasn't the only guy at Seal Land, but he was definitely the guy she needed.

Seal Land backed directly onto the beach and, in winter, the Siberian breezes coming in from the east seemed to pool in its compound walls. Even the Jackass Penguins looked cold.

Sam walked with Guy as he pushed a barrow of hay round to the alpaca enclosure behind the misty-windowed tropical butterfly house.

"Sounds daft if you ask me," he said.

"I am asking you," she said. "Why's it daft?"

"Those animal drills. Don't they have them because of all the earthquakes in Japan? You know – the zoo might fall apart a bit and animals escape. We don't have them in Skeggy. If we build a wall to keep animals in, we'd expect them to stay kept."

"I haven't told you where he's building it yet," said Sam.

Guy hoisted the rectangular bale and, with a thrust of his muscly arm, tossed it a distance into the alpaca's grassy paddock. The mop-haired alpacas, Ant and Dec, trotted over and nibbled experimentally.

"Where's he building it?" he asked.

"You don't want to know. Not even sure if I'm legally allowed to tell you. But are you saying you never have animals escape?"

"Oh, we do. Dec here went for a wander when this gate was accidentally left open. Here…" He led her back up a way to the goat enclosure. "We had a pygmy goat who was fond of jumping out. Climbed up on his friend's back, used him as a platform. We got rid of them to a farm in Worksop."

"Both of them."

Guy gave her a disgusted frown. "They were in it together. Equally guilty. And then, of course, we've got your friend and mine." He turned to the nearest seal pool. A fat grey seal rolled in its depths. With a twist of his body, he jack-knifed upwards and broke the surface.

"Hello, Larry," said Sam.

Larry the seal twitched his whiskers and looked sharply from one human to the other, floating like a corpulent oligarch in his luxury pool.

Larry honked at them – "Blaaaark!"— which sounded very much like the seal equivalent of "Give me all your fish and no one gets hurt."

"Whatever we do with him, he tries to undo," said Guy. "We release him into the wild, he comes back up the beach and terrorises the locals. We keep him here and he tries to smash his way out." He pointed out the gate into the pool area. It was four feet high and so thickly covered in steel braces and supports that it was practically all metal. "If we try to send him off to another reserve or sanctuary, he is such a monumental pain in the arse that he gets sent back, as you know full well."

"So, you do have animal escapes."

"Only due to human error or rogue animals."

"For which my employer requires me to run an escaped animal drill."

"Their money might be better spent on decent staff training and some higher fences."

"Point taken," she said. "Still..."

"You want my advice?" said Guy. "Riot gear for the staff, or cricketing pads if you can't stretch to that. Big panels or nets to block off avenues of escape. And a vet on hand. We used to have Sacha out here twice a month to tranquilise Larry, before he disappeared. Had to switch vets. So, a vet for tranquilisers. A medic to give tetanus shots and antibiotics to staff if they're daft enough to get too close."

"This is great stuff," said Sam, making notes on her phone. "I don't suppose I could ask…"

"What?"

"We need a place to actually hold our mock drill."

Guy laughed. "Way I hear it, you're as much of a disaster magnet as Larry here."

"Is that a no, then?"

Larry, seeing there were no fish forthcoming, snorted a spray of water at them and dived back under the surface.

33

The Christmas decorations went up early at Otterside. Polly sat in the south lounge that morning and watched the staff erect the tree.

"When I was a boy," Jacob said to her, "decorations went up on Christmas Eve and not a day earlier."

Polly looked at the lengths of tinsel and patterned foil chains that adorned the walls. "I think it's perfectly nice. And what if it's early? It gives everyone something to look forward to."

The tidy little man looked horrified. "No. You should never look forward to Christmas."

"What?"

"Statistically, it's the day you're most likely to die. That and your birthday."

"That can't be right. How does Death know when your birthday is?"

Jacob shuffled to the edge of his seat as though about to

divulge a great secret. "It's all to do with expectation and holding on."

"Holding on?"

He nodded. "Mind over matter. People who are near to death might see that their birthday or Christmas or the birth of a grandchild is just around the corner and they 'hold on'. Keep going until the big day and then—" he sagged "—they let go."

"I'll try and avoid holding on then," said Polly.

"And then," said Jacob, "there's the dangerous changes in behaviour one might exhibit at Christmas."

"I wasn't planning on dancing on the tables."

"Overeating. Drinking. Excess."

"Oh, I don't mind a little excess every now and then," she said. "As long as I don't overdo it." She spotted Erin entering the room. "Besides, I'm going to be on my best behaviour this Christmas. If you'll excuse me."

Jacob nodded. "I have a committee meeting to get to."

Polly stood up to greet her niece.

Erin gave her a hug and a kiss on the cheek, a hug that barely touched her shoulders, if anywhere, and a kiss that missed by at least four inches. "Can't stay long," she said, which had become her standard greeting.

"Work busy?" said Polly.

"Places to be," agreed Erin. She made a show of looking round as she sat. "This looks nice. Festive."

Polly nodded towards Jacob, who had moved off to observe the chess game going on in the corner. "Jacob was just telling me how much likelier people are to die at Christmas."

Erin frowned unhappily. "Does this place have a record of Christmas-related deaths?"

"Not just here. Everywhere."

Erin was unconvinced. "You shouldn't listen to what these old people say. They talk nonsense half the time."

"Me included?"

Erin gave her a steady appraisal. "Been looking after yourself recently?"

"I have. You been looking at the activities on my bill?"

"I don't snoop, Aunt Polly," Erin tutted. "I have a bit more respect. Confidentiality. How have you been? Any more lapses?"

It had been weeks but Polly knew what she meant. The confusion. The poor young man she'd shouted at in the supermarket.

"Those pills you gave me worked a treat," said Polly. "I finished the ones you gave me over a week ago. Can you get me some more?"

Erin shook her head. "I should think the infection has cleared up. We shouldn't overuse antibiotics."

"Antibiotics?" said Polly. "I thought they were dementia tablets."

Erin tried not to look condescending, or perhaps chose to let a modicum of condescension shine through. "Dementia tablets? What would they be, Polly? Donepezil? Memantine?"

"I don't know. I'm not the doctor. I'm—"

"You had a urinary infection. That was all. It can cause agitation, confusion, even hallucinations in the elderly."

Polly tried to think. "We sold my house."

"You sold your house."

"For a knock down price."

"For a speedy sale."

"I was moved in here."

"That's right."

"But it was all fixed with some antibiotics?"

"We discussed it. We thought it was for the best."

This was not how Polly had remembered the conversations over the preceding months.

"You were struggling," said Erin. "You couldn't maintain the house. I was coming over every other day."

"Once a week, maybe..." Polly murmured but she suddenly couldn't marshal her thoughts, find any certainty in her memories.

"And you're happy here," said Erin firmly.

That much was true. Polly was happy here. Day to day, the move to Otterside had been a positive one. The other residents were a social bunch, a right laugh. And yet, like a stone caught in her shoe, something did not feel right.

"I want to see the family at Christmas," she said. "I haven't seen Jack and Iris since—"

"I sent you those photos on the family WhatsApp group."

"I don't have WhatsApp, do I?" said Polly.

Erin tutted. "You see? Family's for all year round, not just Christmas. So, I was thinking, Christmas Eve or the day before?"

"For what?"

"To see the family."

"Am I staying over?"

The look that flickered across Erin's face was naked

disgust. "No," she said fiercely. "To meet up. Exchange presents."

"Am I not invited for Christmas?"

Erin sighed. "It's a busy day. The kids get up early. There's presents. A roast to do. I'm cooking for seven this year."

"Seven..."

"David. My practice partner. It's our turn. We'd love to have you over, but...."

"Not enough chairs?" said Polly. She meant it bitterly but the upset robbed it of any punch.

"No, silly," laughed Erin. "It's just very busy and we don't want to spoil your little routine here. The dance classes, the yoga. You've really settled in."

"You said you hadn't looked."

"And they do a lovely Christmas dinner here, don't they?"

"But my family..."

"They love you very much," said Erin with patronising emphasis. "I'll get the children to do you a card. A lovely Christmas card." She looked at her watch and attempted to appear surprised. "Must be off."

"Work," nodded Polly. "Sure."

"Iris's nativity play," said Erin. "Yawn, eh?"

"That's this afternoon? I could—"

Erin was shaking her head. "It's a ticketed event, Polly. And you'd only be bored." She stood and smiled. "Glitter."

"What?" said Polly.

"I'll get them to put extra glitter on their card to you. That will be nice, won't it?"

"The fuck it will," said Polly, once Erin had gone.

34

While Margaret and Strawb waited for the third member of the resident's social committee to arrive, Strawb considered the four jigsaw pieces in his hands. He pushed them round like Chinese worry balls for some seconds before selecting one and putting the other three back in his pocket.

"What's that for?" said Margaret, giving him a sly look.

"Shush. Here he comes," said Strawb, sitting up perfectly straight in a very poor effort to appear casual.

Jacob walked into the north lounge, sat down at his usual chair and opened his minute-taking book in front of him. He checked his FitMeUp watch against the clock on the wall and nodded with satisfaction.

He looked at Strawb. "Is there something wrong with you?"

"Trapped wind," said Strawb.

"To business," said Margaret. "It is the annual outing to

Candlebroke Hall for the Christmas Fayre tomorrow. The coach is booked."

"It is," said Strawb. "And I've requested our specific driver."

"Very good. We've got forty one residents booked to go. Polly Gilpin?"

Strawb nodded. "She jumped at the chance. Think we might even have a spot of fun on the back seat on the way home—"

"Disgusting man," said Jacob.

"—By which I meant we might have a bit of a sing-song. You've got a dirty mind, Jakey boy."

"Question is, does Strawb need to have a *meaningful* conversation with her?" said Margaret.

Jacob leafed back through the notes in his book. "As you know, this isn't an exact science," he said, which is what he had said the last dozen times they'd had a discussion about inviting a resident to join their most select of circles. "However, there are a lot of strong positives. Polly Gilpin is clearly not averse to breaking rules. The midnight trip to look at the golf course, swapping her resident's card with Alison, our fitness tracker fun. From what you say, Strawb, there's been plenty of other examples from her life."

"Is it enough?" said Margaret.

Jacob sucked a backward whistle, like a mechanic assessing a dodgy motor. "There's a lot of negativity between her and the niece. Witnessed the two of them meeting just now. Just the mildest suggestion that she was tricked into selling her home to move here."

"Did the niece profit from that?"

"If not financially, then certainly socially. Have the aunt shipped off to the retirement village so she can abdicate responsibility."

"Whatever the case," said Strawb, "old Poll's got a lot of pent up anger."

Margaret nodded approvingly. "And we can use that. I say we go ahead."

"Right-o," said Strawb. "What could go wrong?"

Jacob gave him a shocked look. "Quite a lot really. She might tell someone. We could go to prison."

Strawb dismissed the notion with a wave. "It'll be fine."

"Even though Sam Applewhite has been snooping around?" said Jacob.

Margaret considered the two men and how, caught between the carefree optimism of one and the joyless realism of the other, she had always felt like the fulcrum on a set of scales, the balance between opposite excesses. In truth, it was where she felt happiest. Justice, with her scales and her sword, not blind but with eyes wide open.

"It is decided," she said. "Next, we still have a couple of open slots in the social calendar between now and the end of the year."

"You got the entertainment booked from your friend at Carnage Hall?" said Strawb.

"Friend of a friend," nodded Margaret. "All in hand. We need to fill in some minor things. Thursday afternoons in the south lounge."

"Poker tournament?" suggested Strawb.

"No one will play with you," said Margaret.

"Cos I'm too good."

"Because you think it's an excuse to act like you're in a wild west saloon."

"Because I brought hats?"

"I think it was the chewing tobacco and spittoon which put them off."

Strawb tutted. "Board games then?"

Margaret pursed her lips and looked from one man to the other. "It appears that Jacob here has confiscated a number of them."

"It doesn't appear I have," said Jacob haughtily. "I *have*. Monopoly—"

"I love a bit of Monopoly," said Strawb.

"Aside from the fact that you borrowed the money for the poker tournament, there's no point in a game which favours blind luck and the rich."

"Sounds like real life."

"And Cluedo?" asked Margaret.

"No one solves a murder by bumbling around a house and loudly accusing people until one of them confesses," said Jacob.

"Ah, I do like a murder though," said Strawb. "What about a murder mystery movie marathon on the big screen telly?"

Margaret raised her eyebrows, intrigued.

"*Murder on the Orient Express*?" suggested Strawb.

"Which version?" said Jacob.

"Does it matter? It's the same story in them all."

"Or we could watch *Strangers on a Train*."

"No, I don't think that would be appropriate," said

Margaret, then realised this was one of the rare occasions when Jacob was joking. "I see."

"Speaking of mysteries," said Strawb, "look what I found on the floor immediately outside Chesney's office." He placed the jigsaw piece he had been holding on the table in front of Jacob.

Jacob gasped and picked it up to inspect.

"Perhaps," said Strawb lightly, "it's one of the ones that went missing."

"Chesney's office you say?" said Jacob.

"Maybe," said Strawb, and Margaret could hear him hamming it up, "Chesney knows where the other three have gone?" His hand even went to his pocket where the other pieces were hidden.

Jacob's face was a combination of fury and wonder. "But why...?"

"Who can say?" said Strawb.

Jacob thrust himself up and stalked out of the lounge purposefully.

Margaret shook her head. "Why do you do this, Strawb?"

Strawb grinned. "Why do we do any of it? It entertains us."

35

B eing unable to clock out from work due to the unfinished community payback task was surprisingly freeing. It was true Sam had received several automated messages telling her that her overtime was unauthorised and wouldn't be paid, but that aside, the fact she could never officially be 'out' of the office meant wherever she was, she was deemed to be 'in'. She took advantage of that by choosing to work at home for the day. She assumed Doug Junior could hold down the fort for at least one day.

Her tasks for the day were manifold. She had a venue, equipment and some pretend zoo staff to source for the Doggerland animal escape drill. The conversations she'd had with Guy at the Seal Land sanctuary up in Anderby Creek had been illuminating, but her subtle hints that maybe Seal Land could be used as the venue were met with a cold hard refusal. Guy had pointed out they had no intention of closing

Seal Land for the day, and that several people chasing pretend mammoths or whatever would be too distressing for the real animals, and too bloody hilarious for the Seal Land staff to cope with.

Sourcing equipment was also difficult. Despite having an actual budget with which to buy nets and prods and such, spending that budget was proving a little tricky. She had in front of her a DefCon4 requisition form. She'd filled in what she wanted – that was easy enough – but it was the other questions on the form that threw her. Answering the question *How does this request meet the company's mission statement?* had taken her four hours of head scratching and re-reading of the company's website. The following question, *How does this request meet the company's vision statement?* utterly flummoxed her, mostly because the website listed a single incomprehensibly worded thing called a 'mission vision' and Sam couldn't work out if both questions referred to the same thing or not. In the end, she answered the question with a simple *As above* and moved on.

The current barrier was a supplementary question which read.

ARE THE REQUESTED ITEMS FOR:

- *OPERATIONAL PURPOSES?*
- *PROCEDURAL PURPOSES?*
- *ROUTINE USE?*

CIRCLE ONE

THIS WAS a riddle worthy of the Sphinx. Sam instinctively felt whatever answer she put would be wrong; that a clever answer was required.

She stared at it for a long while and tried to put her mind in a zen monk riddle-solving frame of mind. Ten minutes later, with no answer forthcoming, she picked up the phone and dialled regional head office. She did this on a daily basis, but could not necessarily say why, as it was generally nothing more than a form of self-torture. She clicked her way through various options and, once the hold music had started, put the phone to one side.

Marvin came into the kitchen with a large storage box and placed it on the counter.

"Where'd that come from?" she asked.

He looked at the faded sticker on the side of the box. "Woolworths."

"I meant..." Since her return to Skegness and the subsequent uncovering of her dad's financial concerns, Sam had been subtly (and not so subtly) streamlining his possessions in readiness for the day when financial collapse came and the pair of them were forced to move out to much smaller accommodation. A career's-worth of magical gizmos and paraphernalia had been sorted – some sold on, some binned, and the absolute essentials re-boxed and safely stored. And yet her dad was always finding a fresh box of tricks and trinkets from somewhere.

"Continuing the great sort out?" she said.

"It's good to look through these things," he said, holding up a heavily-braided fez. "I can tell you a story about every one of them, you know."

"I don't doubt it," said Sam. She didn't add she had most likely heard them all before.

"Contrary to popular belief, Tommy Cooper was not the first mainstream entertainer to wear a fez. This one here was owned by one of Belgium's most popular magicians, Maurice Hochermaus. He and Tommy Cooper exchanged headgear at many an event, but Maurice insisted that the plainer style was more flattering for his face."

"Dad, I—"

"Anyway, Tommy took this fez of Maurice's down to a haberdashers in the East End and paid them to make it as ornate as they possibly could. They went to town and applied everything they could. Of course Maurice saw it and hit the roof, but he wore it anyway. It was a private joke between them, and secretly I think Maurice adored it. I was so flattered when he left it to me and not Tommy. A proper piece of showbiz history, this."

Sam smiled at her dad. "Put it on then!"

He popped it on his head and grinned at her. "Bright, isn't it? Of course it all helps with the lighting on stage. Linda and I always used to joke about putting sequins on our sequins for best effect."

It was an eye-watering piece. Someone had carefully selected braids of contrasting colours and applied them in a striped zig-zag around the crown. Sam looked around and realised her dad wasn't just playing with his old outfits, he'd fetched numerous boxes of props into the kitchen as well.

"Wow, you're having a proper trip down memory lane," she said, indicating all of the things. "Either that or you're planning a show."

Maurice gave her a small grin and turned to put the hat down.

"What? No! Are you doing a show? Really?"

"Mr Marvellous might tread the boards again. I have been approached to perform a small intimate set in the local area. Just to get my hand back in."

"Where?"

"A friend of a friend has asked me to do a Christmas turn at this retirement village place off Roman Bank. Otterside."

"I know it well."

"Apparently the residents are big on nostalgia, and they're just the right age to remember my glory days."

"That sounds really great, dad."

"Why thank you, patronising daughter."

"You are medically cleared to perform?"

Marvin whipped a printed letter from behind the box. "Blood pressure mildly elevated. Too much salt in the diet probably. Blood sugars are at prediabetic levels."

"Prediabetic is still not good, right?"

"*Pre*diabetic," he insisted. "But I have the heart and lungs of a young man, apparently."

"Doesn't he want them back?"

"Ha ha. You should take that humour on stage."

"I'm genuinely pleased for you, dad. So, this gig. Are they paying you?"

"Of course they are. I'm a professional. Gone are the days

when I'd send them over to Botherwicks, so those old sharks could negotiate a better deal for me."

"Botherwicks! I couldn't remember the name of your agents. Are they still going?" Sam asked. "I need to hire some actors to perform a fake animal drill."

Marvin nodded. "How many and how long for?" he asked.

Sam had pondered this. "I need a crowd and a few key players. Somewhere between thirty and fifty I'd say. Just for the day."

"In which case I suggest you give Botherwicks a wide berth. Tony died, of course, and ever since the youngster's been in charge they've become horribly corporate."

Sam knew that 'the youngster' was at least in his sixties. She also knew Marvin did not approve of his business practices, which had something to do with him refusing to sign off on first class travel for Marvin's engagements in the mid-eighties, once his popularity started to wane.

"What would you do?" she asked.

"I'd approach the local am-dram group. Bung them a donation and you'd probably get as many of them as you need."

"Ah, good idea," said Sam. "Cat in the café is a member. All I need now is a venue. Somewhere with grounds and buildings, where we can close off access to the public for a few hours." The germ of an idea lodged in Sam's mind. "When's your performance at Otterside?" she asked.

"Next weekend."

Sam pulled a face and thought. "Broad open spaces.... We

could get everyone to stay inside... Or spectate, it doesn't matter. I'll have a word with Chesney."

"And could you possibly explain to me what an animal drill is?" said Marvin.

"I like to do six impossible things before breakfast," she said, "but explaining this nonsense would be one too many."

Her phone was still on hold with DefCon4. There was also a text from Delia.

"Delia has costumes for me," she said, pleasantly surprised.

Sam looked at the requisition form and pondered the value of staying on the line to speak to someone who would surely only confuse and disappoint her. Her pen hovered over the question on the page.

"Circle one," she mused and then drew a circle around the word ONE. It was an elegant solution, although it was almost certainly wrong.

36

Hilde could see her farfar was up to something.

Ragnar Odinson had many skills, and was a gifted liar when it came to police, council representatives and other Saxons, but he was useless at lying to Hilde. For the past couple of days, he had been drifting from caravan to hut to caravan, chatting to the menfolk, and always averting his gaze when he saw Hilde looking his way.

Whatever he was up to, Hilde realised it was taking shape when she saw Hermod and Gunnolf backing their ridiculous truck out of its garage shed. The modified Ford Super Duty pick-up truck had to remain off-road most of the time, not because it was stolen, but because the US import's four metre wide wheelbase, custom monster tires and bespoke extras made it unsuitable for the narrower Lincolnshire roads and utterly uninsurable. The distinctive cherry red paintwork and custom painted flame motifs only added to its brash excess. Common sense suggested they would do better to find something more subtle to ride around in, but Ragnar's twin nephews were very attached to the truck. They used its open flat back as a large, luxurious bed for much of the time. On the occasional hot day they would put the tailgate up, line it with plastic and host a pool party in it.

"Where are you going with that?" Hilde said, strolling across the muddy compound.

"Lads are just taking it out for ride," said Ragnar unconvincingly. "Might go sea fishing."

Hilde looked at the other burly men climbing into the back of the truck. "Need a bit of muscle, do ya?" she said. "Big fish?"

"Aye."

"And the chainsaws?" She nodded at the gear being loaded into the back.

Ragnar growled in his throat. "May Thor strike down nosey womenfolk with lightning!"

"I'm wearing rubber boots," she said, rocking on her heels.

"Does tha want some wood to build tha ship or not?" he said hotly.

"*My* ship is it now?" She frowned. "Is tha going to steal some oak?"

"Do I look like I intend to buy it?"

"And where are you going to find an oak tree round here?"

Ragnar tapped the side of his large nose with a grubby finger. "Oh, tha farfar's a clever one."

"Oh, I'd like to see what you think is clever." She went to

the truck and stepped onto the tailgate runner to climb in the back.

"Tha's not coming wi' us!" shouted Ragnar.

"Tha's not gonna stop me," she shouted back. "Shift up, Torsten."

She pushed herself in between her cousin Torsten and her uncle Ogendus. Torsten had a bandage wrapped around his upper arm.

"Another tattoo?" she said.

"It's infected," he mumbled.

Ogendus snorted. "I reckon me lad's got a girl's name there and she's already dumped him."

Ragnar stood in the mud. "Tha's not coming wi' us," he repeated firmly.

Hilde just waited. They'd played this game before and Ragnar always caved in when it came to Hilde.

POLLY WATCHED the turkey in the garden visible from her window.

It picked its way, footstep over footstep, along its muddy pen. A layer of frost covered the untidy lawn and the ride-on toys that had not moved in weeks. Even from this distance, Polly could see puffs of frosty air at the turkey's mouth.

"December's a dangerous time to be a turkey," she said softly. "Best be careful."

She hoped the family didn't plan to kill it. Distant and ugly though it might have been, there was something cheering about having a constant companion visible from her window.

She dressed warmly for the coach trip.

Candlebroke Hall was only a short drive away from Skegness, but the social committee were laying on a coach. A festive craft fair was promised – no, a craft fayre with a 'y' which clearly made it all the more crafty – and there was talk of carols and mince pies, too. She had decided she would wear warm practical clothes so that she could take a walk around the grounds if she felt like it. If she was going to be trapped inside with all of the forced Christmas jollity, then she might need an escape hatch. She had no need for Christmas craft gifts. The only people she truly wanted to buy presents for were little Jack and Iris, and craft fayres were not going to fulfil that need. Yes, she might also want to buy a little something for new friends like Strawb or Alison or neighbour Bernard, but it would be uninspired to buy them a gift from a fayre they were all attending.

No, Polly decided she would be more than happy to go along for the ride – it had been some years since she had been there – but they could keep the Christmassy things for themselves.

She descended to the foyer and found a mixed group of residents waiting for the coach. There was a small core who were clearly planning a day of festive fun. All of them wore reindeer antlers on their heads. Earrings with baubles and appalling Christmas jumpers were a recurring theme. They each carried a huge bag with them. Polly suspected the one Strawb was carrying contained a wireless speaker, because Wizzard echoed around the room, wishing it could be Christmas every day.

"Are we all here?" said Margaret, stretching her swan neck to see over the group.

"I have a checklist," said Jacob. He led the way outside, where he proceeded to act as doorman, bouncer and security guard at the coach door.

Polly followed Margaret on board.

"I'll do the safety announcements and then we'll get off," the sandy-haired driver said.

"You will do the driving and nothing more, James Huntley," said Margaret bluntly.

The driver was immediately cowed.

"I shall be doing any announcements," said Margaret. She took the microphone from the front dash and trailed it over the driver's shoulder to the seat immediately behind, where she positioned herself.

The festive fun lovers took the front seats, so Polly moved towards the back to preserve her hearing.

Jacob took two head counts once they were all aboard, although Margaret instructed the driver to set off before he had finished the first. There were whoops and cheers from the front as they pulled out of the gravel drive and onto Roman Bank.

THE ODINSONS' Super Duty truck stopped off at the family's mobility shop over by Chapel St Leonards to pick up Hilde's dad, Sigurd, and a trailer. Sigurd had unlocked the gate leading to the back of the shop, and uncles Yngve and Ogendus had wheeled out the long low trailer and hooked it up to the truck under Hermod and Gunnolf's close supervision. As they did, Ragnar took out a folded newspaper from his back pocket, thrust it into Hilde's hand and tapped a story.

"Lincolnshire Estates Donate Wood For Notre Dame Repairs," she read.

"That there cathedral in Paris burned down, didn't it?"

"I'm aware of that, aye," said Hilde.

"And they need oak to repair the roof. A hundred grand's worth of oak."

"Yes?"

He tapped the story again. "And the daft apeths have listed which stately homes are donating oak trees."

She read to the bottom. "This is a shopping list for anyone who wants to steal oak."

"I know," he said, laughing. "Bloody Saxons have told us where to find it. Candlebroke Hall's nearest."

"And we're just going to roll up and steal it?" said Hilde. "Someone will stop us."

Ragnar slapped a helmet with clear face shield on his face. "Why? We're just tree surgeons going to make much needed repairs."

THE OTTERSIDE LORDS and ladies of revelry worked their way down the coach's aisle of seats.

"All right, love?"

Polly nodded at the woman. She recognised her from the FitMeUp tracker training. "Janine."

The woman grinned. "Polly. Something for the journey?" She raised a thermos flask.

"Tea?"

"On a day like today, we should start with a Bucks Fizz, don't you think?"

Janine handed her a plastic glass and poured a frothy orange cocktail from the thermos.

"Thank you," said Polly.

"You're one of us now," said Janine and moved on.

Polly sipped her drink and felt a surge of warmth for the oddly social group of people who had done this. It was very thoughtful.

"Me again!" Janine was back. Polly wondered if she had some cocktail left in the thermos and lifted her glass, but she was carrying a wicker hamper with a strap. "Now, we've got the picnic we'll have later on in the stable block, but you're probably peckish now, eh?"

"Peckish?"

"Bacon sandwich? Or maybe just a mini-pack of Jaffa Cakes if you're vegetarian?"

"I've just had breakfast."

"But it wouldn't be a coach trip without a snack on the bus."

"We'll be there in a few minutes, won't we?"

The coach had neared the town centre and turned inland. It couldn't be more than five miles.

"No worries, love," said Janine. "Here's your raffle ticket for later on. Hang onto it, cos we've got some surprises. Oh, and a miniature of brandy to slip in your bag. You never know when you might need a little top-up, eh?"

Polly stared at the woman's back as she worked her way down the coach. She was certain that, apart from Strawb, these people were not on the social committee, but clearly they were some sort of self-appointed group of funsters. She could see into one of the other bags they'd piled up on a spare seat: it was filled with Christmas crackers and packaged snacks.

Polly put the brandy into her handbag. She didn't need to resort to the alcohol just yet.

From the Candlebroke roundabout they turned down the long, tree-lined driveway which led to the house proper. There was something to be said for being on a coach, as it gave you a much more elevated view of things. She could see cows grazing. Did they have deer here? She couldn't recall. In a landscape that was either drained fenland or heavily farmed hillsides, Candlebroke Hall was one of the few places in the area where mature trees could be found. It looked very much as if deer ought to be grazing beneath the leafy fronds. She caught a glimpse of a red truck between the trees. It looked rather heavy to be groundkeepers; surely it would leave tyre marks in the grass?

The coach rounded the bend and arrived outside the gate.

Candlebroke Hall was a huge square house of red brick, white stone and tall windows. But for the manicured lawns and sprawling estate it could have passed for an austere boarding school, or a Georgian prison. Such things really didn't matter; it was old and therefore quaint. So therefore desirable for the folks of Otterside's Christmas outing.

"I always judge the quality of a stately home by its tea room," said Bernard, who was polishing off his second bacon sandwich. "An army marches on its stomach."

"Here we are," Margaret announced needlessly over the PA. "We'll get you signed in as soon as possible. Craft fayre is in the tea room. Picnic in the stables at midday."

The driver stood up. "And if I could ask you to take your rubbish with you, ladies and—"

He was drowned out by boos and laughter. There were even items thrown. He hunkered down in his seat to be out of the way.

The group jostled rowdily off the coach.

"I'm all for fun, but that was a bit hard on the old driver there," Polly said as they walked towards the house.

Jacob snorted. "James Huntley? The coach company have a nerve assigning him to us. Should have fired him years ago."

Polly looked back. The driver was half-crouched on the coach steps, picking up wrappers and discarded brandy miniatures that had been kicked down the aisle. He saw her looking and there was a bitter scowl on his face.

"Why? What's wrong with him?" Polly asked, but Jacob had gone.

37

Sam entered *Back to Life*. Delia was behind the counter, a pin between her lips as she rooted through a box of cotton reels. She mumbled something through her tight lips.

"You might want to try that again," said Sam.

Delia put the pin down on the counter. "I'm glad you're here. I've made some proof of concept pieces for the costumes. I need you to assess them and tell me which ones are going to work the best."

"Excellent. I also needed to run some dates by you," said Sam. "I'm planning to run this drill next weekend. Does that give you enough time?"

Delia didn't look entirely horrified, but definitely thirty to forty percent horrified. "Next weekend?"

"Yes. Next weekend."

"The one after this weekend?"

"The one that starts tomorrow? Yes. Next weekend. Eight

days' time. Is that going to be a problem?"

"No, but it might inform some of the choices we make – unless you can rustle up an extra pair of hands for me. Any news on Drumstick?"

Sam pulled a doubtful expression. "Following leads."

"Is that special police talk for no?"

"I had a suspect. Working on the mostly stupid theory it was someone at Otterside who objected to being woken by a turkey in the morning."

"Is it that big guy I sometimes see leaning out of his window to smoke a fag?"

"Could be," Sam shrugged. "Kind of fits. From up there, he'd see how to open the gate from the other side. He'd also know there was a plank in the garden he could use as a murder weapon."

"But?"

"But he has an alibi for the night of the murder. He never left the building."

Delia's nod was one of gratitude that Sam was at least making an effort. "Come through and have a look at what I've got so far."

Sam followed Delia into her workshop. It had undergone a transformation since her last visit. Gone were the Capitalist Whore dolls and all of the Christmas gold-sprayed paraphernalia. In fact, Sam had spied some of it in the shop, labelled as CHRISTMAS SHABBY CHIC, presumably to explain the unfinished paint jobs. What had taken its place was a sewing workshop. Delia's sewing machine and overlocker took centre stage, while the mannequin sported tiger-striped lycra. Other part-made costumes hung on hangers. Delia led Sam over to a table.

"Right, let's talk heads," she said.

"I can see the bodies are well in-hand," said Sam, waving a hand at the various animal onesies hanging up.

"Yeah, those are straightforward, but the heads are what I need guidance on. Let me walk you through the various options."

Delia started at the left of the table and struck a pose like a magician's assistant. "So, my first thought was to go full *Lion King*. An oversized head with a magnificent ruff strikes a really effective note. It says *'Fear me, for I am king of the jungle and although I walk among you, I am to be respected'*."

Sam picked up the headpiece in question as Delia was talking. "Fine. Let's overlook the fact this is clearly a caribou, which is not really the king of any jungle."

"Go on," said Delia. "Would it help if you wore it for a moment?"

Sam slipped it onto her head. "Um, yeah. I have a couple of observations." Her voice was muffled inside the dense and weighty head. "Firstly, I can see why you gave it a magnificent ruff."

"You can?" Delia asked.

"Would it, by any chance, be to counterbalance the monstrous weight of the antlers? This thing weighs a ton, yet it still feels top-heavy. As if it's going to fall and break my neck on the way down."

"That might have been part of it," said Delia, a little defensively. "Although I like it as a design choice as well."

"Secondly, I can't actually see through the eye holes. This

headpiece would be ideally suited to someone with no neck. I'm taking it off."

"Any other thoughts?" asked Delia, helping Sam to steady the enormous head on the table.

"Well yes. It's smiling," said Sam, looking at the face from the outside again. "Why is it smiling? I'm not even sure a real caribou would be capable of an expression like that."

"Ah, that is something we should definitely discuss," said Delia, her face animated with sudden passion. "I've been thinking about this. So, what if a child sees your animal drill?"

"What? There will be no children there."

"But if there were. What we don't want is to traumatise them. If the heads are all smiling, then the kids will think they are amusements or something."

"That is absurd," she said. "Completely absurd."

"Can you give me one good reason why the animals should *not* be smiling?"

"A total lack of muscles which enable them to smile?"

"Now you're just being pedantic," said Delia. "Okay, if we think this head is too much, let's take a look at the next one." She moved down the table. "I had a brainwave that you might need to protect your actors from some rough and tumble."

Sam looked at her. "Rough and tumble?"

"If the zookeepers are shooting at them, trying to take them down. You know, will they need to dive and do roly-polys and so on?"

"That's not my intention," said Sam. "There will be rules,

so the animal actors know how to behave if they get shot, for example. There will be no roly-polys."

Delia looked a little crestfallen. "Well, in case you wanted to build in a bit of live action, I created a test head based on a helmet."

"Interesting idea," said Sam, picking up the next headpiece. "Is this a mammoth?"

"Yes it is! Looks good, doesn't it?"

Sam placed it cautiously over her head. "At least this one lets me see daylight. It's not so heavy, either. In spite of the trunk and the tusks."

"Ah yes. I made those from fibre glass. See how it adheres to the helmet via the central nose piece?"

"Yes. It presents a bit of a problem for properly seeing where I'm going, if I'm honest." The large strips of fibreglass supporting the mammoth's tusks and trunk formed an inverted 'Y' shape on the front of the helmet. If she wasn't afraid of goring onlookers with the outlandish tusks, Sam felt she might be equipped to play American football.

"All good feedback," said Delia. "I aim to please with my creations, so let's look at a different style of head, shall we?"

Sam moved to the last head on the table. This one looked much more wearable. She popped it over her head. It was stretchy, like a ski mask, and the eye holes were big enough to allow for a decent view. "Much better," she said. "I'm a sabre-toothed tiger, right?"

"Hah! Well, right now you're just a tiger," said Delia. "Let's make you sabre-toothed, shall we?" She handed Sam a packet. It was a pair of Dracula fangs.

"Oh, I don't know," said Sam. Delia gave her a stern look,

so she put the teeth into her mouth and posed. "*Rar!*" she said.

Delia took a picture with her phone. "I'm making this the picture which shows when you call me. You make a very good sabre-toothed tiger."

Sam looked at the picture. She looked like an idiotically-smiling cartoon facsimile of a sabre-toothed tiger, but recognisable, all the same. "Yep, well this is definitely the style of head we should use."

"So," said Delia, "just to check what you're approving." She counted off on her fingers. "It's no to papier-mâché, no to fibre glass, no to big heads with ruffs, no to helmets (and roly polys), no to tusks and trunks, but a big yes to smiling animals, right?"

Sam gave a world-weary nod, slightly suspicious that she'd played right into Delia's hands. "And they can all be ready for next weekend?"

"Possibly. I think I need to build some frames or something to bulk out the bodies of the larger animals. Maybe something in a rigid plastic or light metal. Do you know who the actors are?"

"Not yet. I'm going to ask Cat at the café by the office. She's part of the local theatre scene. Um – you know you said things might go smoothly if I could rustle up an extra pair of hands for you?"

"Yes?"

"And you maybe need some metal-working doing."

"Only light stuff."

"Have you ever considered Hilde Odinson?"

"One of the Odinson clan?"

"You've met her."

"When she was doing community service on the beach."

"But she's got a good heart. And she swears she didn't know the telegraph poles belonged to anyone."

"How did one young woman manage to carry off some telegraph poles?"

"She probably roped a daft cousin or something into it. It's surprising what those Odinsons can achieve when they work as a team."

38

Hermod and Gunnolf, with scant consideration for the actual tracks and paths laid out across Candlebroke Hall's grounds, had parked in the shadow of a huge sweeping oak tree. Hilde insisted on checking it actually was an oak before letting them at it with chainsaws, axes and ropes. It wasn't easy to be sure, given the time of year: none of the deciduous trees had any of their leaves left. On the ground beneath there was a good covering of leaf litter, and she could make out oak leaves and a few acorn fragments.

"This is an oak," she confirmed.

"Course it is," said Ragnar airily. "I could have told tha that."

"Sure," she said.

"Now, lass, tha needs to piss off for a bit."

"What?"

"We need to perform the sacred ritual. Man stuff."

There were groans from the other Odinson men. "We're not doing any bloody dancing," said Ogendus.

"Tha'll do what I bloody tell thee!" Ragnar shouted back. "Tha'll not be putting axe to that tree without the proper blessings and permission from Odin himself!"

"Whatever," said Hilde and stalked off up the grassy slope. She was sceptical about some of her granddad's long-standing 'traditions'. She was fairly certain a good many of them were of his own invention.

She'd once come across a manuscript he'd been working on. It was a laboriously handwritten book. Each chapter was headed with a square neon-coloured post-it note, with a ballpen doodle relating to the chapter's content on it. They were really quite charming, like modern-day illuminated letters. The book was entitled SON OF ODIN: LIVE YOUR LIFE THE VIKING WAY and was part memoir, part practical guide, with many instructions about how to weave Ragnar's particular flavour of Viking lore into modern life. He covered everything from making mead with supermarket ingredients (which was fine, as long as the correct runes were inscribed onto the bottles afterwards with a Sharpie), to the organisation and etiquette of family gatherings. There was some bee wisdom, clearly cribbed from Uncle Bjorn's ramblings, which was as wild and eccentric as Ragnar's. Hilde had been tempted to apply edits to some of the practical chapters, to more accurately describe how things were done (pretend the men do all of the work while the women do everything behind the scenes), but she had gently closed the manuscript and never mentioned to Ragnar that she had seen it.

Hilde found a low stone bench by a hedge, close enough that she could keep an eye on the men; far enough away that she didn't actually have to see the embarrassing ritual up close.

"Can I go with her?" she heard Sigurd ask.

"No, tha bloody can't!" yelled Ragnar.

POLLY WAS ENJOYING THE GROUNDS, alone with her thoughts and a brandy miniature. The miniature was still closed, her hand wrapped around it in her coat pocket, but she felt its warming powers, *in potentia* as it were. There were some beautifully laid out formal gardens – the herbaceous borders were pleasant even at the onset of winter – but she wanted to see the slightly wilder parts of the estate and walked out past a long pond towards the great trees further away from the house.

She headed over to where she'd seen the truck earlier. She glimpsed the red bodywork through the trees, a hundred yards away. She slowed as she neared; she could hear chanting.

"We offer mead for the gift of the tree. All hail and dance in its company!"

"Tha's never gunna mek us dance?"

"Tha bloody well will dance."

"But not in the nud this time, eh?"

"If poem says tha's dancing in the nud, tha will!"

"Aye, but ... but tha *wrote* the blummin' poem! Why would tha do that?"

"Odin likes a rhyme, dun't he?"

There were loud protests. "But Odin dun't need us to take our clobber off this time, does he?"

"Always! Always in the nud! Come on now!"

Polly crept forward, keen to see what was going on, yet nervous about what on earth she had stumbled into. She saw six men, all in various stages of undress, lumbering clumsily around a tree, beards and willies swinging. It was a grand old oak tree, fat and gnarly with spreading boughs. The oldest man had a bottle which he sloshed onto the tree's trunk at intervals. Polly had never tasted mead and wondered what it was like. They finished the mead, which seemed to signal the end of the dance. One of the men stamped off, muttering "Thank fuck" and, apart from the oldest (who clearly enjoyed a winter breeze around his nethers) hurried to get their clothes back on.

Polly edged further forward, stepping on a twig, which gave a sharp crack. She looked up, anxious the men should not spot her. At the same moment as her twig snapped, a chainsaw roared into life, followed shortly afterwards by another.

Two of the youngest, very much alike, swung their chainsaws excitedly. Polly (who enjoyed a bit of unexpected nudity, in moderation) was very glad to see they were dressed once more. Nakedness and power tools didn't mix well. Nakedness, power tools and mead even less so.

Now that the embarrassing spectacle of her family dancing in the nude was over, Hilde could see Hermod and Gunnolf starting to take chunks out of the oak's trunk. She wondered how much Ragnar really knew about felling a tree. He was hollering instructions, but he had the look of someone who was winging it.

Hilde spotted a grey-haired Saxon woman watching their activities from a distance. It probably wasn't a concern, but Hilde would watch to see what she did.

Hermod and Gunnolf were both cutting wedges out of the tree with their chainsaws. There was a rhythm to their work, as Ragnar made sure they both took turns. What he probably hadn't intended was that it should turn competitive. Hilde could clearly see the look on Hermod's face as Gunnolf freed a large chunk from his side. When his turn came, Hermod leaned in and carved the chainsaw down, biting off an enormous slab of trunk. If they both carried on like this, the tree would start to look like a pencil balancing on its tip.

POLLY, who was crouched behind a cedar tree, was becoming increasingly certain these people were not doing official work on behalf of Candlebroke Hall. The nakedness had been a big clue.

She looked back towards the house. On a cold day, few had ventured out into the rear gardens, but she wondered if anyone, perhaps looking out from a top storey window, might hear the buzz of chainsaws and see the tree wavering.

And if these men weren't official workers, then what were they? Tree thieves? That didn't sound like a thing, but she could easily imagine it being one.

However, Polly was definitely convinced these men really

didn't know what they were doing. The two twins had got into some sort of macho competition over who could carve the biggest wedge out of the trunk, while the older one seemed to be encouraging them.

A young woman on a bench further off got to her feet and started shouting and waving.

Two of the blokes watching the lumberjacks turned to look at her. Slowly, too slowly, they realised what she was saying.

The one with a red bandana round his head ran towards the truck and opened the driver's door.

The tree creaked.

"The keys!" yelled the man at the truck. "Sigurd! Where's the keys!"

The man with the plaited beard shrugged and began hollering at the chainsaw twins.

The tree groaned and began to lean. It started out looking as if it was going to fall in slow motion – an ancient thing, broad as a house, falling like a wounded warrior – then it was over very quickly. The twins scooted out of the way. The old man pegged it down the hill. Plaited-beard threw himself to the ground just out of range of the longest boughs.

What was not so fortunate was the truck. Its front wheels were high in the air as the back half was crushed beneath tree branches.

"Jesus Christ," Polly whispered.

There was a long silence. The chainsaws were now off. The twins had seen what happened and looked both mesmerised and appalled. The driver's door opened and the bandana man eased himself to the ground.

"Yngve! Tha backed our truck into t' way of the blummin' tree!" yelled one of the twins.

"Tha great idiot! I was trying ter move it, but tha's taken the keys!"

"Yer a liar!" shouted the other twin. "It were never that close! Sigurd! Tell him!"

Moments later the men were throwing punches at each other. Up on the hill, the young woman had the exasperated body language of someone who had to put up with this kind of stupidity on a regular basis.

The oldest man waded into the centre of the fight and shouted at them, his arms raised. They peeled apart with the reluctance of sulky children.

"Chop off them blummin' branches and see what's left o't truck. We came here to do a job, now get back ter work."

Polly stifled a giggle. She recognised it was entirely the wrong response to the death of a mighty old oak, but there was something beautifully karmic about seeing the men's truck crushed.

"What's bladdy Ragnar up to now?" said Strawb at her shoulder.

Polly jumped in surprise, headbutting the cedar tree. "Ow! What are you creeping up on me for?"

Strawb took hold of her shoulders to steady her. "What are you doing lurking in the undergrowth?"

Polly hissed and rubbed her forehead. Strawb helped her up, turning her to face him.

"They're stealing a tree," she said.

"Vikings have a loose sense of property."

"Vikings? They're Yorkshire folk."

"They have Vikings in Yorkshire," he said.

Polly felt her pocket to make sure the brandy was still there.

As Polly and Strawb watched, the twins attempted to extract their truck. One of them revved the engine, while the other attempted to push at any part where he could gain any purchase. As mud splattered up from the spinning wheels, the one at the rear was sprayed in dirt. He emerged, wiping mud from his eyes and spitting it out of his mouth.

"Yer did that on purpose!"

"Rubbish! Yer not pushing hard enough!"

They leapt on each other, throwing punches until the older man split them up again. Eventually, the young girl took the wheel of the truck while all of the men pushed. It crawled free, with much swearing as trapped branches sprang back and slapped faces.

POLLY AND STRAWB walked slowly round the gardens back towards the house and the stable block, where a picnic was apparently waiting for them. At some point they had started walking arm in arm, his large warm hand engulfing hers.

"Nice fat fish in there," said Strawb.

"Carp," said Polly.

"Know your fish, eh?"

"It's called Carp Pond on the map," she said, waggling a leaflet she had picked up. "I heard a rumour that the family have a private menagerie somewhere, too. Tigers and lions and something."

Strawb cocked an ear as though expecting to hear a big cat roar.

Polly studied the map on the leaflet. "And this is the Ghost Walk."

"What is?"

She swept her free hand in an all-encompassing gesture. "This is."

"I heard this place is haunted," said Strawb. "Even had a local psychic feller investigate."

"The wife of Sir Something-something Lettuces," said Polly, who half recalled the story from previous visits. "Seventeen hundreds. She had fallen in love with one of the servants, a postillion, and they were going to run away together. Lettuces found out and killed the servant, possibly his wife too. Dumped one or both in this pond."

"What's a postillion?" said Strawb.

"Something to do with horses?" said Polly, who really had no idea. "Anyway, Lettuces was cursed from beyond the grave: no male descendant would ever inherit the house."

"Justice served."

Polly stopped and turned to look at him, their arms still linked to make an L of their bodies.

"Justice? He gets to murder a man and woman, and his punishment is that his house doesn't get inherited by— I've lost my house; been manoeuvred into coming to Otterside."

"I thought you liked it."

"Irrelevant. Point is, I didn't get to murder someone to balance it up."

Strawb grins. "Oh, murder balances things up?"

Polly was suddenly viewing herself objectively, as though

from an outside perspective. Why was she angry? What did she have to be angry about on a day like this? Strawb had asked her a question. "Some people do deserve to die," she said.

"Violent thoughts," said Strawb, barely a murmur.

"Some people... The world would be a better place without some people in it."

"Amen," said Strawb. "And would you be the person to do it?"

An image of her niece, Erin, flashed across her mind. She shook it away, disgusted with herself. "There's a picnic waiting for us."

"Sandwiches'll be getting cold."

39

S am entered Cat's Café with her usual reluctance.

In many ways the café next door to the DefCon4 entrance was perfectly lovely. A café that had once been an old-fashioned greasy spoon had been brought up to date without ditching any of the things people actually liked. Eggs and bacon had not been replaced with smashed avocado on toast, but the sticky vinyl tablecloths and egg-stained cutlery had been replaced with fresh linen and cutlery you could see your reflection in. The coffee was produced by a whirring, gurgling, steam-spouting machine, but not with a range of silly Italian names that were beyond the Skegness vocabulary. The menu had expanded, but the prices had barely budged an inch.

The perfectly adequate café had only one major drawback: its proprietor. Cat was twenty-something, intelligent and ambitious, and not only wanted to pursue a secondary career as an explosively provocative playwright but assumed everyone would want to hear about it on a daily basis. Poor souls who had just gone in for a milky coffee and a sausage bap would be treated to a forty minute lecture on Brechtian techniques in her latest play. Any fool who showed the slightest interest would find Cat as an unshooable presence by their table, prattling on about plot structures, acting techniques, and the tiniest details of her latest effort.

For once, Sam wanted to actually talk acting. Cat had cornered Vance from the *Who Do You Ink You Are?* tattoo shop next door at his table. He was staring at her with a buttered scone halfway to his mouth while Cat kept up a one-side conversation.

"... said to him that, if I wanted to, I could have a whole play full of nothing but Pinteresque silences. No words, only meaning. You know what I mean?"

Vance looked at her, but said nothing. Sam couldn't tell if it was embarrassment or loathing in his eyes.

"Cat," said Sam. "Could I...? Am I interrupting?"

"Not at all," said Cat, turning from her captive audience. Freed from her Medusa gaze, tattooist Vance almost collapsed with relief. He all but shoved the scone in his mouth. "What can I get you?"

"Um, you know actors, don't you?"

"I've met a few," Cat conceded. "I once auditioned for a role alongside that Jodie Whittaker. But then she went off to become Doctor Who and the rest is history."

"I meant local actors. The Skegness dramatic society thing."

"The SODS," Cat nodded. "I'm their artistic director now. I had creative differences with the last one over my latest play. What do you think, would you say that having murdered parents makes a main character more interesting?"

"I'm sorry?" said Sam. "I was going to ask you about actors."

"I mean, it's not part of the story, but if it had happened in the past, would you be more likely to want to see a play about that person?"

"So is the main character going to track down the murderer, or avenge their deaths?" asked Sam, wary of disappearing into the ever-shifting world of Cat's writerly life.

"No, it's more like she needs to prove her own worth to herself in a post-apocalyptic romance kind-of-thing."

"Right," said Sam. "So the parents thing is irrelevant?"

"Uh-huh. But does it flesh her out and make her a more rounded character? I mean it works for Harry Potter, right?"

"Er." Sam frowned and tried to recall her train of thought. "I was wondering if the Skegness drama people, the SODS, would be interested in a small event I'm organising."

"A production?"

Sam shrugged. "It's definitely being produced. It requires some acting. It's more of a free-form open air exercise."

"Outdoor theatre."

"I'm just sorting out the costumes and the details. It's going to be quite soon. A short turnaround."

"Who's the writer?" said Cat. Sam could see an excited glint in her eye.

"It's more of an improv type thing."

Cat nodded appreciatively. "So, I think I'll go with the dead parents."

"The, er, okay. Yes. Right. I've got to go see a man about unfiled court papers."

Sam's phone began ringing and she turned to go. Cat automatically, instinctively, began to drift back to Vance in the corner.

"If you could phone around now," Sam said to her, "it would be greatly appreciated. I need to know how many of your actor buddies you can rustle up."

"Sure," said Cat, heading for the counter. Vance mouthed a 'Thank you' to Sam. There might even have been a tear in his eye.

Sam picked up the phone call before it went to voicemail.

"Yes," said a man on the other end of the line.

"Yes?" said Sam.

"Yes you can do it."

Sam had no idea who it was. "This is Sam Applewhite from—"

"You can do your zoo animal live action roleplay thing at Otterside."

She realised it was Chesney, the retirement village manager. "Oh, that's great. Thank you. If I can just explain what—"

"But on one condition."

"Oh?" Sam paused to fish around in her pocket for the keys to her van.

"You know Mr Marvellous is coming to perform for us on that very same day."

"Ye-es?"

"I think he needs a support act. Maybe an up and coming singer with a powerful voice?"

Sam grinned involuntarily.

"You are his daughter, aren't you?"

"Last time I looked, but I really don't get involved with that side of his business."

"You could have a word with him? I think I would be an excellent fit."

Sam climbed into the van. Time to go pay Greg Mandyke a visit and see if it was his paperwork stopping her signing off the payback work.

"And if I could get you a slot..." she said.

"A slot!" Chesney made a weird half-giggling noise.

"Okay, I'll see what I can do," she said. "Gotta go."

GREG MANDYKE HAD a house on Derby Avenue. Sam had no idea that he lived just around the corner from her dad's place. It felt odd to know one of her community payback crew – an unrepentant one at that – lived so close to her home. She didn't particularly consider herself to be a representative of the forces of authority, but nonetheless she felt there should be greater geographical distance, if not social distance, between her and the people she was tasked with overseeing.

She rang the doorbell and peered casually through the frosted glass, looking for a shift in the light indicating someone was approaching. She rang again and waited a full minute. Over the past week or more she'd phoned various times and texted.

There was the possibility he had gone on holiday.

She went to the house next door and knocked. The woman who answered looked at her suspiciously, like Sam was about to try to sell her something.

"Hi," said Sam. "I'm trying to get hold of Greg next door."

"You delivering something?" said the woman.

"No." Sam showed her empty hands as evidence. "I'm just need to… It's a work thing. I wondered if you knew if he was away at the moment."

"His car's still here." The woman pointed at a Lexus on the driveway.

"I didn't know if he went on holiday or something."

"Oh, no. He's definitely been around. He was cooking the other night."

"Cooking?"

"Smelled it."

"Oh. Maybe I've just missed him. I've got a phone number for him, but it's ringing out. Do you have another number for him?"

The woman drew herself stiffly to her full height. "I don't go giving out people's private numbers to strangers in the street."

"No. Quite right," Sam agreed politely.

The woman was already closing the door.

Sam went back round to Greg's house. In the good old days – the really old days – you'd be able to tell if someone was away by the build-up of post or milk on the doorstep. But who had their milk delivered these days? In fact, who received more than a smattering of post anymore. More likely to see a collection of *Sorry, we missed you...* notes from parcel companies than actual letters. Nonetheless, Sam levered the letterbox open and peered through.

The hallway was unlit and silent. No sign of life. A pair of moccasin shoes sat halfway down the hall, one on its side. There was a thin scattering of grass clippings on the carpet next to the shoes. Sam recalled Greg had worn those shoes on the last community payback session.

Maybe it was a coincidence, or maybe those shoes and the blades of grass had been there since that day. Sam would hardly have described Greg as house-proud, but she doubted he'd leave the hall in that untidy state for so long.

"Greg," she called through the letterbox and listened.

The silence of the house was a force in itself, blooming outward, filling the space.

"Greg!"

Sam tried the door. She tried (momentarily, before giving up) slipping her hand through the letterbox to reach the latch.

Once her mind was set on the idea of breaking in, the practicalities took over in her mind, pushing aside quibbles about the morality and legality of what she was doing.

She tried getting her fingers round the edges of the living room windows, but they were firmly closed. She looked at the equally closed windows on the first floor, and the sturdiness of the plastic drainpipe, before deciding she'd come back to those. There was a wrought iron gate at the side of the house, all twists and spirals. There was a padlock on the latch, but the intricate design of the gate provided perfect hand and footholds for someone to climb over. Sam gripped the gate tightly as she swung her leg over the top and assured herself she'd be fine – as long as her weight didn't snap the gate off its hinges and crush her underneath when it fell.

Down on the other side, uncrushed, she explored the rear of the house. The summer house or sauna room, or whatever it was down the end of the garden, was an interesting and incongruous addition. Did Greg have his own heated swimming pool? He certainly didn't seem the kind of man to deny himself anything. As for the house, there was no handy open kitchen window or unlocked patio door. There wasn't even a cat flap for her to contemplate. There was, however, a pervasive smell in the air. It had an earthy quality to it, but its top notes were rich and meaty, like a casserole or stew bubbling on the stove.

She stood on tiptoe to better look through the kitchen window. The hob and oven were dark, off. Besides, the window was definitely closed and there was no whirring extractor fan. She looked to the houses on either side.

"That's a strong smell," she told herself quietly and turned to the summer house construction.

Its curved plastic walls were frosted. There also a layer of condensation on the inside.

She gripped the door handle. The door slid aside and a wall of warm, misty air rolled out. Sam coughed at the heat and the sudden stink.

It was like entering a kitchen feverishly engaged in a beef chilli cook-off competition. It was like plunging one's head into a casserole oven. It was a weirdly manly smell: sweaty, farty, meaty. If a dozen unwashed men had gone into a sweat lodge to eat bacon sandwiches, it still wouldn't smell as bad as this. The most perversely disgusting thing about the smell was that despite the weird elements, the off tang, the flatulent aspects, it was an enticing stink, full of umami richness.

There was a swimming pool, not a big one. Only ten metres long, but ten metres longer than any pool Sam had owned. At the far end, in a pine-panelled alcove, was a hot tub. Its surface bubbled.

"Greg," she called.

There was an untidy pile of clothes on her side of the swimming pool. There were grass stains on the trousers. Sam felt a knot in her stomach.

"Greg, are you here?"

She walked the length of the pool. No drowned Greg at the bottom.

There was a thick white froth on the surface of the hot tub. The meaty smell, fading as fresher air circulated through the outer door, was stronger here. It was also half-drowned by a heavier, almost sewage smell. Nausea brewed inside Sam, more from expectation than the smell itself.

The bubbling foam had a shiny, greasy quality, like rendered fat.

"Greg," she whispered. Not because she believed he would answer, but because the air needed to escape her lungs and her mouth was on autopilot.

There was a control panel set into the rim of the hot tub. She edged closer. With an outstretched arm she pressed the power button. The button was slick and oily.

The bubbles stopped. The foam settled in a white-brown web of fatty strings. Now, the stilling surface water cleared, she could see other things in the golden depths. Large flecks of material hung in the water, brown and pink and black, stringy strands of cooked meat. Here and there she saw clumps of hair, held together at the roots by fragments of flesh.

She didn't want to look anymore, but it was irresistible. There was a window-cleaning squeegee blade by the base of the hot tub. She picked it up and carefully stirred the surface. For some reason – for *no good reason* – her curiosity demanded more. More evidence, more confirmation. She drew the foam aside and glimpsed a larger, dark shape just below the surface. It was a ball of boiled flesh. Across one ragged section a pale skull was visible beneath. Her brain released her. It was enough.

Sam stepped back, took a moment to think, and threw up.

She had the self-control to push herself away from the hot tub, stagger to the edge of the swimming pool and vomit there. She coughed, stared, vomited again, then walked outside into the garden and the clear cold air.

She was dialling 999 before she knew it.

"Emergency service operator, what service do you require?"

She blinked, devoid of thought. "Ambulance? I found a body."

"Did you say you found a body? Have you checked if the person is still breathing?"

"No. It's Greg Mandyke. Derby Avenue..." For the life of her, she couldn't remember the house number.

"Where is the person?"

Person? The word sounded so stupid in the circumstances. The man was soup.

"The neighbour said she could smell him cooking," Sam heard herself say.

40

Hilde watched Hermod and Gunnolf cutting through branches with their chainsaws. After about twenty minutes' of slicing away the heaviest boughs the truck bounced free and landed back on its wheels. The bodywork was severely damaged, but they ascertained it was driveable by doing some small circuits. They seemed crestfallen when Ragnar indicated they were to prepare the tree for transportation back to the Odinson compound. This was possibly the first time they had understood quite how much work would be involved.

"They never think, do they?" she said to herself.

POLLY AND STRAWB located the stable block. Polly wasn't sure it was routinely open, but the jolly Christmas crew from the coach had taken it over. Wooden benches and tables were laden with food and drink.

Christmas funster Janine waved Polly over to come sit with them. "Ooh, Polly's come to join us! Get yourself some food, love."

There were several large wine boxes laid out on the benches, along with cans of beer. It seemed likely the party had been in full swing for a while now. Polly helped herself to a cup and filled it with wine from one of the boxes. She grabbed a ham and piccalilli sandwich as a tray went past.

She looked over at some of the purchases the women had made. "Good craft fayre?"

Janine proudly placed an object on the table. It looked like a paper doily with an old-fashion clothes peg shoved through the centre. It *was* a paper doily with an old-fashion clothes peg shoved through the centre. "It's a Christmas angel," said Janine. "It's got a face."

Someone had drawn a wonky smiley face on it in felt tip.

"So it has," said Polly politely.

"Tat," said the next woman along, who Polly thought might have been a Clare. "I bought some genuine craftsmanship." She put a wide wooden ladle thing on the table.

"That's very..." began Polly.

"It's a spoon rest. You put your spoons in it."

"A spoon rest," echoed Polly. "And do spoons need somewhere to rest?"

"Course they don't," said Janine dismissively. "Spoons have been resting by themselves for centuries without needing somewhere special."

"It's a Christmas spoon rest," argued Clare, pointing at the pokerwork snowflake burned into its bowl.

"Ideal for Christmas spoons," said Polly brightly.

"And I bought another for Alison, which I'm sure she'd like."

Polly looked round. "She not here today?"

"No, on account of that Huntley character being given the job. How could she? How could *he*? Should be in prison."

Polly shook her head to express her confusion. At that moment there was a loud "Ho ho ho!" and Father Christmas walked in. Or, to be precise, Bernard walked into the stables in a cheap Santa suit, with a bulging sack on his back. He remembered to flick his cigarette stub out of the door just as he entered.

"Oh, look!" hollered Strawb. "If it ain't Saint facking Nick, in the flesh!"

Santa Bernard sat on a chair which Polly realised had been put out for the occasion. "Who's going to be the first to sit on my knee, eh?"

It was hardly an enticing prospect, but Janine almost physically propelled Polly towards him. "And make sure you tell Santa whether you've been naughty or nice, love!"

This was met with much raucous laughter.

Polly refused to sit on Bernard's knee. Nonetheless he reached into his sack and brought out a present.

"Ho, ho, ho, young lady!" he said. "Here's a little something for you!"

Polly smiled at the idea of her being a young lady and returned to her seat, nibbling on a small pork pie as she went. She pulled the wrapping paper off her present and found it was a colouring book and some pens. A strange present for an older person. These things had been a bit of a fad in recent years, hadn't they? She shrugged inwardly and decided it would be something for the children to do, if ever they paid a visit.

Clare sitting next to her gave her a small nudge. "Look properly," she whispered.

Polly opened the book and looked at the first picture. It was a group scene, although the group was engaged in some sort of sport or perhaps...

"Good grief!" Polly breathed. Now she understood. It was a colouring book most definitely for adults. All of the pictures showed increasingly outrageous sex scenes.

She looked up. "Am I the only one who got a rude colouring book?"

There was a ripple of laughter as dozens of hands lifted copies of the same book.

"Santa's always watching!" said Bernard, tapping the side of his nose. "But this year it seems as though he's decided you're all naughty *and* nice, so you've got presents to suit."

"Cheers!"

As HER RELATIVES trimmed and prepared the oak, Hilde ran through a few calculations in her notebook. They took into account what she had learned of longship construction, the approximate height of the felled tree, the density and weight of oak wood, and the carrying capacity of a Super Duty truck.

Hilde re-checked the calculations.

Hermod gave a shout and waved. The load was ready to go.

Hilde went down the slope, among the piles of chopped oak they could not fit on the truck or trailer, and climbed into the already cramped cab with her male relatives. With a corkscrew jiggle, she wedged her backside between her dad's and her farfar's.

The truck rumbled into life. Gunnolf revved the engine. For a moment it seemed the weighed down truck was not going anywhere. Then it managed to get some traction and pulled slowly away.

Hilde opened her notebook and touched a pencil tip to her notes. "So..." she said.

"Yes?" said Ragnar suspiciously.

"It used to take the average Viking village nine months to build a long ship."

"Aye?"

"Nine months."

"Aye, but they didn't have chainsaws and nail guns."

"And they used up to fourteen oak trees in its construction."

Ragnar frowned. "But none as big as that'un, right?"

"Maybe. Although you've left most of it behind."

"We'll come back for it."

Up front Hermod and Gunnolf grumbled at the notion of putting their truck through further tortures.

"However you do it," said Hilde, "given the carrying capacity of this vehicle..."

"Yes? Spit it out, lass."

She put the pencil back in the book and closed it. "Twelve more trips. At least."

Every man in the truck groaned loudly at that.

"Yeah, but at least there'll be no more dancing, right?" said Yngve. "Right?"

Ragnar didn't answer. As the bickering erupted, Hilde set to working out how big a space they'd need to season the oak while it matured. It was quite probable a new shed would need to be built.

AFTER AN INDULGENT LUNCH and a distinctly half-hearted attempt to potter round the rose gardens (which were dead and empty in winter), the Otterside folk returned to their coach. Polly couldn't help but stare at the driver, Huntley, as she got on, though she had no idea what his crime was.

Loud Christmas carols accompanied them as they pulled away. This time it seemed as though everyone on board was joining in, even Polly. She looked out of the window and was astounded to see Ragnar's truck coming over the grass towards the entrance.

"Hey, someone's been in the wars!" shouted a voice from the front. They all looked out at the truck, which looked very much as if it had suffered a crushing blow from above. Polly wasn't sure how it could still be functioning, but somehow it pulled a trailer behind it. Both truck and trailer were laden with enormous chunks of oak.

"He's a mad bugger that one," said Strawb, dropping into the seat next to her.

In a gap in the singing, after an excruciating whole-coach attempt at *I'm Walking in the Air*, Polly had to ask Strawb.

"The driver..."

"Yes...?" Strawb said darkly.

"What did he do? To Alison."

"Killed her daughter," he said simply.

Polly pictured round-faced, yoga-loving Alison and tried to picture her with a daughter, with a family. "Really?"

"Really," said Strawb.

Polly shook her head. Alison seemed so pleasant, well-balanced. Maybe it had been decades ago, maybe not, but even so... "God," Polly whispered.

"He's got nothing to do with it."

She was still shaking her head, couldn't stop. "How do you move on from something like that?"

Strawb chuckled, but it was a humourless and dry thing. "Alison? She didn't. Not a day goes by when she doesn't wish he was dead." He held up a fist. "You and I were talking about people who deserve to be removed from this world. Imagine if I gave you a magical button, one that if you pressed it made that man—"

Polly slapped the button that was Strawb's fist. "In an instant," she said. "No hesitation."

"Interesting," said Strawb.

41

The police were the first on the scene, beating the ambulance crew by thirty seconds. Sergeant Cesar Hackett got out of the car, saw it was Sam waiting for them on the driveway, and scowled as though everything was her fault. "What did you do?"

Sam bit down on a sharp reply. There was a horrible taste in her mouth and it wasn't just the vomit. Part of her wanted to never talk again. She wondered if she was going into some kind of shock.

She pointed at the gate. "Round the back. In the pool house."

The sirens gave a tiny whoop as the ambulance drew to a halt.

Cesar went to the gate. "It's locked."

"I climbed."

Cesar considered the gate, perhaps weighing it up against his own considerable bulk and meagre athleticism.

The neighbour woman appeared at her front door and stared at Sam. "What did you *do*?" she said.

"Now, now, madam," said Cesar, making calming motions with his hands that would annoy any normal person. "We don't know what she did yet. We're just looking into it."

"Greg is dead," Sam told her simply.

"Nothing is ruled in or ruled out yet," said Cesar.

"The man's casserole," Sam muttered.

Two ambulance paramedics approached. One of them, seemingly built from joints of ham, looked at the small padlock holding the gate, took off his coat to cushion his shoulder and, with two sharp shoulder barges, snapped the lock and forced his way through.

"In the pool house," Sam called after them, but there was little need. They'd find Greg in their own time. He was kind of hard to miss.

"How do you know it was Mr Mandyke?" Detective Constable Camara asked Sam fifteen minutes later.

"Sorry?" said Sam.

The detective constable was a tall, gangly man, with thick black hair that gave him several more inches of height. His long coat and scarf hung shapelessly on his frame, giving Sam the peculiar impression that he looked like a hallway coat stand.

"The individual you found in the tub. Do you know that it was Mr Mandyke?"

Sam stared across the driveway at the meagre flower

borders of Greg's front garden. "I ... assumed. I was looking for him. I saw his shoes in the hallway and when I went round to the back I saw his clothes in a pile and—"

"Through the locked gate," said DC Camara.

"Over," she said. "I went over."

"Keen to find him."

"I needed to check some paperwork had been filed." She reached into her pocket to get her DefCon4 ID to show him, realising she had already done so.

"And you last saw him...?"

"November. Weeks ago." She couldn't remember the exact date so checked her phone. Images of discarded shoes and grass-stained clothes popped into her mind. "You don't think...?"

"They don't encourage it in the modern police force," said Camara drily.

"Do you think he's been in there since the day I last saw him? In there, you know ... *cooking*."

Camara shook his head, slowly and honestly. "Something like this. I don't know how we'll ever work out cause of death, let alone time of death."

Sam nodded. She felt numb.

"What you found was horrible, but he probably didn't suffer. Maybe it was a heart attack or something of that ilk. Something sudden."

"You don't suspect foul play?" she said automatically.

Camara looked surprised, like he truly hadn't considered it. "Do you know of anyone who would have wished Mr Mandyke harm?"

Sam found herself unable to know where to start. The man had been serving a community payback order. Bullying. Threats of assault. She always had the impression he'd been an unscrupulous builder and a ruthless businessman.

"It could be a long list," she said.

"Oh?"

Sam laughed. She didn't know why. It wasn't a laughing situation. Maybe it was the absurdity of the circumstances of Greg's death, maybe it was just her stunned emotions seeking an outlet. Maybe it was the realisation that he had been stewing away in his own juices all the time and the neighbour had simply put the stench down to cooking food.

"I tell you what," she said. "If he has been in there all that time, no one – no friends or loved ones or even workmates – came round and found him. No one reported him missing. That's got to tell you something."

DC Camara paused with pen in police notepad. "That's a depressing thought."

A silence hung between them for a second.

"I'll need to take a full statement from you at some point," the detective said.

"Down the station?"

"Can be. Or I we can do it somewhere convenient for you. It's just to get some details down."

She nodded. "You've got my number. I'm just round the corner at my dad's place. I'm going to go home and tell him what happened."

"Did he know Mr Mandyke?"

"Not at all," said Sam. "I'm going to tell him so that when

I burst into tears and down four strong cocktails in a row, he'll know why."

"Not a terrible plan." Camara closed his notebook and went off to chat with the forensics officers who'd just appeared at the scene.

42

Hermod banged the roof of the truck and pointed ahead as they bounced and rattled down the uneven track of the Elysian Fields caravan park.

Ragnar peered towards the compound. "Saxon alert, lads."

There was a car parked by the chain gate of their compound and a woman stood next to it. The car, whilst not exactly old or battered, had a well-worn look to it. It was a car that had either been loved to bits or not loved enough. The young-ish Saxon woman had a similar air about her, tired yet bright-eyed.

"Ay up, lass," said Ragnar as the wood laden truck stopped at the gate.

Several of the Odinson men tried without success to stand in such a way as to conceal the huge cargo of stolen oak.

The woman smiled nervously. "It's Ragnar, isn't it?"

"Aye. And who are you?"

"It's that woman with the shop," said Hilde.

"Delia," said the woman. "And I was wondering if I could ask..." She gestured at Hilde. "I wanted to ask Hilde about some work she might do for me."

Ragnar wasn't sure what was going on here. Strangers didn't turn up at the Odinson compound – police, yes, social workers, yes, other representatives of the Saxon authorities with their demands and questions, yes, but not ordinary Saxon folk. He was immediately suspicious and stroked his beard as he stared.

The woman, Delia, tried another smile. "My, that's a lot of wood you've got on your truck there."

"No, it isn't," said Sigurd automatically, leaning against a chunk of tree trunk as though to normalise it and make it vanish.

"Isn't it?" said Delia.

"Perfectly normal amount of wood," said Yngve.

"Oh. Right."

"Not even worth mentioning," said Torsten.

Hilde jumped over the side of the truck and onto the muddy ground. "What work?"

"I've got a mammoth's belly that won't stay on and I think I need to construct a supporting framework. Maybe out of light metal."

Hermod had moved the chain barrier. As the truck rumbled forward, Ragnar pushed his way to the rear and jumped off. No way was his granddaughter going to discuss any sort of deal without her farfar to look after her.

"Hilde's services don't come cheap," he said.

"Well, I don't have much in the way of funds," said Delia. "But I don't have much time, either."

"Then she's not interested."

"I thought you could come down to the shop. I've probably got all the tools you'd need in the workshop."

"As I said, she's not interested—" said Ragnar.

Hilde stepped in front of him. "Workshop, you say?"

"Yes."

Hilde frowned. "Are you talking about an actual job?"

Ragnar quivered a little inside. The Odinsons worked, after a fashion. Indeed, after a fashion they were very hard working workers. But an actual job? The Odinsons pretty much prided themselves on the fact none of them had real jobs. They were free Viking folk, not Saxon peasants.

"As I say," said Delia. "You could come take a look, if your family can spare you while they unload all that wood."

Ragnar looked to the compound. Hermod and Gunnolf were already bickering about how to unload the wood.

"Aye, aye," said Ragnar. "Maybe just go and have a look with her. While we just get on with our general business."

Hilde first gave him a firm look, then Delia. "I'll take a look and then I'll decide. No promises."

"Super," said Delia and gestured for her to get in the car.

43

S am poured Detective Constable Camara a coffee from her cafetière.

"Nice ... cosy," he said, politely.

Sam flicked the bobble on the coffee pot's hat. "You think so?"

He considered it. "Not really."

Across the kitchen at the counter, Marvin chuckled, but didn't look up from the stage dummy he was oiling. "Orville had a hat like that."

"Orville?" said Camara.

"Keith Harris's duck."

Camara was frowning.

"Orville the Duck?" said Marvin. "Cuddles the Monkey? Keith Harris? Ventriloquist? We did panto together at the Sunderland Empire in eighty six. Lovely chap. No? Never heard of him?"

Camara gave an apologetic shrug.

"And so stage ventriloquism dies," sighed Marvin and twisted the dummy's head. "Disgraceful," he squeaked in a poor attempt to give the dummy voice.

"You have to forgive my dad," said Sam. "Toast?"

"I've had breakfast. If I may...?" He took out his notepad. Camara, an elongated figure of a man, had equally elongated fingers and there was a certain grace to the way he handled pen and pad. "I need to get a clearer picture for this investigation."

Sam's hand paused in the act of reaching for toast from the rack. "Investigation? You no longer think it was an accident?"

He pulled a face. "We need to cover all the angles."

"You *don't* think it was an accident."

"Be careful, constable," said Marvin. "My girl can be a sharp one. Takes a while for her to get up to speed but..."

"Thanks, dad."

"If you could just go over the events of the day you last saw Mr Mandyke, then the day you found— You went to his house."

With DC Camara occasionally prompting or asking for clarification, Sam went over the day of the community payback session at Otterside.

"Odinson?" he said when she mentioned Hilde and the Odinson van that had come to collect her. "They were there at the same time as Mandyke?"

She did not need to ask if Camara was aware of the Odinsons. The family had a reputation which permeated the local area like an urban legend. In Skegness, mothers didn't tell naughty children the bogeyman would get them; it would be the Odinsons stealing them in the night.

"I don't think he had any dealings with them," she said. "And he left Otterside well before them. I saw him go."

"And would anyone else there have seen him when he departed?"

Sam remembered the childish and deliberate spray of gravel from his car wheels as his Lexus pulled away, and another memory dropped into her mind. "Greg knew or knew of someone who was at Otterside."

"Who?"

Sam struggled to recall any details. She sighed and bit into her toast. "He gave the impression it was a woman. An old client."

The DC patted the folder on the table beneath his notepad. "I've got some of his business records. If I showed you some names would you be able to tell me?"

"I can look," she said.

He flicked through his notes and asked her further questions about the days that followed, the fruitless phone calls she'd made. Then he took her through the day she went to Mandyke's house. This involved a little background information, including her visit to Delia's to look at the animal costumes.

"This is Delia who also knits hats for ducks?" said Camara.

"Coffee cosies."

"Sure. But these animal costumes..."

"Are for an escape drill for an Ice Age theme park that's going to be built at the bottom of the North Sea. Yes."

"And, just to check," said Camara. "This is your *job*?"

"It's a wide and varied remit," she admitted.

"I think she makes it all up," said Marvin. "Earns her money as a high stakes poker player."

"I wish," she said.

Camara listened to her account, double-checking facts and rephrasing questions until she feared she was starting to make up extra details just to make him happy. He did indeed seem happy.

"Does that help?" she said.

"It does and it doesn't."

"Oh?"

"It matches with what we found at the scene."

"But...?"

There was a moment's hesitation. "We still don't have confirmation that the body is Greg Mandyke, although it seems likely. It's a male. The hair in the – I'm going to say water – is a match to photos we have of him. There was water in the lungs. He drowned, ultimately. But there was also an electrical wire leading into the tub."

"Oh, my," said Marvin.

"Suicide?" said Sam.

Camara's graceful finger flexed, a gesture of ambiguity. "The doors to the house were locked. Nothing out of place inside. Forensics haven't finished, but there's no obvious signs of an intruder."

"But...?" Sam repeated.

"There were no keys to the house in Mr Mandyke's clothes pockets. None at all in the pool area or around it."

"He was locked out of his own house."

"Indeed."

"Which means he either did it accidentally on his way out..."

Camara shook his head. "The back door isn't on a latch system. It needs a key."

"So that means someone locked up the back door and front door on their way out." Sam recalled the front door, the uPVC door lock. No Yale-style latch on that either. "The front door keys?"

"On the door mat."

"Posted back through the letterbox," Sam and Marvin said at the same time.

"Is what it looks like," agreed Camara.

"He was murdered," said Sam.

"Is a possibility," Camara conceded. He opened the folder on the table in front of him. "If we're looking for a suspect, it may be among these people he's done work for."

Sam held her hands out to take it. DC Camara slid it over. She leafed through the pages. She didn't expect to see anything, but on the second page a name leapt out at her.

"Janine Slater."

"Who?" Camara leaned forward.

"I did some training for a fitness app with her the other day. She's at Otterside. And..." She frowned.

"What?"

Sam hardly knew how to phrase it. "I saw her behaving oddly the day Drumstick died."

"Is that slang for something?" said Camara.

44

Jacob appeared in the south lounge with half a tennis ball. "I've got it," he said to Polly and Strawb.

"That's half a tennis ball," said Polly.

"It is," said Jacob, undeniably pleased with himself. "So, we can go now." He held it like it was the cup of Christ.

Polly looked to Strawb. Strawb shrugged.

"He's got a tennis ball. Which apparently means we can go."

He stood and, none the wiser, Polly stood also. "Where are we going?" she said.

"The main drain in Ingoldmells," said Jacob.

"If that's a pub name, someone should be fired."

"It's a short drive, so we need to use Chesney's car."

Polly was vaguely aware that the Otterside site manager had an alleged sideline as a local taxi driver (and as a second rate cabaret act).

"We're going to pay him in bits of tennis ball?" she said. "Or maybe he already has the other half and this is the final payment."

Jacob, unable to perceive a facetious remark when he heard one, shook his head. "It's a well-known fault on the two thousand and two Transport-Es that the exterior lock is connected to the door latch through an airtight tube."

"Yes?" said Polly who didn't understand a word, but wanted to be polite.

"Therefore, if a sharp blast of air is applied to the exterior keyhole, the latch inside should pop open."

"Ah."

Perhaps her 'ah' didn't express sufficient awe, or perhaps Jacob realised she didn't understand or wasn't making enough effort to understand.

"Half a tennis ball against the keyhole of the car," said Jacob, miming. "And then – whack." He flexed the tennis ball as though it had been struck. "Sudden rush of air and the lock pops open."

"Our friend has been watching a lot of YouTube videos," said Strawb.

"It will definitely work."

Polly walked with them along the central corridor towards the reception and exit. "So we're stealing Chesney's car to go on a drive to Ingoldmells."

"Yes," said Strawb.

"Excellent."

They went out into the car park to find Margaret sitting at the wheel of a yellow people carrier, engine idling.

Strawb opened the door for Polly. "Hop in."

Jacob stared at Margaret. "I was going to break in." He sounded affronted.

"I did it first," she said.

Jacob held up his half tennis ball.

"I went into the office and borrowed his keys," she said.

"The tennis ball would have worked."

"I'm sure it would."

"It really would."

"You can show me later if you like."

"But you've already done it," sulked Jacob. "What would be the point?"

"Scientific curiosity."

Jacob, dejected, climbed into the front with Margaret. In the back, Polly buckled up.

Margaret drove like a woman who hadn't driven in ten years but was confident it would all come back to her if she approached the matter with sufficient gusto.

Polly was still unclear where they were going or why, but made the effort to enjoy the drive. The road from Skegness to the seaside village of Ingoldmells – several hundred yards inland from the beach and lined by caravan parks on both sides – was a short one. In summer season, tens of thousands of families would be living, frolicking and feuding in these semi-permanent townships. In winter, most of the caravans were empty shells. Ingoldmells itself felt like a nothing place, a couple of pubs and a supermarket, a placeholder to give some sense of geography to the caravan parks claiming an Ingoldmells address.

"Where are we going again?" she said.

"Just up here," said Strawb as Margaret indicated and pulled over into a lay-by near a bridge.

"I'll show Polly," said Margaret to Strawb. It wasn't said sternly, but there was the sense of an order being given.

"Then I will watch and marvel while Jacob demonstrates his bladdy tennis ball method."

"I know it will work," said Jacob.

Margaret gestured for Polly to walk with her. A cool breeze was blowing in from the direction of the sea. Polly wished she had brought a coat, but said nothing.

"James Huntley," said Margaret.

It took Polly a good second or two to recognise the name. "The coach driver."

Margaret nodded. "It was three years ago."

"When he killed Alison's daughter?"

Another nod. "Her name was Rachel. She'd been visiting the area and staying at a caravan park some distance up that way. Like our Chesney, Huntley had a sideline as a taxi driver. Lots of people do."

The bridge was a flat span across a dyke, fifteen feet across. Margaret stood at the green railings and looked out across its still surface. "Rachel had been out with friends in town. Pubs and bars. She was thirty-three I think. Late in the night, she called a taxi to bring her back to the caravan."

"Huntley."

"He'd been drinking as well."

"Oh."

Margaret pointed along the road back to Skegness. "He came down here. The road was empty as far as anyone knows. No hidden bends. No surprises. And yet..." She drew a line along the road towards where they stood. "He drove through that wooden fence there, cutting across the rear of that grassy bit and..." Her pointing finger went to the dyke. "The car rolled and went into the water upside down. Four feet of water."

There was a hiss and a shout from back along the road. Strawb was rocking with laughter as Jacob evidently failed to open the car lock.

"Four feet," said Margaret. "James Huntley got out. I believe he later claimed he'd tried to get Rachel out. People were on the scene within five minutes. Huntley had crawled up the bank and was walking up the road that way. Looking for a phone box, he said."

"You said he'd been drinking."

"The police breath test showed thirty seven micrograms of alcohol. The legal limit is thirty five."

"So he was drunk driving."

"The second test at the station showed thirty four. When asked about the crash, Huntley said an 'animal' had run out in front of them and he'd swerved." Margaret took a deep breath. Cold winter air misted around her lips. "The police and fire crews got Rachel out quarter of an hour after the initial crash. She'd stopped breathing, but there was still a heartbeat. For a time."

Back at the people carrier, Jacob gave a little cheer and Strawb starting arguing.

"Recorded time of death was fifty minutes after the initial crash," said Margaret.

Polly looked down into the water. There was a grey-silver sheen on the surface. "This is terrible. Fascinating too, but definitely terrible. Why are you telling me this?" She gave Margaret a quizzical look. "It's not exactly a cheery outing."

Margaret gave a tiny grunt of laughter. "I need to ask you two questions."

"Okay," said Polly.

"Do you think a man like James Huntley, who drunkenly drove his vehicle into this dyke and left his passenger to die while he walked *away* from the nearest houses and telephones, a man who had drink driving convictions before — Do you think a man like James Huntley deserves to live?"

"No," said Polly simply. "It should have been him that drowned."

Margaret nodded. "Second question. Please answer honestly and seriously."

Polly felt a sudden and foolish urge to cross her heart as testament, but that would hardly have been serious. "Okay," she said.

Margaret faced her properly so she could look her in the eye. "If we asked you to kill him, would you do it?"

An obvious and flippant answer rose to Polly's lips but she suppressed it. "We?" she said.

Margaret nodded, indicating the two men arguing genially beside the stolen vehicle. "Could you do it?"

Polly looked at Margaret's face. It seemed the woman was being perfectly serious.

45

Saturday was the day of the escaped animal drill. Sam was up early for there was a lot to do. Any kind of large scale drill would require considerable effort and manpower, but making the patently ridiculous seem credible was doubly hard.

Marvin came into the kitchen of *Duncastin'* as she cooked up a batch of pancakes. "Smells good," he said.

"A nice treat to set us up. We both have a busy day today."

He nodded. There was a glint of glee in his eyes.

"Nervous?" she said.

About what?" he said. "I'm quite excited to be treading the boards again, I must say."

"It'll be more like treading the community lounge, but at least the lighting should be flattering," said Sam.

"True. A small intimate gig. I'm going to throw in some of my old time stories."

"Like the night you stole Jimmy Cricket's wellies? Or that

one where you had to hitchhike up the A1 with, er, Lena Zavaroni?"

"Bonnie Langford. Yes, that kind of thing."

"Showbiz stories from a real showbiz legend? They'll love it."

She put the latest pancake on the pile she was creating, only then noticing the suit and gold bow tie her dad was wearing. "Good choice. You look suitably glamorous, but not too shiny."

"Mr Marvellous – not too shiny. They should put that on the posters."

"Just right for an intimate gig." Sam looked at the various boxes of props that had taken up temporary residence in the kitchen. "Which of these boxes needs to go in?"

"All of them," said Marvin.

Sam stared in dismay. She was certain, in Marvin's mind's eye, her van was the same size as a normal one. In truth, the Piaggio Ape 50 had about the same capacity as the teak sideboard her dad insisted was a cocktail bar (maybe it was, but Sam had never seen a cocktail anywhere near it).

"Can we maybe get the things you need into one or two boxes?" she asked.

"I suppose we could leave the saw the lady in half box."

"Yeah." She nodded slowly. "Let's leave geriatric dismemberment for another day, eh? But bring the levitation table."

In the end they got everything Marvin needed into the van, but Sam had a real fear the tiny engine would fail to move the weight. She inched down the drive and they crawled to Otterside at a little over ten miles an hour.

Chesney the manager came out to meet them. He was wearing a shiny lilac shirt that was more flouncy blouse than shirt, and more fire hazard than anything else.

"Spotted your sweet ride from inside. Taking it nice and steady I see!" he said. "Can I help you with your props, Mr Marvellous?"

"That would be helpful," said Marvin. "And it's Marvin, please."

Chesney giggled and blushed like a lovestruck teen. "Oh, I couldn't. Can I? Can I? And you're fine for me to open for you, Marvin?"

"Open...?" said Marvin.

"Just a couple of numbers. Get them warmed up."

"Er..."

"Two maximum," said Sam. "As his stand-in manager, that's a direct order. And you did get his list of riders, didn't you?"

"Riders?"

Sam caught her dad's suspicious look, but she kept a straight face. "Mr Marvellous insists on five hot chocolates prepared for him in advance of every performance. He will only drink one. The rest must be disposed of securely. And he needs a private dressing room. With a bouquet of lilies on his dressing table."

Marvin frowned. "Aren't they a sign of death?" he whispered.

"As a reminder not to die on stage," said Sam, making it up on the spot.

"Of course," said Chesney.

"And a bottle of scotch," said Marvin, joining in with the silliness.

"I don't think Mr Marvellous has scotch as a contract rider," said Sam.

"Oh, he does," said Marvin, deadpan.

"Anything. Anything. Of course," said Chesney.

"And you're not to sing any songs with the letter 'a' in the title," said Sam, because the more Chesney agreed to the demands, the more she wanted to make up.

Chesney's brow creased.

"Well known stage tradition," she said.

"Oh. Oh, is it? I knew that. Of course, I knew that."

Marvin squeezed her hand. "I think this young man is going to look after me perfectly well," he said.

Chesney gestured to the corner of the building. "Your actors have arrived. They're over by the rose garden. Dunno if they're doing tai chi or something."

Sam walked over. The group was a large one, at least thirty people. Sam recognised Sergeant Cesar Hackett (out of uniform) among them. Like the rest, he was dressed in loose gym wear. All of them were facing Cat from the café, who was bellowing instructions at them.

"Right, it's the Ice Age, so I don't want to hear anybody else suggest that we get a nice cup of tea, is that clear? I want you to *feel* that glacier under your feet! You are animals. This is your world, your truth. Remember that half hour we did on Meisner technique. I want you to look up and *see* the snow falling from the pewter sky! Can you see it?"

A hand went up. It was a young woman with auburn ringlets. "If we're animals who lived in the Ice Age, we're not actually going to feel cold are we? We've got thick coats and we're adapted to—"

"Thank you for your thoughts Rhianna, but were you there?"

"Was I where...?"

"In the Ice Age!"

"No, but science suggests—"

"There is no place for science when we're easing our way into a role!" Cat snipped. Sam was some distance away, and she was a bit too loud even for her. "Feeling is everything. We immerse ourselves in the world of our subject. Go totally Stanislavski on this, okay?"

"Yes, but science can—"

Sam strode forward to insert herself before Cat could respond to the unwanted insubordination of her troupe.

"Ah, Sam. Good to see you. The Skegness Operatic and Dramatic Society are delighted to be here. Aren't we everybody?" There was a vague mumble of assent. "We were just warming up our acting chops."

"There are some things we need to go through," said Sam. "The residents have kindly given us the use of their summer house. There are chairs and tea-making facilities in there." She indicated where that was, and there was a surge towards the building. Cat frowned slightly. Sam wondered if she was peeved at how quickly her troupe had forgotten the icy glacier under their feet.

"I've got to mark some things out," Sam said, jiggling the heavy rucksack on her back. "Then I'll come give some instructions."

"Acting suggestions," said Cat.

"The rules of the activity."

Cat gave her a haughty look. "Any production can only have one director."

She smiled. "You're the director?"

Cat inclined her head regally.

"Which makes me the producer," said Sam. "And, er, the producer is the one who writes all the cheques, yes?"

There was a minute change in Cat's expression. Not so much a direct acknowledgement that Sam was in charge, but a concession she might have some very minor but conceivably important role to play in proceedings.

"I must make sure our caribou does not have too many cups of tea," said Cat. "Otherwise, he'll be excusing himself every five minutes to go to the loo. Played havoc in our production of *Sweeney Todd* having a bloody corpse get up, apologise to the audience, and go off to go have a tinkle." She ran to summer house. "Cesar! One cup only! Half a cup!"

POLLY STOOD in the north lounge and read the poster the woman, Sam, had stuck on the door.

DO NOT LEAVE THE BUILDING BY THIS EXIT. PRACTICE DRILL
TAKING PLACE.
DO NOT BE ALARMED. THE ANIMALS ARE NOT REAL.
IN THE EVENT OF A REAL EMERGENCY, PLEASE GO AROUND TO THE
FRONT OF THE BUILDING.

"WHAT ANIMALS AREN'T REAL?" she mused, looking around for animals, real or otherwise.

Sam had placed similar posters on all doors and fire exits along the rear of the building, and was now working along the lawns with metal stakes and lengths of twine.

"Is she constructing a maze?" asked Jacob.

"Or possibly having a mental breakdown," said Polly. "Hard to tell."

"My uncle Jack made a replica of the Blackpool Tower out of bulldog clips when he was having a nervous breakdown."

Polly nodded, conceding the point.

There was a squeal of electronic feedback. "Right everyone," said Chesney on the mic. "Do you want to gather round?"

The chairs in the north lounge had all been rearranged into a circle, focusing on a central spot where Chesney had set up a microphone and PA.

"He's not going to bladdy sing to us, is he?" said Strawb.

"Is he bad?" said Polly.

Strawb nodded. "I got us front row seats."

"Come on, come on," said Chesney to the more reluctant residents. "Find a spot."

"I was looking for the animals," said Jacob, tapping the window.

Chesney squinted. "What animals?"

Jacob shrugged. "They're not real."

There was a distant buzz. A white helicopter started to descend behind the trees separating the Otterside lawns from the beach beyond.

"And there's a helicopter too," said Jacob.

Chesney railed at the implication that a helicopter and non-real animals could possibly compete with his singing skills.

"Here's one you'll all like," he said, tapping the phone plugged into the PA. "*Looking Through the Eyes of Love.*" He said it in a peculiar measured way, as though checking each word as it came out of his mouth.

Polly sat down next to Strawb as the intro music began. She put her hand on the armrest and her fingers brushed up against Strawb's. She didn't pull away politely as she might normally have done.

"In the eyes of the world I'm a loser..." Chesney crooned.

Strawb lifted his hand and gently took Polly's hand in his. He leaned in. "Awful, isn't it?" he whispered.

46

Rich and his impeccably attired butler, Peninsula, entered the grounds of Otterside retirement village from where their helicopter had landed on the beach. Peninsula carried an old-fashioned picnic hamper. Sam finished spooling out the cord and markers delineating the enclosures and walls of their imaginary Ice Age zoo.

Rich clapped his hands. "This all looks very clever. Don't understand a bit of it, mind."

She thrust a folded map against his chest and kept on with the job in hand. She wouldn't normally treat a client with such rudeness, but Rich was her ex and warranted special treatment.

He wore an expensive suit jacket over a loose cotton shirt that didn't have enough buttons. He might be slumming it in mid-winter Skeggy, but he was dressed like he was lunching in sunny St Tropez. He didn't seem to notice the cold. He unfolded the map.

"This is Chester Zoo," he said. "Why is this Chester Zoo?"

"I'm using it as a stand-in plan for your theme park, since you don't have one yet and— Does your Ice Age theme park even have a name yet?"

"I'm tossing up between Doggerland and Ice Land," said Rich.

"There is already an Iceland, if you recall, sir," said Peninsula.

"Right. The shop."

"*And* the country."

"Yeah, that too. We're working on it."

"Today's layout is all scaled down," Sam explained. "Miniature versions of the real thing. Eurasian cave lion enclosure there. Irish elk paddock there. Giant cow things here."

"Madam means the aurochs," said Peninsula.

Sam resisted the obvious comeback. "That's what I said. Giant cow things."

"With the massive steak house next door," Rich grinned.

Sam waved at the map and gestured across the lawns. "Hot dog stands. Ice creams. Toilets."

"This looks very good," said Rich. "I'm impressed."

"We're recording everything with DefCon4 bodycams and I'll be monitoring, so—" she carefully took the map from him and took a step back, smiling genially "—why are you here?"

"Oh, just observers," said Rich, grinning. "Aren't we?"

Peninsula opened the picnic hamper and produced a pair of binoculars. "Observers, madam."

"With a delightful selection of goodies from Cartwright and Butlers to enjoy while we watch," said Rich. "Their onion chutney is to die for."

A picnic in the middle of December... There was a fine line between madness and eccentricity and apparently the only difference was wealth.

Sam pointed out a distant damp bench to her eccentric ex. "Sit there. Eat chutney. Do not get in the way."

There was a text on her phone. Delia had arrived. Sam went up to the main building and round to the car park.

Delia was lifting plastic-wrapped animal costumes out of the car, struggling with some of the papier-mâché heads. Sam had agreed the heads could form a useful part of the scenery, while the more practical ski masks would be on the moving animal actors. Hilde Odinson was helping Delia, and a tall figure with a shock of black hair had also been roped in, apparently.

"DC Camara," said Sam. "I did not expect to see you here."

"He's helping," Delia grunted. "Leave him alone."

The gangly detective gestured helplessly. "When you told me you were holding an emergency escaped mammoth drill, I just had to come down to see."

"Professional curiosity?"

"Cruel fascination. I gather one of my colleagues is among the actors." He regarded the wolf head he was holding. "Wonderful craftsmanship ... Delia, isn't it? I was only admiring your coffee pot cosies the other day."

"Ideal Christmas present," said Delia. "I'm sure Mrs Camara would love one."

"My mum, you mean. Maybe she would."

Sam gathered up as much as she could, which amounted to two bucket-like animal heads with costumes stuffed inside. "The actors are in the summer house. Round here."

Delia scurried to catch up with Sam. "See how I did that?"

"Did what?" said Hilde close behind.

Delia jigged her head. "The detective isn't married. He's single. Sam's single."

Sam was blindsided by the suddenly new conversation. "Who are you? The village matchmaker?" She looked back. "I'd get a crick in my neck trying to kiss him. And, God, think of the children."

"The ability to reach high shelves is an underrated attribute," said Delia. "Trust me."

Sam laughed her comment away, but knew the thought had been lodged in her head now.

In the summer house, actorly types milled and drank tea. Breath misted in the cold air. Condensation clung to the windows. Sam put her costumes down on a lounger that had been put in there for storage.

"So," she said loudly, trying to draw everyone's attention, "I have blu-tacked some posters around the room. They give the basic rules for the roles you will have today."

"Acting guidance," said Cat, equally loudly, positioning herself next to Sam within the zone of authority.

"Rules," said Sam. "Different rules for every role. There will be costumes for some—"

"Courtesy of *Back to Life*," added Delia, equally loudly. "Quality creations for every occasion."

"Thank you, yes – and everyone will be equipped with one of these body cams." Sam opened a plastic briefcase. Inside thirty of the devices nestled in foam compartments. "So, can we spend a few minutes assigning roles to each of you please?"

"I'll do that," said Cat. "I know my people and have assigned roles already."

"Well, the starring roles, if we're going to call them that, are the five animals," said Sam. The mammoth, the sabre-toothed tiger, the bison, the wolf and the caribou. Then we will need ten zookeepers. Everybody else will be members of the public."

"Right! Step up!" said Cat. She pointed at various people in the group. "Bison, caribou, mammoth, wolf, sabre-toothed tiger."

Sam wondered what had informed Cat's choices. A large dose of type-casting might have been involved. The bison and the mammoth were both big hairy men. The wolf was a grey-haired woman with a permanent scowl. The caribou was Sergeant Cesar, a suitably doughy and doe-eyed man. While the sabre-toothed tiger was the young woman who had argued for a scientific approach earlier. Cat strode through the group appointing zookeepers, then told everyone else they were members of the public.

"You will all need to carefully study and follow the rules," said Sam. "There is also an indicative timeline that tells you when tranquiliser guns will become available, and other key details. Cat here will issue the guns from the stores located within this room."

Cat realised she was effectively being removed from the action. "How can I offer feedback on the actors' performance if I'm based in here?" she asked.

"You will get to view the collated footage," Sam said. "Consider this to be part of your professional showreel."

Cat nodded, although she still looked slightly peeved. Sam really didn't want her holding up the exercise while she admonished the actors for some perceived shortcoming.

"One last thing," Sam shouted, as everyone milled around reading the posters, "I will arrive on scene and represent the local law enforcement agencies. If I issue an instruction, I expect it to be followed. Understood?"

There was a murmur of assent. Sam looked to DC Camara, half-expecting him to step in with a 'I'm a real copper so do what she says' but he just nodded happily as though accepting her instructions.

The actors familiarised themselves with the rules, and discussed the exercise in their groups. Delia moved around the actors who were playing the animals, making sure the costumes and masks fitted properly. With a few safety pins she soon transformed them into grinning Ice Age beasts.

"There's no zipper," said the caribou.

"Sorry?" said Delia.

"What if I'm, you know, caught short during proceedings?"

"Do not mess this up, Cesar," growled Cat. "We're not having another *Sweeney Todd* incident." She sighed and helped Cesar out of his costume so he could go off for a preparatory wee.

Sam set up the weapons store, which was a table laid out with some Nerf guns, some sticks and some nets. Cat took up position behind the table like a proud shopkeeper.

"We should line them up for a picture," said Delia, once they had Caribou Cesar back in costume.

The five animals stood obediently side by side, arms around each other like a bizarre chorus line. Sam took a picture with her phone and saw DC Camara was taking one too.

"Purely for my own amusement," he said.

Sam looked around. Everything was ready. Weeks of hurried preparation, some insightful use of outside expertise, and her very best attempt to plan a project that had never been attempted before. This was the moment. Either it was going to be one of the highlights of her DefCon4 career, or what followed would be the damning evidence at her firing.

"Okay, everyone," she called. "It's showtime!"

POLLY HADN'T SEEN Mr Marvellous for some years. As he stepped into the central stage area she was mildly shocked to see how much he'd aged. Then she admonished herself. Was she turning into one of those old people who got all judgey and mean? Possibly.

Mr Marvellous patted Chesney on a sweaty shoulder. "Wasn't he astounding, ladies and gentlemen? That last number. It just seemed to go on forever, didn't it?"

The audience applauded. Polly wasn't sure if it was

because of the appearance of Mr Marvellous in glitzy bowtie, or because Chesney's turn was finally over. Even the most charitable person wouldn't think it was for Chesney's actual talent – which wasn't so much bad as painfully mediocre. Whichever, it was considerable applause.

Polly was surprised at the turnout of Otterside residents. She had never seen so many of them all together before. A celebrity could do that, though. Sure, he wasn't a superstar, but there wasn't a single person of their age who didn't know and remember Marvin 'Mr Marvellous' Applewhite.

Marvin stood in the centre of the residents' lounge, his arms raised as he basked in the applause. "A very good day to you, ladies and gentlemen. I've played the Royal Exchange in Manchester, the Sheffield Crucible, the Liverpool Playhouse, I've played to British troops at sea during the Falklands War, I've been on stage with the good and great." He put his hands on his hips and turned a full circle, giving them all a scrutinising look. "But nothing compares to the honour of performing here at—" He frowned, pulled a piece of paper from his hand and pretended to read. "—Otterside!"

There was light laughter and a little groaning. Marvin rolled his eyes, screwed up the paper, slammed it between his hands and confetti flew out. There were hardly gasps of wonder, but there was silence as everyone sat up and gave him their full attention.

Polly relaxed. The man's act might be a little corny, but he clearly still had, ahem, a few tricks up his sleeve.

"As you can see," said Marvin, "today I will be performing 'in the round', as you're quite a large crowd. You can be sure that a lesser magician would be nervous about this. Eyes will be on me from every angle." He gave a comic wink to those behind him, turning slowly as he spoke, making eye contact with the whole crowd. "Now, before I start there's something missing. As you can see, I am without an assistant. I wonder if someone from the audience would care to help me with my show today?"

Many hands went up, and Polly found hers shooting up as well, held firmly in Strawb's grip. She didn't resist. Marvin's gaze passed over the crowd and came to rest on her. "Can I ask your name?" he asked.

"Polly," she said.

Marvin nodded sagely. "Yes, Polly. I think I'll be able to remember that. A hand for Polly please."

As the audience clapped, Polly stood and walked over.

"Polly, what a perfect name for a glamorous assistant!" he said. "Now I won't make you wear the outfit." He studied her face for a moment. "Unless you want to, that is?"

Polly gave a small nod. In for a penny, in for a pound.

"Ladies and gentlemen, we have a real trouper on our hands! Please show your appreciation for Polly!"

As the crowd cheered and clapped, Marvin bent and whispered that she would find some outfit options in the ladies' toilet outside the lounge, inviting her to choose whatever she liked.

47

S am had signalled the start of scenario one: the escape of the mammoth. The actors who were playing members of the public milled dutifully around the pathways. Zookeepers were spread out at various points, then came the 'escape'.

The mammoth burst out from behind a shed with a loud trumpeting sound. Nearly everyone stopped what they were doing and stared in astonishment at the noise it made as it capered along the path.

"Very impressive," said Rich, appearing at Sam's elbow with a small bowl of dip and crackers in his hand. "Did you hire that person knowing they were able to make the sound of a trumpeting elephant, or did you get them to practise?"

"I told you to stay on your bench," she said.

"Rye cracker and relish?" he said.

Sam pointed sternly. "Back to your bench."

The mammoth's rules declared that any members of the

public directly touched by the escaping animal would sustain injury, and were required to sit down and wait for medical assistance. The rapid progress of the mammoth, teamed with the startled response of the public, meant there were already a high number of casualties. Zookeepers were charged primarily with the safety of the public. Once they sprang into action they quickly evacuated the remaining people and carried temporary fencing to try and contain the mammoth. The mammoth knew the rules – once it was completely surrounded by fence panels, it was to remain still – but this particular specimen had the agility of a rugby forward and dodged the approaching zookeepers with a keen glint in its eye. Sam might have to amend the rules slightly there, although who knew how nifty a real mammoth could be?

She gave the signal for the release of the weapons. Even with this particularly determined escapee, the zookeepers were fairly close to pinning it down so they could administer the tranquiliser.

MARVIN LED AN ADMIRING round of applause when Polly emerged in the outfit she had selected. She'd been delighted to find that the tights provided were thicker than some of the trousers she owned, so what looked like a rather immodest swimsuit outfit was actually pretty warm, transforming her mottled legs into those of a tanned supermodel. The costume was so heavily sequinned that it was slightly scratchy, but she was prepared to put up with that. She had crowned the whole ensemble with a feather headdress, in the style of a Vegas showgirl. In the mirror of the ladies' loo, she had rather liked what she saw.

"Spectacular, my dear!" said Marvin. "Simply spectacular. Now your main job is to help me look good. If you don't mind indulging an old man, I'm of the opinion that a bright smile and an outstretched arm are the tools that are likely to work best. What do you think, Polly?"

"I can help you look good," she said, emboldened by the lavish outfit. She spotted his bow tie had moved out of place slightly. It seemed like the right time to correct it, so she leaned forward and gave it a tweak. She chucked him under the chin and gave him a wink as an afterthought. The crowd laughed loudly at her boldness.

"An absolute natural. Thank you, Polly! Now, I would like to show you a few little things I can do with a pack of cards. Polly, would you mind bringing that tray over here? Now, is anyone familiar with Busby's card warp?"

SAM MADE notes as quickly as she could. She had numerous observations and thoughts for improving the response to the mammoth drill. She'd write them all up later. Right now it was time for the next two scenarios, featuring multiple animal escapes. This time it was the turn of the wolf and the caribou. Sam signalled, and the two animals burst from their starting places. There was a built-in assumption that the wolf might chase the caribou, although this wasn't necessarily a given, if the wolf was well-fed. The man playing the wolf swaggered down the path, howling aggressively at the public. The public were faster to respond this time and took off at speed. When the caribou cantered jauntily onto the path (Sam was impressed by the moves Sergeant Cesar had improvised. She was prepared to believe it was how a caribou genuinely walked) the wolf yowled enthusiastically and gave chase at top speed. Sam realised a valuable lesson she should take from this was if you gave an actor the choice between doing a fun and interesting thing and *not* doing the thing, it was pointless. During their performance, all they wanted to chase was any glory they could.

"Daddy, come with me. I'll save you from the wolf!" shouted a voice from behind.

Sam spun round and came face to face with a girl, no more than six or seven years old, in a severe and old fashioned pinafore dress, holding an orange teddy in her hand. Apparently Caribou Cesar was her dad. The girl ran swiftly towards the wolf, dodged it, grabbed its tail and as the actor stumbled, kicked him heavily between the legs. The wolf went down with an exclamation of *"Jesus! Man down! Man down!"*

Cesar turned to the girl. "What are you doing here, Iris? Aren't you with mummy and Jack?"

"Someone take the kid inside while the zookeepers capture the caribou!" shouted Sam. "The wolf has been, er, neutralised and is no longer a threat."

The scenario completed without further compromise, although Sam wasn't sure how future drills might mitigate against an actor's child disturbing the proceedings. Delia came over to whisper in Sam's ear. "It seems as though Cat put that picture up on social media. The kid saw it and came to help her dad fight the good fight."

"I think the mum must be around here somewhere."

"She's just round the front," said Cesar.

"I'll take care of her," said DC Camara.

Sam nodded and added *Social media blackout* to her list.

POLLY WAS VERY MUCH ENJOYING BEING a magician's assistant. She had briefly wondered if it might give her an insight into how Marvin's tricks were carried out, but even up close, she couldn't tell how his 'circus card trick' or 'chink-a-chink' worked.

"Right, stand right here Polly, while I wave my wand over the bag of gold you're holding. Right close. Don't take your eye— Not *that* close. We don't want to make your boyfriend jealous."

The audience laughed, Strawb laughing the loudest.

"He's not really my boyfriend," Polly whispered to Marvin.

"Careful," Marvin told Strawb. "If you want to keep a hold on this one, you'd better put a ring on her."

Marvin gave a wand flick and turned the bag inside out. Gold glitter fell out.

"Where's it gone?" said Polly, automatically.

Marvin pointed at her hand. There was a thick gold band on her ring finger.

"How the...!"

Strawb chortled and literally slapped his knee. "Bladdy hell, mate. You've still got it!"

"Thank you, I believe I have," grinned Marvin who was either a supreme performer or having the time of his life.

"The problem with half the things I've got these days is I can't remember where I got it from or what it's for."

Strawb wagged a finger. "I saw this guy in summer season in Clacton."

"Did you? I think I shared the bill with Dennis Waterman that year," said Marvin. "Seventy ... nine? It was shortly after we all found out he could sing as well as act. 'Dennis!' I used to say, 'Dennis! You do all that running around on the television and then you come over here to Clacton and you sing as well. What's your secret? Do you eat a special diet?' Do you know what he said to me? The secret of his success? Avocados! Or it might have been bananas. I forget now. It was something mushy that I don't like all that much."

"You are a national treasure," guffawed Strawb.

"And speaking of treasure," said Marvin, "I'm going to have to alleviate your lady friend of this sparkly finger jewellery.

Polly twisted at the ring. "I think it's stuck."

Marvin produced a hacksaw and a chopping block. "Not to worry."

SAM HAD rounded everyone up for the final scenario of the day. All of the actors seemed to have relaxed into their roles after two 'escapes', and Sam found it challenging to be heard above their chatter.

"Can I have your attention please? We'll be getting underway with the final scenario in a moment. The bison and the sabre-toothed tiger. You've all done a great job so far, and I need you to keep to the rules as we do this last drill.

Now, we shouldn't have any more interruptions from outside. Are you all ready to go?"

There was a cheer from the actors. Sam hoped they weren't getting carried away.

She gave the signal to begin and watched carefully. The actors playing members of the public were on the lookout for the escapees, but that was fine. First into the public area was the sabre-toothed tiger, played by the young girl – Rhianna, was it? Sam watched as she sashayed down the path. She had clearly modelled her performance on an actual cat, as she displayed a distinctly feline arrogance. Sam hoped she wasn't going to indulge in a paw-washing display, or belt out *Memories*. She kept walking serenely until she came close to some members of the public, when she lashed out with a claw, tapping them both on the arm, even though they thought they were out of reach. They sat down, scowling, and the tiger moved on. The bison was out of its cage now. A large, lumbering presence, it clattered along paths, trying to give the tiger a wide berth. The tiger pretended not to notice at first, but the already grinning face became more animated as the bison took out some crowd members with its clumsy movements. The zookeepers were closing in now, able to move more swiftly this time because the public had been cleared (apart from the casualties who were still down). They had Nerf guns and some wire mesh panels to contain the animals. Sam observed a slight breakdown in teamwork. It looked as if the zookeepers were not clear which of them was tackling the tiger and which was taking care of the bison.

The tiger took advantage of everyone being distracted, creeping up behind the zookeepers and taking out nearly all of them with a neat series of swipes. The tiger grinned and turned its attention to the bison who looked around nervously. It was largely unprotected.

The bison saw a gap between two buildings and ran through, desperate to evade the tiger.

POLLY FOUND her face was starting to hurt from all the smiling, but she couldn't stop. She had enjoyed being Marvin's assistant more than she could have imagined. She'd thrown herself into the role after the interval, with exaggerated poses and wide hand gestures to accompany every trick and bad joke that Marvin made.

"Let me show you a trick I once performed for Mr Frank Sinatra at a Hollywood charity gala in seventy-four," said Marvin. "He was a fine gentleman and gave me a hundred dollar bill to use in the trick. Does anybody here have one of those?"

Marvin stopped. Polly followed his gaze. A beanpole of man was stood by the door, waving.

"Sorry to interrupt, folks," he said. "I'm DC Lucas Camara. Does anyone know who this little girl belongs to?"

"That's not the kind of bill I had in mind," said Marvin with a brief wave at the policemen.

Polly wanted to clap in admiration at his quick wit, but she was frozen in surprise, her mouth dry. "Iris?"

Her great-niece blinked.

"It's me. Great aunt Polly."

The girl mushed her teddy bear to her mouth and giggled. "You look funny."

Polly gave her a chorus girl wiggle. "Not used to seeing your aunty look like this, are you?"

"So she does belong to you?" said the policeman.

"Yes," said Polly, then felt a large stupid lump in her throat. "Oh, God, I'm going to cry."

Marvin clicked his fingers and a handkerchief appeared in his hands.

Polly ignored it and held out her arms. "Are you going to give your Aunt Polly a hug then?" she said.

SAM AND DELIA found themselves trying to explain to the tired and understandably angry woman, the doctor from her dad's medical, where the woman's daughter might now be.

"She was here, but then the policeman offered to take her to find her mum," said Delia "Well, you."

"What policeman?" Dr Hackett demanded between aggressive puffs on her e-cig. Her whole body shook in fury as she spoke. She was practically crushing the hand of the little boy beside her in her own. "Was he even a real policeman?"

"I'm fairly sure he was," said Sam.

"Fairly?!"

"He was. He is. He's probably gone into the care home."

"I was only parked round front, waiting for their daddy."

"I see. I think..." Sam scanned the animals still in play. "Is it your husband? Cesar? I think he's around here somewhere."

"He's a caribou," added Delia helpfully.

The woman's expression became one of profound

abhorrence. "I will not be speaking to that man while he's engaging in such shenanigans. What is that one even meant to be?"

Delia looked. "Sabre-toothed tiger. It's stalking the bison."

"But it's smiling! Why is it smiling?"

"It's happy to be here." Delia looked at the glum-faced boy who was barely visible beneath the vapour clouds the woman was producing. "Are you happy to be here?"

"He doesn't talk to strangers," snapped the doctor. "I don't approve of the activities I see you conducting here and I refuse to let either of the children get involved."

"What we are doing here is a piece of commissioned work," said Sam.

"Pornography for plushies, is it? I'm not stupid."

"It's part of a risk assessment and will help to inform best practice for my client's new venture."

"So, knowingly putting a child at risk, are we?" Dr Hackett said and dragged the boy away.

Sam was debating whether to follow when there was a sudden shout of *"Get down!"*

The bison, in a bid to escape the sabre-toothed tiger, had climbed up onto the low roof at the south end of the Otterside building. There was a step ladder which the bison had used to get up there, surely very un-bison-like behaviour.

"That's cheating!" shouted the tiger woman.

A pair of zookeepers took the opportunity to shoot the tiger with their Nerf gun tranquilisers. The tiger, incensed, was having none of it. She wrested a Nerf gun off one of the zookeepers and began firing up at the bison.

"Die, you cheat!"

"Come on," said a zookeeper. "It's just theatre."

Whether this comment was directed at the tiger or the bison, the tiger took exception to it and turned the gun on the zookeepers, shooting them one by one with tranquilisers. There were groans and tuts, then one of them, as the rules dictated, fell to the ground as though sedated. The others took this as their cue and tried to outdo one another in falling with an over-theatrical manner.

"Tigers can't shoot keepers!" Sam shouted.

The tiger wasn't done. She ran to the ladder. Further along the roof, the bison jigged among the aircon outlets and skylights, trying to make his escape.

MARVIN APPLEWHITE HAD of course invited Iris to join him and Polly in the stage area as their new assistant. An older audience liked little more than seeing a little girl doing something cute. They cooed and chuckled as she helped Mr Marvellous with his next trick. Iris had been equipped with a floppy hat and an over-sized wand, and was waving it over a decorator's table where her teddy had been placed beneath a velvet cloth.

"You're not going to chop it in half, are you?" Polly whispered aside to Marvin.

"Nothing so gruesome," Marvin grinned. "The lady has a tender heart, doesn't she? Now, to make sure I don't interfere with this trick, I will ask you to handcuff me securely to the table with these handcuffs."

"What is going on here?"

Erin stood in the doorway, Jack at her side, a furious look on her face.

"Gosh," said Marvin, almost hiding his own annoyance at yet another interruption. "It's like Piccadilly Circus in here, isn't it?"

Erin ignored him. Her attention and her anger were focussed entirely on Polly. At once Polly could see herself as Erin now clearly saw her: a foolish old woman wearing inappropriate clothing and showing off in front of a crowd.

Polly put a hand on Iris's shoulder. "We were just entertaining her while we waited."

The lanky police detective tried to speak to Erin. "I found your daughter round the back. Perhaps if we could have a word..."

"Iris. Come here."

"But we haven't finished the trick," said Iris.

"Dr Hackett. We'll just be a moment," said Marvin.

"Now," said Erin.

Marvin pulled a face for the audience. "She's a busy lady. Just moving house."

Polly had felt herself drowning, sinking in the hateful gaze of her niece but Marvin's words jolted her back to the room. Moving?

Iris dragged her heels as she walked over to her mum.

"Well, that's the end of that trick, then," said Marvin with just a hint of bitterness.

There was a thump and a crack from above. Suddenly, in

a shower of skylight safety glass, the teddy on the table was replaced by not one but two human-sized teddies. The table collapsed instantly under their weight. Handcuffs and wand flew aside. Polly hollered in shock. She was not the only one.

One of the figures, some sort of buffalo creature, groaned loudly as it rolled on the carpet. The big orange cat coughed and grunted. "Ow. That hurt."

"Magic!" yelled Iris in delight.

"Jesus facking hell!" exclaimed Strawb and started to clap. Half the stunned audience joined in.

48

L ater, in the front car park, Sam collected body cameras from actors and tried to comprehend and compartmentalise the day's events.

An ambulance had been called and the bison and tiger were being checked out by paramedics. A few of the retirement village residents had been alarmed by the sight of two squabbling Ice Age animals crashing through their ceiling but, by pure luck, no one had been hurt or suffered a heart attack.

Cesar and his foul-tempered wife had taken their children and were off before Sam could offer her sincerest 'Please don't sue us' apologies. She'd wait for any fallout that might strike DefCon4, but since she could barely get a word of communication out of her employers, Sam doubted Dr Hackett would have much luck making a complaint.

She made notes on the key takeaways from the day, adding three items to her list.

- *Somehow prevent competitive element between animals*
- *Clarify rules on climbing (even if realistic)*
- *Animals not allowed to use weapons*

"MARVELLOUS SHOW. MARVELLOUS SHOW," said Rich. Peninsula was by his side, empty picnic hamper on his arm.

"I think we might need to do another one," said Sam.

"Of course. Without a doubt." Rich picked at something stuck between his teeth. "I'd pay good money to see all that again."

"I'd rather we didn't have that again," said Camara, strolling over.

Rich frowned at the taller man.

"DC Camara," said the policeman. "You're Rich Raynor."

"One and only," said Rich proudly.

Camara turned to take in the scene of excitable residents, equally excitable actors, partially unclothed ice beasts and perplexed staff. "I'd struggle to explain what happened here," he said. "No one's reported a crime being committed, but I'm sure if I thought about it long enough I'll find one." He smiled brightly at Rich. "I'd probably start by querying whether you had permission to land your helicopter on the beach."

"I have nothing but the highest respect for the law," Rich assured him, drawing himself up to his full height, which was nowhere near enough to even approach Camara's.

"Glad to hear it. Now, I wonder if I can steal Ms Applewhite here..."

He gestured for Sam to come with him. She was perfectly happy to go. Anything that took her away from this car crash of an afternoon was preferable.

"I'm not in trouble, am I?" she asked Camara.

"No. I just wonder if now might be the time for you to point out the woman who was one of Greg's clients."

"No closer to working out who killed him?"

"The wheels of justice turn slowly..." he said.

"But they turn," said Sam and pointed. "There. Janine Slater. In the pink hoodie."

Janine was with some of the other residents, consoling the woman, Polly, who was quite overcome with emotion. Sam had no idea if those emotions had anything to do with the fact Polly was squeezed into one of Linda's old magician's assistant outfits.

"And you said you saw her sneaking out of the premises one night," said Camara thoughtfully.

"Not the night Greg died," said Sam, then corrected herself. "Not the day I last saw Greg. I was the last one to see him alive, wasn't I?"

"He paid a visit to a house he had recently finished working on, maybe an hour after he saw you. The gentlemen there did not have complimentary things to say about him."

"A hard man to like," she agreed.

"You have access to the CCTV here?" he said.

"Don't you?"

"I'd have to ask."

"But it would be easier to ask me." She gave him a shrewd look. "Suddenly, I don't think you came here to look at the Ice Age escape drill."

"I can multitask."

She led him inside. At the door they were confronted by a bespectacled woman. Camara stiffened, almost stumbled. The look the woman gave him was unreadable, but it was not a nice one.

"Mrs Duncliffe," he said, nodded, and slipped past.

"What was that about?" said Sam, intrigued.

Camara shook his head. "Dealt with an incident involving her family some time ago. Nasty business."

She gestured towards the manager's office and security cupboard next to it. Chesney, still in his blousy show gear, was haranguing a pair of cleaners. Something about dealing with the mess in the south lounge. Sam ignored him completely.

"Here." She dropped into the seat in front of the screen and brought up the video. "First, the night of Drumstick's murder."

"And Drumstick is a turkey, yes?"

"Yes."

A few minutes searching relocated the imagery of Janine creeping along the corridor in her burglar gear.

"She's watched too many cheesy crime dramas," said Camara.

"Right," nodded Sam. "Let's fast forward to the day Greg died. Maybe we'll see her again."

There was a practical choice to be made, whether to try

to locate Janine and follow her throughout the day, or focus on the CCTV near the exit and try to spot her amongst the flow of people going in and out. The latter was nearly impossible; these were not stay-at-home old people. They were out and about until the evening. Watching Janine's apartment door was easier.

She didn't emerge until mid-morning. Sam and Camara followed her to the swimming pool entrance, then back to her rooms. The door remained closed until mid-afternoon, when she went to the café. Half an hour later she returned to her rooms. Sam fast forwarded through the footage, but the door remained closed until long after midnight and into the next day.

"If he died that day, it wasn't by her hand," said Camara.

"Unlikely anyway, I suppose."

There was a presence at the doorway. The bloke in the black trilby, Strawb, popped his head round the doorframe.

"Are you Mr Marvellous's manager?" he asked.

"Roadie, agent, generally dogsbody and, oh, daughter," said Sam.

"Right," Strawb nodded. "He says he's packed up and ready to go home."

"Is he now?" said Sam and sighed.

Strawb glanced at the screen of CCTV cameras. "Big Brother spying on us, eh?"

"Just checking everything's in order, sir," said Camara, turning the screen off.

49

Without asking for permission, Polly pulled a narrow armchair over and sat at the north lounge table with Margaret, Strawb and Jacob. The south lounge was out of action while glaziers repaired the damaged skylight. She'd been to have a look.

"We were in the middle of a committee meeting," said Margaret, not unkindly.

Jacob pointed to his book of minutes as evidence of this.

"All hell will break loose if we can't discuss the Boxing Day sequence dancing evening in secret," said Strawb.

"Oh, I don't think it will be as bad as that," said Jacob, failing to note the sarcasm.

Polly ignored their words. She had come here to speak and had lined up what she wanted to say. "Let's say you're not joking. Let's say you really are asking me to kill that man. What do you want me to do?"

Margaret placed her hands on her lap. "Killing people is against the law." She paused as though Polly might need time to let that sink in.

"Yes...?" said Polly.

"If you were caught you would probably go to prison for the rest of your life. Naturally, we would claim to have no knowledge of what you were up to."

Polly thought about this a second. "Okay."

"This would be something you do alone. Without any practical assistance from us. There would be no physical evidence to implicate anyone but yourself."

"But I'd want to get away with it," said Polly.

"And, to that end, we can offer you advice," said Jacob.

"You have a lot of experience killing people?"

"I wouldn't say 'a lot'. What's 'a lot'? Personally, I've—"

Strawb squeezed Jacob's shoulder to stop him talking. "We know what works and what doesn't."

"We know why murders are sometimes unsuccessful," said Margaret. "Mostly it boils down to lacking the conviction to go through with it."

"Let's pretend – and we're still pretending, just for now – let's pretend I think he really deserves to die," said Polly.

"Squeamishness is your enemy," said Margaret. "Squeamishness and cowardice."

"And physical strength," added Strawb. "If that's going to be required."

"Any murder method requiring you to do something and keep on doing it until the person is dead – strangulation for example – has the drawback of you possibly losing your nerve partway through. Or think you've finished the job when you haven't."

"Short, sharp and irreversible is often the best way," nodded Strawb.

"So shooting him," said Polly.

"If you have a gun."

"Pushing him in front of a speeding train."

"If only Skegness wasn't the end of the line and the trains moved at anything other than a crawl."

"Off a tall building."

"If you can get off the roof before the police arrive," said Jacob.

"Or you can go subtle," said Strawb. "Poison."

"Like ricin."

"Or something that isn't impossible to source. Sleeping tablets will get you fifty percent of the way there."

"You can get cyanide from apple seeds or cassava," said Jacob.

"Assuming you can get someone to ingest facking huge quantities of crushed apple seeds."

"Carbon monoxide poisoning would be effective," said Polly. "And painless."

Margaret *hmphed* lightly. "You would need access to the home, or the car, and know what you were doing. And does the man deserve a painless death?"

"He deserves to drown," said Polly.

"And there's your problem with enough physical strength to hold someone under water," said Strawb.

"You could utilise the 'brides in the bath' technique," said

Jacob. "Grab the legs and lift sharply. The shock of water rushing in causes instant loss of consciousness."

"Which begs the question why Polly is in the man's bathroom while he's having a bath," said Margaret.

Jacob nodded. "You're right. Most people have showers these days."

"Not *quite* the point I was making." Margaret looked at Polly, and Polly realised she was being studied. Was Margaret looking for a reaction to this conversation? A flicker of fear, doubt or disgust?

"If you were to kill James Huntley," Margaret said with slow precision, "then you have the distinct advantage of there being no link between you. You have no personal motive. You are not an obvious suspect. But if your murder method requires you to get close to him personally – to slip him that poison, drown him in that bathtub—"

"Or shower," said Jacob.

"—then that advantage is lost. And if you kill him in public then, in this day and age, you have a strong chance of being caught on security cameras."

"So," said Polly, "I have to get to know him intimately but remain a stranger, be part of his life but keep my distance, kill him in private but not be part of his private life."

"It's quite a conundrum," Margaret agreed.

"Yeah, but the thing you've got to remember," said Strawb, "is that you're an older person now."

"No one suspects little old ladies?" said Polly.

"That as well. But what I meant is this is a chance to do something new, something unique, at a time of life when we don't get to do things for the first time." He smiled. "So, however you do it, you've got to remember to have a bit of fun. Do it the way you want to. Have no regrets."

"Murder can be fun?" she said.

"That's the spirit!"

50

The nights were drawing in fast. Midwinter was approaching. Dark a couple of hours before six, with wintry winds rattling the wooden window frames of *Duncastin'*. Friday night was clearly a night for snuggling down in front of a fire in the living room, with a cocktail and crappy television. Sam sat with her feet up on the sofa and two pairs of socks on for warmth.

"What do you call this one?" said Marvin.

"Gogglebox," said Sam.

"I meant the cocktail."

Sam tried to remember. She believed drunkenness should always be approached with a level of creativity. Only a few select favourites made repeat appearances. "An East India gimlet. Gin, lime, dill and celery bitters."

"We had celery bitters in?"

"I had to improvise. Blended celery and vodka sieved through a tea strainer."

Marvin sipped and coughed. "Smooth. Called a gimlet because it's like having holes gouged in your taste buds."

"If you don't want yours…"

Marvin cradled his glass protectively. He nodded at the television. "And just to be certain, this programme is us watching other people watching television programmes that we're currently not watching?"

"It's what passes for entertainment these days. The alcohol helps."

"We had proper telly in my day," he said.

"Oh, hazy reveries," said Sam. "Alcohol helps me deal with those, too."

"Hush, child," he said, smiling as he said it. "Friday night, we had *The Duchess of Duke Street, Dick Emery, The Rag Trade, Mr and Mrs, Starsky and Hutch.* Real programmes."

"*Mr and Mrs Starsky and Hutch*? That was a spin-off?"

He scowled at her. "You know. *Mr and Mrs.* Derek Batey asking couples what their favourite flower is, or where they're most ticklish, and seeing if they give the same answer. Lovely chap. An accomplished ventriloquist, you know. I did a few nights with him on Blackpool Central Pier."

"We'd be rubbish on *Mr and Mrs*," said Sam.

"Well, we're not married for one," said Marvin.

She reached across the sofa and tapped him with her foot. "I meant we don't have other halves."

"You had that Rich for a while," he said.

"A while was long enough."

"And I had, um, you know…"

"My mum?"

"That's the one!"

"Anyway, you and Linda would have been better on *Mr and Mrs* than you and mum."

Marvin looked scandalised. "I can assure you that nothing ever happened—"

"I *meant*," she cut in loudly before he could embarrass her with any protestations about whatever sexual or romantic antics did or did not go on between him and his former magician's assistant. "I *meant* you knew each other better than any other married couple."

He tilted his head and considered it. "You stuff a woman inside a box and chop her in half every Saturday night for fifteen years, you kind of get to know each other."

"Exactly. What was her favourite flower?"

"Self-raising."

Sam snorted. "Where was she most ticklish?"

Marvin paused in thought, then chuckled darkly but said nothing. Sam grunted and sipped her gimlet. The homemade celery bitters didn't taste half bad, although that possibly said more about her personal standards than her cocktail making skills.

"Speaking of partners, Delia tells me you ought to ask out that young detective. You know – the lanky one."

"Bloody hell. Are you guys in cahoots?"

"Seemed a nice lad."

"A full foot taller than me."

"If it starts raining, he'd know two minutes before anyone else. Handy."

"I don't need a boyfriend."

Marvin laughed. "You know, that night the feller from the bank came over, Tel—"

"Tez."

"—Tez, right. I swear you thought I was trying to set you up with him."

"No, I didn't," she said quickly, burying her face in her drink.

"Ah," said Marvin, expelling a heavy sigh. "We small families are fragile things. And I'm not going to be around forever."

"Heart and lungs of a young man, you said," she said.

"It'll be a quiet Christmas with just the two of us."

"A cheap Christmas," she corrected. "Could do to be a bit cheaper."

"I'm earning again," he pointed out.

"One afternoon with the oldiewonks is not going to settle all our debts."

"*My* debts."

She shook her head. The wind was picking up outside. "Christmas always costs. Even when you try to do nothing."

"We've already got a turkey."

"A murder victim."

"Buy some sprouts and a figgy pudding and we're sorted, surely."

"Oh, you wait," said Sam. "The costs will mount. They always do."

Marvin licked his lips and pulled a string of celery from the edge of the glass.

51

The Lucky Strike arcade on Skegness promenade was three floors of video games, coin cascades, pool tables, ball pools and ticket-spewing games machines. A hundred dinky game tunes competed with and nullified each other; a thousand lights merged into a background Christmas twinkle. Polly could understand how other people, particularly of her age, would find it an appalling sensory mess. But in truth, there was a distilled sense of child-like wonder to the place that touched her soul sufficiently to make it all bearable. Besides, the café-restaurant on the first floor had quite possibly the finest views in the town.

From the table she shared with Strawb and Jacob, the view encompassed the promenade, the compass rockery garden and, in the spaces visible between Carnage Hall and the seafront fairground, the beach and the sea. The few dog-walkers on the wintry beach were individual specks of colour. Beyond, the North Sea was nearly the same grey as the sky. The row of wind farm turbines out to sea were like a row of white stitches, holding the horizon together.

Jacob looked round to the window, and the Tower Esplanade which ran down to the sea between shuttered fish and chip shops and donut stands. "She should be here by now," he muttered.

'She' was Margaret who had gone to collect a vital component of Polly's plan.

"It's a fair walk to the boat yard," said Strawb, who had ordered and devoured most of a plate of scampi and chips during Margaret's absence.

"So it's her boat," said Polly.

"Her husband's," said Strawb. "Pat. But he's been dead ... ooh, years."

"Fifteen years," said Jacob. His eyes tick-tocked from side to side for a moment. "And eight months."

"So, I guess it's her boat now," said Strawb. "We've been out on it a few times, 'aven't we, Jakey?"

"It's an impressive cruiser," Jacob nodded. "Six berth. Could get you to Europe and back, easy."

Strawb pushed his plate a little closer to Polly. "Go on, have a chip."

"I'm watching my figure," she said, taking one anyway.

"You need facking feeding up, girl," said Strawb, and squeezed her knee under the table.

"I shall be performing soon," said Polly in a stiff, received pronunciation tone, like she was a ballet dancer preparing for her big debut. Butterflies fluttered in her stomach. She was feeling pre-show nerves, days before the planned event. "I must look my best for my performance."

"You'll be amazing," said Strawb.

Jacob opened his notebook. "We should check the details again."

"Put that bladdy thing away. She knows what she's doing."

"No," said Polly. "I'm happy to go over it. Helps with the nerves."

There had been days of planning and preparation. Polly had been past James Huntley's house half a dozen times in the past week alone. He lived alone in a two-bedroomed bungalow in Beckett Close. The house backed onto Beresford Field park and had an attached garage, a rarity in this day and age, rarer still that Huntley kept his car in it. It was a quiet close, mostly working families, and all but deserted for much of the day.

Jacob had magicked Huntley's work rota from somewhere. School Christmas holidays began on the twentieth of the month. There would be more people in the close from then on. There were three weekdays between now and then in which Huntley would not be at work during the day. Three windows of opportunity.

"I've got most of my equipment," said Polly. "Did I show you these?" She took a set of closed handcuffs from her handbag and placed them carefully on the table.

"You got a key?" said Strawb.

Polly shook her head, then pinched and twisted the lock. The cuff sprang open.

"Trick handcuffs. I think Mr Marvellous was in a hurry

to pack up after the hoo-hah. These were under the curtain by the window. I'm surprised they didn't find them while sweeping up the glass from the broken skylight. I've still got the costume as well. He didn't remember to ask for it back."

"You looked proper dazzling in that," said Strawb.

"I looked wonderfully preposterous," she said. "I wish I had one of those head dresses with the ostrich feather plumes. Oh, but I do have some fans." She produced two lacey Spanish fans from her handbag. She felt a bit like Mary Poppins and would have liked to whip out a standard lamp or a pot plant next.

"What are the fans for?" said Jacob.

"A bit of distraction," she said and snapped one open in front of her face.

Jacob consulted his notebook. "They are not on the list," he said sternly.

"Give her a chance to facking improvise," said Strawb.

Jacob's face twisted unhappily. "Improvisation is for people who do not plan adequately. The list is clear. Bicycle, yes. Handcuffs, yes. Costume, yes. Cake, Polly will buy from the supermarket. The kazoo we have. The bottles of alcohol will be acquired from a corner shop out of town. Duct tape. There is a list and we stick to it."

"Put fans on the bottom," said Strawb.

"Please," said Polly.

Jacob looked truly pained, but eventually relented and added 'fans (2)' to the bottom of the list in his notebook. "We have to consider all eventualities," he said, still smarting. "What if he puts up a fight?"

"Then he will have attacked a defenceless doddery old woman in his own home," said Polly. "He won't."

"What if the car won't start? What if it's out of petrol?"

"Who puts a car with no petrol in a garage?" said Strawb.

"I will take a small cannister of petrol with me and leave it with the bike in Beresford Field."

"Very well," said Jacob and made a further note.

"Oi oi," said Strawb softly, nodding to the café area entrance.

Margaret had entered, removing the scarf she had put on to protect her hair against the blustery winds outside. She stopped a serving girl.

"Tea," she said, then looked across at the table. "For four of us." The girl started to protest but Margaret was having none of it. "Quick as you can," she said before joining them. She passed Polly a carrier bag as she sat. "Took me an age to find. Will it suit?"

Polly looked inside at the snorkel and visor. It was large and chunky. The thick rubber strap looked reassuringly sturdy.

"Why my Pat thought anyone would want to go snorkelling in Skegness is quite beyond me," said Margaret.

"It's perfect," said Polly.

Margaret touched one of the folded fans on the table. "Fans?"

"A late addition to the plan," said Jacob testily.

"A bit of creative finessing is to be admired," said Margaret.

The weather worsened as they drank their tea and they agreed to the luxury of taking a taxi back to Otterside, even though it was scarcely a mile. At Polly's request, they made a detour inland to Wickenby Way and pulled up outside a three-bedroomed semi-detached. The estate agent's SOLD sign was still in the front garden.

"Are ya getting out?" asked the taxi driver.

Polly looked at the half drawn curtains. A figure passed by the window briefly, not full adult height. Jack or Iris, she couldn't tell. She imagined toys scattered across the Axminster carpet, a house full of life that she would have invited in if she'd been allowed.

"No," she said. "You can drive on."

52

Hilde stood next to Ragnar. He had summoned a meeting of the Odinsons.

"Seems like there's more mead than usual, farfar," she said casually, her voice lower than the drumming of the rain on the roof.

"Aye. It's a useful persuader," said Ragnar, looking out across the crowd. "We'll give 'em a few minutes to sup up. You drinking yourn?"

"Eventually," she said.

He eyed her suspiciously. "Wondered if taking a job with that Delia woman had turned you Saxon."

"Being a Saxon isn't an infectious disease."

"Don't believe a word of it."

The mead hall was more crowded than usual. It was called the mead hall because mead shed didn't have the same ring to it. The benches were crowded together in the centre, because planks of oak were stacked around the edges. Steam rose from those closest to the open fire at the centre of the hall. The hall stank of woodsmoke and the dense comforting fug that was the natural smell of the Odinson clan.

Dozens of Hilde's relatives jostled on the benches, exchanging gossip and passing bottles around. Hilde was proud to see everyone had brought their goblets. One of her earliest projects, after she had first built herself a lathe at the age of twelve, was to turn chunks of wood into goblets for everybody. Ragnar had now firmly embedded wooden goblets into the Odinson tradition, and insisted they were brought along for any mead-based gathering. He had the largest, most ornate goblet. He held it high and addressed the crowd.

"Has tha all got tha goblets charged? We drink to the beginnings of a new era for t' Odinsons." Everyone raised their goblets in a solemn toast. "When we tek to the seas, we'll go where we please, when we please. 'Tis the Viking way. None of this blether about Saxon licences and insurance, like with the blummin' cars."

Hilde was fairly certain there would be licences and insurance for boat-related activities, but she knew better than to interrupt her farfar.

"We can fish! We can travel abroad as we like, in the true Viking way. We'll do all of this in a craft built of Odin's sacred oak, with a fearsome dragon's head to strike fear and awe in the hearts of all as lay eyes on her." There was a cheer at this. The mead was working its magic. "But there's work to be done, to mek this a reality. Who's in?"

There was another cheer from the crowd. Hilde stepped forward.

Ragnar held up a hand. "In a moment, Hilde will explain how we will build this ship and what help we need. First though, I want to read out some of the suggestions you've all made for this project."

The suggestion box. This was a new thing. One of the Odinsons had been somewhere and seen the idea. Either prison or the council offices; Hilde couldn't remember. She was surprised that Ragnar had agreed so readily. He pulled a sheaf of papers from his pocket.

"So, none of these are signed. All anonymous like. This one says 'I've heard that boats can be built quickly and cheaply with fibre glass. Why don't we do that?'" Ragnar looked up from the paper. "Well, I'll address that one. I reckon I already mentioned Odin's sacred oak. We want some pride in this ship on ours, don't we? Now, I'm not an unreasonable man, and I think we can do a few modernisations, but oak is what it's going to be built from, and that's the end of it."

Ragnar looked fiercely round the room, daring anyone to speak up, but there was silence. He pulled out the next paper.

"Ah, interesting idea. This one says 'Why not put an outboard motor on each oar, so's the craft can go a bit faster?' Seems like a popular idea, that one." He looked across at Hilde.

Hilde leaned across to see the paper. As she expected, the careful writing was in the runic script that Ragnar favoured. He was fooling nobody. "We can look at some ideas for making it go faster," she said, "but this one is just not going to work. It will de-stabilise the boat, and don't get me started on how dangerous it could—"

"So, in summary, we'll think about it," said Ragnar. "Now we have one final idea. This one says 'Can we have a glass bottom in the ship so we can look at the fishes as we travel along?'." There was a series of appreciative 'Oohs' from the crowd.

"Now, I'm just going to repeat," shouted Ragnar above the excited chatter. "This will be made from the sacred wood of Odin, not the sacred glass of Odin. Do I mek meself clear?"

"As a functional improvement," said Hilde, thinking on her feet, "I think Odin would always approve of increased visibility."

Ragnar scowled at her. She could tell he was teetering on the brink of reprimanding her for suspected mockery of Odin's most famous injury.

"Now, tha knows Odin lost an eye to gain knowledge," he said. "But happen tha's right. We can have some portholes or summat." The crowd relaxed, pleased at this. "Now young Hilde's going to tell us all about the jobs as need doing. We'll all need to do our bit, so pay attention."

Hilde smiled around at the rows of faces. "We'll be building the ship with the clinker technique. It's what the Vikings used."

A hand went up, the trademark rollup between the knuckles.

"Yes, Yngve?"

"Why's it called clinker?"

Hilde knew the answer to this. "We're going to be hearing

a lot of clinking while we build this ship. Each nail we use to fasten t'boat together needs a hundred hammer bashes to fix it in place."

"Cool!" There were murmurs of delight from around the hall. All Odinsons loved the idea of hitting things with a hammer. Hilde could almost hear the cogs turning in her farfar's mind. He was sure to pick up on—

"Hammer work is a sacred honour!" bellowed Ragnar. "I throw down a challenge to the best of you. Go out into the world and come back with a hammer. When we start work, Hilde will show you where your efforts are needed and then you will each fulfil your personal quest. Select your tool with care, as there will be a reckoning at the end. We will bestow the blessing of mighty Thor upon the best hammer-wielding warrior amongst you."

Hilde was filled with admiration. She had lots more detail about construction techniques to share with the group, but it very much seemed as though they didn't care about that. They did care about hitting things with hammers and her clever farfar had just turned it into a competition. She would need to channel the enthusiasm, but she had all of the labour that she'd need to build the longship. She briefly wondered if the people of Skegness might notice the inevitable rash of hammer thefts that was about to hit them. Hopefully not, if everyone managed to keep their heads and be discreet.

53

On the morning of the planned murder, Polly bumped into Alison Duncliffe on the ground floor corridor. Polly must have walked past her several times on any given morning but today, as she prepared to avenge Rachel Duncliffe's death, it felt abruptly significant. Staged even.

"Alison," said Polly.

"Polly," said Alison.

Was that a sadness in Alison's eyes? A welling of emotion? Did Alison know what was about to happen? Had one of the social committee told her? Or was it just Polly's imagination?

They had been silently looking at each other for several seconds.

"Well, I'm off to yoga," said Alison and waved her resident's card. "Or you are," she added with a conspiratorial wink.

"Yes. Yes. Have a good…"

Alison moved on. It had been a fleeting moment, but it stayed with Polly far longer than it should.

She continued, thoughtfully, to the north lounge and, seeing Margaret sitting alone with a book, approached her.

"Good morning, Polly," said Margaret without looking up.

"Can I join you?"

"I would have thought it best to stick to our usual routines on a day such as this," said Margaret, only then lifting her gaze from the book. She closed it: *Principles of Criminology* by Edwin Sutherland.

Polly tittered.

"Second thoughts?" said Margaret, in a tone clearly disapproving of the possibility.

"No." said Polly. "I have questions. Only two questions."

"Glad to hear you've thought about it," said Margaret.

Polly sat in front of Margaret. "Why me?"

Margaret sat up. She had a long neck and sharp watchful eyes, like a heron in the shallows of a lake, waiting for a fish to swim by. "Why do you think we picked you?"

"Well, there's the flattering answer and the not-so flattering answer," said Polly, who had truly thought about it. "Maybe you think I'm resourceful and determined and clever, or maybe you think I'm a pliable fool who'll do anything to gain the approval of others."

"And which do you believe?"

Polly shook her head. "I suppose I'm more concerned as to why you think I would do this. Most people would say no, wouldn't they?"

"Not in my experience," said Margaret. "There is a general fallacy most people hold to be true: that murderers and criminals are different to the rest of us. Look at the newspaper headlines. Scumbags, monsters, devils. The media, and we too, wish to paint those who break society's rules as something *other*. It's one of the reasons we are generally fascinated with murder, serial killers especially. We want to point. Look at that, look at that. Isn't it horrible? Isn't it disgusting? Burn the witch." She put the book to one side and joined her hands in her lap. "No, murderers and criminals are people just like you and I. Give them the right incentive, a little push in the right direction, and everyday folk will commit all manner of atrocities." She looked at Polly. "No, you're not committing an atrocity, just a little light killing."

A little light killing. Margaret spoke of it with an ease that was chilling.

"Murder serves a valuable function in society, you know," she went on. "It's akin to... Back in the days before television and radio, our ancestors had to make their own entertainment, sitting around the fire and telling stories. Tales of dragons, of ogres. Little Red Riding Hood. Hansel and Gretel. They weren't just stories to entertain. They unified the little community sitting around that fire. They were a way of codifying behaviour. *This* is who you should hate. *This* is what constitutes anti-social behaviour. If you do X then Y will happen. Little girls who disobey grandma *will* get eaten. We tell stories so people can go on believing they are normal and that, out there, are the monsters."

"And I'm to be a monster?" said Polly, not sure she followed the analogy.

"No, Polly Gilpin. You're the storyteller. When James Huntley's body is found and reported in the press, it won't say specifically why he died, but people will know. They will read the unspoken clues and know this man deserved everything that happened to him. What's the other?"

"Pardon?"

"You said you had two questions."

"Oh. Yes. Why you?"

"Why am I encouraging you to do this? Why would I even suggest the idea in the first place? Don't you think James Huntley deserves to die?"

"That's not what I meant," said Polly, guessing Margaret already knew this.

Margaret nodded, an understanding between them. "There are no good people and there are no monsters. But there are people who have a net positive effect on the world. No, not me. I might flatter myself to imagine I'm in that group, but I'm probably not. Simply by living in a wealthy, wasteful country, I'm probably in the bad half. But there are people – kind people, clever people, industrious people – who by simply doing what they do, are making the world a marginally better place than it would be if they didn't exist. And I don't mean Mother Teresa-type idiots who slap a bandage on someone dying of a curable illness while perpetuating the old, bad ways. I mean truly good people."

"Okay," said Polly. "I suppose so…"

"And by the same logic, there are people who— Well, the world would simply be a better place if they didn't exist."

"Absolutely."

"If I could snap my fingers and those net detractors, ourselves included, could simply vanish from the world..." She clicked her fingers, and a visible shudder ran through her as if this was a genuine and fervent wish. "But I can't."

She smiled. Polly saw it was a tiny smile of embarrassment, because Polly had momentarily been allowed to see through to the real Margaret below the composed manner.

"I realised, as I reached retirement, that I had achieved nothing truly good in life. Donations to charity, kindness to neighbours – these were nothing against the waste and harm my sixty years of mere existence has caused. I decided to use whatever time I have left to make the world a better place, not by injecting good into it, but by deleting the bad."

"Murder."

"Murder."

"You've done this before."

"Eighteen times. This will be number nineteen." She tilted her head. "Some less significant than others."

Polly thought. "Strawb and Jacob..."

Margaret nodded. "None of us would ask anyone to do something we hadn't already done ourselves. That's one of our rules. No one person ends more than one life. I admit I had to break that recently when a man betrayed our trust. You now have his apartment, by the way."

Polly felt horrified disgust swelling within her. The need to know what Margaret had done with the man – Bob, wasn't it? – but the reaction was almost immediately replaced by the knowledge that Polly herself was about to carry out an act of murder.

"And that's it?" said Polly, not sure if she was surprised or not. "You chose to set up this ... this murder club because you decided the world would be a better place without certain people in it."

"And a turkey."

"What?"

Margaret frowned irritably, but it was irritation at herself – at the non-human blip in her grand plan. "There was much wheedling and whining, but one of ours members practically begged."

"Bernard."

"Yes. The blasted creature was apparently ruining his lie-ins with its warbling." Margaret saw the look in Polly's eye. "Not our proudest moment, I assure you. Although I'm convinced all sublime works have some note of the ridiculous in them. I hope so." She reached for her book. "Was that everything?"

"Yes, I think so," said Polly.

"Good. Then you perhaps need to be on your way."

54

When Rich arrived unannounced at the DefCon4 offices, Sam felt an irrational urge to tidy up, immediately feeling deeply angry with herself. The office was tidy. This was not some bedsit apartment which a prospective boyfriend had just entered. And he was definitely not her boyfriend. Her conscious mind had been quite clear on that point for many months; clear and without equivocation. Her subconscious mind seemed to have occasional lapses.

"Ah," said Rich, clapping his hands expressively as he strode about the office. "This is where the hi-tech hi-security magic happens, eh?"

Sam wasn't sure if there was anything notably hi-tech or hi-security about this place. There were four desks: hers, Doug Junior's, and two empty desks which she tried and failed to avoid using as dumping space for parcels and paperwork. There was a bank of filing cabinets and a kitchen area with a kettle and a cafetière with a knitted cosy. There were various posters and brochures, many of which were starting to look faded and dog-eared.

"Can I help you?" said Sam.

"Quick and to the point," said Rich. "Can't I just pop in and see how my newest ... er, not employee..."

"Contracted service provider."

"Indeed. Can't I see how my ... that thing you said, is getting on?"

"Not when I'm busy." She knew she was being quick with him, grumpy even. That was standard operating procedure with Rich, but on top of that, she was hungry. When she'd gone down to Cat's café that morning to pick up a sandwich, the smell of cooking sausages had instantly reminded her of the smell of Greg Mandyke simmering in his hot tub. The stink had filled her nostrils and her throat. She had to leave immediately or throw up.

"Got a lot of work today," she said.

"Do tell."

She groaned. He simply wasn't going to take a hint. "I've got fire extinguisher servicing to do at the public swimming pool..."

"Do they have many fires at the swimming pool?"

"I've got to give the fairground management company a quote for an improved security system. Because someone managed to hide a dead body in the ghost train for several days..."

"Ideal place."

"And I'm busy transferring data from your Ice Age park

drill." She pointed at one of the desks where a score of bodycams clustered around a work laptop.

The bodycam footage had been of a superb quality. This, however, made for large file sizes and slow transfer rates. Whether it was the cameras or (as she suspected) the DefCon4-tweaked operating system the laptop was using, it was taking nearly an hour for each camera to upload its data.

"Oh, superb," said Rich.

"It should be, when it's done," she said. "The software should sync the timestamps, which means we'll be able to get a sort of compound view of the various bits of video. A good few hours of it."

"We can watch it like a Christmas movie while we're recovering from Peninsula's superior Christmas pud."

"Pardon?"

"Oh." He grinned sheepishly and dipped into his designer jacket pocket to produce an envelope. "Merry Christmas!"

Sam looked at the envelope but did not touch it.

"It's two tickets for an all-expenses paid trip out to the Valhalla gas platform, soon to be the world's premier hotel slash casino slash resort experience."

"It's what?" She took the envelope cautiously.

"Helicopter transport. Christmas day, Boxing day. The finest cooking you'll find anywhere in the North Sea."

Sam opened the envelope. Inside were two tickets and a brochure. The brochure cover, showing a drilling platform above a moonlit sea, somehow made the place look moderately attractive. Yes, it did look a bit like Castle Dracula had gone through an industrial upgrade, but it did have an inviting air. The inside pictures showed an interior transformed – bedrooms and suites like luxury cruise cabins, a wide casino and club lounge in warm pinks and peaches where the glitterati played roulette and blackjack, a stunning restaurant with what looked like panoramic views of a mist-dusted sea at sunset.

"Looks impressive."

"When the first paying guests arrive, they will have their socks knocked off, I tell you," said Rich.

The two tickets were simply strips of plain paper on which someone had written 'Ticket for Christmas' in biro. The words were framed by amateurish drawings of a gas platform on one side and a picture of Father Christmas on the other. In the same biro, a loopy border had been drawn round it.

"You made these tickets?" said Sam.

"You don't actually need proper tickets to come visit my rig yet."

They looked like they had been drawn by a six-year-old. That was Rich; the soul of a six-year-old.

"Two tickets?" said Sam.

"You'll bring your dad, right?" he grinned. "No one's leaving Marvin alone at Christmas."

Sam sighed deeply. Richard bloody Raynor, as thoughtless as a toddler on a sugar high, yet still capable of huge touching gestures. She jiggled her head, which was halfway to a yes. She was sure she'd regret it when she finally agreed.

55

Polly cycled to Beresford Field and chained her bicycle to the fence near the cut-through to Beckett Close. The playing field was deserted. Her bag of props was tied to the pannier. She unstrapped the bungee around the supermarket bag-for-life, slipped off the thin full-length mac she'd worn to cycle over and, bag over arm, walked down the cut-through and to the front door of James Huntley's red brick bungalow.

"Surprise is on my side. Keep moving forward. Make it my own. Have fun."

She murmured her personal mantra as she knocked the door. She was out of breath. She didn't know if it was nerves or the exertion of the cycle ride. She wasn't as fit as her fake aqua-aerobics attendance suggested she ought to be.

She refused to reflect on the gravity of what she was about to do. She had already mentally squared that away and now it was showtime. She had a plan sketched out in her mind, but a key part of that plan was being able to react to James Huntley's own behaviour. It required some creative flair and quick thinking. She buzzed not only with nervousness but with excitement.

James Huntley came to the door wearing a polo shirt and crumpled trousers. She recognised him from the Candlebroke Hall trip all right and wondered if he might recognise her in return. His face registered confusion as he took in the sight before him. Polly was currently dressed in the magician's assistant outfit, complete with a feather headdress. She had added a pair of satin opera length gloves, which conveniently hid the latex gloves she wore underneath. She carried a cake in her hands, which she raised up to show James. It was a supermarket cake decorated with lavish amounts of icing, and dotted with Disney figures from Delia's shop. Polly smiled as brightly as she could. She'd applied cartoonish quantities of red lipstick and dramatic eye makeup, extending the Disney motif to her own face.

"Ta dah!" she said.

"Pardon?" he said.

"Ta dah! I bet you're surprised to see me, aren't you?" she trilled in the strident falsetto belonging to her new, invented persona. She wasn't expecting any neighbours to hear her, as the houses here were not close together. Families were out at work or school. "I'm here for the biiiig celebration!"

"I think you might have the wrong house," said James. There was a waver of uncertainty in his voice. That was good. She could work with that.

"Ooh, you're a cheeky one, aren't you?" said Polly,

dabbing a finger on the end of his nose. It made him take a step backwards, so Polly took a step forward.

"I don't know which house you want..." he began uncertainly.

"I'm bringing the cake and the party and the whole celebration, so let the festivities begin!" She balanced the cake and hooked a finger into her cleavage, bringing out a kazoo. She tooted a part improvised version of *Spanish Flea* and danced along with her shoulders and her feet, using the opportunity to expand the space she occupied, nudging slightly further over the threshold.

"Come on, join in!" she said around the kazoo.

"I do think you need to be somewhere else."

"Remember, life's what you make it, and today, we're making magical memories!" She did another round of tooting, this time making a big show of which shoulder wiggles she expected James to perform. Her routine, she realised, owed more than a little to the dance she and her sister used to perform to *Tiger Feet* by Mud.

"Come on. With me," she said.

"This is not the right house..."

"You can do it. Give a little shake..."

To her utter delight, he started to join in, simply caving to the pressure. She just needed to ramp it up a little, and she'd be in.

"Oh, good job! Great job!" she said. "Now we're cooking on gas! Come on, let's go and put this cake down shall we?" She thrust it forward, hoping he would either take it off her or step back and allow her to pass. He took the cake. This was good. He'd taken possession, which was a step closer, but was hesitating to let her inside.

She had her hands free now, so she gave a series of dainty claps. "What is better than cake? Can you tell me, James?" She used his name deliberately.

He frowned. James had no clue. The panic in his eyes said he was searching for an answer, and coming up empty. "Did someone put you up to this?"

"What's better than cake?" Polly said, smiling even more widely. "Anyone? It's easy: cake with friends in your own house! Can you believe that someone would be kind enough to do this for you?"

He looked around as though expecting to see a host of people behind him in the gloomy hallway.

"Cake and friends and celebration," said Polly. "I'm so excited for you! We're going to have such a fun time!"

A dawning of comprehension passed over James' face. "What friends?"

"And what friends they are! Now can you see how precious this is?" She put the kazoo back to her lips and started tooting again.

He stepped back quickly, indicating she should follow him inside. She had the distinct impression he wanted her to stop playing the kazoo, which was disappointing. She thought she held a pretty good tune with it.

"Um, right. I'm not sure anyone else is here yet," he said. "Who is it that sent you? Was it my brother? Evan?"

She made generic motions of agreeableness without confirming. She picked up the bag from the side of the door and followed him inside.

"Oh this is perfect, just perfect!" said Polly, doing a circuit of James' lounge. She fussed with some detail, moving a lamp away from the wall, angling it slightly. "Lighting is important for the show, very important. You don't mind me making some small adjustments, do you?"

"Er, what shall I do with this?" James asked, still holding the cake.

"Ah, well remembered. Let me take that. Where's the kitchen?"

He pointed through a door.

"Thank you, James." She popped the kazoo in her mouth and tooted out a tune as she went through to the kitchen. She put the cake down on a table and straightened, looking round. The kitchen was small and dilapidated, but it was fully-functioning. There was a tiny map of sauce and gravy stains on the counter by the microwave, and a tell-tale smattering of food crumbs in front of the grill oven. Microwave ready meals and oven tray food. Consistent cooking for one. Polly imagined he had one favourite mug and none of the others got any use.

"Are you sure this is for me?" he called from the lounge, voice tremoring. "I don't think it's the kind of thing my brother would— What are you doing in there?"

"I'm preparing things."

She opened a couple of cupboards, needing to know where she would find the key ingredients to make this mission successful. She spotted what she needed after a couple of tries. She carried on around the room, in case anything else looked useful. She had got halfway through the cupboards when he appeared in the doorway.

"But who *are* you?" His voice was rising, initial confusion being replaced by the certainty that this situation was profoundly wrong.

"I'm mother," she said.

"What?"

"I said, I'll be mother when we're ready for a slice of cake." She gave a loud whoop.

"Are you drunk?"

"I don't know about you, but I'm always ready for a slice of cake!"

"What are you doing?" he asked.

"Plates, James! Where do you keep your plates?"

He pointed wordlessly to a cupboard and Polly opened the door. "Perfect!" She clattered inside the cupboard and removed a small pile of plates. She wanted to keep alive the notion this was some sort of surprise arranged by a friend, although she suspected actual friends were thin on the ground. "I'm going to leave these here for a moment. Back into the lounge!"

She shooed him through as though he was a rabble of children rather than a tired, bewildered man. As she left the kitchen, she pulled a chair along with her. "Just borrowing this for a moment."

She put the kitchen chair down in the centre of his lounge. She stepped back a little way, stared at it thoughtfully, then adjusted its position. "I want to make sure you're sitting in the perfect spot for the entertainment.

"I normally just sit there," said James, pointing at the sofa. It had a greasy sheen on the velour seat cushions, clearly marking his favourite spot.

Polly put her hands on her hips. "It's a little bit like those old-fashioned shops that sell high-end stereo systems. They make you sit where the speakers sound best. I'm just doing the same thing here." She turned the chair slightly. "Nearly there."

He had a phone out. "I'm calling my brother. Was it Evan who booked you?"

"No, no, no," she said, not sure if she was channelling the spirit of a headmistress or a dominatrix. "Put that down at once."

"I don't think he knew what he was doing if..."

She steered him to the chair, gently but insistently pushing the phone and his hand to one side. "We don't want to spoil it for everyone," she said, almost simpering.

"I'm not spoiling anything," he said, neither angry nor apologetic. "It's not even my birthday."

Polly giggled. "Of course it's not. Just sit, give me a moment and all will become transparently clear."

James allowed himself to be sat down. Polly stepped back and eyed his position critically. She walked back and forth, using her hands to make a viewfinder.

"Do we need to do this?" he asked.

"Not bad." She walked around behind him and pulled the handcuffs from her bag. She bent behind, took hold of his left wrist.

"Are you a proper party entertainer?" he asked. She clicked the bracelet around his wrist, let the chain drop over the chair back strut, and grabbed his right hand. He resisted too late. She had him before he could pull away.

"What are you doing?" he said loudly, his voice strangled to a squeak.

"Oh silly," she said, stepping back. "You've heard of a captive audience, surely?"

He tried to stand and shake himself free, then sat down clumsily, twisting an arm. "Ah!"

"Be still, James. It's to help you focus."

His head whipped side to side to try to see her out of the corners of his eyes. "Is this – is this a kinky thing?"

She pulled a face, amused, saucy, and shocked. "Let's see. Now, you must concentrate please, and save any questions for the end."

"Who paid you to do this? You're not a children's entertainer at all."

"Oh, no. This is strictly a show for adults." She wondered where the words were coming from. She had slipped into a persona, a dark and mischievous persona, and she was loving it.

56

Hilde walked the length of the mead hall, making sure all was in order. The keel of the ship filled the entire building. Construction had been forced to move from her shed to the mead hall once it had become clear that her farfar would not budge on the monstrous dimensions.

The keel was crafted from enormous pieces of interlocking oak. She had cut those pieces herself, knowing how critical they were as they formed the backbone of the ship. The horizontal strakes were now in progress, and she had delegated work on those to various hammer-wielding Odinsons as there was a great deal to be done. As predicted, the noise of a dozen Odinsons hammering the iron nails was overwhelming. Hilde wore ear defenders, but she found it difficult to persuade her male relatives to consider their well-being above their self-image of manly swagger.

"Farfar," she called when Ragnar strolled in. "We need to persuade everyone to wear their PPE."

"PPE?" said Ragnar.

"Personal protective equipment," shouted Hilde. "They'll all be deaf by Yule if they don't protect their ears. They should wear glasses for hammering, as well."

"I'll sort it," said Ragnar. He walked across to Hilde's planning table, which was covered with diagrams and timetables. She had schedules for everything from the sawing of the wood (so that the build was kept supplied with planks as they were needed) to the procurement of specialist tools (where they would either need to engage with a hire firm, or discreetly borrow what they needed while the owner wasn't paying attention). There was also an overall project plan that carefully spliced in the building of the vessel with other activities that traditionally involved the mead hall. The biggest headache was the upcoming Yule celebrations. There would be feasting for the whole community, so Hilde had planned for the ship to have reached a point where it would contain benches, so that they could have their traditional celebrations inside the body of the ship. It was the only viable option as it would, by then, fill the entire hall.

As Hilde watched, Ragnar grabbed a sheet of blank paper and a felt tip pen. He inscribed a poster in bold runic script.

BY ORDER OF ODIN

FOR ALL WHO WANT TO BE BLIND AND/OR DEAF,

WE WILL PERFORM THE CEREMONY WITH THE SACRED SPEAR AS PART

OF THE YULE SACRIFICE.

TO BE CONSIDERED FOR THIS HONOUR, LEAVE OFF THE EQUIPMENT
HILDE RECOMMENDS FOR PROTECTION.

HILDE NODDED with approval as Ragnar pinned the sign where everyone would see it.

"What was that?" said Hilde, as she heard a different noise below the *tink tink tink* of hammers.

"Dint hear owt," said Ragnar.

Hilde eyed him. The air of studied innocence was a dead giveaway. "It were a pneumatic tool," she said. The tell-tale hiss-thump formed a bass note which shuddered through her feet as it sounded again. She walked off to see where it was coming from. As she suspected, she found Yngve with a pneumatic nail gun. He was firing them into the strakes.

"What are you doing?" she shouted.

"Ragnar said we should do what we can to speed things up," said Yngve, more than a little defensively.

"I did that," said Ragnar, coming up behind them. "Lad's been and got this. Ingenious, no?"

Hilde sighed. "It'll be great for benches and internal fitments and such like, but we need the strakes to be riveted, with the nails going into them roves behind. The entire hull will flex when it's at sea. We can't afford to have weak joints."

Yngve looked to Ragnar. "But it's a top machine, this is. Quality!"

"Do as Hilde says," said Ragnar. "It's a fine machine, no doubt, but we'll use it another time. Back to hammering."

Yngve lugged the nail gun away, crestfallen.

"Tha'd best come and see this other machine," said Ragnar, clapping a hand on Hilde's shoulder.

Hilde feared the worst. Ragnar led her out of the mead hall and into one of the smaller buildings nearby. Gunnolf was inside, poring over a workbench. He looked up as they entered.

"I reckon I've got the hang of this thing now."

"Oh, a router," said Hilde. She had one in her own workshop, but she didn't mention that, as Gunnolf had obviously sourced his own.

"Gunnolf's practising carving the sacred runes, so's he can do them on the ship when it's time," said Ragnar.

"Good idea," said Hilde. It made a lot of sense. The runes would have been chiselled by the Vikings, and a router was a modern, electric chisel of sorts. It would speed up one small part of the job. "What are you carving?"

"Well," said Ragnar, his chest swelling with pride. "Don't want to waste wood, so Gunnolf's creating a saga that'll go round the wall of t' mead hall." He drew a hand across the wall at shoulder height to illustrate his vision.

"A saga?" Hilde asked. "Of Vikings of old?"

"Well, yes and no," said Ragnar. "It'll not be long. Just a short saga. It'll detail the exploits of us Odinsons on us ship."

"But ... but how can we have exploits when we haven't built it yet?" Hilde was confused.

"Ach, we can do most of it wi' a little bit of poetic licence," said Ragnar. "Tek a look."

Hilde saw there were already three planks stacked to one side, carved with writing. She inclined her head to read what they said. The execution of the lettering visibly improved along the length of the first plank.

GULLS AND SEALS SCREECHED A WARNING AS THE FEARSOME DRAGEN WAS SEEN THROUGH THE WAVES.

"YOU'VE SPELLED DRAGON WRONG," she said.

"That'll be the Viking spelling," said Ragnar automatically. "None of tha Saxon spellings here."

Hilde just about stopped herself from rolling her eyes. "And do seals screech? I'm not sure—"

"—You do the building, we'll tek care o' the writing, lass," said Ragnar firmly. "Now, Gunnolf lad, mebbe you should write t' saga out on paper before doing the routing, eh?"

Hilde returned to her planning table, as she had a few wrinkles to sort out in the overall project plan. An unexpected figure was waiting there.

"Hey, Farmor."

Astrid Odinson – Hilde's grandma and Ragnar's wife – was like no other Odinson. Hilde had once come across the word 'sanguine' in a book and, after looking it up in a dictionary, concluded it was a word that entirely described her farmor. Whereas every other Odinson tended to a greasy and emaciated look, like they had been raised on a diet of gruel and engine oil, Astrid was round and rosy-cheeked. She was filled with colour and hope and life itself. She loved the Viking lifestyle, but loved it a little *differently* to everyone else. There were those who loved quaffing and feasting, and then there was Farmor Astrid who brewed the finest quaffing mead and the lightest feasting bread. Every one of her grandchildren would receive a decidedly Viking soft toy, stitched by farmor's hands – cloth doll warrior men and warrior women, cuddly goats and sea serpents. In her hammock (hidden between two pillows), Hilde still had her plump eight-legged horse, Sleipnir. Old Slippy was made from neatly stitched denim, with red button eyes.

Astrid was as Viking as the rest of them, but Viking like none of them.

Hilde bent to give her a kiss. "What brings you into this noisy place?"

If there was one thing Hilde associated her grandmother with, it was peace and quiet. She was the calm anchor to Ragnar's crazy ambitions.

"I heard that the build is getting along nicely, so I thought I'd come and see for myself. It's starting to look like a boat."

"It is," said Hilde. "A ship."

"Yes, said her grandmother peering across at the structure. "So where will the benches go?"

"Across the width of it," said Hilde, pointing. "Why do you ask?"

"I thought I'd make a start on some cushions," said Astrid.

"Cushions?" Hilde was stunned, then realised this was her farmor, and of course there would be cushions. Possibly embroidered with hearts and flowers (along with the expected dragons and lightning and such). "I see. Everyone will be so pleased if you do, although maybe there's something you could do that might be of more practical value—?"

Astrid gave her a look.

"—Or cushions. Yes of course."

57

J ames Huntley looked up at Polly. His sweaty face reflected anguish, confusion and fear. He was little more than half her age, but time had not been kind to that face. A pitiful, ravaged, lonely man. A guilty and cowardly man.

Polly took measured steps across the room, like a gymnast about to perform a floor routine. "And now! The fans!" she shouted. She held a fold-out fan in each hand and flicked them out to display them fully. She held them aloft and stalked across the room. She was certain her moves were more attention-seeking than erotic, but James had widened his eyes, assuming perhaps that she was about to perform some sort of strip tease. She continued, striking lots of different poses to keep his attention. She added a song to the mix, turning to *These Boots are Made for Walking* as it struck the right tone. She didn't think it mattered that she wearing a pair of comfortable ladies Skechers shoes rather than actual boots. Once she'd started thinking about Nancy Sinatra, it seemed natural to turn to Frank. She segued into *New York, New York*, and added plenty of kicks. They were not quite as high as she would have liked, but she didn't want to get carried away and injure herself by having too much fun.

"How are we liking the show?" she called at James. "Any requests?" She peered at him over the top of her fan, fluttering it lightly.

He muttered faintly.

"Sorry James, speak up! What was that?"

"*Ferry Cross the Mersey*," he said. "I always liked that one."

"Of course!" Polly pulled a feather boa from the bag and held it aloft, channelling a hybrid of burlesque performer and football hooligan. It took her a few moments to remember how the song started, but as soon as her mind had plucked the opening line from her memory, she crooned her way through the entire song. She added in vocal flourishes, based on every terrible pub singer she'd ever heard, building to an impassioned climax.

"So, now I will astound you with some close up magic. I will need your car keys. Where will I find those, James?"

James started to move his arms, grunting with frustration when he remembered he was tied to the chair. "You going to steal it?" he said.

"An old Vauxhall? Hardly worth stealing, wouldn't you say?"

He frowned.

"Ah," she said. "Probably wondering how I knew what car you had, eh?"

"The keys are—"

"Yes!" she said, grabbing them from the table nearby. She repositioned the table in front of him with the keys at their centre.

"I will now cover these up with a cloth," she said. "I want you to watch them very, very closely, otherwise you'll miss the good part. Are you watching?"

He grunted, a possible affirmative. Polly reached down into her bag, removed the snorkel mask and popped it over his head. He gave a small shriek of shock.

"What the— *Mmmph!*"

She wiggled the mouthpiece between his lips. "Do not spit it out, or I shall be very angry," she said.

There was another brief *mmph* from James, but he complied.

"Doing the magic now, keep your eyes on the cloth."

She found her roll of duct tape, located the end and pulled it free of the roll. The sound made James turn his head slightly, but before he could react, the duct tape was around his head, securing the snorkel in place. Round she went, two, three times. She made sure she kept his nostrils free, so that he could breathe, but there were no gaps around his mouth.

"Isn't this fun?" she said, giving his cheek a little waggle.

"*Mmph!*" he honked down the snorkel tube.

She fanned herself. "Time for some refreshments, I say."

James tried to speak and shout through the snorkel, but all that came out was a drowning tuba sound. "*Mwamph! Mwamph! Mwamph!*"

She slipped into the kitchen, returning with the small bottle of cheap vodka she'd spotted in there earlier, and a tumbler. She poured a very generous measure and held it out to him. "A drink, James?"

Through the glass visor, he gave her a perplexed and hateful look. She took hold of his snorkel and tipped the shot down. He coughed a second, then swallowed hard.

"Gosh, you were a thirsty boy, weren't you? Another?"

She held the vodka bottle up to pour more. He was ready this time and lashed out with his feet. The edge of his heel clipped her ankle painfully. She stepped away round his side, out of reach. He screamed – "*Mwaph-a! Mwamph! Mmmf!*" – and tried to tear his head away. Polly poured another generous measure of vodka into the snorkel.

James tried to tilt his head so that it would pour out. Gravity was against him, and Polly was able to keep the tube upright with no trouble. He started coughing and retching. Vodka sputtered and sprayed from the pipe, but it mostly went down.

When the coughing and panting had ended, Polly stepped back to give him a break.

"Now, you need to take better care than that. We don't want you choking, do we?"

His eyes watered. A trickle of vodka ran from his nose, but he had his breath back.

"Best to just drink it straight down, wouldn't you say?" Polly asked.

There was a panic in his eyes now, but she ignored it. She poured straight from the bottle this time, bracing the snorkel firmly in the crook of her other arm. It was an oddly intimate moment as she clutched his head to her bosom. She saw his Adam's apple working as he drank it down, keen to avoid choking. She gave him a small break before tipping the bottle again. She stopped when it was empty.

She stepped away. James was keening in distress.

"Just breathe, James."

"Mwamph! Mwaph!"

She went to the kitchen, found a towel and came back to wipe the trickles of vodka that had poured down his face.

"Just settle down," she said. "Do not throw up because I don't know how you'd breathe with a snorkel full of sick."

Whether he saw the wisdom in that or simply had no choice, he sat still and watched her.

She sat on the arm of the sofa, realising she also needed to get her breath back. This whole charade was turning out to be thoroughly exhausting. "Round two in a minute," she said.

James tried to twist in his chair to better see her. Polly dipped into her bag and withdrew full sized bottles of vodka and whisky.

"Vodka man, right?" she said.

James hollered and protested, but there was no making sense of any of it.

She put the whisky back in the bag, unscrewed the vodka and gave him a third of the bottle, straight down the pipe. Polly had never heard someone simultaneously drinking hard while sobbing into a snorkel pipe. It was a horrible sound, but rather than be disgusted, she found herself thrilling in it.

"Running out of air there?" she said, patting him on the shoulder.

"*Mmph,*" he panted, miserably. The inside of his goggles were splashed with tears.

"Drinking. Drowning." She looked at the bottle. "Two more should do it."

He shook his head groggily and wheezed down his snorkel.

"Two more," she said and gave him half of what was left.

As he desperately swallowed, she crouched before him, safely out of kicking range and watched. "Shall I tell you why I'm doing this?" she asked.

"*Mmph?*"

"I could. I could tell you, but you wouldn't like it. Or we could just pretend this is a weird little party with vodka and cake." She twitched her lips. "I thought it would be important that you know why I'm doing this, but I'm not so sure anymore." She stood and fed him the last of the bottle. "What does it matter what you know or think, James?"

She mopped his face with the towel again, tenderly, like he was child. Like she was a nurse or nanny. "You've got to promise to not throw up, and then I'll take it off in a bit."

"*Mwaph-a mmf?*"

"In a bit."

She needed to go and check out the next part of the plan. She picked up his car keys and went through into the kitchen. There was a door off to the side that could only lead into the garage. She found the key for it on the same ring as the car keys, opened the door, and turned on the light.

The garage was the usual size for a British suburban home, which meant you could either fill it with a modestly sized car, or you could use it for storage. James Huntley had opted to house his old Vauxhall in there. Only by sliding carefully sideways could an adult human get in between the car and the walls. In fact, the gap at the rear of the car was barely any wider. James had implemented the time-honoured system of hanging a tennis ball from the ceiling, so that when he reversed into the garage he knew to stop when it appeared at the top of his windscreen.

Polly opened the car door, slipped in and let the handbrake off. It rolled forward until it nudged the garage door. She went round to the boot, opened it and looked inside. There was nothing in there except for some shopping bags and a small tool box. It would do. She went back into the house.

James sat where she'd left him, naturally, but he sagged in the chair. Behind the mask, his eyes were unfocused, and there was a sheen of sweat on his face. She shook his shoulder.

"Smmph mmph?"

He was, of course, incomprehensible, but she suspected after all that vodka he would be without the snorkel.

"I'm going to help you feel a bit better," she said. "If we go for a little walk, then you'll soon be right as rain, yes?"

He nodded. She undid the handcuffs, put them aside and brought his hands together. She held them in hers and clapped them gently to get his circulation going.

"Up you get. Come on," she said.

He staggered to his feet, but he was very unsteady. Clumsily, he felt for the tape around his face.

"Leave that for now."

"Mwaph fuff-a mmph."

"No, leave it," she said. "Movement will help, come on." She took his arm across her shoulder. He wasn't a heavy man, but he was heavy enough to make her grunt as they moved. "There, that's better already, isn't it?"

She walked him out to the kitchen and then through the door to the garage.

"Mmmf fa wah?" he slurred.

"I'll take you to a doctor, shall I?"

"Ma!" he said which meant nothing.

"A nice drive, eh?"

He wasn't fighting her. He could barely stand. He couldn't stand at all. He slumped against the car and began to sink to his knees.

"No, not yet," she said, getting down to prop him up. "Let's take you round to the passenger side. I'll need to drive."

She manhandled him round to the back of the car.

Munph pff!" he noted.

"So it is," said Polly. "You wait here, and I'll be back in a jiffy."

She draped him over the edge of the boot. He slumped back like it was a bed. Polly went round to the driver's door. The keys were in the ignition. She started the engine. The petrol gauge showed three quarters full. She reversed slowly until a muffled scream of pain told her she had reached the back wall. She didn't need a dangling tennis ball to help her.

She left the engine running and got out. James was rolling and moaning. His lower legs were pinned between the boot lip and the wall. He was upright now, thrown vertical by pain or alarm or the crushing of his leg tendons.

He was moaning at high pitch through the snorkel, the tuba become a bugle.

"Okay," said Polly. "Let's actually get this off."

She reached for the tape around his face and he feebly swatted at her. She pushed back. She wasn't hideously drunk and was currently stronger.

"Here." She found an edge and pulled hard. He gasped as the snorkel came away with a stream of vodka-infused spit.

"N'legs," he mumbled.

"Yes," she agreed and ripped the mask and remaining tape from his head. His skin was flushed and mottled pink – tape abrasion, tears and nausea.

He tried to say something more but he couldn't control his mouth. Polly surveyed her handiwork, making sure there was no more evidence of her on him. He attempted to move but he was fixed, tight. He'd be pinned in place as the exhaust fumes poisoned him.

"You left Rachel Duncliffe to drown in the dark," she said to him, even though she doubted he could understand anymore. "There has to be justice, you see."

She turned off the light as she went back into the kitchen and shut the door behind her.

She collected the party cake (too incongruous to be left in the house) and the bag with the whisky inside it. She collected her fans and her feather boa. She took out her long coat and wrapped it over her costume. Everything else went in the bag.

A little peek out of the front door and she was out, down the cut-through and back to the bike she'd left in Beresford Field.

58

The Friday before Christmas seemed to be the day when most of those leaving Otterside for the festive season left. It wasn't a huge exodus, but a noticeable number of residents had departed, to visit family or fly to warmer climes. Nearly midwinter, the sun didn't rise until gone eight and was set again at four, the day in between generally sunless and grey. The remaining residents tended to venture out only when they needed to, bracing walks and rounds of golf were reserved for incurable fanatics. The season of quiet crafts, card games and endless daytime television was upon them.

"Look what I found," said Jacob, approaching the table where Strawb and Margaret sat. He held out a jigsaw corner piece.

"What's that then?" said Strawb with polite interest.

Jacob brought it close to his eye. "I think it's *World*

Landmarks, a thousand piece Ravensburger. And I found it outside Chesney's office."

"And why would it be there?" said Strawb.

For a man with such a relaxed manner and easy wit he was a shocking liar, Margaret thought. And yet Jacob, a man with a literalist's brain and such an eye for details that he frequently failed to see a larger picture, did not notice.

"I have several theories," said Jacob. "None confirmed."

Tired of Strawb's silly tricks, Margaret took the newspaper from the chair arm pocket next to her and placed it on the table. "Strawb and I were just discussing the news regarding Mr Huntley."

Jacob pulled back. "You started the meeting without me?" He checked the time. "It's not time for the meeting to start yet."

"We happened to be here," she said. "This is just a pre-meeting chat."

Jacob was not mollified. "But I'm always here for the pre-meeting meeting."

"Ah, but this is a pre-pre-meeting meeting," said Strawb. "We've not even started the pre-meeting yet."

Jacob sat down with a measured formality that made it clear he was not best pleased.

"The news," said Margaret, opening the paper so Jacob could see the story on page six.

LOCAL MAN FOUND DEAD IN HIS OWN GARAGE, read the headline.

"Three days after he died," said Strawb. "Found by his brother."

Jacob read then re-read, placing his finger on key words. "Doesn't say if the police are treating it as suspicious."

"They never do," said Margaret. "We know this. There will be a coroner's inquest. The police will not show any interest unless there is some anomaly."

"I say our girl, Polly, has done a bladdy good job," said Strawb.

Margaret offered a small nod of agreement. The others knew this was as good as a rapturous round of applause from her. "And so I've decided to put our next project into action," she said.

"So soon?" said Jacob.

"Bernard owes the collective, and I was disturbed by his somewhat blasé attitude to the seriousness of our endeavours."

"She's still smarting over the fact he asked us to kill a turkey," Strawb translated. "Let's not forget that as an ex-military man, he's been very helpful to us. Weapons, electronics, et cetera."

"We have a target: Dr Erin Hackett. Bernard is already planning how to do it."

"Her crimes?" said Jacob.

"Elder abuse," said Margaret. "Emotional, psychological, financial. We have checked. When Polly was 'strongly encouraged' to sell her house, it was bought up through a series of transactions that ultimately put it in the hands of Polly's niece. And the sale price..."

"Sixty percent of the facking market value," said Strawb. The man's hands twitched restlessly with emotion. Margaret considered he was, perhaps, genuinely smitten with Polly Gilpin.

"Theft then," said Jacob.

"Ah, but it gets worse," said Margaret. "Erin Hackett has been showing a surprising level of interest in Polly's health."

"Doesn't want her knocking back the gins," said Strawb.

"Yes?" said Jacob. "Does this fit into the fraudulent sale?"

"I have a theory," said Margaret.

"And it's a facking bastard," said Strawb hotly.

Jacob pulled his chair nearer to the table, intrigued.

59

Sam was modelling outfits in her bedroom while Delia lent moral support, which she claimed was fuelled most effectively with cocktails. Sam had whipped up a batch of Christmassy cranberry and cherry liqueur based drinks which she christened Jingle Juice.

"What about this?" Sam twirled in a long burgundy dress.

"It's a good colour for Christmas," said Delia. "Very festive."

"It needs high heels though, and I'm going to be on an oil rig."

Delia rolled her eyes. "It's not as if you're going to be swimming to the place, is it? You said he's got a casino out there. People turn up to a casino in high heels, don't they?"

"Yes, that's true," said Sam. "What dress code do you have in a casino? I feel as if this isn't glitzy enough."

"I've got time to sew you some sequins on," said Delia.

"No, wait, what am I saying? There must be loads of sequinned things in this house from your dad's stage act."

"I have a love/hate relationship with sequins," said Sam. "They can be very scratchy. I think this dress is a definite maybe. I wonder how warm it's going to be in the middle of the North Sea, though?"

"Again," said Delia, "I'm going to mention the casino. You don't expect to take a cardigan when you're playing high-stakes roulette or whatever, do you?"

"You're right," said Sam. "I'm going to squeeze in a jumper, if it'll fit. Rich said Dad and I should each plan to take one smallish bag."

"Has he come over all Ryanair for a reason?" asked Delia. "That seems a bit harsh."

"We have to get there by helicopter. I guess there isn't that much room."

"Don't you need to do one of those ditch-in-the-water safety drills if you're going to be flying to the rigs?"

"We're not oil rig workers," said Sam and sipped her cocktail. It might have been festive, but the sharp flavours were going straight to her stomach. "Now, what else do I need to take?"

Delia looked to the ceiling as she counted off on her fingers. "If all the practical things are going to be taken care of out there, then you're looking at clothes, toiletries, jewellery. What else? Lingerie, obviously."

"Stop it."

"A book to read, or a game to play? Anything like that?"

Sam thought for a moment. "It would be a bit rude for me to sit and read when I'm spending Christmas with Rich and my dad. I'll pop a deck of cards in there, just in case anyone wants to play."

"Cards? Don't you think they'll have those in the casino?"

"I guess so. Although, if you were running a casino, would you let a magician borrow your cards for a quick game of patience?"

"Fair point," said Delia. "Card games always end in arguments in our house."

"And what will Christmas Day be like in your house?" asked Sam, wondering how she should inflect such a question in the light of the super posh Christmas she was about to enjoy.

"Being woken at five a.m. by screaming children," said Delia. "Ripping off wrapping paper. Laughter. Tears. My parents and some singular aunts and uncles coming over for Christmas dinner."

"Ah. Christmas dinner? Twizzler is....?"

"Off the menu," said Delia firmly. "We've gone meat free this year."

"Oh." Sam tried not to sound like a judgemental carnivore.

"It's just a case of starting Veganuary a month early," said Delia. "We will have a delicious beetroot and lentil bake with sweet potato parcels on Christmas Day."

"Does sound rather lovely," said Sam. "And the kids will like that?"

"I bought in some pigs in blankets, in case they go into meat-withdrawal. Cheap sausages, mind. Hardly any meat in those. And then its Secret Santa for the adults. Done that for years. Five pound limit, everyone gets a surprise gift. Are you taking presents with you to the gas platform?"

"Well, I do have a small gift for Rich, and one for my dad, but the food and drink should all be taken care of. He's got this super-efficient butler called Peninsula, who makes Jeeves look like a slacker."

"Never mind the butler, tell me about the gifts! What did you get for Rich?"

Sam sighed. "It's always tricky buying something for a multi-millionaire. I like to get something that will surprise him."

"Oh yes?" Delia waggled her eyebrows in the most lascivious way she could.

"Not that kind of surprise. A funny surprise."

"I could have totally found you something in the shop," scolded Delia. "He would not have expected a banana stand, would he?"

"You still not sold that?" Sam asked.

"Stop changing the subject. Come, on, tell me. What did you get him?"

"A shirt that's printed all over with Nicholas Cage's face," said Sam.

Delia looked at her. "What? That actually exists in the world? Were you drunk shopping on the internet or something?"

Sam wasn't sure how to respond to that. She had bought it off the internet, it was true. "How are we defining 'drunk'? I was relaxing while I was shopping, that's all."

"You were drunk shopping!" crowed Delia. "God, I wish I

could get a few customers to buy my stuff when they were doing that."

"You haven't got a website," Sam pointed out. She pulled a top out of her wardrobe. "What about this?"

"Oh, that's nice," said Delia. "With wispy things like that you can have a few changes of outfit and still get everything into your Ryanair baggage allowance."

"Yeah, that's what I was thinking," said Sam. "There's nothing worse than feeling uncomfortable at a swanky event."

"Ah, so when you spill gravy down yourself you can whip out a spare," said Delia. "It beats wearing a bib."

"Not quite what I meant," said Sam with a sideways glance.

60

When there was a knock at the front door of *Duncastin'* that evening, Sam looked to her dad. "Carol singers?"

"Dah, you beat me to it," he said.

She pushed herself out of the living room armchair. "I don't know if I should feel proud or horrified. You've turned me into a mini-you."

"You should be so lucky," he grunted.

"Oh, well, this reminds me of the time I shared a wimpy burger with Larry Grayson in nineteen seventy-three..." she warbled in a silly voice as she walked to the door.

It wasn't carol singers.

"Detective Camara," said Sam. "What a nice surprise."

He shrugged, which was quite an expressive gesture with those angular shoulders and long arms.

"Not nice?" she said.

"Couldn't say. May I...?"

She stepped back to let him in. He involuntarily stooped to get through the front door.

"Get them to sing Good King Wenceslas!" Marvin called from the lounge.

"I can't. It's DC Camara," she called back.

"Right," said Marvin. "Doesn't he know the words?"

"We're in a festive mood, by which I mean silly, and we haven't even started drinking yet. You like one?"

"Ah, no," he said, hand raised. "I'm still on duty."

"This is a formal call?"

There was a deep, pensive air about him. "I need to talk to you about a body we've found."

"Greg?"

"James Huntley."

The name meant nothing to her.

"Actually, I'll take a tea if you're offering one," he said.

"Sure."

He waited until she'd filled the kettle and put it on. "A local man. Very local to you. Just off Beresford Avenue. He was found in his garage, killed by carbon monoxide fumes from his car."

"A suicide?"

"Accident, probably. The car had rolled back, pinning his legs. There was an astonishing amount of alcohol in his system."

"Christ."

"Yeah. I knew of him. Had met him. There was a drink driving incident up towards Ingoldmells a few years back. The car rolled into a dyke. A passenger drowned. Alison Duncliffe up at Otterside was the dead girl's mum."

Sam put tea bags in the pot for the three of them. "The Otterside connection," she mused.

Camara shook his head. "In a town like Skeg, and a retirement place like Otterside with a hundred residents, you're going to find a link between the residents and any person you'd care to name in the town."

"So, you've come to speak to me because ... I'm a good listener? What?"

"In truth, I just wanted to pick your dad's brains about these." Camara held a pair of handcuffs sealed in a clear plastic evidence bag. "We found these in Huntley's house. Just discarded and to one side."

"Handcuffs."

Camara twisted them through the plastic and a cuff sprang open. "Trick handcuffs. American import. Not many of them about. Magician's handcuffs." He said these last words heavily and distinctly. "Do you mind if I...?"

He made to go to the lounge. Sam instinctively wanted to leap up and bar his way, demanding he produce a warrant, even though that was utterly foolish. She followed him through with a hurriedly made pot of tea.

Camara explained himself patiently to Marvin, the background to his visit and the presence of a pair of stage handcuffs in a dead man's house. Marvin asked to look at them. Camara asked him to not remove them from the bag.

"Yes, stage handcuffs. Good ones. None of that cheap mail order rubbish," said Marvin. "Was the man a magician?"

"No. There are, however, marks on his wrists to indicate

he was wearing them shortly before he died. Did you know a James Huntley, Marvin?"

Sam watched her dad do a good five second impression of someone searching their memory just so the detective could see he was trying to be helpful, then he shook his head.

"Do you own such a pair of handcuffs?" Camara tried to keep his tone light.

"I have done," Marvin said readily. "At least two pairs. Bought them from Tannen's magic shop. That's New York."

"Do you still have them?"

"I might have used a set like these recently. I've got a couple of boxes of props."

"A couple?" said Sam, scoffing lightly.

Marvin scoffed back. "My villainous daughter keeps trying to sell off my old memorabilia."

"That's tat to you and me," said Sam. "And I'm not selling anything you don't want me to."

"Not sure it feels like that," said Marvin in good humour. "Most of it went to Delia's junk shop."

"She doesn't like it being called a junk shop."

"So," suggested Camara, "these could actually have been yours?"

"Sorry?"

"Sold through Delia's shop. That's the one opposite the pier, right?"

Marvin reached for the tea Sam had poured. "Constable, is this evidence in a crime?"

"It's possible."

"Am I a suspect?"

"We're just trying to find out what happened."

"Are you going to tell me not to leave the country in the next seventy two hours?" He was now hamming it up like a bad actor.

Camara laughed. "Is that likely?"

"We're being flown out to a luxury oil rig in a few days."

Camara frowned. "Really?"

"It's a gas platform," said Sam. "Converted."

The frown deepened. "Really?"

"Do you need to take my fingerprints, officer?" said Marvin.

"No, that's all right. There are no fingerprints on the handcuffs anyway."

Sam held her tea to warm her hands but did not drink. "That's unusual, isn't it?"

"Not a single print on the handcuffs? Not even a partial?" he said. "That's very unusual, yes."

61

B ernard Babcock believed in preparedness and the rewards of preparedness.

A career in the British Army, from infantry training through to the 33rd Engineers Regiment, had shown him that those who did not prepare had no one but themselves to blame. A badly packed pack, an unserviced engine, a doorway not checked – any of these could cost you big style, and it'd be all your own fault. When the failure to determine if that little Belfast girl was carrying a weapon or not had cost a good friend his life, Bernard had decided it was time to prepare for the long term, and a long and happy retirement.

After twenty years in the army and ten years as a quarrying engineer, his preparations had paid off. His retirement nest egg had bought him an apartment at Otterside, with the funds to enjoy each and every day as it came. A morning fag, a decent fry up, a chance to catch up on his suntan, a snooze under the open pages of The Sun, and a few beers in the evening. That bloody noisy turkey had put a dent in his perfectly happy retirement for a few weeks, but the committee had sorted that out and it was back to business as usual.

If that snooty Margaret and her cronies needed a return favour it was no problem to Bernard. Just a little side project, something he could squeeze in between meals and sessions under a sunlamp. Plus it allowed him to flex some of those creative skills he'd honed over his long career. Once he'd devised a plan, he went round and knocked on his neighbour's door. Polly was a game bird, but had made it clear that she didn't like the sight of too much bronzed flesh, so Bernard made a special effort. Before he went round he tied up his dressing grown (or 'leisure robe' as he liked to think of it).

When Polly opened the door, she was smiling, laughing even, her head turned to someone within. Bernard heard the fading sounds of a man's voice, Strawb perhaps. The smile faded somewhat when Polly saw it was Bernard at her door. She consciously straightened her cardigan and gave him the politest smile.

"Am I interrupting?" he said.

"Yes," she said genially.

"Right you are," he said. "I wondered if you could help me with these." He held out a bunch of printed sheets.

Polly gave them a confused inspection. "These are e-cigarettes," she said.

"Yes, they are," he nodded. "I was thinking perhaps it was

time I cut down on the old fags and switched to something a bit healthier."

"About time?" The critical up-and-down she gave him seemed to suggest the time to cut down had long since passed.

Bernard ignored the insult. "I saw that your – it's your niece, isn't it? – had one and I thought it looked the dog's bollocks. I wondered if you knew which one it was."

Polly looked at the papers again. "Out of these?"

"These are the top sellers," he said. "Researched them myself."

"Did you not read any reviews?"

"I thought it might be this one."

"No. Hers has got these cartridges that load in the middle. They click in."

"Ah." He shuffled his sheets. "Like this one? Or this one?"

"That one."

"Definitely?"

She nodded. "They're all the same. All quite ridiculous."

"Better than dying."

Bernard didn't appreciate the look she gave him, but he was capable of rising above such things. Besides, she'd change her tune when she realised what a favour he was doing for her.

Strawb said something from inside the apartment that Bernard didn't catch. Polly blushed.

"Are we done?" she said. Before he could answer, she closed the door.

He returned to his own apartment. His kitchenette table had

been turned into a little workbench. Wires and components sat in a rack. There was a little plastic bag of red Tovex, a water-gel explosive. He'd treated himself to a kilo of the stuff as a retirement present from his quarry job. He'd barely used any since then, and he'd need no more than a teaspoon for this job.

He looked at the e-cigarette Polly had pointed out. "It'll work," he said.

62

Margaret recognised the man in reception as a police detective, specifically as the one who had brought Polly's great niece into the south lounge on the day of the magic show. The man was at least six and a half feet tall and gawkily angular with it, like a teenager going through an embarrassing growth spurt. Such a man was easily recognised. Margaret suspected he didn't get to do much undercover work.

Police visiting Otterside wasn't something to be specifically worried about, but Margaret was curious and idly followed him down to the café bar, where he spotted and made a bee-line for Alison Duncliffe. She was sitting in the wicker chairs by the French windows, drinking a lurid-coloured smoothie through a straw.

As the detective approached Alison respectfully, practically stooped in deference, Margaret moved to the bar.

"Another one of those smoothies for Alison there," she

told the serving girl. "And a snowball for me."

It was perhaps too early in the day to be indulging in cocktails, but it was Christmas Eve for goodness sake, and if she was buying a joyless vegetable smoothie for Alison, Margaret felt it only right that she should balance things up.

As the girl mixed two drinks, Margaret watched the conversation. Alison had become quite still as the detective spoke to her. Relaying the facts of James Huntleys death, presumably. Quite possibly revealing nothing that hadn't already been reported in the local papers. Margaret watched their body language. Yes, the detective was piling on the sympathy – what painful memories this must bring back for Alison, condolences once again on the death of her daughter, apologies that the police hadn't been able to provide the family with justice at the time, hope that this might bring some sort of closure to the matter. Empty and meaningless words. Alison nodded but said almost nothing.

But soon he would start to ask questions. Clearly the death was being treated as suspicious.

Margaret had placed herself at the bar where Alison could clearly see her. Alison glanced her way a couple of times. Margaret saw her role as a comforting presence, but also a reminder to Alison that she was part of a wider enterprise; that others were relying on her.

Margaret paid for the drinks and sipped her snowball.

The police officer asked Alison something. Alison went into an explanation, offering the detective the residents card attached to her key ring. She glanced to Margaret once more. The detective caught the action and looked round.

Margaret was ready and took both drinks over to the

table. "I didn't want to interrupt while you were chatting," she said, as blandly as possible. "It looked serious. A Lean Green Detoxing Machine for you, Alison, wasn't it?"

Alison took the drink and a look passed between them. Margaret made sure that look said, 'Stay strong, he knows nothing.' Margaret didn't sit, but she didn't move away. She stood, waiting, impressing upon the detective that this situation was fleeting, the conversation soon to be over.

"Mrs Duncliffe," said the detective, "this card isn't yours."

"Isn't it?"

"It belongs to a Polly Gilpin."

"Oh, we must have got them swapped at some point," said Alison. "But even if it's not on my record, you can ask anyone who was there. I'm always at the Pilates in the morning and the guided meditation in the afternoon."

"Of course," he said and returned the card. "Make sure Ms Gilpin gets her card back."

He looked up at Margaret. Was that irritation in his face? Good.

"Mrs Duncliffe, we will be conducting a thorough investigation. Obviously, if we learn anything, I will personally make sure you're informed." Perfectly hollow words, a perfect match for the hollow effort the police had made in investigating Rachel Duncliffe's death.

Alison said her thanks to him nonetheless.

The detective nodded in acknowledgement at Margaret. She gave him a thin and fleeting smile. Margaret watched him walk out and then took his seat.

"Are you holding up?"

Alison nodded and in lieu of words or any outward

expression of emotion, took an overlong suck on the smoothie.

There was a noise from the corridor just outside the bar. Polly Gilpin stormed into view, turned and said loudly. "They're not even coming now! Not at all."

"Okay, sweetheart," said Strawb, approaching, reaching to put his hands on her shoulders.

"I'll not fucking do it," she spat. "I'll not be cut off like this! I'll not go without a fight!"

Seeing that a good three quarters of the café bar were looking at her now, Polly threw her arms up dramatically and stormed away.

Strawb was about to follow when he spotted Margaret. He wove through the bar, apologising for the scene, offering jokey conciliatory remarks to the more affronted residents, until he reached Margaret.

"The facking niece," he said simply. "Hello, Alison. That's a bladdy colourful drink you've got there. Looks like someone put Kermit the Frog in the blender."

"I don't normally have more than one," said Alison.

Margaret gave Strawb a questioning look. He saw it and nodded.

"The niece isn't even coming to see her before Christmas. Boxing Day. Can you believe it?"

"Good," said Margaret. When Strawb frowned she added, "It means we were right. She's a worthy target. I will see how Bernard is getting on with the preparations."

Alison pushed aside her smoothie. "You know, I think I actually need something stronger today."

Strawb whistled and gestured to the woman at the bar.

63

Bernard found Jacob in the restaurant, the notebook he always carried with him open on the table and several sheets of writing paper before him. He appeared deep in thought, so Bernard gave him a respectful second or two before sitting down opposite him.

"You busy?"

Jacob blinked as though returning from a distant place. "Yes. I am. I am writing a letter to Ravensburger, suggesting they should offer a service by which customers can order up single jigsaw pieces which they have lost."

"Still looking for those missing ones?" said Bernard. He'd seen the posters Jacob had put up.

"I've gone on to suggest that, if they are unwilling to offer such a service, it would suggest they want customers to lose pieces so that they are forced to buy entirely new jigsaws. A scandalous business practice."

"That's great," said Bernard uninterested. "I need your

help. I need something specific and I think you're exactly the man to help."

Jacob's nodded, conceding that Bernard was probably right and he set down his pen.

"I need a halfpence piece," said Bernard.

"A halfpenny?"

"Uh-huh." Bernard held up his fingers, a short distance apart as though holding one.

"They went out of circulation in 1984," said Jacob.

"Is that so?"

"It is."

"But you don't happen to have one lying around?"

"I'm not a hoarder, Bernard. Why, may I ask, do you want one?"

"I need a thin metal disc, no wider than twenty mil. It needs to fit inside this." He held up a short metal tube.

"And what is that?" said Jacob.

"It's the heating element and battery compartment for a VapourMax e-cigarette. Do you know what an explosively formed penetrator is?" said Bernard.

Jacob gave it some thought. "I could speculate. It's a shell or bullet formed by an explosion."

"Exactly. A big one took out several mates of mine in Yugoslavia, back in the day. You get a concave metal disc and pack it in front of a short-barrelled metal cylinder."

"I'm picturing something like a Caribbean steel drum."

"Yeah, except this one doesn't play *Yellow Bird*, it explodes. The explosive force turns the metal disc into a bullet-shaped, self-forged warhead that can penetrate tank side armour. That one was a couple of metres across. I need something—"

"Less than twenty millimetres, like a halfpenny coin."

"Exactly."

"Or a euro one cent coin."

"Really?" said Bernard.

"Sixteen millimetres in diameter."

Bernard grinned. "You see! I knew you'd be the man with the answer. Clever bastard. It's the specs."

Jacob adjusted his round glasses. "There is no correlation between spectacles and intelligence, Bernard. That it was literate people who were the first to make full use of them is another example of how people misunderstand cause and effect."

"You crack me up," said Bernard. "Right. Off to find some euros. And I'll feel happier destroying them rather than decent British coins. Pissing fiddly things."

Bernard left him to it. Jacob picked up his pen, apparently to resume his campaign to right the wrongs in the world of jigsaws.

64

S am and Marvin each had a small overnight case for their Christmas trip to Rich's offshore luxury pad. Sam had watched a series of videos on the internet on the most space-saving ways to pack a suitcase. There was some dispute as to whether rolling or folding was best, but Sam opted to roll all of her clothes into sausage shapes. She layered them carefully into her case, using the tiny gaps to accommodate toiletries. It was deemed essential to use the dead space inside shoes, so Sam stuffed her underwear tightly inside.

"Can I put some stuff in your case?" asked Marvin as they plonked them down by the front door, just before Rich was due to pick them up.

Sam looked at him in alarm. "If I said there's no room in my case, I think I'd be understating it. If the zip bursts, we could all be killed by tightly-rolled undies."

"Just a pair of shoes," said Marvin. "You must have room for that, surely?"

"Why must I?"

"Because men's shoes are bigger than women's. It stands to reason you'd have some spare space."

"It really doesn't," said Sam. "How many pairs of shoes are you taking?"

"Only four," said Marvin.

"Four pairs of shoes? We're there for two nights. How could you possibly need four pairs of shoes?"

"It's not good for the leather if you wear the same pair every day."

"Nope, still doesn't add up."

"A pair for relaxing and a formal pair. It certainly does add up."

"Can you do without them, dad? I really haven't got any spare room in my case. I've also got my laptop in there in case Rich decides he wants to look over his animal drill footage."

"How about your handbag?"

Sam sighed. Her dad always seemed to imagine a woman's handbag was the size of a small valise. She held up her tiny bag. "If I emptied everything out of it, you still wouldn't get a pair of shoes in there."

The doorbell went and Sam was saved from any further discussion. She opened the door and Rich beamed at the pair of them.

As always, he didn't seem appropriately dressed, as though weather was something that only happened to poor people. Despite the cold breeze his jacket and shirt were open enough to display the shell on a leather thong that hung at his neck. He said he'd got it freediving with some foreign catwalk model on a tropical island, or somesuch. Another bullshit story.

"Ready?" asked Rich

"Very much so," said Marvin, his spare shoes forgotten. "A helicopter ride is something special."

"I hope you enjoy it," said Rich, picking up their cases and leading them down to a large four wheel drive.

"It's been a while," said Marvin. "Can't think who it was that used to have one. Tarbuck or maybe Cheggers. Actually, it could have been Dusty. I once remember going over for a picnic on Anglesey, just because the sun was out. I daresay that's not allowed since the royals moved in."

They drove north through the town. Glimpses of the sea showed wave tops whipped into white foam by a stiff wind. Christmas Eve in Skegness was all greys and whites.

"How come you're driving, Rich?" Sam asked. "I thought we were going over with your butler chap."

"Peninsula is making his way there separately," said Rich. "He's been to collect some equipment and catering supplies from Grimsby, so he'll be bringing everything across from there."

"Cool."

"He's got a load of specialist contacts pulling out all of the stops. Expect some seriously gourmet meals over the next couple of days. Game bird, fish, the finest wine. Did you know he's a Master Sommelier?"

"He's good then?"

"It's the highest level of proficiency you can get. Trained in Australia. The man is an expert."

Sam grinned at her dad. They were going well and truly outside their comfort zone. The Christmases she'd grown up with were a straightforward ritual involving food, presents and telly. The house would be littered with fruit, nuts and liqueur chocolates for in-between snacking, but the basics were always the same. Sure, not many houses had the occasional celebrity in for Christmas dinner (there was one memorably crowded Christmas where there were five Grumbleweeds at the family table) but, that aside, the Applewhites were used to distinctly ordinary Christmases.

This year held the promise of something very different, with the frisson of excitement that came with the short, dramatic flight they were about to make out across the North Sea. The road north out of town turned inland at Seathorne, to an airfield. Sam could tell it was an airfield because there was a scattering of tiny planes, but there didn't seem to be very much else there.

A helicopter was parked on a pad near the squat control building. It was larger than the car they were in, but not by much. Was it irrational to want a helicopter to be bigger than that? Sam had only ever been on commercial flights, where the aeroplane was the size of an office building.

A man in a flight suit walked around and shook Rich's hand.

"This is Gregor, the finest commercial chopper pilot in the business," said Rich.

The pilot glanced at Sam and Marvin. "These two done the HUET training?"

"No they haven't, they are my guests," said Rich. "I've applied for a waiver for visitors to my—"

"I can't take you out if there are people in the group who are unprepared to ditch into the water," said Gregor.

"I am definitely unprepared to ditch into the water," said Marvin.

"It's just a drill," said Rich to Marvin and Sam. "Nobody's going into the water."

"HUET?" Sam asked.

"Helicopter Underwater Escape Training," said Rich. "If you're working on the rigs you'd definitely do it, but I'm not sure we really need—"

"It's important," said the pilot. "I mean, I'm already overlooking the fact that none of you are wearing rubber immersion suits."

Sam could see he wasn't budging on this. "How long does it take to do the training?" she asked.

"It's half a day," said Rich, "but you need to go to a specialist centre that has the facilities."

"Is there a video we can watch on the internet or something?" Sam asked. If DefCon4 had taught her anything, it was the value of self-learning.

The pilot rolled his eyes, but Rich caught his arm. "Great idea. I can run them through everything in fifteen minutes or so."

"It's supposed to be physical training," said Gregor, "so that it's embedded firmly into your muscle memory."

"We both have a great imagination," said Marvin. "If we see a video, I guarantee it will be as if we've lived it ourselves. There was this time back in Eastbourne when I was doing a summer season with The Barron Knights. There was a strong man appearing on the same bill and he tore a ligament. Or it might have been a tendon. Anyway, I swear I still get twinges in the same spot when the weather's—"

"Fine!" said Gregor. "Show them the video. Hurry up though, there's a major weather system moving in and I don't want to be stuck out in it." He walked away towards a small building nearby.

"Does he work for you?" asked Marvin.

"Sort of. No," sighed Rich. "He does private charter work. Very safety conscious. Come on now, pay attention to this video, he will almost certainly ask questions when he comes back."

Rich played them a video that showed four trainees strapped into a mocked-up helicopter cabin. When the shot changed, Sam realised it was positioned above something like a swimming pool.

"Oh wow, are they actually going to get a dunking?" she asked.

"Yep."

The video made it clear the dunking was going to happen multiple times, and the trainees would evacuate the helicopter in different ways, as each particular scenario dictated. The first one was straightforward, where they would each evacuate through the window nearest to them. Sam watched in horror as the trainees sat calmly in their seats, the water coming up their legs, over their laps, and eventually over their heads. They didn't move until the cabin was entirely filled with water.

"Such self-control," said Marvin, echoing Sam's thoughts.

"Listen to the commentary," said Rich. "It's drilled into you that you shouldn't waste your energy until the water fills up the cabin, as you won't be able to get the windows out. The pressure's equal when there's water on both sides of the glass. You also need to wait until the rotors have stopped as well, obviously, or they'd slice and dice you as you swam to the surface."

Sam felt herself shiver involuntarily as the trainees on the video held their breath while they removed the windows and swam to the surface. The idea of doing all of that in the frigid waters off Skegness was beyond appalling.

"That's not all though," said Rich. "The scariest thing is, in real life, you wouldn't know which way was up. Something to do with the action of the rotors flips the whole helicopter upside down, more often than not. You need to focus on a reference point to try and tell which way is up. Got it?"

Before Sam and Marvin could respond, Rich was waving at the pilot to come back over.

"Don't go through with this just to save face," whispered Marvin. "We've got cottage pie in the freezer. We could eat that for Christmas dinner."

"It will be fine, dad. Crashes are so rare, but we just need to be mentally prepared."

Luckily nobody asked her whether she was mentally prepared, but they all took their places in the helicopter. There was no getting away from the fact that they were stepping into a bubble. A bubble that looked tiny against the pewter grey backdrop of the North Sea.

65

"Come."

Dr Erin Hackett glanced up at the wall clock as the penultimate patient of the day entered. It was four-fifty and the man had a four-fifty appointment. This was right and proper. She fully intended to finish her clinic at the appropriate time. This had nothing to do with it being Christmas Eve; it was her standard operating procedure.

The NHS guidance that GPs must allocate at least ten minutes to each patient had been rightly scrapped, and Erin saw no reason why she couldn't rattle through the obvious and easy cases as fast as she wished. As a busy frontline health service, her role was one of winnowing out the malingerers, prescribing to those who could be medicated and referring on those who could not. In many ways, she envied veterinaries whose patients didn't cloud matters and waste time with idle chat.

She looked at this latest one. A rotund man who wore old age badly. If he had been a dog or a horse, she would have already implemented a strict diet and made a note recommending he be put down sooner rather than later. Of course, such a course of actions was neither moral nor professional for humans. She was going to have to steer him towards more palatable and less effective remedies.

"Mr Babcock. Bernard," she said, waiting for him to waddle across and sit down. "What can I do for you?"

"I've come with my chest," he said.

"Experiencing pains?" she asked. A heart attack in the surgery, at this point in her day, would put paid to all her evening plans. There were presents to wrap, a table to lay, and a house to tidy (even though her husband would claim he had already tidied it). Cesar didn't seem to understand the importance of David coming over for dinner on Christmas day.

"Trouble breathing," said Bernard Babcock. "A bit chesty. A cough."

She already had her stethoscope out and he was reaching for his shirt buttons.

He was a physically repulsive man, one of the many fat and tattooed who seemed to congregate in this corner of the world and plague her surgery door. He was tanned: a deeply unnatural complexion for this climate and time of year.

She listened to his chest. He did that stilted, self-conscious breathing that all patients did when they were being examined, as though they might get brownie points for the quality of their inhalations.

"Relatively clear," she commented. "You've no history of asthma. Do you smoke?"

"Thirty a day," he said with apparent glee. "Should I cut down?"

"You should stop. Do your shirt up."

"You see I was thinking about that. I thought I ought to get me one of those e-cigarette thingymajigs."

"They do considerably less harm than regular cigarettes," Erin nodded. "Now, there is an NHS smoking cessation service which—"

"I was wondering if you knew what e-cigarette I should get."

"We don't prescribe e-cigs, Mr Babcock."

"No. But I was wondering if you had any ideas." The man's eyes flicked to Erin's bag on the floor.

It took Erin a moment or two to work out what he was hinting at. Clearly he'd seen her smoking her e-cig, either leaving or arriving in her car. He'd seen his GP using an e-cig and wanted to follow suit. Hers wasn't even in her bag, but in her desk drawer. She felt a tired irritability – the man thinking she was some sort of e-cig saleswoman. He could simply have gone to one of the growing number of vaping shops in town.

"Smoking cessation services are the best place to start," she said. "I have a leaflet."

"In the waiting room?" he said. "Would you fetch it for me?" Did he have something in his closed fist? He was holding it tightly.

"I have one here." She slipped one off the rack behind

her and passed it to him. There was a look of nervous disappointment on his face which she couldn't comprehend.

"Perhaps I can write you a prescription for your cough," she suggested. "Although you can simply buy tickly cough medicine at the pharmacist."

Mr Babcock nodded but he didn't seem ready to leave. "I just ... I just..." He clutched at his coat pocket and pulled out a phone. He put it straight to his ear. "Hello?"

"You will need to take your phone call outside," Erin said. The man had taken up enough of her time already. There was little need for him to stay any longer.

"You're what?" He stood and took a step towards the window. "Mary! What's happened?"

"Mr Babcock..."

There was now full-blown panic on his face. "Doctor! Mary who dropped me off. She's having a heart attack. In her car."

"What?"

He peered out of the window. "Oh, Mary!"

Erin tried to see where he was looking.

"The blue car," he said. "The Honda."

Erin hesitated for a second before grabbing her own phone from the top drawer and the medical responder kit from the wall' Leaving the man, she dashed out along the corridor and past reception.

"Sofia!" she called to the receptionist. "I may need you to call an ambulance!" Then she was outside and hurrying towards the little blue Honda that Mr Babcock had pointed out.

It was empty.

She peered through the windows in case the occupant was lying flat along the seats. She circled the vehicle in case the person had gotten out. There was no sign. She looked toward the window of her consulting room, but Mr Babcock was no longer there. Erin moved along the row of parked cars, looking at each, even stepping onto the pavement to check the verge for any signs of a recent heart attack victim. There was none.

As she made her way back inside, Mr Babcock was coming down the corridor from the consultation room.

"I must apologise, doctor," he said. "She was telling me about something that had happened on *The Archers*. Silly moo."

"What?"

"Total confusion," he said and smiled tightly. "Right. I've got my leaflet. Off to buy some Robitussin, yeah?"

He left, which was at least a good thing. Erin sighed, annoyed, and returned to her office. She had left the man alone in there for a minute or two, but nothing was out of place. There were no drugs or expensive equipment he could have stolen. He hardly looked the type, anyway. As she sat down she saw that her top drawer was closed. She thought she had left it open when she'd grabbed her phone. Clearly that was not the case.

She clicked on her computer and told Sofia to send the last patient in.

66

The drone of the helicopter rotors made ordinary speech inside the cabin impossible. Conversation was possible only through headphones connected to the intercom. Marvin was merrily telling everyone about the time he rode in a helicopter with Noel Edmonds, shortly before making an appearance on Noel's Late, Late Breakfast Show. It was droning of a different sort.

Sam stared down at the sea. From this height the waves almost looked static, lines of cotton-wool wave tops in a teal grey sea. She suspected it was an optical illusion. When they'd passed the wind farm, Sam looked back at the coast. The buildings of the town merged into one another, a mould growing on the edge of the flat Lincolnshire landscape. She wanted to ask how high they were flying, but she didn't want to distract the pilot from his important job of not ditching the helicopter into the sea.

For the rest of the journey, Sam drifted into a sleepless

reverie, watching the impossibly still sea. When Rich tapped her arm, she looked ahead and saw the Valhalla gas platform. It was a box or a series of boxes, a Lego construction, balanced on girder legs that didn't seem big enough to support its bulk. Crane arms, scaffolding and pipework for the old gas mining operation wrapped around the outside of the superstructure. The helipad was huge in comparison to the working spaces, a parasol covering almost the entirety of the upper levels.

"Is the helipad really big or is the rig really small?" she asked. No one answered.

"We've got forty mile an hour winds down there," came the pilot's voice in her headphones. *"Stay low, stay away from the edge, and once you've got your bags, head straight for the stairs."*

The helicopter swung around onto the helipad with apparent ease. The rotors slowed but did not stop.

As they climbed out, Sam felt the full force of the wind – brutal and cleansing – and it took her breath away. Travel bag in hand, checking her dad was okay, she followed Rich to the shelter of a metal staircase. Ten steps down and they were through a metal door. As it clanged shut behind them, the sudden silence was like being plunged underwater.

"That was bracing," she said.

"Skegness is bracing. That was downright offensive," commented Marvin, but he was smiling as he said it.

Sam heard the now muffled sound of the helicopter taking off. "The pilot's leaving?"

"Yeah, he'll come back on Boxing Day to take us home," said Rich. "Let's go and make ourselves comfortable." With clanging footsteps, he led the way down metal corridors.

"I thought there would be a welcoming committee," said Sam.

"Peninsula should have already flown in from Humberside Airport."

"I meant the other staff," said Sam.

"Staff?"

They entered what had to be the main section of the platform building. Sam's mental images of luxury casinos and swanky hotels were not being met so far. There were hard-wearing floors and fibreglass panelled walls. It looked very much like a budget hotel or student accommodation.

"Is there no one else here?" Sam said.

"We're operating on a skeleton crew," said Rich. "And Peninsula is worth ten people."

"So a skeleton crew of one butler."

"Here's the living quarters." Rich held open a door. "It doesn't look as though Peninsula's made up any of the beds yet. Hey, that means you get to choose whichever room you like. Cool, huh?"

As Sam walked along the corridor, peering into all of the possible bedrooms, she felt very far away from the civilised world. Skegness was unreachable without the helicopter, which had gone. There was no mobile signal here, either. Her father edged close, and she wondered if he felt it too. She thought she heard a sound coming through the structure. She touched the wall.

"What's that?" she asked Rich.

"There's always some background noise," he said. "This platform is built to withstand waves of over twenty metres, but still, when a storm hits, it's going to be quite dramatic."

Sam tried to picture a twenty metre wave. Surely Skegness would never see that? It would demolish the pier. How far out to sea were waves of that size found?

"Suddenly, a frozen cottage pie for Christmas dinner doesn't seem so bad," she murmured.

"This is fun," said Marvin. "Bit of an adventure."

"So, if no one else is here, is the casino open over Christmas?" she asked.

Rich gave her an odd look. "The casino isn't open at all yet."

"The brochure you gave me."

He grinned. "Architect's vision."

Sam processed this. No casino yet. Bedrooms that were functional but hardly plush. "Oh, so we have a vision of the casino, not the real thing."

"We'll just have to imagine really hard," said Marvin. "I might even imagine I've won the jackpot."

"It's just the three of us for Christmas," said Rich. "Plus Peninsula, of course."

"Not much of a Christmas for him if he's running after us, doing the work of ten people."

Rich pushed out his bottom lip as though he hadn't thought of that. "He's not a Christmassy person anyway. His people are into ancestor worship. I think."

"So how much work has been done to turn this into a luxury playground for wealthy tourists?" she asked.

"None of the development's actually started yet," said Rich.

"None?"

"None. The lab's out here of course, that was the priority.

The rest of it will be done in the coming weeks."

Sam wanted to ask a follow-up question, something that went along the lines of "Why did you invite us out here when we could have just had a nice meal at home?", but she didn't. Apart from being rude and more than a little ungrateful, she knew the answer. This was Rich's latest toy, and he was very excited about it. He would not understand why anyone else might not be equally excited. Expectations of a high-class Christmas in the lap of luxury evaporated.

"Well, I don't know about either of you two, but I feel like celebrating not having to swim out of a crashed helicopter," said Marvin. "Where will we find a tipple, Rich?"

"That's the spirit! Let's do the tour, then see where Peninsula's got to with all the provisions, shall we?"

They walked down a maze of corridors. Rich indicated the office spaces, gym area, smoking room and radio room, all of which would be transformed into something far more luxurious, eventually.

"This here is the lab complex," he said, indicating a door. Sam peered through the glass and saw a large clinical-looking space, fitted with workbenches and racks of equipment.

"Lab complex?" said Marvin.

"For cooking up beasts to populate Rich's Ice Age theme park," said Sam.

"I remember you telling me," said Marvin. "I just assumed it was a joke. Or a dream. Or I was having a mini-stroke."

"You and me both, dad."

"The science is sound," said Rich, unoffended. "With all

resources now securely kept here, we can operate without fear of our glorious specimens being stolen."

Sam wasn't sure anyone wanted to steal frozen animal bits, but decided to keep such thoughts to herself.

Rich led them on.

"And last but not least, here's the kitchen and stores, where Peninsula's going to work his magic." Rich looked around. "Peninsula! Are you here?" There was no response. The large kitchen space was decidedly void of people, activity and, specifically, butlers.

"Busy elsewhere," Rich shrugged. "I'm sure he's about. Right. Let's find that drink."

67

Yule had arrived in the Odinson compound. Hilde could literally hear it approaching, as Hermod and Gunnolf tooted the horn on their truck to announce their return with the midwinter sacrifice.

That it was already three days past the actual midwinter was a point Hilde was not going to raise with her farfar. He would only say something like "Ah, that's the Saxon midwinter. Tha' should pay no attention to that." Hilde could have also pointed out that a number of features from the Saxon Christmas had crept in, but Astrid's knitted nativity scene was cute (with a baby Thor in the manger and a visit from the three wise warriors), and it would have been churlish to point out that gift giving, especially with Christmas wrapping paper, was not really the Viking way. Hilde had given her dad a string of crystal beads to weave into his beard and her farfar an old brass telescope, both from Delia's shop as part payment for the work she'd done there.

As the traditional Odinson Yule drinks of spicy mead (and Ribena for the kids) were passed one way, and the traditional Odinson Yule snacks of Doritos, cocktail sausages and Jaffa cakes were passed the other, Hilde looked at the splashes of colour that Astrid's cushions made on the benches. There was no doubt her cushions lent a festive touch to the place, even if the Viking subject matter was a little grim – a depiction of a blood eagle sacrifice was unpleasant to behold, even if it was executed in pastel coloured cross-stitch and everyone (even the cartoon victim) was smiling cheerily.

The work on the longship had progressed at a very pleasing pace, and they were about to commence Yule celebrations in a space that was very clearly identifiable as the hull of a Viking longboat. Gunnolf had mounted the planks containing his saga around the edges for the occasion. It was a florid account of modern-day seafaring that really didn't boil down to much more than launching a boat, sailing around on the sea, and snarling at the passengers on the Hull to Zeebrugge ferry. But the tone of it was impressive.

As Hermod and Gunnolf led the bleating sacrifice into the hall, Hilde heard voices raised in anger outside. Hilde went out to investigate. She found Astrid facing off with Ragnar.

"Tha' can't tek away the traditions as have been there fer generations!" Ragnar shouted. "Since time immemorial, us Odinsons have made a sacrifice to Odin fer midwinter!"

"Nobody's saying we can't honour Odin," said Astrid, in a measured, reasonable tone, "but there's to be no killing. It upsets the young uns."

"What?" blustered Ragnar. "Never heard such nonsense! When I were a lad there'd be no talking back about tradition. It's just something young uns need to get used to."

"There were no traditions back in your day. Your mum and dad lived in Peterborough. Your dad was a gas fitter and you went to Sunday school at St Peter and All Souls."

"Blasphemy, woman!"

"Times change, Ragnar," said Astrid. "Freyella's a vegan now and she's—"

"A vegan? I should cast her out."

Hilde watched Ragnar's frown. It was likely he was trying to remember exactly who Freyella was, out of the countless rabble of grandchildren scattered around the Odinson complex.

"You do that and I'll be following her straight out the gate," said Astrid. "And I'll be telling everyone that your name ain't Ragnar Odinson but—"

"Woah there, woman," said Ragnar shaking open hands to ward off her words. "Let's not get hasty, eh? Vegans, is it? Well put her on the side with her lentils or what have you, and t' rest of us will get on with the traditions."

"Ragnar, it's not that simple and you know it. She's very popular with the other young uns. You'll have a big problem on your hands if you don't pay attention to this. I have some suggestions, if you 'd like to hear them. Or maybe I should go and mention that mead's not vegan?"

"Fine!" roared Ragnar. "Let nobody say that an Odinson's not adaptable."

He looked round to see the whole clan was watching him in the afternoon gloom. The Odinsons liked a Christmas show like everyone else.

68

Sam, Rich and Marvin looked everywhere for Peninsula, even beyond the point at which it was clear the butler was nowhere on board the gas platform, unless he was deliberately hiding somewhere. Sam felt mounting concern as the search lengthened. Rich seemed to be treating it as some sort of grand game of hide-and-seek.

"Perhaps he fell overboard," said Marvin warily.

"Ah," said Rich, quite inspired by the thought. "That would explain *a lot*."

"And it would be a bad thing," Sam pointed out.

Rich nodded, reluctantly conceding the point. "So we ought to go look for him down there?"

"And hope to see a little pair of butler gloves floating on the sea?" said Marvin, dubiously.

Rich glanced at his phone. "Oh, I missed some calls. From Peninsula indeed."

The concern growing in Sam took on a different flavour.

"He's left me a voice message," said Rich. He put the phone to his ear and his expressive, child-like face went blank.

He's not coming, thought Sam.

"He's not coming," said Rich.

"What?" said Marvin.

Rich replayed the message on loudspeaker, so that Sam and Marvin could hear.

"I had hoped to speak to you before you took off, sir," said Peninsula's voice. *"There is a storm approaching. Storm Wendy is the official designation. It appears that Wendy is much worse than they initially expected. All aircraft from Humberside Airport have been grounded for the day, possibly longer. I've called around, sir, and it is the same story everywhere else. I will not be able to get out to join you at this stage."*

"That's not good," said Marvin.

"Please tell me he wasn't bringing *all* the food," said Sam.

An hour later, after a thorough inspection of the rooms, Sam was beginning to understand the scale of the problems facing all three of them. Not only were they stranded without the skills of Peninsula, who was supposed to be providing them with the finest food and drink, they were also stranded without the ingredients he was bringing. The storm meant there was no prospect of Peninsula joining them until after Christmas Day. It also meant that there was no prospect of them getting off the platform until after Christmas Day.

While Rich made endless calls on his satellite phone trying to solve the unsolvable, Sam went exploring, to see what little they had to work with. Marvin accompanied her.

They quickly discovered that the inner sanctum of the rig was where all of the human comforts were located. The outside edges were dominated by machinery and lots of signs insisting a hard hat should be worn.

"At times like these, it would be so useful if you could do real magic," said Sam.

"All magic is real!" said Marvin. "Lives have been transformed by the power of stagecraft. Jeanette Krankie used to tell me that she saw a conjuror as a child. It instilled in her a life-long love of the stage, after he pulled a live rabbit from a top hat."

"I know, dad," said Sam. "But pulling Christmas dinner out of a hat might be slightly more difficult."

Sam found a walk-in store cupboard next to the kitchens. It was a sizeable cupboard, the sort that would see a working crew through an extended period of isolation if it was fully stocked. Right now it was empty. Why would a decommissioned gas platform keep a food store, just on the off-chance that its slightly hopeless millionaire buyer would find himself stuck out here without fresh supplies? Sam scoured the shelves and opened all of the containers to check whether anything remained. After fifteen minutes she had completed an exhaustive search, and gathered all of the useable things onto a table. There was a tin of mushroom soup (dented), four packets of ramen noodles, half a jar of chilli powder, a packet of pudding rice, and a multipack of chewing gum.

"Well that's a start," she said. She tried to inject a cheery note into her voice. "I expect there are some other supplies somewhere else. This place is massive."

She checked the taps. There was running water. It tasted a little stale but the platform at least had some fresh water. They weren't going to die of dehydration.

She went out to the corridor and into a large communal room. There was a big TV screen on the wall, a couple of battered sofas and comfy chairs, a bookcase full of DVDs and boardgames, and table football. Out of interest she scanned the faded posters and flyers on a wall-mounted noticeboard. Many of them promoted safe ways of working. Sam resolved not to stand under any suspended loads. There were timetables for something that might have been a sporting fixture, or might have been a quiz league. She couldn't be certain. With team names like *Norfolk n Luck* and *Twilley's Twonks* it could have gone either way. There was also a slimming club, which made Sam pause. It was perfectly reasonable there should be a slimming club for workers out here on a gas platform, but it was something she hadn't expected to see. They all looked faded, but none of them contained a date.

"There's a storage room here," said Marvin, peering round a doorway. "Coming?"

Sam hurried over. It was encouraging. There was a row of deep chests in one half of the room, and the other half was given over to lockers.

"What do we think, general storage and personal storage?" she said.

"I would say so," said Marvin with a nod.

They went over and opened the chests.

The first contained nothing but life vests. After reading all of the safety notices, she was primed to take personal responsibility for the safety of herself and others. Knowing where the life vests were was definitely a notch in the bedpost of personal safety, but right now she would have been happier with a giant stash of tinned food. She started to picture the things she'd ideally like to find. She'd always had a soft spot for tinned peaches. Tinned potatoes were an intriguing thing to eat: nice in their own way but not very much like actual potatoes. Then she remembered that it was Christmas.

"Didn't they used to sell whole Christmas dinners in a tin?" she said.

"Wasn't that just for dogs?" said Marvin.

"Was it?"

"I hope we don't have to resort to eating dog food."

"Dad, why would there be a dog on a gas platform?"

"Cat maybe. To catch the rats."

She didn't know whether to scoff at the thought of there being rats on a gas platform, or shudder because it might conceivably be true.

"Best food you can get in a tin, dad?" she said, poking between life vests in the forlorn hope that something was hiding. "What are you hoping for?"

"Artichoke hearts," he said after a pause.

"Really?"

"Really. Nice in a salad."

"Well if we find some of those you can keep them all," Sam said with feeling. She dropped the lid on the life vest storage chest, looking across at the one Marvin held open.

"Shall we look in the lockers?" asked Marvin.

"How can we do that?" Sam asked. "The open ones are empty and the locked ones are, um, locked."

"We can do it Sam, because magic is real," said Marvin. "I just need you to believe in me." He gave her the faux-sincere look that worked on stage, but definitely not on her and hadn't since the age of nine. Sam eyed him carefully. Was the stress of the situation getting to him? He did love to wallow in the past. Right now, it sounded as though he'd been transported back to a fictitious past, perhaps an old Disney movie, the way he was wheeling out his fairy dust stage patter.

She stood with her hands on her hips. "Go on then, can you seriously open these doors?"

He gave a mysterious waggle of his eyebrows and pulled a handkerchief from his pocket. He approached a locked door and flapped his hanky over the lock, obscuring the view. "Now, before we continue, I need you to say it with me."

"You can just—"

"Say it with me!" urged her father.

"Fine. Mr bloody Marvellous."

"Don't you sully the name that has made our fortune."

"Fortune? Ha! We're broke."

"Shut up and say the words."

"Abracadabra!" said Sam, making it sound more like an expletive than a word of conjuration.

There was a brief movement, the hanky twitched away and the door was open.

Sam gaped. "How did you do that?"

Marvin gave a smug grin and held up a key. It had a label

hanging off that read *Master Locker Key.* "It was on the table when we came in."

Sam laughed. "Nicely played!"

Sam reached into the locker while Marvin unlocked the others. For a moment she wondered if she was invading the personal space of some long-departed engineer, She quickly got over it when she discovered most of the detritus in the lockers was rubbish. The scale was wide, encompassing mummified fruit, a dog-eared manual for a large industrial pump, a selection of ancient porn magazines ("Jazzle! Amazing Grace wants to sit on your face!") and a battery that had leaked acid, corroding the locker base into a rusty puddle.

"Oh, now here's a find," said Marvin, reaching inside a locker right at the end. He pulled out a tin. Sam's eyebrows shot up in surprise. "A treacle pudding? No way!"

Marvin held it up. "I can't see the date on it."

Sam crossed the room to take a look. "It's still in date! I can barely believe it!"

Rich appeared. "It's not looking good for getting out of here. We're going to feel the full force of Wendy tonight and no one can come out."

"Windy Wendy, eh?" said Marvin.

"But you've found some food, yeah? I should think there's plenty here we can use."

"There really isn't plenty of anything, Rich," said Sam.

"Hey, there's no need to be downbeat. Worst case scenario is we have to stay here for a couple of days," said Rich. "There's some sort of rainwater filtration system, so we'll have enough water."

"I checked. There is."

"The electric's working and there's gas for cooking. I see you've already found the tinned provisions, so we're good, yeah? We shouldn't get bored, there's a DVD library and a table football. I hereby challenge you both to a game as soon as we've found something to drink!"

"How can you sound so chipper at a time like this?" said Sam. Even after having been the man's girlfriend for far longer than was sane, she still couldn't get over his unbearable optimism.

"Winner gets to choose a restaurant when we get back to the mainland!"

"Slap up dinner," nodded Marvin.

"He'll be buying me a fucking restaurant at this rate," said Sam.

"Either, both," grinned Rich. "So how does that sound?"

Sam rolled her eyes. Maybe Rich was happy with not eating over Christmas, as long as he had table football. She wasn't sure Marvin would be. She certainly wasn't.

"You're on, lad!" said Marvin, taking her by surprise. "You coming, Sam?"

"I'll just have a bit more of a scout round," she said. "I'll come and find you in a few minutes."

She went back into the kitchen and tried the gas. It seemed to be working. She searched around to see if there were supplies of any sort. She found a bottle of cooking oil that smelled slightly rancid, but nothing else. She searched the remaining communal areas. In the canteen seating area there was a drinks machine, but she couldn't tell if there was anything inside as it was powered down. She decided to come back later and investigate. She found some board games, which she left on the table for later, but no more food. There was a brief moment of excitement when she found a Pringles tube; then she opened it and found it was being used to store a jigsaw.

She explored the laundry area and found washing machine pods and some ancient dryer lint, but no food.

She went back through the corridors until she came to the lab complex. The old signage made her realise it was a repurposed sick bay. She peered through the glass and wondered how safe it was. If she came across a cage with baby velociraptors inside she would definitely leave.

She nurtured a hopeful theory that whoever had set up or was operating the lab facility might have left some snacks behind. The door wasn't locked so she entered. She looked inside the cupboards. There was scientific glassware, electronics, and boxes of things called Eppendorf tubes. She started to check cabinets that might possibly double as storage cupboards. Most of them turned out to hold more equipment, but when she pulled open a large upright cabinet she struck gold. It was a freezer!

She eagerly pulled open the internal drawers to see what was in there. Not much that looked useful. Lots of reagents, according to the labels. The last drawer was labelled samples, and she pulled it open just to check for a rogue box of choc ices. She was surprised to see a familiar shape: it was the mammoth specimen she had fetched from Hull. She lifted it out, feeling a sudden, nostalgic warmth towards it. It was like meeting an old friend in this isolated and hostile place. There was a section missing from one corner. Presumably Rich's pet scientists had started using it.

She glanced around, struck by the sudden irrational idea she had missed a tiny cloned mammoth. "If there are any tiny mammoths in here, you'd better come out right now," she said to the empty room.

No. She placed the sample back into the freezer. It had such a strong resemblance to a nice piece of roasting beef that she suddenly found herself quite hungry. She stood in the centre of the lab and had a final look round. There was a storage unit near one of the machines that she hadn't checked. She opened it up and was stunned to find numerous packets of dried milk. She was suspicious it wasn't the real deal, but on turning a packet over she found serving suggestions – including a warming mug of hot chocolate. The unexpected discovery lifted her mood, and she put the packets with the rest of her very small stash. Then she went to join the table football fun.

"Here she is!" said Marvin with a wink.

"Your dad's wiping the floor with me," said Rich. "I think he's using magic."

"There's nothing in the rules that forbids a little sleight of hand! Come and have a go, Sam. Did you find anything else?"

"Yeah, some milk powder." She took over the handles of the game from her dad and locked eyes with Rich. "Show me how we do this then Rich."

"It's pretty simple. You turn the handles to make the – what—?"

Sam grinned smugly. She had knocked the ball into his goal while he was explaining the game. "Sorry, couldn't resist!"

They laughed.

"Nip of scotch, Sam?" asked Marvin. Suddenly there was full bottle of single malt in his hand.

"Scotch? Where did that come from?" she asked.

"Do you want the magical answer or the real answer?"

"Magical!" said Rich.

"The truth," said Sam.

"My case," he said. "I popped it in on a whim. Glad I did now."

Sam smiled. It was a cheering thought. "Hey Rich, how far have your scientists got with their work?" she asked.

"Hmmm?"

"Recreating Ice Age creatures."

"They tell me they're most of the way there with the current samples, apparently they extracted some viable material."

"Cool!" said Sam. Her mind was considering something and she hated herself for even entertaining the thought. "So it's fairly fresh then? The mammoth?"

"Oh yeah! Honestly, it's amazing how well-preserved it is. But it's barely fifteen thousand years old."

"Must be rare? Irreplaceable even?" Sam asked.

"Not irreplaceable, you'd be surprised," said Rich. "Mammoth flesh is found fairly regularly in deep ice. Now, can we play a sensible game this time, where you let me get ready?"

"Will you be ready at the count of three? Three!" Sam whizzed another ball into Rich's goal. "Two nil!"

They played some more and Sam retired victorious after a few short minutes.

"You take over dad, I'll be back soon," she said. "Just need to do a bit of Christmas dinner prep."

69

At nightfall the Odinson mead hall was full, and everybody was talking excitedly as food and drink was circulated. Torsten had given Ragnar a massive drinking horn worked with shiny filigree as a Yule gift. Hilde wasn't sure where her cousin could have possibly got it from – the Odinsons bought a lot of their Viking amulets and ornaments from a pagan shop in Lincoln run by a guy who called himself Runesplicer (but whose real name was Nigel). Wherever Torsten had got such a lovely horn from it certainly made their farfar happy. The thing could hold a whole litre of mead and Ragnar demonstrated that to the family repeatedly.

Hilde watched with mild disapproval as crumbs were strewn and drink was spilt on the longship's woodwork. It would doubtless see a good deal of mess during its service, but it seemed somehow disrespectful to soil it before its launch. However, she soon realised there were worse things than food that could be spilt on the floor.

The petting corner was a new feature in the Odinson's yule, invented about thirty minutes earlier, and was proving very popular with the children. A belligerent goat was the centrepiece, having just arrived courtesy of Gunnolf and Hermod. Hilde had initially assumed they had stolen it, but was beginning to suspect someone had given it to them, just to be rid of it. It ran at the children, butting them violently and bleating loudly. The kids loved it and kept going back for more, taking scraps of food for the goat to eat. It had just vomited copiously onto the floor, and Hilde suspected she'd be finding nuggets of goat poop for weeks.

Ragnar stood and raised an arm to get everyone's attention. "We will raise a toast to Odin!"

There were hearty shouts of agreement from around the hall, and mead was sloshed into goblets.

"But first we must prepare the sacrifice, as demanded by tradition!" Ragnar shouted.

Hilde shifted in her seat.

Ragnar stalked over to the prow of the boat which bore a carved dragon's head. His position elevated him above the rest of the crowd. "We have always spilled the blood of a sacrifice to honour the Yule father, and this year will be no different!"

He bent down and picked up a huge sword. Hilde gasped.

"Who best to perform this act of ritual slaughter than the youngest people amongst us?" he shouted. "Come forward if you're under twelve and you want to honour Odin."

Some of the children headed straight up. A few others had to be shoved by their parents. Moments later a group of eight children stood with Ragnar. He held the sword aloft and swiped it at a rope that was slung across the ceiling, severing it.

"Behold the sacrifice!" he yelled as a huge piñata in the shape of a donkey swung down. "Children, take up your weapons!"

He indicated a row of little sticks and the children each picked one up.

"Odin! Odin!" Ragnar began the chant and the entire hall joined in. Ragnar gave the signal to the children and they attacked the piñata with their sticks, giving squeals of delight as sweets and presents dropped out of its belly. They carried on going until the cardboard donkey figure was smashed and distorted, then Ragnar turned the children to the crowd.

"Tek a bow, that was a fine job."

There was much cheering and clapping. Hilde doubted any heard Ragnar say to his wife among the hubbub, "But next year we're having a piñata of Jörmungandr the world serpent or we're going back to goat."

70

Sam got up early on Christmas day.

It hardly felt Christmassy at this point. There was no stocking hanging at the end of her bunk bed. There was no rushing to the window to see if, hope against hope, there was any snow. There were no windows in the accommodation block for one thing. And definitely no snow. There was no tree festooned with decorations. The only festooning in sight was the entirely unsuitable clothes she had brought with her, hanging on the metal clothes hooks on the wall.

She hadn't slept well in this strange environment: it vibrated with the violence of the wind and the sea. They had eaten ramen noodles the previous evening, followed by Sam's best attempt at rice pudding, but it was a joyless sludge as there was no sugar to sweeten it.

She looked through her clothes and decided to wear yesterday's jeans and jumper. It wasn't a festive outfit, but it was practical. She wandered out of her room to find she was the only one up.

She wished she could bring a little Christmas spirit to the place. If Delia was here she would have whipped up a Christmas tree out of an old mop by now. Sam wandered into the room with the lockers. She shuffled through the well-thumbed porn magazines ("Oiled Up Babes! Tina wants to work in YOUR hard hat area!") She could make some crackers, maybe? Just the idea of porno crackers made her smile. She dropped the magazine onto the table, not all that sure how she would go about it.

"Morning sweetheart," her dad said as he shuffled into the dining room. "We haven't got any tea or coffee, have we?"

"No. I can do you a cup of warm milk if you want?" she said.

"Sounds lovely. Merry Christmas!"

She kissed his cheek.

The man was wearing slippers – actual comfy tartan slippers – which either meant he'd found them here or had wasted valuable packing space bringing them. Sam didn't know if she felt disgust or jealousy.

"I thought we should make some crackers." She indicated the porn magazines.

"Interesting idea," said Marvin. "I'll take care of it while you whip up some warm milk. Would I be correct in thinking we might be having rice pudding for breakfast?"

"Excellent choice," said Sam.

She moved into the galley kitchen and got busy with the milk powder while Marvin started cutting up the porn magazine.

"Ah, morning, Rich," she heard him say. "Happy Christmas! Tell me, which is more festive out of these two pictures?"

It went very quiet for several long moments. Sam was on the brink of going to see what was the matter, then Rich walked into the kitchen.

"Your dad has some strange hobbies," he said.

"He's trying to make us feel a bit more Christmassy," said Sam.

"Lovely. Well, a happy Christmas to you."

"Cup of warm milk followed by rice pudding?" said Sam.

"Sounds good," said Rich. "I've been phoning around again. I can't believe nobody will come out to us. I've offered some pretty tempting fees, but nobody's budging."

"You don't want someone putting themselves at risk," said Sam. "We can wait it out."

"I know, I know. I just can't bear that I promised you and your dad a special Christmas, yet it's going to be worse than staying at home and eating beans on toast. A lot worse."

"It won't be that bad," said Sam. "I saw *The Great Escape* and *The Magnificent Seven* in that pile of DVDs. It will be just like a normal Christmas."

"No queen's speech though."

"How about I do an alternative one?" said Sam. "I'll be queen of – what's this platform called again?"

"It's known as *Valhalla*," said Rich. "All the platforms round here have 'V' names. *Viking, Vampire...*"

"Vaginormous," said Marvin from the dining room.

Sam peered through the doorway.

"Sorry," he said, holding up a magazine. "I was just reading."

"I'll be queen of Valhalla and I will make my speech at three o'clock."

"Cool! Just after lun— Ah. Yes. What are we doing for lunch...?"

"I'll sort something," said Sam with a confident smile. "Seriously, don't fret."

Rich smiled. "You're brilliant, did you know that?"

"Yes, I did."

"It doesn't matter if we have rice pudding three times a day until we get off here, I'm happy I'm spending time with you."

Sam didn't like to break it to him that the rice was nearly gone. Or that the feeling wasn't wholly mutual.

"Shall we exchange presents?" Rich asked.

"What? It's morning!" said Sam. "I thought posh people all waited until the afternoon?"

Rich gave her a pained look. "I might have lots of money, but I would never call myself posh," he said. "Let's do presents after breakfast."

They all ate the thin, rice-based gruel and pretended to enjoy it. Sam felt her face starting to ache, as she strained to stop it pulling into a rice-hating rictus.

"Right!" said Rich brightly. "I'll pop out and get the pressies."

They all got up to retrieve their gifts from their rooms and gathered in the community room. They each took a seat and exchanged packages. All three of them had brought neatly wrapped parcels. Marvin's were done with the precision and care of a manually dextrous performer. Rich's were clearly the work of an expert butler. If anything, Sam's thoroughly competent wrapping was the poorest of the lot.

"Marvin, you go first," urged Rich.

Marvin unwrapped his first package. He held up socks, a sweater and a book by Dynamo, the magician.

"Thanks darling," he said to Sam. "Never met this chap, but he seems like an interesting character. It's all about stamping your own personality onto the act, as I used to say to Ray Allen, back in the day."

"You should write your own book one of the days, dad." Sam wasn't sure how much money could be made from books, but another income stream couldn't hurt Marvin's financial problems. He clearly had a wealth of stories to share – if only he could be encouraged to share them in a coherent and linear format.

"Oh the tales I could tell!" said Marvin. "But my lips are very much sealed. It wouldn't be right to gossip about my old friends and colleagues."

Sam didn't like to disagree. Marvin gossiped about his old showbiz contacts every time he opened his mouth. Perhaps he kept quiet about the really juicy stuff? She would ask him at some point.

"This one's from you, Rich," said Marvin with a nod, pulling ribbon off something that had clearly been professionally wrapped. "Good lord, it's a bottle of eighteen year old Laphroaig. How utterly fantastic! Thank you."

Sam watched Marvin glance between the bottle and the clock on the wall. "It's Christmas day, dad. It's definitely not too early for scotch."

He beamed at her. "You opening your presents next?"

Sam looked down at the parcels on her lap. Two were immaculately presented in a tasteful low-key paper, embellished with some artfully-tied raffia. The other was wrapped in paper featuring kittens on a tartan background, and was held together with tiny and precisely placed squares of sellotape. The kitten wrapping paper was a family joke: there was a roll of it in Marvin's loft so large it had been in use for as long as she could remember.

"Tell Rich the story about this wrapping paper," she said, holding it up.

"I was in the local Woolworths store," began Marvin. "This was back in the seventies, or early eighties. I was recognised, of course. It happened a lot back then. I worked up a bit of a routine with the pick 'n' mix, and before I knew it I'd drawn in quite a crowd. They had record sales, would you believe? Ran out of chocolate coins after I showed everyone how to roll them across their knuckles. Anyway, the store manager wanted to give me something in return. I told them I just needed some wrapping paper, so they gave me the roll from the gift wrapping station. It was almost too heavy to carry, and it's still going strong."

Rich laughed. "I love your stories, Marvin."

Sam opened the present. There was a box of chocolate-covered marzipan, and a long-sleeved t-shirt with a cheerful teddy bear motif.

"Nice! Thanks Dad, we've got something else to eat!" Sam's mouth watered at the idea of the sweet snacks.

"The t-shirt is a thermal fabric, for when you're out and about with work," said Marvin.

Sam smiled, Marvin worried about the small things, which made her feel loved and unexpectedly Christmassy.

"This is from Rich. The wrapping is so nice, I'm not sure if I want to open it," she said.

She unwrapped the flat one, and pulled out a box. It contained a silk scarf. She held it up. It was richly coloured and featured a design like an ornate compass. The centre of the scarf had text surrounding a circle, and Sam turned it to read the words *Jeanne D'Arc*. "Joan of Arc? I never realised she had her own range of merch," said Sam with a smile.

"I think of you as Skegness's answer to Joan of Arc," said Rich. "Although your battles are possibly more subtle."

Sam didn't quite know what to make of that. She suspected the scarf was probably eye-wateringly expensive, but Rich was jabbing a finger towards the second package. She opened it to discover a box containing three bottles of wine.

"Oh, how wonderful," she said.

"It's English wine," said Rich.

"Right now, I'm just focusing on the fact it's wine!" said Sam gleefully.

"I'll open mine," said Rich. He picked up an oddly-shaped parcel and pointed at the tartan kittens. "I too have some of the heritage wrapping paper. It's a gift experience all by itself." He ripped it open to reveal a piggy bank, with a smiling face and a cheeky wink. Rich passed it from hand to hand, examining it. "It's gorgeous, Marvin."

"I thought it might be fun for you to collect up some coins," said Marvin. "Maybe you don't see them much anymore, in the cashless billionaires' world. Sometimes we need a touchstone, to keep us grounded."

"That's profound, truly profound," said Rich with a nod.

"Delia came up with the idea," said Marvin.

"I knew I'd seen that pig somewhere before," said Sam. "It was in Delia's shop. Damn, that woman can work up a story to sell anything!"

They all laughed, and Rich placed the pig on the table. "All donations gratefully received."

He opened the last gift, and pulled out the shirt Sam had bought off the internet, whilst in a playful mood (definitely not drunk).

"Is that ... is that Nicholas Cage?" he asked.

Sam nodded.

"Oh. My. God. I had no idea I needed this in my life, but it's amazing. I love how it's a proper shirt as well. I can wear it for business meetings."

Sam couldn't be totally sure, but she thought he was sincere in his appreciation of the peculiar gift.

"Well, I plan to dress up in my new shirt," said Rich. "Maybe we should re-convene in a few minutes and work through some of the entertainment options?"

Sam put her new scarf around her neck, tying it in the cowboy bandana style because it was Christmas. She went to find a corkscrew. She paused outside the lab before going inside. She had left the mammoth meat out of the freezer last night, in a metal sink. By doing so she had committed to a course of action that she did not want to acknowledge. Not yet. It sat, defrosted, in a puddle of mammoth blood. She picked it up and sniffed deeply. It had a rich gamey scent, but didn't smell rotten. She carried it through to the kitchen, weighing it in her hands. She reckoned it was about three kilos. Would she cook it like beef? It seemed like the closest possibility, until she considered the idea of eating it rare. That was a terrible idea. Maybe it would be better to treat it more like pork? It would need something like three hours' worth of cooking. She would start it now, on the basis that she was much more likely to back away from the idea if she thought about it too hard. It was just a joint. Just a joint.

She ploughed ahead, on autopilot, forcing herself to think about Joan of Arc and Nicholas Cage rather than what she was actually doing. Who would win in a fight? She lit the oven and searched through the cupboards for a roasting tin. Joan of Arc would bring military prowess, but could she beat up a man who was physically much bigger than her?

"Which do you prefer, Sam, draughts or Cluedo?"

Her dad's voice from the kitchen doorway made her spin guiltily, almost knocking the mammoth joint onto the floor. She stood in front of it, so it was hidden from his view.

"Either will be fine by me," she said. "I'll be along in a minute, just looking at what we might have for lunch."

She checked her dad had gone and put the joint into the oven. She'd defrosted it now, so it was of no use to the scientists. She might as well cook it. As she slammed the oven door closed, she was flushed with a sense of mild shock at what she'd done. She found a corkscrew and opened a bottle of wine, taking a hefty swig straight from the bottle. It was beginning to feel a lot like Christmas.

71

In Otterside, Christmas was a varied and mildly chaotic sequence of celebrations. Yes, there was a single large tree in the re-opened south lounge. Yes, there were sittings in the one on-site restaurant at noon and two for Christmas dinner. But beyond that there were as many celebrations as there were residents.

Strawb had tried to corral a number into a dawn game of crazy golf, although it had to be abandoned when the wild winds stole the first ball struck out of doors. There were carols in the north lounge. Friends and neighbours exchanged presents. Many wore their finest clothes for the day. Bernard wore a festive dressing gown and not much else. Party games started early. For many, the drinking started even earlier. There were arguments in the lounge over whether *It's A Wonderful Life* or *Love, Actually* was more appropriate Christmas Day viewing. Otterside was filled with noise and life.

As Polly took her seat in the restaurant for dinner, a thought struck her. "Huh."

"What?" said Strawb.

She allowed the puzzlement to show on her face. "I've just realised something. I'm happy."

"Does that come as a surprise?" said Strawb, waiting for her to sit before he took the seat opposite.

"Surprisingly, it does."

"Today of all days," he said, pretending to be mystified.

Polly interrogated her mental state while others took their seats. There was the usual kerfuffle over whose cutlery was whose, which cracker belonged to which place setting, and the important business of pouring the wine.

She was happy. Despite the fact she was now a murderer, despite the fact her nearest family had utterly abandoned her at this festive time. No, she told herself. *Because* she was now a murderer and *because* her family had abandoned her. Killing James Huntley had excited her, positively invigorated her. It was possibly the single greatest achievement of her seventy-odd years. It had been technically difficult, had required courage and improvisation, and she had made the world a moderately better place by removing James Huntley from it. She had enjoyed killing him and it had made her feel good about herself.

On top of that, here she was, among people who liked her, approved of her, and having a good time without the family she notionally ought to be with right now. Fuck Erin and fuck Cesar. Yes, it would have been nice to have Jack and Iris in her life, but they couldn't miss what they hadn't known. Mad Aunt Polly would just be a vague family story they would share long after she was gone. Right now, Polly was having the best of times with Margaret, Alison, Janine, Jacob, Bernard and Strawb.

She reached across the table and squeezed his hand. Strawb cracked a smile and tilted his hat back on his head like he was a fifties crooner. Strawb didn't know it yet, but Polly had decided she would be dragging that man into her bed one of these nights. Even if 'Little Strawb' had gone into permanent hibernation, they'd have fun trying to wake him.

Strawb squeezed her hand back and raised his wineglass. "Here's a merry facking Christmas to us all!" he toasted the long table. "Gawd bless us, every one!"

There were toasts and cheers.

"Straight out of Dickens," said Margaret softly.

"He's a regular Tiny facking Tim," said Polly.

Strawb laughed. "Are you mocking my accent, darling?"

"I'm happy to mock anything about you," she replied. "What have you got?"

"Sprouts," he said, passing the bowl down.

Bernard heaped sprouts high on his plate as though he was planning to compete with the howling winds presently vibrating the windows. Sprouts were followed by glazed carrots, peas, broccoli, roasted parsnips, potatoes (two kinds, of course), pigs in blankets, stuffing balls, sliced turkey, Yorkshire puddings, gravy, bread sauce and cranberry sauce.

"I'm going to explode if I eat all this," Polly said.

"You wouldn't actually explode if you overeat," said Jacob. "You could rupture your stomach, or even theoretically tear your oesophagus. But you wouldn't actually explode."

Strawb rolled his eyes. "You should make a note of that

for a future project, Jakey boy," he said and pointed at Jacob's notebook.

"Actually, speaking of explosions..." Bernard mumbled. He pulled a small cylindrical package from his dressing gown pocket and put it on the table.

"Or," suggested Margaret with a quiet authority that drew everyone's attention, "we could all just eat sensibly."

Polly shook her head, smiling. "Even though I might regret it later, I want to enjoy every last bite of this. I don't think I've ever seen a Christmas dinner quite like it."

72

"We're laying the table!" called Rich. "How long's lunch going to be?"

Sam went to the kitchen and opened the oven. "Nearly done," she called. She inhaled deeply. It was an undeniable fact that roasting meat smelled good, whatever it was. She looked around, hoping to be inspired for accompaniments.

"Come on Rich, I need your help with these crackers," called Marvin. "I can't decide on how much pornography is inappropriate for Christmas lunch."

Soon enough, Sam wheeled a serving trolley into the social area. She passed plates to Rich and Marvin and placed three covered tureens on the table.

"Here we have some mushroom served *a la crème*," she said, indicating the mushroom soup. "And here we have Valhalla pudding. Don't ask."

She had mixed some ground-up rice with milk powder,

water and meat juices, in the hope she might create something like a Yorkshire pudding. What she had made were tough, beige discs, but she was prepared to serve them up, given there was no alternative.

"And the *pièce de résistance*, ta-da!" She unveiled the meat, being careful to avoid naming it. She lifted it out and cut some slices, all the while talking, in the hope nobody would ask what it was. "Who's hungry then? Let's tuck in before it gets cold. A toast to those who can't be with us today, perhaps? Would you fill our glasses, Rich?"

Rich filled the glasses. While Sam distributed slices of meat he stood with his glass raised.

"First of all, let's toast the chef, who has created a minor miracle here with so little material. Well done Sam!"

Sam lifted her glass in response and they all chinked a toast.

"So where did you find—?"

"Let's not forget poor Peninsula, who must be frantic with worry about you!" said Sam hurriedly.

They toasted Peninsula.

"And Delia too!" said Marvin. "She might have created crackers without quite so many breasts."

"Yes, talk us through these crackers," said Sam, delighted to move the conversation away from the meat.

"Well, there's not much to tell," said Marvin. "We should pull them, and shout 'bang' as they obviously won't do that on their own. There is no gift contained within, but there might be a hat."

"Cool!" said Sam brightly. "And they each have their own,

er, character too. I have Melissa, who's clearly quite the athlete. Who do you have Rich?"

"Mine is called Cindy-Lee," he said. "She loves music and long walks in the country."

"How do you know?" Sam asked.

"I can tell by looking."

"What about you Dad?"

"The young lady on my cracker is Annabelle. She reminds me of someone from the seventies with long hair. It's on the tip of my tongue." Marvin mimed luxurious long hair with his hands.

"Rula Lenska?" Sam tried.

"No. Paul Nicholas, that's who I was thinking of."

Sam had no response to that so she held out her cracker to Rich. They pulled and shouted 'bang' and Sam picked her hat out of the paper while Marvin and Rich pulled their crackers.

"Lovely hat!" she said, as she perched the folded paper on her head. "Tuck in everyone!"

For some reason, she didn't want to be the first to try the meat. Was it cowardice? Probably. It was also something else, something she couldn't quite identify. Something to do with the honour of being the first to sample meat that was thousands of years old. Rich had paid for the privilege, so maybe he should have the bragging rights, if there was such a thing. She nibbled on the brittle edges of a Valhalla pudding, pretending to savour it, then took a hefty swig of wine.

"Where did you find the meat, Sam?" asked Rich.

She froze. It was a direct question; one she couldn't easily ignore or deflect. Now she had to decide whether a bare-faced lie was in order. Or a semi-truth. Yes, semi-truth was surely the way to go.

"I checked some other freezers and found this joint. Can you believe how lucky that was? We owe someone big time. One of your lab staff, probably." She grinned brightly. Too brightly. She pointed at Marvin's plate. "The mushroom *a la crème* isn't bad, is it?"

Marvin made a lip-smacking noise in agreement as he tried it. It was a teeny bit panto, but Sam loved her dad for supporting her efforts. She glanced across at Rich. He was turning over a slice of meat with his knife and fork. She pretended not to notice and ate some more mushroom.

"Sam, is this the mammoth?" Rich asked.

Well, at least it was finally out there. "Is it the mammoth? Yes. Yes, it is," she said.

Rich nodded at her, his face inscrutable. "Huh." There was a long pause while they all considered their plates.

Finally Marvin cut off a piece and held it up to his face, peering and sniffing lightly. He popped it into his mouth and chewed.

"Well it's not bad," he said. He cut off another piece.

Rich followed suit. Sam did the same. They all chewed thoughtfully.

"What do you think it tastes like?" asked Marvin. "I'm put in mind of the time that Faith Brown overcooked something like emu steaks. Or it might have been gammon."

"I have no idea," said Sam. "It's like weird beef, or something."

"More gamey than I normally like," said Rich. "Not

unlike reindeer. To be honest, I think we should all be grateful that Sam's resourcefulness has provided us with this meal." He chuckled. "Maybe this was what Christmas dinner was like during the stone age."

"I don't think they had Christmas dinner in the stone age," suggested Marvin.

"Why not? All the tribe, gathered round a big chunk of roast mammoth, stone age roasties and stone age veg."

"I don't think they had Christmas day at all."

Rich frowned, then nodded. "No calendars. Wouldn't have known what day it was. I'm sure they'd have done their best. It's a bloody good meal anyway, Sam."

"Thank you, Rich," said Sam, with a surge of warmth. It felt as if the typical British Christmas was being played out here, as it no doubt was throughout the rest of the country. Everyone had different expectations of the day and was probably living through a series of mild disappointments. Social pressure forced them all to interact as cheerfully as they knew how, at least until someone broke ranks and either stormed out or pretended to fall asleep.

"When do we get to hear your speech, Sam?" asked Marvin.

"Oh, yeah." She'd put that from her mind, and had failed to prepare something uplifting or amusing. She thought for a moment. "As temporary queen of Valhalla gas platform—"

"It's a post for life, I reckon," said Rich.

"Fine, as your ruler until death, I would like to start by celebrating our pioneering North Sea Christmas. Let us raise a glass to a Christmas that will never fail to provide future anecdotes and cautionary tales."

They all solemnly raised a toast.

"The year ahead promises to be a startling one for Valhalla," continued Sam. "I do hope we haven't set back the programme for the introduction of the woolly mammoth by eating the sample, but it won't be long before Doggerland is restored, and Rich can introduce the world to a long lost ecosystem."

"With the addition of a luxury hotel and casino," said Rich.

"I suppose modern sensibilities will forbid the use of hostesses in animal skin bikinis?" Marvin asked, turning to Rich with sudden interest. "Raquel Welch carried off the look quite well in that film about cave men, as I recall. Lovely girl, I met her once at the Birmingham Alexandra."

"No dad," said Sam firmly. "Now I wanted to wish us all a very merry Christmas and a safe return to the mainland when the storm dies down. In the meantime, we will return to the board game tournament this afternoon. May the odds be ever in your favour!"

"It's not about the odds, it's about the skills," said Marvin with a wink. "The most masterful players of any game are the ones who make it look as though someone else is in control."

"You might very well be right there, dad," said Sam.

It was true in life as well. There were people who rushed around, busily messing with the everyday detail, when unseen players were engaged at a higher level.

73

Turkey and all the trimmings had been eaten, followed by extra trimmings, Christmas pudding with brandy sauce, an unexpected cheese course and several more glasses of wine. Crackers had been pulled, paper crowns put on, and more than a couple of belts loosened to ease the indigestion (or a dressing gown cord in Bernard's case).

Polly groaned and plucked a crumb of dark pudding from her cardigan.

"Eaten too much?" said Margaret, who seemed to have only picked at her food like a fussy bird, but who had an empty plate nonetheless.

"I regret nothing," Polly said.

"Life's for living," nodded Strawb. "That said, it might be time to fall asleep in front of the Queen's Speech."

Jacob tapped his watch. "I think we've missed the Queen's Speech."

"We can watch it on catch-up."

"And then sleep through it," said Polly.

"And then sleep through it," agreed Strawb.

"Before we do..." said Bernard. He looked left and right along the long table. Several diners had already excused themselves and most of the others were engaged in private conversations. Apart from the three social committee members and Polly there was no one within earshot of Bernard. He pushed the narrow package he had put on the table earlier over to Polly.

Polly looked along the table just as Bernard had done. "Is this a secret present?" she asked.

He nodded.

"It's the wrong shape to be an engagement ring."

"Open it."

She peeled open the neatly sealed ends and opened it up. "A used toilet roll! How thoughtful!"

Bernard tutted. "Within."

She teased out the plastic and wire thing within the tube. It looked a bit like a TV remote, or a car component. One of those weird conjunctions of black plastic and LEDs that seemed to lurk behind dashboards these days. There were two lights on it and a toggle switch. Neither of the lights were lit.

"Careful with the switch for now," he said.

"What is it?"

Bernard leaned across Margaret, an act she clearly didn't appreciate, and tapped the lights. "That one comes on if your niece's e-cigarette is turned on and within range of this controller."

"My ... my niece?" She remembered him coming to her a door with e-cig pictures. "Is this some sort of tracking device?"

"This light comes on if she is sucking on it and the heating plate is activated. So when she's got it in her mouth."

"I don't quite follow..."

He tapped the switch. "And this detonates the device inside it."

Polly sat back, drawing the control device out of Bernard's reach. She stared at it for some time. "You put a bomb in my niece's e-cig."

"It's a tiny device. Grams of explosive and a one cent euro coin that will deform into a projectile. It will fire up the barrel and into the mouth, sort of like a dum-dum bullet. Probably quite a powerful splatter effect. The controller, twenty-seven megahertz, kind of neat, came out of a garage door controller. Real small and—"

Polly pushed herself away and stood, the chair scraping on the floor. She could feel nausea welling rapidly inside her along with the prospect of chucking up the wine, the cheese, the pudding, the trimmings and the turkey.

"Enough, Bernard," said Margaret.

Polly blinked and stared from each of them to the next. Bernard, Margaret, Jacob, Strawb.

"Strawb...?"

"It's your decision, darling," he said.

"You knew about this?"

"I was aware of the plans. We help each other out. We look after one another."

She felt light-headed: the combination of shock and too

much wine. "You think I want to kill my niece?" she whispered.

"You don't have to do it yourself," said Bernard, totally failing to understand her.

"I..." She reached out to the wall for support. Strawb stood to take her arm. She violently shrugged him away. "She has made me so miserable. She has cheated me. I think."

"She has," said Margaret.

"She's shut me out and shut me off and..." She stared at the remote in her hand, fully aware that she had slipped into a 'Is this a dagger I see before me?' piece of over-acting. "But kill her? I have a grand-niece and a grand-nephew. Children."

"Who would be better off without her," said Jacob.

"Have you seen their dad?" Polly scoffed. "A pathetic incompetent."

"At least he actually loves them," said Strawb.

Polly shook her head, not because she disagreed, but because there was an unpleasantly attractive note of truth in that.

The nausea and horror and the stares were too much. "You evil murdering fucks," she gasped and fled from the room as fast as her legs would carry her.

74

The suggestion they go for an afternoon walk to blow away the cobwebs and work off their lunch had been derailed almost instantly. The three of them had crowded round one of the external doors and looked through the window. Storm Wendy's gale force winds shrieked and whistled through the platform structure. Wordlessly, they agreed a walk around Valhalla would probably blow more than the cobwebs away, and they'd have to work off their dinner in other ways.

A games tournament was decided upon.

"Checkers!" said Rich as Marvin pulled out the box.

"Draughts, please," said Marvin.

"Whatever. Same difference. I haven't played this since I was a kid. Pretty sure it's like riding a bike though. It will all come back to me."

"Don't be so sure," said Marvin. "A game like draughts favours the stage craft of the magician. Planning moves in advance, with a little misdirection thrown in for good measure. You don't see me coming for you because I'm always one step removed from the kill." Marvin made an exaggerated pouncing movement with his hands, then set up the board, inviting Rich to be his opponent.

Sam sashayed across the social room with the wine and three tumblers. "Who's for a drink while we play?" she asked.

A few minutes later, as predicted, Marvin executed a killer move, jumping over three of Rich's playing pieces to capture them. He swirled his wine in his tumbler and gave Rich a cool look, as if he'd just beaten a supercomputer at chess, and not a mildly sozzled millionaire at draughts.

"Beginner's luck," said Rich, good-naturedly.

"No, not that," said Marvin. "Possibly the exact opposite."

"Best of three then."

While the draughts battle raged. Sam opened the Cluedo box. Sadly a good proportion of the cards were missing, along with a number of the counters and murder weapon props. That was disappointing but not a disaster. There were three character cards and most of the weapons still. If she could improvise with counters and make her own cards.

Her eyes alighted on the selection of porn magazines that had been cannibalised for cracker material. She picked up a copy of *Honkers* ("Chelsea is more than a handful!") and flicked through. She just needed some pictures for suitable suspects and implements of murder.

As Sam set to work with scissors, she listened to the men play. Rich's growls and groans were ample commentary on how well he was doing in his attempt to defeat Marvin 'King Me!' Applewhite. In the quiet isolation, she felt a faint but sustained Christmassy sense of time pleasantly spent among loved ones.

"Maybe we should watch a film," said Sam once she'd finished her Cluedo creation. She walked over to the DVD collection and picked up a box. "Ah, we have *Die Hard*. A Christmas classic. Shall we start with this?"

"Fire it up," said Marvin. "I'll have this whippersnapper beat in a trice."

"I don't think so," said Rich. "I think I've got the measure of you this— Hey, you can't do that. That's ... that's..."

"King me," said Marvin.

The *Die Hard* DVD box was empty. "Oh, no *Die Hard*. So it's *The Great Escape* maybe..."

Sam found that box was empty too. She worked her way through all the boxes. They were all empty.

"Well, that's rubbish," she said, holding up two empty boxes.

Marvin grunted. "I remember when we had a DVD player at home, you'd just take a DVD out and put it in whatever box you had left over. *Lion King* in the *Little Mermaid* box. *Little Mermaid* in the *Cinderella* box."

"A bit of a Disney girl were you?" said Rich.

"Ah, she was also a fan of older films," said Marvin. "I seem to recall a fondness for Inspector Clouseau."

"Once I got over the disappointment that the Pink Panther never actually appeared in any of the films," she said.

They all flopped back into their chairs.

"No telly then, I guess," said Rich. "I'll get satellite put in at some point, but that doesn't help us now."

"Hang on. I do have something we could use," said Sam. "In terms of entertainment value, we might have to get creative, but let's have a look."

She went back to her room to fetch her laptop, then sought out the right cables on the side of the television so she could connect the two.

"Technically, this is your material anyway, Rich," she said.

"What is it?"

"A dozen body cameras and their recordings from the animal escape drill. So – let's play a game where I show a chunk of film and then stop it. I'll ask you questions and you have to guess what happens next. Yeah?"

They both nodded. Sam had already reviewed the footage, so she had a pretty good idea of how it flowed. The software package had spliced the various pieces together using the timestamps and it was an unexpectedly coherent narrative.

She clicked on the video player program and the TV came to life, showing a paused image of the rear lawns of Otterside retirement village.

"We start with the escape of a mammoth." She played a few seconds of the mammoth coming down the path. "You will see this mammoth is ably represented by a local am-dram player. Now my question to you is this: how many casualties will the mammoth cause before being captured?"

"Hmmmm," said Marvin, having found a notepad and pencil so he could look like he was being studious and professional. "Looks like a sturdy sort. I once did panto with Beefy Botham, did I tell you that? Ninety-three, Theatre

Royal in Bath. He has the same sort of build. I'm going to say eight."

"Well there's the thing, Marvin," said Rich. "I say a big target's easier to hit. I reckon it's going to be more like six."

"Well, let's watch the film then!" said Sam, aware she sounded like a game show host trying to ramp up the fun. She counted them down as the mammoth reached out and tapped people before being sedated. "What do you know? That was actually fourteen! Marvin's our winner for that round."

She paused the film. "Now for the next scenario, we have a wolf and a caribou. I'm going to introduce a multiple choice element to this round. You need to choose from answer one, two or three when I ask you how this scenario ends. Answer one: the wolf and the caribou are both tranquilised and caught by the zookeepers. Answer two: the wolf kills the caribou and is then captured by the zookeepers. Answer three: the wolf is neutralised by a member of the public, and the caribou is captured separately."

Rich nodded thoughtfully. Sam knew he had actually witnessed this part of the action, and however distracted he'd been by Peninsula's excellent picnic, he couldn't have missed the spectacular intrusion of the child. He was keeping up the pretence of ignorance for Marvin. "I'm going to say answer one. What do you think Marvin?"

"I'd better go with answer two," said Marvin.

Sam played the film and enjoyed the expression on Marvin's face as the action played out and the girl with the teddy bear kicked the wolf between the legs.

"Well I never!" said Marvin.

"No points awarded for that round," said Sam. She played the film for a few more moments. "Now, you are both aware that things took a colourful turn at the end of the final scenario. The question you need to answer, because I'm not sure that either of you saw this part, is this: what happened to the zookeepers in this final scenario?"

They watched the film. Sam wasn't sure if it was the wine they'd all drunk, but they all laughed uncontrollably at the footage captured from the bison. There were snippets of audio that had escaped them all on the day, but which revealed the flustered panic of the bison as he turned this way and that as the sabre-toothed tiger chased him. There were *oohs* and *aahs* and (most memorably) several *oh shits* as the incensed tiger wrenched the Nerf tranquiliser gun from a zookeeper and shot down several would-be captors.

"Well, that's better than an *Only Fools and Horses* Christmas special," said Marvin, wiping tears of laughter. "Couldn't ask for better entertainment!"

The footage automatically cut between participants inside and out as the tiger and bison crashed through the skylight of the residents lounge. A blur of rapid cuts filled the screen.

"I swear I saw your face there," said Rich.

"Mine?" said Marvin.

Sam rewound and replayed it a frame at a time. In between a flash of white and a scene from outside, there was a split second shot, mostly a blur of sabre-tooth tiger fur, but in which Marvin and his temporary stage assistant simply stared as magic props and fragments of table flew up into the air.

"I don't even look surprised," said Marvin.

"Surprise comes later, when you actually work out what's going on," said Sam.

"That the doctor lady?" said Marvin, pointing to an out of focus face in the background. "It was her little girl who was assisting us. I think she thought she'd conjured the costumed characters. The mother wasn't impressed though."

"Dr Hackett," nodded Sam.

"She seemed a very tightly wound woman. Barely concealed rage. I've known stage performers like that. There was one I was doing the cruise ships with, back in the nineties. He wasn't happy with his room and got so het up that he threatened to throw the purser overboard."

"Who was that?" said Rich.

"My lips are sealed," said Marvin. "But let's just say he's no longer on this planet and he's not mourned."

"I bet we could guess."

"Who am I!" Marvin declared loudly.

"That's it," said Sam. "His mind's gone."

Marvin threw up his hands irascibly. "We play *Who Am I*. We'll get—" He grabbed his pencil and paper. "Each of us comes up with a name, a famous person and—"

"Twenty questions," said Rich. "Stick the names on each other's foreheads and ask yes-no questions."

"This requires more alcohol," said Sam and reached for a fresh bottle of wine.

Sam scribbled a name down for Marvin. Marvin passed one to Rich. Rich passed one to Sam which she licked and slapped on her forehead.

"Right," said Rich, taking a tumbler of wine from Sam.

"Am I someone who got so angry on a cruise ship that I threatened to throw the purser overboard?"

The name on Rich's forehead was *Nana Mouskouri*. Sam couldn't imagine the woman had it in her.

"Nope," said Marvin.

"But you said..." Rich's frown was almost enough to dislodge the paper on his brow.

"It was the inspiration for this game, but as I say, my lips are sealed."

Sam pointed at the name Rich had given her. "Am I a beautiful international celebrity?"

"No," said Rich.

"Oh, then that forestalls my follow up question – have you slept with her?"

"Hey, not fair," said Rich. "Marvin?"

Marvin thought deeply and waggled the name *Greta Thunberg* childishly. "Am I a man?"

"At last a sensible question," said Sam. "No."

"A lady of the female persuasion then? Am I a singer?"

"One question each," said Rich. "Now, let me think."

"We should instigate a drink-while-you-think rule," said Sam. Rich took that as a direct instruction.

Thirty minutes and a whole bottle of wine later none of them were any closer to guessing who they were.

"Right," said Sam, struggling to recall. "I'm a man. A real man, not fictional. I'm not a celebrity and I don't do sport and I'm famous because I've done something that's made me rich but that's not anything creative or to do with the internet. I'm definitely not Bill Gates or that Amazon guy." She shrugged. "Am I Russian?"

Marvin blew out his lips. "I can see it and even I don't know who you are."

"Oh, that's no use then," she said and impulsively ripped the paper off her head. "Jim Ratcliffe? Who's that?"

"Come on," said Rich. "Jim Ratcliffe. Chemicals and finance. He's a billionaire! Possibly the richest man in Britain."

"Not a clue," said Sam.

Rich huffed and in response tore his own off. "Nana who?"

"Mouskouri," said Marvin.

"That's a Greek dish, isn't it?"

"She certainly was," said Marvin with an uncharacteristic leer. "Possibly still is, although she must be eighty something now."

"If she's alive," said Sam.

"Oh, those Greeks," said Marvin with the self-assured wisdom that only drunks could summon. "All that olive oil and tomatoes and whatnot. Very long lived." He sniffed and pointed at the *Greta Thunberg* label on his head. "I'm female and Swedish and, apparently, some people don't like me. But I'm not Agnetha from ABBA?"

"No."

He mushed his lips. "And I'm not Ingrid Bergman or Greta Garbo." He saw the twitch on Rich's face. "I'm not Greta Garbo, but I'm like her? Another Greta?"

"Yes," said Sam.

"*Another* Greta? But not Greta Garbo?"

"You're like the most famous Greta in the world," said Sam.

He stared blankly, then took his name down. "Not a clue," he said frankly.

"The girl with pigtails trying to save the planet?" said Sam. "Sailing round the world, getting angry at the politicians? *That* Greta!"

Marvin shook his head. "Is this a TV series or something? You know I don't do Netflix."

Sam sighed and emptied the last of the bottle into the tumblers. "You know what our mistake was. We each came up with famous people who we knew but not ones that everyone should know."

"It's not my fault you're not up to date with business news," said Rich.

"We didn't have a chance, did we?"

She groaned as she picked herself up off the floor where she'd been sat. No windows in the rig meant no natural light, but something told her that it was well past nightfall. She blearily sought out a clock on a wall and saw that she was right. She could feel the room spinning slightly, but didn't think it had anything to do with Storm Wendy.

"I might have to go to bed," she said.

"With such palatial rooms, they're hard to resist," said Marvin.

Sam laughed, but it was forced. She was tired and had her fill of life on a tiny gas platform. "Rich, please tell me we're being picked up tomorrow."

"Depends on the weather report," he said. "But if Peninsula can get a chopper out to us, he will."

"He'd better," she said and wandered off in search of a bunkbed to call her own. She had plenty to pick from.

75

"Right!" declared Ragnar in a drunken shout that woke many of the Odinson folk who were bedded down for the night in the longship's hull. "'Tis time to launch this beauty!"

Hilde sat up and made an unhappy noise.

The Odinson Yule celebrations had been going on for a full day and two nights. There might have been some brief intervals on Christmas Day when people returned to their caravans to find fresh sustenance or make use of toilet facilities, but there was a storm howling outside. The community had spent the last thirty-plus hours feasting and carousing in the longship; it was now ankle-deep in party detritus and goat poop.

Hilde looked at her watch in the dim light of the burning lamps. "It's the middle of the night, farfar."

"And I feel a stirring in me that says Odin wants us to tek the ship to the beach to greet the dawn," said Ragnar.

Sigurd rolled over, looking a little green around the gills. "Something's stirring in me," he muttered, "and it ain't bloody Odin."

"I've gone blind," slurred Yngve.

"Tha bandana's slipped, tha daft apeth," said Sigurd, pushing the bandana back up his kin's forehead.

"Come on, come on!" shouted Ragnar, clapping his hands and kicking the boots of the drunk and dozy.

"The kiddies need their sleep, you fool," said his wife, comforting a grubby toddler who was not happy at being awoken.

"Aye, aye," nodded Ragnar astutely. "Womenfolk, get tha babbies to bed. This is not work for women and children."

Astrid snorted. Hilde stood up sharply.

"No one is taking this vessel anywhere unless it's under my strict instructions."

"Is tha denying my authority?" said Ragnar.

"Not at all, farfar," she said sweetly. "But I suspect you might need a little help removing that wall so we can get the longship out of here. Then across a caravan park, a road and a hundred metres of dunes before we actually get to the sea."

"Aye. Fair enough. Lads, tha's to listen to Hilde here, who is acting under my guidance. Now, get the kiddies out of here. *And can someone take away this flamin' goat that's trying to butt me shins!*"

While many of the young uns shuffled off towards their beds, certain they had the better part of the deal, Hilde supervised the moving of the longship. With the aid of the burliest and most sober of the family, she directed the removal of the eastern wall. There were many strong young

Vikings to do the heavy lifting, but she was the one who would stop the roof falling in by insisting upon dull but essential details, like the installation of roof props.

There were several dozen men ready to carry the vessel, but it was made from oak and it was tough work. Together, they eased the ship up and out into the compound.

Ragnar was doing none of the carrying. He stood alongside Hilde, wearing his ceremonial robes, which affirmed his position of authority. They were grand robes indeed, only a little spoiled by the mead stains around the bottom half, and the squished mince pie stuck to his elbow. He was ready to begin the celebrations that would accompany the launch of the longship. He knew it would be prudent to get the riskier parts of the job out of the way before mead was consumed, although Hilde guessed he would also insist several of the remaining barrels of mead be carried to the shore.

"We need to get this part into the saga," he said. "Where's Gunnolf? He's in charge of t' saga. What do you reckon sounds better, that the sky shone fair upon the warrior Vikings, or that stormy skies loomed over the upcoming raid?"

Hilde looked up to the sky, which was black, what with it being night and all.

"I reckon you can tell it however you like farfar," she said. "But pay attention everyone! We're coming up to the tricky part now. If we can get clear of the buildings without breaking anything, that would be wonderful."

"Leave it to me," said Ragnar. He addressed the Viking warriors who were carrying the ship, hefting the enormous wooden structure upon their shoulders, gripping the hull as Hilde had shown them. "There will be mead before launching. Mind, we must do this right. There is to be a steady procession behind me, so we can make sure Odin blesses our sacred raid upon Cleethorpes."

"Cleethorpes?" said one voice, hidden behind the ship.

"Yes. Cleethorpes."

"Why Cleethorpes? Skegness is nearer."

"Aye, but Cleethorpes town is full of them hoity-toity folks, and they deserve a good raiding."

"Do they have decent pubs in Cleethorpes?" asked another voice.

"They've got a miniature railway."

"Aye," said Ragnar, leaping upon the comment. "And Hilde needs some new engine parts. So we're gonna raid them and steal their miniature locomotive and—"

"They've got that new fish and chip place on the end of the pier," threw in another voice. This drew some oohs and aahs.

"Right! Right!" shouted Ragnar. "And we'll get us some fish and chips an' all. Now quit tha mithering and let's go."

The longship wobbled its way across the compound like a tipsy centipede and through the gap in the chain link fence separating the Odinson compound from the rest of the Elysian Fields caravan park.

76

Sam woke with a throbbing head and a mouth so foul-tasting she thought it would take a whole tube of toothpaste to put right. She sat up and looked for a glass of water that wasn't there. As she stood, she realised she was in that rare state of being hungover and still a little drunk.

Unimpressed with herself, she went in search of a bathroom and a drink. The hard floors were slightly tacky under her bare feet. The living quarters might have been very basic, but they were well-insulated. With the near-Arctic weather conditions just beyond the walls, she was perfectly toasty wandering about in just T-shirt and pants.

She somehow bypassed the bathrooms and found the kitchen first. Leftover mammoth roast and sloppy rice sat in tins on the cooker hob. She picked out a glass and poured herself some water. She gulped it down and poured herself another. The clock on the wall said it was eight in the morning.

"There'd better be a helicopter today," she muttered.

Stretching, working on her personal and unscientific belief that movement would work the alcohol (and hangover) from her system more quickly, Sam wandered through to the communal area. Marvin and Rich had left it pretty much as it had been all evening. The TV screen was on, still frozen on that clip of Marvin and Polly's faces. The draughts board was still out, cleared of all red pieces in a pitifully one-sided game. The Cluedo box was open. Had the two men tried to play it? She inspected the cards.

"Reverend Green in the ballroom with the butt plug," she nodded. "Thought as much."

She sipped water and contemplated her hangover. She wasn't sure how much she'd drunk. There had definitely been several bottles of wine, and some whisky as well. She didn't want to go back to bed – the bunks were serviceable but hardly welcoming – but she didn't particularly want to loiter here, either. She'd only end up tidying the place.

She should at least turn the video footage off. It was doing neither the TV nor the laptop any harm, but some perversely old-fashioned part of her felt that a frozen image was like a needle stuck in a groove: a thing held unhealthily paused, a car riding on the clutch.

As she bent to unplug the cables, she glanced at the image. The blur gave the people's faces a ghostly appearance. Fragments of flying debris scored lines across the image. She could see Marvin's wand, black and white, and a vaguely bird-like shape in silver.

Sam unpaused it.

One of the creatures groaned.

"Magic!" squealed the little girl in delight.

"Jesus facking hell!" shouted a man in the audience.

Sam wound the recording back ten seconds and watched it again. The crash. The smashed table. *"Magic!" "Jesus facking hell!"*. Sam re-ran it. Crash, smash – she paused it, then went through a frame at a time as the magic show flew apart. A teddy, a cloth, the wand, and that silver item. Two wing-like hoops joined together.

It was a pair of handcuffs. And Sam knew, with a concrete certainty that the facts didn't warrant, they would be the same handcuffs later found in the dead drink-driver's house.

They flew out of sight. Sam kept the video running, hoping to see more. Her only eyes inside the room were the tiger and bison bodycams. There was applause and confusion, a little shouting, even more confusion as residents were carefully moved out of the room across the glass-strewn floor. The tiger continued to moan and groan. It was interesting to see that the sabre-toothed tiger, played by a young and feisty female actor, seemed to get many more offers of assistance than the bison. On the poor unloved bison's camera, Sam saw Caribou Cesar run into the room. Sam paused, narrowed the feed down to those three inside cameras, and continued playing.

"I think I've bruised my coccyx," grunted the tiger.

"I could take a look for you," offered an unseen voice.

The Otterside manager, Chesney, trit-totted over the debris, calling *"Mr Marvellous"* in worried tones.

None of the three cameras were looking at where the handcuffs had gone.

Cesar was with his wife, his bodycam showing nothing but Dr Hackett's torso and the top of the little girl's head.

"That fool of a magician just told her we had moved house," Dr Hackett hissed.

"Told who?" said Cesar.

"Polly! She knows!"

Cesar twisted to look round the lounge, presumably in search of Polly Gilpin. He turned too fast for Sam to get any decent view of the people still in the room. It was all blobs and blurs. The tiger and the bison were making for the exit, a very happy older man providing the tiger with perhaps a little more physical support than necessary.

"If she starts asking questions about how much that house is worth—" Dr Hackett said, off-screen.

"How much is Aunt Polly's house worth?" said the little girl. There was a high-pitched grunt of pain, small and fleeting, maybe a hand sharply squeezed, or an arm roughly shook.

"The woman's an embarrassment," said the doctor and then tutted. *"You're an embarrassment."*

Cesar turned. Dr Hackett was dragging their daughter from the room. Cesar hurriedly followed.

Sam stopped the video and exhaled heavily, partly from what she'd just seen, but mostly from the hangover brewing in her head and her gut. She tried to think.

"The handcuffs at Otterside. That drink-driver dead." She blinked and frowned. She crossed back to the Cluedo board and shuffled three random counters together into a space.

"Alison Hinchliffe with the handcuffs in the dead guy's garage."

She looked at it and moved three more counter together.

"Janine with the electrical wire in Greg Mandyke's hot tub. Except..."

It didn't work. She persevered and moved three more.

"Bernard the liar with a wooden plank in Drumstick's turkey pen."

Greg Mandyke had thrown Janine Slater out of her house, but CCTV pretty much proved she couldn't have killed him. There was even Bernard, who hated Drumstick the murdered turkey, but *he* wasn't the one caught on camera sneaking around on the night of the crime. James Huntley was a drunk driver who'd killed Alison Duncliffe's daughter. What were the chances that her alibi was equally tight?

"Hang on..." Sam moved a piece. "Janine snuck out the night Drumstick was killed. And if Janine did Bernard's murder ... well, turkey-cide..."

She shuffled pieces. Was it as simple and as crazy as that? Three murders, three murderers. A three-way swap. No links between murderer and victim.

It might be right. It might actually be correct.

"Three murders," she said and then, gripped by a deeper suspicion, "That we know of."

She pushed herself away from the table, a little giddy (spilling drink over 'Double-D Desiree' who may or may not have committed murder in the billiards room with a candlestick) and hurried back to the bedrooms. On the fourth attempt she found Rich's room. He was in the top bunk, an arm dangling over the side as he slept.

"Hey, I need your satellite phone," she said.

He cleared his throat and opened bleary eyes. "Whut?"

"I need your help."

He blinked. "You coming up here? Not sure if there's much room."

"Your phone! Where is it? I need to call the police."

That woke him. "What's happened?"

"Phone."

He reached under his pillow and pulled out the satellite phone. She snatched it from him and started to dial 999, then stopped. It wasn't exactly that kind of emergency.

"Hang on," she said, went to her own room and found her own phone. It had no signal, but did have a contact number for Skegness police station. She keyed in the number on the satellite phone and heard it ring.

"I need to get through to Detective Constable Camara," she said to the operator.

"Your name please."

"Applewhite. Sam Applewhite. I need to speak to DC Camara. I have information regarding a crime."

"You wish to report a crime?"

"No. He's investigating a murder. Well, a death. But it's murder. I'm sure of it. All three of them."

"What murders would those be?"

"If you could put me through to DC Camara..."

"He's off duty at the moment—"

"You can't put me through?"

"If you'd like to give me some details. Murders, you said."

"Yes. Greg Mandyke, Huntley – the man they found in

the garage off Beresford Avenue – and Drumstick. Drumstick's a turkey."

"A turkey? That's been murdered?"

"That's not the headline, here," said Sam.

"Miss Applewhite, are you drunk?"

"Only a little. This is not a prank call. Can you tell DC Camara that Alison and Janine and Bernard – they're all at Otterside – tell him I think they did each other's murders."

"As in?"

"They swapped them. You know, like that Hitchcock film."

"Psycho?"

"Not *Psycho*. Can you just tell him?"

"And could I perhaps get your details? What number are you calling from?"

Sam stared at the phone and then put it back to her ear. "I don't know. I borrowed it. It's a satellite phone. I'm on a gas platform in Doggerland."

"Doggerland. And that's...?"

"In the sea. I'm out at sea."

"Right."

Sam could hear utter disbelief in the operator's tone. "Please. Just tell him. As soon as you can. I don't know if it's just them. There may be others."

There was a long pause. *"Of course,"* said the operator. *"Let me get some of those details down again."*

77

Odin might have wanted the ship to be on the beach to greet the dawn, but Odin clearly hadn't taken into consideration how long it would take two dozen men to get the longship from its shed to the shore. The dying blasts of the passing storm buffeted them to and fro as they moved. The ship pitched and yawed as though it was already at sea.

There had been casualties. A little light crushing as men got their bodies, hands and faces mashed between the ship and various caravans, trees and lampposts. The major non-human casualty was a poor Honda Civic they'd rested the ship on for a while so they could have a breather, and which now had a one foot deep indentation in its roof.

Thus it was that the longship and the Odinsons greeted the dawn while trying to navigate their way across the Seacroft road.

"Right!" bellowed Ragnar in the grey and uninspiring light of a December morn. "Not far to go!"

"You said that an hour ago!" someone shouted, in the safe knowledge that Ragnar could not see them behind the hulking ship.

"I'll have none of that treasonous talk!" Ragnar snapped. Then he frowned. "What's tha farsa doing up there?"

Hilde looked ahead towards the dunes. Sigurd was on a dune top, hands on his knees. To her eyes, it looked like he had either just thrown up or was preparing to. "I reckon he's trying to get a good view of the scene so he can immortalise it in the sagas."

"Aye, right you are," said Ragnar. "Come on, lads! Have at it! All aiming for the path!"

"Sign 'ere says this area is a nature reserve of special scientific interest," said Gunnolf, up front.

"Too bloody right," said Ragnar. "This vessel is a bloody scientific miracle."

"Be a miracle if we can get it to the beach in one piece," muttered a voice which Ragnar either didn't hear or pretended not to.

There was a defiant bleat. Hilde looked up to where the no-longer-sacrificial goat stood in a commanding position atop the carried ship.

"We should've killed that flamin' thing, I tell thee," said Ragnar with a rueful shake of his head.

78

Sam, Rich and Marvin weren't on the helipad to see the arrival of their lift home. The winds were still strong, and no one wanted to be blown off the platform into the sea in their moment of liberation. All three of them gathered together in the arrivals corridor with their luggage (much lighter now that all the booze had been drunk). They even managed an un-British cheer as they heard the helicopter come overhead and swing round to land.

"Let's go," said Rich. "Sam, lead the way. Marvin, you next."

Sam scurried along the covered walkway to the stairs leading up to the helipad. Many metres below, the waves swirled around the platform legs. Sam struggled to believe that no more than twice that distance down there was a prehistoric landscape of stone age settlements and animal remains waiting to be uncovered. A reclaimed Doggerland seemed even more of a fool's dream than when Rich had first mentioned it.

She was so focused on her feet and her balance, she almost collided with Rich's butler – coming down the stairs to meet them. Peninsula was not in his butlering clobber, but wearing a bright orange survival suit.

"If I may, miss," he said. He took both her suitcase and Marvin's. "Let's get you on board."

He jogged up to the pad and, with both hands free, Sam gladly followed. She ducked instinctively as they passed underneath the thrumming rotor blades. Once she was sure she had her dad close behind, Sam threw herself inside as though leaping aboard a life raft.

Once everyone was inside, with the doors shut and checked, the helicopter pilot peeled away with an assured speed that made Sam's stomach flip. She put on her seatbelt, ensured Marvin had his, then grabbed a set of headphones.

"*—can only repeat my most heartfelt apologies, sir,*" Peninsula was saying.

Rich laughed. "*Oh, think nothing of it. We coped admirably in adversity, didn't we, Sam?*"

Sam didn't have an answer.

"*We coped,*" agreed Marvin, adjusting his microphone.

"*We had quizzes and games,*" enthused Rich. "*And we had some rather sexy Christmas crackers. And we ate well.*"

"*We ate,*" agreed Marvin.

Peninsula lifted a blue pail hamper from the floor and opened one side. "*I thought you might appreciate some sandwiches for the journey home.*"

Marvin's hand was in and out like a striking cobra.

"*Roasted turkey sandwiches with honey crackling, cranberry chutney and pepper seasoning,*" said Peninsula.

The cabin comms channel was soon filled with the sound of chewing and grateful murmurs of culinary delight.

"*Oh, and Sam reckons she solved several murders,*" mumbled Rich around his second sandwich.

Peninsula's thin moustache twitched and he gave Sam an unreadable look.

"Several murders?" she said. "Maybe. There's something going on, and I think I have at least half of it right."

Rich made a complicated movement in the air. "*Everyone swapped their murder victims. Including the turkey.*"

"*Turkey, sir?*"

Sam looked through the cabin to the cockpit and the flat seascape beyond. "Mr Pilot, sir. How long until we're back in Skegness?"

"*Now that we don't have a winter storm bearing down on us, it's going to be a much quicker journey. We'll be at the airfield well before eleven.*"

"Thanks." She tapped Rich's foot with hers. "Did the police call you back on your satellite phone?" She checked her own phone to see if they had come back within the mobile signal range or any messages had helpfully popped up.

"Do you think you could land us near Otterside retirement village?" she asked the pilot.

"*You planning on arresting them yourself?*" said Marvin.

She shook her head. "I don't have all the pieces yet."

"*Your theory is bizarre but sound,*" he replied. "*Those men and women had some wrongs to right in their own lives — I'm not saying I'm condoning it — and they came up with a plan."*

"I'm not sure." Sam looked to the horizon again, willing it to come closer. "What was it you said about masterful players of games?"

He smiled. *"Was I drunk when I said it? No idea."*

79

The rest of the Odinson clan, the women, the children and the workshy who'd had a good few hours' sleep while the men hauled their ship to the shore, came back in dribs and drabs to line the rest of the route through the dunes and cheer them on. Hilde walked alongside Ragnar, making sure the pace was steady, monitoring the ship carefully as it made its slow progress towards the beach. As they came down the last of the dunes, Hilde was surprised to see an ice cream truck on the beach, selling cornets at this early hour.

"What the hell? It's Boxing day!" she said. She caught a look from her farfar. "I mean, as far as the Saxons are concerned it is. I'm surprised they turned up today."

"It's all part of mekking it an event they'll treasure," said Ragnar, tapping the side of his head.

Hilde understood. The ice cream truck was there by invitation. Indeed, all the little Odinsons were running up to get ice creams She scanned the horizon, wary of any other unexpected surprises. Sigrid was up in the dunes, capturing the scene on an easel, or at least pretending to, while quelling his rebellious innards. Ragnar was keen to have pictures to accompany the saga and appeared glad to see him so enthusiastic.

From the edge of the grassy dunes, they reached the flat part of the beach and set the longship carefully down. It sat heavily in the sand. Skegness town was a full mile to the north. The pier was just a smear of dark lines in the distance, the town almost entirely hidden behind dunes, the fenced off compound of the Skegness boating club, and the trees and concrete walls that fringed the children's boating lake. Out here, against the vast backdrop of the North Sea and the miles of sand that stretched away in both directions, the ship didn't look as enormous as it had done during construction. If anything, it looked small and fragile. Hilde knew the design was good and the construction sound. It was a good ship and she felt pride swell in her heart.

The Viking warriors all looked to Ragnar for further instruction. Hilde looked down the beach and saw Hermod approaching from the north in his red truck. He pulled up alongside. Hilde organised a group to remove the hoist from the flatbed of Hermod's truck so they could place it onto the longship.

"What's tha crane thing for?" asked an Odinson child as it licked a Mr Whippy with raspberry sauce.

"Farfar needs a hoist to bring our raiding treasure on board," said Hilde. "Woah! You! Stop!" She ran over to the burly oafs who were trying to shift the hoist from the flatbed to the ship hull. "I need to be sure we hold the ship good and steady while we bolt this into place. If it topples over it's going to hurt someone."

The goat in the boat bleated in agreement.

Hilde boarded the ship, and had her burly assistants line up the base of the hoist with the wooden platform she'd had built for it. She wasn't certain this was even slightly authentic for the period, but it was the best she'd been able to come up with for Ragnar's planned raid.

"We're nearly ready for launch, farfar," she said. "I need to do the safety briefing now."

Ragnar nodded. He turned to Gunnolf, who was jotting notes for the saga. "I reckon we can put this down as 'The women stood by the ocean-side sobbing for the safe return of their men'."

"Don't you dare!" exclaimed Hilde. "Tha can say something like 'Each proud warrior made certain they were fully prepared for every possible turn of fate, and much wisdom was exchanged at the seashore'."

"Yep. What Hilde said," said Ragnar, with a nod.

Hilde walked down the beach until she stood between the longship and the sea. Ragnar stood beside her.

"Think it'll float?" he said.

"It'll be fine," she replied.

"It looks blummin' marvellous, dun't it? Like a great big dragon in the sand."

"A sand drake," said Hilde.

"Oh, I do like that." He cupped his hands to his mouth. "Gunnolf! We're calling it *Sandraker*! Put that in the saga!"

Not many of the Odinsons were listening. Someone had

cracked open more mead and the drinking horns were being passed round for a celebratory drink.

Hilde blew loudly on a whistle. "Pay attention to me! All of you! Conditions are good for launch, but we need to make it soon. It will not happen until we've completed the safety briefing and Ragnar is satisfied you all understand what I'm about to tell you."

There was some foot shuffling, but Hilde saw that everyone's gaze was on her. "Now, is everyone wearing their life jacket?"

There was some indistinct grumbling.

"It's essential that you all wear your traditional Viking robes," bellowed Ragnar.

"Traditional Viking robes?" said an Odinson, holding an orange life jacket aloft.

"Your ceremonial Viking robe is a modified life jacket, that you must wear at all times when on board," said Hilde.

"Orange, like the flames of victory!" said Ragnar. "Gives you a big chest like Thor the mighty!"

Hilde nodded in approval. "In the event of an evacuation, your emergency exit is over the side," she said, indicating with an outstretched arms. "You can inflate the life jacket by pulling on the leather toggle, like so. You can top up the air by blowing into this tube. Your life jacket also has a light and a whistle. Please do not inflate your life jacket on board the longship as it may impede your exit. In the event of an emergency evacuation, you should also take with you the nearest flotation device. These are the decorative shields situated around the edges of the ship, which you're all familiar with. Please secure your own device before helping others."

She paused to let all of that sink in. Many of them were exploring the features of their life jackets.

"Any questions on keeping safe?" she called. "Just in case this needs saying, do not bail into the sea unless you have absolutely no choice. It's cold out there."

As the Odinsons considered the real dangers of going to sea, and a team worked to get the hoist into place, a Land Rover rolled along the damp compacted beach.

"It's the fuzz!" shouted a gaggle of Odinsons, pointing.

Hilde looked and nodded. It looked like the police.

Ragnar stroked his hairy chin. "Stay sharp, lads. Saxons ahoy."

80

Polly couldn't rightly say how long she'd been awake.

Boxing Day morning and she sat at the little table in the little lounge in her little apartment at Otterside. The cup of tea she'd made herself had gone cold, undrunk. The misshapen remote control device that Bernard had passed her sat in the centre of the table. She had not touched it since she'd placed it there the day before.

At some point, a light had come on the side. Polly couldn't recall what that light meant. She couldn't even be sure how long it had been on.

Her mind was full and empty at the same time. She was confused, disgusted, angry and excited, and nothing at all. She was tired and perhaps needed to go back to bed.

She massaged the bridge of her nose and, as she did so, there was a knock at the door.

She stood automatically. Finding she was upright, went to answer the door.

It was Erin.

"Merry Christmas, Aunt Polly," said Erin.

"Christmas was yesterday," said Polly.

"Still in the twelve days of Christmas."

"You were going to come before Christmas."

"It was always going to be before Christmas, or after. We'd not decided, had we? But here I am. Merry Christmas."

There was a forced note of Christmas jollity, but her face had either failed to receive the message or struggled to maintain the charade.

So, Erin had come as promised to exchange Christmas presents. A fleeting moment of contact between family members, brushing past but not connecting. Polly had her neat stack of presents ready on the side in the lounge area. It had been ready for the past forty-eight hours.

"Merry Christmas," said Polly and looked past Erin. "Are they here?"

Erin looked behind her. "Who?"

"Jack? Iris?"

"No. I didn't want to stress them out by bringing them in here."

"Stress them?"

"Oh, you know. Co-ordinating children. It's like a full-scale military operation."

"Not even brought them in the car?"

"They were so worn out from yesterday. Big Christmas lunch. Some naughty treats. David brought over a sinful pavlova."

Polly simply looked at her.

"Are you not inviting me in?" said Erin. "I've brought

mince pies." She waggled a box of Marks and Spencers mince pies in demonstration.

"You're staying for a mince pie but you didn't think to bring the children—"

"Oh, these are for you," said Erin with assured generosity. "Every one of them. Something to enjoy at Christmas."

"It was Christmas yesterday."

"You said."

"I wanted to see my family."

Erin dropped all pretence of festive cheer, her face become cold and tense. "Fine."

She shoved the mince pies back in a carrier bag and stepped back into the corridor, taking her phone out as she did. Her hand went involuntarily to her jacket pocket and the e-cig there.

"Yes, Jack," she said. "It's mummy. Yes. Get Iris."

As she waited, Erin gave Polly a candid stare, one that said, 'Look at what you're putting me through. I hope you're happy now.'

Polly found herself about to say something, but then tinny voices came from Erin's phone. Erin put it on speaker.

"Hi, Auntie Polly. Hi."

"I wanted to speak to them," she whispered to Erin, realising she was very much in danger of crying.

Erin continued to hold the phone.

"Hi, darlings," said Polly, unable to control the tremble in her voice. "Merry Christmas."

"Merry Christmas!"

"Did you get some nice presents? I've got a couple of presents for you here. I'll..." She turned and went into the apartment and picked up the pile. Why she was picking them up now she could not say; she couldn't pass them down the line.

When she came out again, Erin had the phone to her ear once more. "Yes, yes. That's fine. Tell dad there are to be no more biscuits until I get home." She ended the call.

"I wanted to *speak* to them," said Polly.

"I offered."

"Spend time with them then."

Erin glanced at the wrapped presents. She held open the carrier bag for Polly to drop them in, a bin held out for waste.

"They're not toys, Polly. They're not here for our amusement. Do you think they're interested in you? Or me, for that matter?" She took out her e-cig and puffed on it.

Polly closed her eyes and tried to maintain a semblance of calm. She had just wanted to see her family, be part of them for a while, exchange gifts, share chocolates. She'd had every intention of keeping it to that and not bringing up anything else. But Erin had denied her even a sliver of proper happiness, had only offered her shop-bought mince pies and human connection at a distance so...

"Are you living in my old house?" she said.

"Pardon?" said Erin. The clouds of steam vapour around her smelled of cinnamon and fruits.

Polly pursed her lips. "I misspoke. You *are* living in my old house."

Erin snorted. "Who told you that?"

"I saw it. I was there."

"You left this place?"

"I'm not a prisoner, Erin. I went out, I saw the house. You live there."

Erin held her gaze, face frozen, an android malfunctioning. "You couldn't support yourself," she said eventually. "You were having episodes."

"A bladder infection. A passing illness."

"You made the decision to sell."

"You told me to."

"I *advised*," said Erin firmly. "You weren't coping. The place was too big and too expensive and—"

"And you made me sell it for less than the market value. Far less."

"A place became available here."

"And you bought my house."

"We purchased it from the property company, a third party."

"And if we looked at whose company that was. A friend? Maybe you even own it."

"David's wife runs—"

"Who's David?"

"My practice partner, I told you. She has a property business."

"This is theft."

"Polly, please," Erin scoffed. "I'll not have hysteria."

"No one will believe the amount you paid me was a genuine or fair offer."

Erin shook her head, displeased. "And I brought you mince pies."

"Well," said Polly sourly, "you wouldn't want me to get fat, would you? A friend pointed something out to me."

"One of your do-lally friends here?"

"If I die within seven years of the sale then the Inland Revenue might look at that house sale and decide you paid me so little it could constitute a gift. A taxable gift."

"The house comes nowhere near the threshold for inheritance tax. Do not kid yourself, Polly."

"If I died within seven years. That's the period of time they look at. And if it's not taxable, they might just look at it and wonder what kind of scam you pulled on me. Best to keep me healthy and whole into my eighties, eh?"

Erin huffed and, in doing so, huffed a great cloud of vapour between them. "Fanciful nonsense, Polly."

"I could get a solicitor. I could get you struck off as a GP."

"Which reminds me, I do have a shift to do later."

"I could call the police."

Erin snorted in derision. "Now, you're being silly. No one's done anything wrong and the police have much better things to do."

"Like investigate murders," said Polly.

"Er, yes."

Polly had a vivid mental flash of that snivelling murderer James Huntley, bound and helpless in the chair, and she felt a surge of power course through her. She could picture herself with a knife in her hand, showing this bitch of a niece what she was truly capable of. But she didn't need a knife.

"You need to be careful," she said in a low, menacing whisper.

"Threats?" said Erin, unfazed. "One could almost believe you were having another episode. Remember that poor young man you shouted at in the supermarket? I don't know if we can trust anything you say or do."

"Oh, you'd be surprised at what I can do." She didn't care that now she did sound like a crazy lady. "You stole my house from me and put me in here."

"But you're happy here."

"You want to deny me every pleasure in life just to suit your own needs."

"This is no way to behave at Christmas."

"You are an appalling mother."

"I keep my family safe."

"You don't deserve a family. You don't deserve to live."

There was no crack at all in Erin's emotional armour, just the patient rebuttal of everything Polly said. "This is no way for us to behave at this time of year," Erin smiled. Oh, it was almost a human smile. "Here. I brought you something else. Something to bring you some cheer."

Erin offered Polly a heavy envelope. Then with a nod, she turned and left.

The envelope was thick and constructed from heavy sugar paper, held together by a square of Sellotape. It came open with almost no effort. Inside was a card.

Glitter cascaded from the card as Polly removed it. She didn't know if it had been made by Jack or Iris. The mountains of glitter stuck to it made it impossible for her to decipher the picture. It could conceivably have been Father Christmas with a reindeer. It could have equally been a fireman having a fight with a picnic table.

Merry Xmas was written across the front in wobbly felt tip.

"Christmas was yesterday," she said quietly. "Yesterday."

Glitter came away on her hands as she moved them, red and sparkling white. She instinctively wiped them on her cardigan, which only meant she now had glitter on her cardigan and her hands.

"Fucking, fucking glitter," she said. She had tears in her eyes now.

She went back into the apartment, ostensibly to clean her hands, but the moment she saw the little detonator device on the table, she understood what she had truly intended. There were two lights on it now, one continuously, the other winking intermittently.

She picked it up and strode out again, only realising on the stairs that she was still wearing her nightie under her cardigan and had fluffy slippers on her feet. She went to the main entrance.

Automatic doors slid open for her. Erin was in the car park, beside her car, the boot open. She dropped the carrier bag inside with little care. Poor mince pies squashed at the bottom, went a little thought through Polly's head. It was drowned out by her roaring rage.

A car was pulling off the main road and into the car park but there was no one else around.

Erin closed the boot and saw Polly down by the entrance.

"Why did you do this?" Polly called to her. "What did I ever do?"

Erin gestured vaguely with her e-cig. "Just ... just look at you," she said and took a drag.

Polly flicked the switch.

The bang was no louder than a Christmas cracker. The

plastic casing of the e-cig shattered in Erin's hands. Her cheeks bulged instantly, her eyes too, and the back of her head burst apart, throwing out a shower of blood, brain and bone – red and white.

It was, all in all, quite beautiful.

81

"Oh, my good giddy God!" yelled Rich, stalling the car in surprise. "Did you just see that?"

Of course, Sam had seen it. They had all seen it. How could they have not seen it?

The woman in the car park. Her head had just exploded. There was even a spatter of blood on the windscreen.

The woman – it was Dr Hackett – fell, twisting like a helter-skelter as she bounced to her knees and then onto her face. What remained of her face.

"I don't understand," said Marvin numbly from the back seat.

They had landed at the airfield ten minutes earlier. Peninsula had offered to drive them home, but Rich's car was also parked there. Peninsula had been sent on ahead to prepare yet more food for them at Rich's apartments in the defunct Hotel Splendid. Rich offered to drive Sam and Marvin to Otterside. Sam had agreed, although she had little idea how she was going to prove her theory or challenge the suspects.

The conundrum had been taken from her hands in an instant.

She unclipped her seatbelt and ran out to the fallen doctor.

Her eyes scanned the building as though expecting to see a hidden sniper. Her hand was already clutching her phone. It only took a moment to switch to the keypad and call 999. Her mind gabbled through her first aid training – recovery position, the ABCs of CPR...

She crouched beside the woman who was obviously dead – she was missing the back half of her skull – putting her hands to her neck to feel for a pulse anyway.

"Hello. Emergency service operator. Which service do you require?"

"Ambulance. I don't know. There's been a terrible accident. Her head..."

There were people coming out of the retirement village building now. General staff, the manager and at least two women in nurses' overalls.

"I'm at the Otterside retirement village," said Sam into the phone. "It's Dr Erin Hackett. She..." She couldn't say that the doctor's head had exploded, no matter how true it was. "She's suffered a massive head injury. She's dead. I'm..."

Nurses, pausing momentarily at the shocking scene, pushed Sam firmly aside and knelt beside the corpse.

"There's an ambulance on its way," said the operator. *"What kind of injury?"*

"I don't know," said Sam, standing back. A nurse looked

at her and mouthed 'Nine nine nine?'. Sam nodded. She turned away and, looking to the building, saw Polly Gilpin stock still among the staff and residents who were blocking the door.

"It's like a firework went off in her face," said Sam.

She took one step towards the building. Polly saw her and immediately withdrew back into the crowd.

"I don't think it was an accident," said Sam and followed.

There was a press of on-lookers to get through, a mixture of the horrified and the fascinated. Once she had pushed through, the corridor beyond was relatively free. She looked left and right and could see no sign of Polly.

Regardless of what DC Camara might think, Sam had encountered death upon death upon death linked to Otterside. Each one different, each one too unusual to be initially seen as murder. What would they say about Dr Hackett? That her e-cig had exploded. Such things were known to happen. But Sam didn't believe it for an instant. There was a plan in action here, a plot.

She knew where Polly's room was and took the stairs.

If Polly was involved then what did that mean for her theory? Had Polly picked up the discarded handcuffs after the calamitous conclusion to the magic show? Maybe that meant she was the architect of the drink-driver's death. Janine had snuck out on the night of Drumstick's death. So had Alison killed Greg Mandyke for Janine, and Bernard killed Dr Hackett for Polly or vice versa?

Sam reached Polly's door, hesitated only a second, and knocked.

But how did these people, all with murderous intents, all

find one another? This wasn't just *Strangers on a Train*, this was a whole organised murder outing.

There was no answer. Sam knocked again.

"Polly. It's Sam Applewhite. From DefCon4. I just want to check that you're okay."

No response.

Maybe she was hiding, maybe she was elsewhere. Sam set out to look.

The 999 call on her phone had dropped, forgotten. She called the number for the Skegness police station. Camara had not yet got back in touch with her, but it definitely felt like it was time to call the cavalry.

82

The three members of the Otterside social committee sat in the north lounge.

"It's almost as if Chesney is stealing the pieces to deliberately torment us," said Jacob, turning over a recently reclaimed jigsaw piece in his hands. "He says he knows nothing of it, but they still keep going missing and they keep turning up one by one near his office."

"Torment us," said Strawb. "Oh, quite probably."

"I've made people sign a liability form when they take the jigsaws out now, and keep them locked away in the cupboard only we have keys for. But it's clearly still occurring."

"If we may return to the matter of the sequence dancing which should be taking place this evening," said Margaret.

Jacob, in the manner of a man who felt missing jigsaw pieces was a higher priority than any mere social activity, grumbled but settled into silence. Margaret Gainsborough decided the meeting agenda and brooked no arguments.

There was evidently some sort of hoo-hah going on in the corridor beyond the lounge, even some medical staff running full sprint towards the epicentre, but Margaret was not going to have her meetings disturbed by such things.

"Now, we traditionally make use of the old gym, but that currently contains holes fifteen to nineteen of the new crazy golf course—" she began. She was halted by the sight of Polly Gilpin rushing in, bouncing off the open door as she came.

Margaret would not have normally stopped for such an interruption, but there was a wild alarm in Polly's eyes that cut right through her.

"I did it," Polly panted.

Strawb stood and took hold of her with supporting hands.

"What's happened?" said Margaret.

"I flicked the switch," Polly said. "Erin. I did it. But the woman saw me."

"Who saw you, love?" said Strawb.

"That Sam. From the company that did our fitness trackers. She's asked questions before, and she saw me. I know she saw me."

"I see," said Margaret.

"Ambulances and the police are coming," said Polly. "They'll know. They'll know."

Margaret nodded slowly. "I think we might have to call this meeting to an unscheduled stop."

"She's here now," said Polly and there was an unbecoming panic in her voice. Margaret had thought her made of sterner stuff.

"We don't know this Sam character knows anything," said Jacob.

"We facking do," said Strawb. "Poll's just said."

"Then we silence her," said Margaret. "Like we did Dennis."

Jacob shook his head. "I don't think we have any more weather balloons, and there's hardly any air in the cannister."

"Like we did with Dennis *generally*," hissed Margaret. "Not specifically. We take a boat trip and—"

She stopped, interrupted for the second time in a minute.

Sam Applewhite, that young and earnest women from DefCon4, stood in the doorway. Her right hand was covered with blood. She held a phone to her ear in her left hand.

"Are you all right, dear?" said Margaret, nodding at her hand.

"I was hoping to speak to Polly." Sam looked at her phone, then put it away, a twitch of her nose suggesting it wasn't giving her any joy anyway. A call unconnected.

"We just heard the news of the terrible accident," said Strawb. "Bladdy awful. Those e-cig things are dangerous."

Sam blinked and frowned and blinked again, then a half-smile creased her lips. "Organisation and dissemination," she said.

"Pardon?" said Margaret.

"Your role. You organise and disseminate." She laughed bitterly. "My dad said – my dad is Mr Marvellous, the man whose handcuffs you stole – my dad said the most masterful players of games are the ones who make it look like someone else is in control."

"Not following you, love," said Strawb.

Jacob interjected. "What she's saying is that—"

"Do shut up, Jacob," said Margaret. "What exactly is it you're suggesting, Miss Applewhite?"

The woman hesitated, but only an instant. "You organise murders."

"The social committee?" said Margaret.

"Yes. You arrange to have people killed – and turkeys – and you find the people to do it."

Strawb tried to laugh it off. "You hear yourself? That's crazy."

"Definitely crazy," agreed Sam, "but I think it's true. Maybe you've all watched too many episodes of *Murder She Wrote* or something. All those daytime murder mystery shows gave you ideas."

"Getting a touch ageist now," said Margaret. She caught Strawb's eye and looked aside to the cupboard in the corner.

"I know Janine killed Drumstick. That's the turkey. Bernard must have – the exploding vape thing. He was a military man, wasn't he?"

Strawb carefully let go of Polly and went towards the cupboard. "How many murders are you actually accusing us of?" Margaret saw how he put a little bit of old-age dodder in his movements to emphasise his harmlessness.

"I don't understand the ins and outs," said Sam. "And I can't believe you think it's okay to do this."

"What we think is okay," said Margaret as Strawb fiddled with the lock on the cupboard. "Getting older does that for you."

"Makes you lose your grip on morality?" said Sam, not deliberately offensive but merely bewildered.

"Age gives you time and distance and perspective, Miss Applewhite."

"That's not an excuse to kill three people. And a turkey."

Margaret winced. She wished the woman would stop mentioning the turkey. It was embarrassing.

Strawb had the cupboard open, along with the shoebox at the back. He turned with Bernard's revolver in his hand. Margaret had no idea if it was loaded, but the threat of it was probably enough.

"Oh, come on," said Sam. She sounded both afraid and irritated as she put her hands up. "There's no need for that."

"I'm sorry, but there is, little lady," said Strawb gently with a glint of his white teeth.

"You think we killed three people?" said Margaret. "You have no idea."

83

Hilde and a couple of uncles were remonstrating with the unhappy police detective who'd come down to interfere with their honest and harmless business of launching their longship. He was a lanky fellow, a full head higher than either Yngve or Gunnolf, but he had that Saxon manner of trying to be reasonable when he should be stamping his authority and he was easy to counter. Ragnar was continuing with the launch preparations while the Saxon cop was kept at bay.

"Are we doing anything illegal, detective?" said Hilde.

"Well, no, not specifically, but in terms of your own safety—"

"And who says we should follow your laws anyway?" demanded Yngve loudly.

"Well, the law says you should follow the law. As citizens of the United Kingdom, we should all—"

"I recognise no kingdom but that we have declared for ourselves!"

"That ... that doesn't really matter," said the detective. "Point is, this boat looks possibly unseaworthy and we don't want to have to call out the lifeboats if you get into—"

"Are you saying my niece here does not know how to build a ship?" said Gunnolf, clapping a meaty hand on Hilde's shoulder.

"I'm sure it's lovely and, if we can get it checked out by the proper authorities—"

"Authorities?" scoffed Yngve.

"Concerned local residents called us because—"

"Busy bodies!"

"We just want you to be safe."

"It's you who should be afraid, not us!"

"And the people of Cleethorpes!" said Gunnolf.

The detective was perplexed. "You're sailing it to Cleethorpes—?" He hesitated, distracted by the phone buzzing at his belt. He gave them all a bewildered look and stepped back to take the call. "Camara, here. What was that, central? Otterside? I'm kind of up to my neck in things down on the beach. Seacroft end. I could do with a couple of uniforms at the scene. Yes? I do know a Sam Applewhite."

The detective drew away further and Hilde was able to turn her attention back to her own folk and Ragnar, who was truly getting into the swing of things as Master of Ceremonies.

. . .

MARVIN STEPPED out of Rich's car to better see what was going on. "Where did Sam go?"

"I think I saw her go inside," said Rich.

Marvin walked forward, but gave the scene of the accident a wide berth. There was no point getting in the way of the emergency crew.

"Watch out!" Rich firmly but gently pulled him aside as a yellow people carrier drove hurriedly out of the car park. "Christ, that thing nearly had you."

"At least there's already an ambulance on stand-by," said Marvin.

They continued forward toward Otterside, but they were walking against the tide. Most of the residents were pressing forward to see what was happening outside.

A man grabbed Marvin's arm. "You saw it, didn't you?"

It was Chesney, the manager and enthusiastic amateur singer.

"The accident?"

"My car." He pointed to an empty parking space.

"The big yellow monstrosity?" said Marvin.

Marvin knew that age brought with it a certain propensity to worry unnecessarily, and he generally thought he did well at keeping senior anxieties at bay, but his brain had suddenly put two and two together and coming up with an alarmingly large number.

He turned to Rich. "Get after it."

"Get after what?" said Rich.

"The yellow people carrier thing."

"We didn't see where it—"

"In all likelihood it went towards town. It's a long straight road for I don't know how long. It's bright yellow, man! Phone me!"

Marvin's urgent tone must have had an impact because Rich nodded dumbly and stumbled and ran for his car.

"We should call the police," said Chesney.

"You and I are going to check every room to see if my daughter is here."

84

S am sat in the front passenger seat of the people carrier. She didn't know whose vehicle it was but got the impression it might be Chesney's part-time taxi, and this was not the first time these elderly residents had borrowed it.

They had skirted the on-going scene in the car park. All eyes were still on the spot where Dr Hackett had died, and the paramedics going through the motions of dealing with someone who was beyond saving. Sam could have shouted out for help as the social committee slowly kidnapped her, but something held her back; and it wasn't just the fear of being shot. Despite all reasonable evidence to the contrary, part of her struggled to believe this was anything other than a charade, a grand pantomime.

In the people carrier, Strawb sat immediately behind her. There was the insistent pressure of the pistol barrel through the car seat, pointed directly at her spine. Polly and Margaret sat on the back seat with Strawb. Jacob drove. They were heading to the southern end of town. The roads were nearly empty. It was Boxing Day after all.

"It won't be long," said Jacob. "Not far to go."

It won't be long, sounded ominous.

"RAISE your horns and we shall all drink mead in celebration of this glorious day!" Ragnar shouted, his own huge horn held aloft. Bottles of mead were passed around the crowd, and there was much joyous shouting.

"We have long dreamed of this. We now have the means to expand our horizons. Today's raid will be upon Cleethorpes. They'll never expect a raid from the sea, and we'll be away with their miniature locomotive before they know what's hit them."

A loud cheer went up.

"Will this be the adventure of a lifetime?" Ragnar asked. "No, this is just the beginning! We want to test the capabilities of our fine craft. I want every man to come back inspired!"

"And woman," came a firm voice from within the longship.

"Astrid?" Ragnar said, surprised. "Astrid my love, this is no place for you."

"Of course it is. Who else will make sure everyone is fed and comfortable? And in case you hadn't noticed, quite a number of your Viking warriors are women."

Hilde saw her farfar reach for his glasses to check, but he remembered himself in time. "Of course I knew that! I was speaking figuratively. So anyway, I want every man and woman to come back inspired! Our coming adventures will know no bounds!"

There was more cheering. Ragnar acknowledged the adulation of the crowd with his hands held high in the air. "We shall set sail in a few minutes. Let us have music! Our enemies will cower at the approach of our mighty vessel as they hear the fearsome sound!"

Hilde had installed a high spec public address system. It was capable of volume sufficient to render everyone on board permanently deaf, so she had cautioned Ragnar not to turn it up to its full capacity. The sound blasting out was from the Viking Metal band Meat-Heads, which was young Kalf, Erik and Horik Odinson. They had enjoyed moderate success on the internet with songs like *Blood, Mead, Death* and *Goreheart.*

As the music boomed, the goat in the boat bleated in distress and, even better, the police detective was forced to move further away to be able to continue his phone conversation.

For the longship's first journey to sea, Hilde had selected the thumping anthem *Dragon Bait.* She could see from her farfar's face that he wasn't a fan of the music, but he certainly appreciated the drama of it. If enemies could be crushed by harsh, growling vocals and a bass line that banged their teeth together from half a mile away, then Meat-Heads were a force to be reckoned with.

. . .

MARVIN CUPPED his hands to his mouth and called out for Sam.

It felt a silly gesture. Otterside might have been just one building, built around a single horseshoe corridor, but it was a large place nonetheless. Residents who had not gone and congregated outside to gawp at the accident were in the corridors, chatting with one another.

The sight of a man wandering around shouting, "Sam! Sam!" repeatedly drew their attention.

A number of well-meaning but useless individuals tried to stop and ask him if he was all right. Marvin shrugged these off and moved onward. The last of these was a rotund chap in shorts and a dressing gown who tried to block Marvin's way.

"Enough of that," he said with brusque authority. "Can't go around shouting at everyone."

"Bernard," said Chesney. This man is looking for his daughter, Miss Applewhite. Apparently, it's important."

"Bernard?" said Marvin. "Who swapped his murder with Janine or Alison?"

The words came out of Marvin's mouth unbidden. They were a seeming nonsense, and despite Marvin's current fears he didn't even know if they were remotely true. But the look on Bernard's face when he said them, the panic that appeared in the fat man's eyes, shot a bolt of dread through Marvin.

"Must be about my business," said Bernard hurriedly. "Plenty to do."

Marvin took hold of Chesney. He suspected if he didn't he would simply fall. "You must call the police."

"My car, yes."

"I think Sam's been kidnapped."

"What?"

"And I have to tell you about the murders." Marvin felt around in his pockets for his phone and called Rich. Rich picked up on the second ring, which was too slow.

"*Hi—*"

"Tell me you've seen it," said Marvin.

"*Well, I did. Several cars ahead. And I saw it turn onto that boulevard towards the sea front with the Sea Castle at the end and then...*"

"Then?" said Marvin. "Then?"

"*And now I'm looking. I really am.*"

"Look harder."

"*They'd only come down here if they were going somewhere. I mean there's no through road really. They could have turned into a car park or... I am looking, Marvin.*"

85

The people carrier had come down along the seafront and was now making its way along one of the tracks that cut through the dunes to a quieter part of the beach. The empty boating lake was off to the left and, to the right, a compound surrounded by high blue fencing and containing rows of white boats. Fishing boats and cruisers sat on trailers.

Jacob got out and hurried to the gates of the compound. Strawb indicated for Sam to follow.

"So, tell me," she said, "how many people have you killed?"

Strawb blew out his lips. "I couldn't say."

"I measure it in time rather than numbers," said Margaret.

"Twenty three," Jacob called from the gate.

"That many?" whispered Polly.

"It's hard to put a number on things when accidents

happen all the time," said Margaret. "Ten years ago, Jacob here killed my Pat for me, didn't you, Jacob?"

"I did," said Jacob and disappeared into the compound.

"He was a vile and abusive husband. Denied me the family I might have wanted. Spent his money on his own pet projects. We'll see his boat in a minute or two. I kept it. Then Strawb joined us and did for those punks who had been such horrible neighbours to Jacob."

"Carbon monoxide poisoning," said Strawb. Sam saw him lean close to Polly in the rear view mirror. "They didn't feel a thing."

"Then there was Linda, who was most creative in dealing with that loan shark. In return we asked Charles to do away with that scumbag burglar who ruined her nerves. Carol then David then Nancy – these were the perpetrators, not the victims. We don't bother remembering the names of the human waste we do away with. Ronald and Judith and Donald—"

"I thought it was Donald then Ronald," said Strawb.

"No, Ronald then Donald," said Margaret. "Ronald ran that pervert over – took him weeks to die. Donald managed to get that swindling gardener chap to somehow drown himself upside down in a water butt. I liked that one."

"All helping each other. In a chain," said Polly. The way she said it told Sam she was discovering this for the first time. "I once belonged to a tea towel club. You sent off one tea towel to the address at the top of the list and then you got sent six tea towels by other people in return."

"A pyramid scheme," said Strawb.

"Pyramid scheme murder club," said Sam and could have laughed.

"Except we kept it very tightly under control," said Margaret. "Ten years and many deaths—"

"Twenty three," said Jacob.

"—and we haven't been caught. No one's even come close."

"The police were asking round," said Sam.

With a low engine thrum, a tractor and trailer reversed out of the compound. On the trailer was a white cabin cruiser boat. Despite having lived in Skegness for a while, and spent much of her life at various coastal towns, Sam didn't know much about boats. It had a pointy end and a squat stern, with a little deck and a piled up cabin area in the middle that made the boat seem almost as tall as it was long. The name *Calypso* was painted on the side in a jolly flowing script.

"What are we doing?" said Sam.

"Use your imagination," said Margaret. "That's what we're going to do."

"LET US LAUNCH WITH ALL HASTE!" bellowed Ragnar, then swiftly deferred to Hilde.

Under her supervision, the Odinson men lifted *Sandraker* once more and carried it down to the surf. They carried it until the lapping waves lifted and supported it.

It fair cheered the hearts of everyone to see the ship fully afloat and not sinking at all. It was a proud moment for the Odinsons, definitely something for the sagas, and Hilde was certain the occasional squeals from the men and exclamations of "Ooh, the water's cold!" would not make it into their proud history, soon to be forgotten.

A gangway plank was laid at an awkward angle and the men and women of the raiding party climbed aboard. There were cheers from the onlookers, and the Odinson children, with ice-cream smeared faces, yelled in delight.

The Saxon copper, Camara, was still on the beach, on his phone as though he could magically summon forces to stop them. Hilde, stood in the prow and laughed at that thought.

Her farfar clapped his hand on her shoulder. "Tis a fine day for the Odinsons," he said.

She leaned in against him and wrapped her arms around his considerable chest. "You know, we might actually do this. Now, shall I show you the gas-fired grappling hooks I've installed?"

Ragnar held her at arm's length and looked at her with shining eyes. "For boarding enemy ships?"

"Well, I thought for mooring ourselves to Cleethorpes pier. But sure."

Astrid moved along the deck promising her brave Viking sailors that she'd have the kettle on for a cup of tea soon enough.

ONCE THE CABIN cruiser *Calypso* was released into the sea swells with Margaret at the helm, Jacob waded out to join them. Strawb passed the pistol to Polly and told Sam to sit on a deckchair on the little aft deck. He had a roll of silver-backed tape in his hands.

"Yeah, I don't think I'm going to do that," said Sam.

Gun or no gun, Sam preferred her chances if she threw herself overboard and swam up the coast. If these crooks were planning on a quick getaway, they wouldn't bother chasing her down.

Strawb tutted "This is the facking problem with young people."

He stepped forward. With a speed she didn't expect he slammed his fist into Sam's nose. She sat down hard on the chair, her nose already throbbing and bloody. She gasped in shock.

"Oh, Strawb," said Polly.

"Just because our best years are behind us, they think we're harmless," he seethed, then shook his hand. "Fack. Gone and hurt my hand now."

Polly took the tape from him and securely bound Sam's wrists to the aluminium arms of the deckchair.

Jacob shook his wet legs out on the deck once he'd climbed aboard, then lifted up the lid of one of the seats on the rear deck. He took out a rucksack and removed a pair of dry trousers. Blinking against the tears and pain dominating her face, Sam thought the emergency grab bag was very telling. They'd been planning this for a while.

The engine rose in volume, sea churned and the boat pulled away.

There was movement on the shore, up by the compound and the yellow people carrier. There was a car parked next to it now and a man stood in the open doorway. His arm was cocked as though holding a phone to his ear.

Too late, she thought.

.   .   .

THE SAXON DETECTIVE, Camara, came running down to the waterline, waving his hands.

"Too late, my friend!" Ragnar chortled at him. "We set sail!"

"Well, we're actually rowing for now," said Hilde. "I want to get out a-ways before we raise the sails."

It had occurred to Hilde during the planning and construction of the ship, that despite their Viking bravado, none of the Odinsons had any sailing experience. She had spent much of the past year reading up on the mechanics and techniques, but feared research was no replacement for actual practice.

"Ragnar! I need you!"

Ragnar stepped up onto the prow, his ceremonial cloak flapping about him in the stiff breeze. "Tha'll not get in the way of us launching this magnificent ship, so tha might as well—"

"—Ragnar, I'm not going to stop you," said Camara. "I'm coming with you. I need to commandeer this vessel for police business."

"What?"

"I need you to follow another boat." He swivelled and pointed at a white-grey shape a half mile up the shore. "That boat!"

"What for? We'll be having no truck with thee."

"They're murder suspects."

"Then let tha Saxon coastguard deal with it."

"They've got Sam Applewhite hostage."

Ragnar stared at Camara for a moment.

"Farfar," said Hilde.

Ragnar nodded and then turned back to the crowd surrounding the ship. "Gunnolf! Gunnolf! New chapter for the saga. We'll be joined by a—" he gestured at Camara "—what'll we call you? A renegade priest? Yes a renegade priest, sent to capture pirates."

Camara shook his head. "A renegade what?" He scrambled on board, getting soaked to the waist. "How quickly can we set sail in this?"

"We're actually going to be rowing at first," said Ragnar.

"If we want to go quickly," said Hilde. "I suggest you all help with the rowing and I will provide steering instructions until we've made up the distance."

Ragnar looked like he was about to protest, before dropping to a bench and pulling Camara down beside him.

Hilde instructed all the new sailors to find their oars.

"The coastguard and lifeboats have been notified," said Camara, almost as though he was trying to justify all this to himself, knowing he was in the hands of this band of fools in an untested ship on the chilly vastness of the North Sea. "But the nearest rescue helicopter is in Humberside and the RNLI have only just been alerted."

Hilde shouted out her clearest instructions and oars were lowered into the water. She was doubtful they could catch the motor boat. If her family could get this vessel going without clouting each other around their heads with their oars, that would be victory of a sort.

86

S trawb brought a thick waterproof coat out for Polly and, once it was on, passed her a life jacket.

Polly kept focus on the tallest of the rides at Fantasy Island as they rapidly diminished. The coast was fading into the grey sky and sea. Ahead, the only visible landmarks were the giant posts and whirling blades of the wind farms. In other circumstances it might be pleasant to be on a boat like this, but the freezing Boxing Day wind, and the fact she was now a wanted murderess on the run, kind of took the shine off things.

"You okay, love?" said Strawb and pressed a dry kiss to her cold cheek.

She turned and looked at the man she had thrown her lot in with. His eyes met hers. He was smiling. Despite all the craziness and the horror, Strawb was smiling at her. But it was a handsome, roguish smile and – Christ! – it had been years since a man had looked at her like that.

A new sensation crept over her, like the cold winter chill and the warm winter coat, hot and cold all at once. It was a new sensation, and a new realisation. She had killed her niece, her thieving, swindling, loveless niece. She had fought back against the woman who had oppressed and abused her for too long, and now she was on the run with a man who she maybe – no, *definitely* – definitely had fallen in love with.

She glanced at the DefCon4 woman, Sam, strapped helplessly in the deckchair, huffing and swallowing as the blood from her broken nose trickled over her lips and chin.

"We're like Bonnie and Clyde," said Polly. "From the movies."

"I'm no Warren Beatty," said Strawb. "And you're far more beautiful than whatserface."

"Faye Dunaway. I saw that with my sister at the Tower Ballroom. My twenty-first birthday, I think. And you're a liar."

He winced and sucked hard through his teeth. He raised his hand. His knuckles were red and swollen from when he'd punched the DefCon4 woman.

"You might have broken it," she said.

"That would be a bladdy foolish thing to have done," he said.

"Let Nurse Polly find a first aid kit."

The cabin cruiser *Calypso* had a split level cabin. Down below was the tiny accommodation. Margaret did something to the controls and came away, down the short steps to the deck level.

"You're not steering?" said Polly.

"Autopilot," said Margaret.

"I thought that was just planes."

Strawb laughed.

"Course set in for the marina in Ijmuiden," said Margaret.

"Holland?" Polly hazarded.

"And is that it?" said Sam from her seat. "You're going to push me overboard and sail across the North Sea to the Netherlands?"

Margaret moved so Sam could see her. "That is more or less the plan, yes. The details do not concern you. Your part in this requires very little planning."

"You're crazy."

"Thorough. I even chose my least favourite deckchair to fasten you to."

"People are looking for me."

Margaret gave a hollow laugh. "Were you about to add that we'll never get away with it? We've been getting away with things for a long time. We're careful in our planning, and using this boat as an escape route was always a part of that plan. Jacob has even got a little house rented for us on Saturnusstraat."

"*Ja. Oost West thuis best,*" said Jacob coming up from below.

"We have taken into account every eventuality," said Margaret primly. "Polly, see to Strawb's hand. Jacob, it might be time to make some sandwiches. Sea travel always makes me hungry."

HILDE LOOKED out across the rows of oars with some pride. There was a rhythm emerging and the ship was surging through the waves. The keel kept the ship steady and there was sufficient off-shore wind that she was tempted to raise the sail. Ragnar stood at the prow, calling out every poetic phrase that occurred to him for the saga, but Gunnolf couldn't hear him. As they rowed, the family shouted the lines back along the ship in a relay, although they were definitely getting muddled, because slightly deaf Uncle Bjorn was sitting nearby.

"The gulls and gannets soared overhead!" said Ragnar, an arm pointing dramatically at the sky.

"The gulls and gannets sawed off a head!" said Bjorn.

"The girl sawed off her own head!" said Kalf further back, his voice hushed slightly at the news.

Hilde scanned the water. Nothing was in sight apart from the wind farm dominating the shore off Skegness. The cabin cruiser had temporarily gone from sight. Not knowing where it was heading was a problem. There was a lot of sea out there.

"I see the boat!" yelled Ragnar. He had his folding brass telescope with him and was squinting through it now. Hilde looked to see where he was pointing. She saw something smudging the horizon. She indicated to Hermod who was operating the steerboard at the back of the ship and he adjusted the course.

"We have sighted our enemy!" declared Ragnar.

"We have signs for Outer Hebrides!" Bjorn reported.

"Hey, we're in Scotland already!"

A cheer went up, and Hilde shook her head. Perhaps she should move Bjorn.

She made her way towards the mast and gestured for

Torsten and Yngve to step up and help raise the sail. She hoped she had the measurements right. With a square sailed ship, she'd read, if the sail was too wide or too narrow it would be near impossible to sail.

"Bring me up to date with what tha mission is, renegade priest," Gunnolf said to the Saxon detective behind Hilde.

"You know I'm not actually a renegade priest," said Camara, puffing with exertion. "I'm not a priest at all, I'm a policeman."

"Yes, I know that. But I've got to add this extra plot line into t' saga, so I best have a bit of an idea what's going on, don't tha reckon?"

"The current hypothesis is—" the DC started.

"Hold up. I'm not right sure a saga can have fancy words like hypothesis."

"Fine. The idea we're looking at right now is that a bunch of senior citizens have committed a number of murders."

"Oh aye? People they didn't like?"

"Apparently they blew a woman's head off. So they abducted the witness on a boat and that's where we're going."

"Oh aye? Exploding heads I can work with. Did anything else explode?" Gunnolf looked hopeful.

Camara sighed and shook his head as he rowed. "No, not yet. It's early days though, right?"

"Yeah!" said Gunnolf, oblivious to sarcasm.

SAM WORKED her wrists back and forth on the deckchair to see whether it would loosen, but so far it wasn't budging. Her captors weren't paying her a great deal of attention. Margaret and Jacob were up at the controls, apparently in discussion over the weather, or the course. Strawb and Polly, the runaway lovers, were below deck and seemed to be in no hurry to re-emerge.

Sam flexed her wrists and was heartened by the small amount of movement she'd created. A few more minutes and she might have some space. Although there was no sign the tape would tear or stretch, it was simply bunching up.

A movement in the distance caught her eye. She strained to sit as upright as she could to see better. It was a boat. Its hull was a barely visible smudge against the sea, but it had raised a dark red sail and it stood out against the muted palette of landscape like a drop of blood on a tissue.

It appeared to be coming towards them on an interception course.

"Hey, what's that?" Strawb had appeared on the stairs, fastening a coat as he came. Margaret came down to look with him. Sam sat still and tried not to remind them she existed.

"Well it's definitely a boat, but it's a funny-looking one," said Polly, taking Strawb's arm.

With the four of them looking over the rear rail, Sam used the opportunity to wrestle more forcefully against her hand restraints. She managed to get the tape scrunched up into a single loose bracelet on each arm. Sadly, it was still fastened to the chair beneath her, so she wasn't free yet.

"It's the fackin' Vikings!" said Strawb.

"Pardon?" said Margaret.

"Ragnar and his kin. It's gotta be a wind-up!"

"Well, I'm not laughing," said Jacob.

"It is what it is," said Margaret. "Do we think this boat is coming after us?"

Sam was unable to read their expressions, but their body language was clear. None of them wanted to be the one to say yes, the peculiar wooden Viking ship was coming after them.

It was Polly who spoke first. "Whether it's following us or not. It's powered with a sail and oars. If it doesn't have an engine then surely we can easily outrun it?"

She was right. If this was any sort of rescue mission, then it was a rescue mission without an internal combustion engine.

Sam wondered if she folded the chair she was strapped to, she could move about. She inched her bum forward in the seat, her wrists still fastened to the arms. She needed to tip her weight onto her feet, so she could stand up. She managed it, with only the smallest of grunts, although it didn't feel like an improvement in her current situation. She was standing in a painful crouch, with the edge of the seat digging into the backs of her legs, and her arms pinned uselessly at her sides, straining at tape bracelets which showed no sign of giving way. She thought carefully about her next move. What she couldn't afford to do was fall into the usual trap of not remembering exactly which way to fold a deckchair. She peered behind (which was easier than usual, given her position) and saw this was the kind of chair where the back and the seat came together and the legs took care of themselves. She could use her legs to push the edge of the seat, but what about the back?

She crabbed across the tiny deck, praying the others would not turn around. The boat pitched and rocked in the increasingly choppy waters. They couldn't have been more than a few miles out and the waves were slapping the boat about. At least the sounds of the wind and the swell managed to mask the noises she made. She felt the back of the deckchair hit the cabin wall and she wriggled into position, pushing her legs back against the seat and hoping her bottom wouldn't prevent the seat from closing. It took more wriggling, but luckily the slack she'd created around her wrists meant she could shuffle things into place. The chair snapped shut with a light thunk.

87

Aboard the *Sandraker*, Hilde could see that the life of a seafaring Viking was working out better for some than for others. Astrid walked between the benches, passing goblets of water wherever she detected a queasy face. Several of Hilde's cousins had a greenish shine to their complexion. They kept glancing around at each other, determined not to be the first to complain or to vomit. The music blaring from the speakers wasn't helping. It was highly likely everyone on board already had a headache, if not permanent hearing loss. The Meat-Heads tracks had come to an end and it seemed the source of the music had gone onto a shuffle setting. They approached the enemy vessel with the terrifying sound of *Chariots of Fire* by Vangelis.

Hilde didn't have time to attend to the music, but she was delighted with the ship's performance and seaworthiness. They had made astonishing progress across the sea, closing the distance between themselves and their target. She approached the Saxon policeman. He was not suffering as badly from seasickness as some of the others, but he swayed slightly as the ship raced across the waves.

"What's your plan when we reach the boat?" she asked.

He looked up. "Are we actually closing in on it?"

Hilde nodded. "Should be there in a few minutes."

The Saxon looked around him. "It's a remarkable vessel."

"Aye. My design."

He nodded, impressed. "I don't have a plan. We have reason to believe the people on that boat intend to harm Sam, but if we show them they have no chance of escape, then they won't want to compound their crimes. Possibly."

"Right. Then tha'd best come and have a look then. We're almost there."

Camara and Hilde moved up through the rows of Odinsons. Sea spray splashed them with rhythmic regularity. The *Sandraker* was a knife on the sea, cutting through waves as much as riding over them. Camara was clinging to the gunnel rail by the time he reached Ragnar in the prow.

Ragnar stared fiercely ahead. Saltwater shone in his beard and he had a grin on his face like a man reborn. Hilde could not think of a time when she'd seem him look happier.

"I can't believe how quickly we've covered the distance," Camara said to Ragnar.

"Aye. That'll go down in't saga, that will," he said and began to sing. "*We are raiding, we are raiding!*"

In truth it wasn't so much singing as bellowing raspily into the wind, an old man pitting himself, voice and soul, against the elements.

"He does love to sing," Hilde said to Camara, mildly embarrassed.

"I think he might have borrowed the tune from Rod Stewart," said Camara. The Saxon name meant nothing to Hilde.

"*We are raiding, chasing pirates. To be Vikings, to be free!*" Ragnar was definitely enjoying himself.

POLLY FOUND herself utterly absorbed with the weird pirate ship, which was now quite close. She could see someone at the prow of the ship wearing long robes.

"That's gotta be Ragnar there," said Strawb. "And who's that long streak of nothing next to him?"

"Detective Constable Camara," said Margaret.

"Police on a sailing boat?" said Polly. "Incredible. But can they do anything, once we're in international waters?"

"We've got to get three miles out," said Strawb.

"Twelve," said Jacob. "The wind turbines there are about — Hey!" He'd looked back down the boat as he pointed at the line of wind turbines.

Polly looked. Sam stood upright with a folded deckchair suspended from her wrists, like a really inconvenient pair of handcuffs. She'd managed to step through the chair and bring it in front of her without catching it and tipping herself completely over.

"What the fack is she trying to do?" said Strawb, fumbling in his pockets for the pistol he'd put somewhere.

Sam moved quickly. She stumbled up the steps to the tiny cockpit, the chair held high, and smashed it down onto the controls. She smashed again and again. Polly realised if the interfering woman could stall the cruiser, then the sailing boat (and police helicopter and coastguard!) would be upon them before they got anywhere near international waters. Her life on the run with Strawb would be over before it had begun.

Something sparked on the dashboard and the deckchair split apart in Sam's hands. Seeming to think her sabotage job was done, Sam forced herself through the upper side window to reach the front deck.

"I'll get her!" said Strawb and moved along the narrow bit of deck skirting the cabin. Polly watched him gripping the cabin rail against the tossing of the boat in the waves.

"Be careful!" she shouted.

Margaret and Jacob hurried to the controls.

"Leave her!" snapped Margaret. "It's not as if she can go anywhere, is it? What damage do we have? Steering will be challenging but not impossible. Jacob, you'll need to try to mend that display. Without maps—"

"I don't know anything about these things—"

"I know you're a fast learner Jacob. Needs must."

88

"Trouble brewing on t'ship," said Ragnar as they neared.

"Time for the grappling irons," said Hilde.

"Grappling irons?" said Camara.

"I designed a system to fire grappling irons using compressed air. Farsa! The guns!"

Sigurd reached under his seat and brought out something that looked very much like a metal tube bound to a gas cannister.

"Pneumatic-powered grappling irons?" Camara said. "I'm struggling to imagine a use for that sort of set-up that's sensible or even legal."

"Yeah, I can see that," said Hilde.

SAM WORMED her way onto the front deck and stood on the prow of the cruiser. She worked to get the remains of the deckchair off her. It had come apart when she made her attack on the controls, now she was able to rip the remainder away from her sticky tape bracelets. As a bonus, she had an aluminium leg with a jagged end as a weapon. Although in an actual fight it was not going to get her very far.

She could see two figures in the spray-misted cockpit and could hear someone else making a big deal of coming round the side of the cabin. She crept around the opposite side of the cabin, without any real hope of staying hidden from the others. The boat was a very small place, and she had to tread carefully to avoid being pitched into the sea.

She had never been more conscious in her life of how valuable a life jacket could be. Images from the ditched helicopter training video flashed unhelpfully before her. How long could an unprotected person survive in the North Sea? Was it five minutes? Two?

She glanced over at the wooden ship. It was now quite close and she could hear loud music coming from it, some cheesy instrumental song. She risked a brief wave at Camara – not a jaunty 'Hello' wave, more a definite 'I am here, come get me' wave – and hoped he had a good plan. On the face of it, he was a passenger on a weird Viking longship that had to belong to the Odinsons, so perhaps his plan was not all that sound.

Sam risked a peek. Two of the Odinson men were pointing some sort of mounted weapon at them.

"What the—?"

Abruptly, her wrist tape was grabbed and she was dragged along the edge of the boat and back down onto the rear deck. Polly had the tape loop firmly in her hand.

"Now, that's enough of that, gal," said Strawb, coming round with the pistol aimed. "Stay still so's we can keep an eye on you. I liked you. Don't make me change my mind."

Sam was chilled by the use of the past tense.

There was a thumping noise followed by a loud, nearby crack. Something dark and arrow-fast shot directly over the deck at head height and splashed into the sea.

"They're shooting at us!" shouted Polly.

"They can't be!" said Strawb. He was immediately contradicted by another thump-boom.

This time the projectile crashed onto the deck. It was a big metal hook, a grappling iron. Sam watched as it slithered across the deck, jamming in place by the back rail, one of its claw fingers embedded in the fibreglass bodywork.

Strawb laughed. "These lot think they're the pirates of the fackin Caribbean!"

"What's going on?" called Margaret.

"They think they're going to board by shimmying along this bit of rope!" grunted Strawb. "Don't fancy their chances of that!"

Sam wondered whether it was the plan. The steel wire attached to the grappling hook tightened, and the cruiser jerked. Jacob gave a shout of alarm. The Viking ship might be slower, but it was bigger and definitely heavier.

"GOOD SHOT, FARSA!" Hilde shouted.

"A remarkable piece of equipment," said Camara, pointing at the launchers. Sigurd and Torsten put them down carefully and made the spooled wire fast around a metal stanchion.

"Aye, well we needed a way to grab hold of, you know, things," said Hilde.

"Of course." Camara's face told her he could very well imagine what things they might need to grab.

"It's based on the same sort of principle as a paintball gun, made with some bits and pieces I found lying around." Hilde felt the deck shift beneath her feet. It was tilting forward, which loosened the rope. She saw what had caused it: most of the Odinsons were coming forward to see what was happening. "Hey, farfar! They need to sit down!"

Ragnar strode forward, his arms raised and his robes flowing. "Back to your seats! 'Appen we might need to move quickly, so take your places at your oars. In the reading of the saga you will all want to be known as the crew who reacted with the speed of a striking cobra, yes?"

A hand went up. "Are cobras allowed in't sagas? Aren't they from India or summat?"

"We can talk later about what goes in, but I'll have final word," said Ragnar. "If us Odinsons want to be world travellers, then we must embrace the unusual and exotic."

Hilde rolled her eyes. She had once suggested that her farfar might like to try an Indian takeaway and he had railed against the idea as if it undermined his very being.

"We've got them snared. What next?" Camara asked.

"When's your backup coming?" said Hilde.

Camara sucked his teeth. "I can't get a signal on my phone."

"Another ship!" shouted Hermod from the ship's stern,

pointing. He was right. An orange speck was coming towards them from the coast.

"The lifeboat," said Camara.

Not backup as such, thought Hilde, but some actual competent seamen coming to the rescue couldn't be a bad thing.

"We can hold them 'em a while," said Ragnar. "There's nothing they can do about it."

"And we could slide a life jacket and a line down to Sam," said Hilde.

"Ship to ship rescue?" said Ragnar, intrigued rather than doubtful.

Camara wasn't paying attention. He was staring, open-mouthed at the other boat. "Shit! Has he got a gun?"

He tried to push Hilde down below the safety of the gunnel wall, but Hilde wanted to look.

89

S trawb took aim with his pistol and fired at the Odinson ship. He was using his good left hand, his grip was wrong and the pistol recoil nearly knocked him over.

"Bladdy hell, that hurts!"

As the ship rolled, Sam clung to the handle of one of the aft deck locker seats. She was happy to keep low.

The boat engines accelerated as the *Calypso* tried to pull away.

Margaret came onto the deck with a pair of brightly coloured plastic tubes.

"Ooh, you're full of surprises, aren't you, Margaret!" said Strawb.

Margaret ignored him, pointed a tube and twisted. A flare fired out at the sailing ship.

"Ooh!" said Polly, possibly out of some Pavlovian response to fireworks.

The fireball didn't hit the sail or the side, but slid onto the deck. Odinsons scattered.

On the *Sandraker*, most of the novice sailors demonstrated what not to do when a fire starts on deck. The men bunched together, collided with each other and got in the way of anyone who might have tried to extinguish it.

As the pink-red ball skittered on the deck, leaving scorch marks and throwing sparks, Astrid tried to smother it with a cushion and stamped on it.

"Mormor!" shouted Hilde in warning, forcing her way down through the men to get to her.

The flare was too hot and needed no oxygen to burn. There was no smothering, with cushions or anything else. Hilde scooped up a bailing bucket, wet with sea spray, and came at the flare. She inserted herself between Astrid and the flare and, with a fluid action, with more luck than skill, scooped it up. She tossed bucket and flare over the side together.

"You can't stamp it out," she panted to her grandmother.

Astrid, wet grey hair stuck to her face, looked at her scorched cushion. "That has ruined my needlepoint."

Hilde yelled up to Sigurd. "Let's get a life jacket and line over to Sam!"

Torsten grabbed a spare life jacket and looked about for a rope.

"Shields up everyone!" Ragnar bellowed.

There was a brief scramble as everybody retrieved their shields. Ragnar directed them to form a makeshift roof to deflect any more incoming flares. Another one came fizzing over their heads, but it skidded harmlessly off the shields and into the sea. A cheer went up.

"Look at that Polly! They've only gone and put a lid on the whole boat!" declared Strawb. "You gotta admit, this is pure gold."

Polly seemed unimpressed. "I just wish we could get out of here."

"Just you wait girl, we'll be fine."

At the helm, Jacob was over-revving the engine. Was he hoping enough force would rip the hook from their stern? By the cracks in the rear deck wall, it might be possible. The taut wire sang a high note, discernible above the waves and the wind.

"There's more flares in one of the lockers," said Margaret.

Strawb had his back to Sam, while Polly was as fascinated by the exchange of grappling hooks, gunfire and flarefire as any of them.

Sam shoved Polly aside, leaping forward to grab the gun from Strawb's dangling hand. Polly stumbled and slid against the rear rail, crying out, but not before Sam had grabbed the gun from Strawb's weak grip.

Margaret yelled, "No!" Not so much in alarm, but as though to say, "How dare you! On *my* boat!"

Strawb tried to grab the gun back from Sam, but she managed to stumble clear. They were too close for her to point it and threaten him.

Polly sat in an untidy slump in the rear corner of the

deck, groaning and pulling a face as seawater ran across the deck and soaked her clothes.

Margaret flung open under-seat lockers in search of more flares.

Strawb, taller than Sam, tried to reach round and snag the gun from her. He overbalanced and Sam pushed. She was not generally in favour of giving open-palmed shoves to older members of society, but she was in the mood to make exceptions.

Strawb's legs went from under him and he came down hard on his knees. Amid the roaring elements, Sam imagined she heard them crack against the deck like dry branches. Sam sidestepped, trying to stay upright on the pitching deck.

Margaret was rooting through the lockers with wild abandon, the location of the flares forgotten in the chaos. She had lifted up a seat at the very rear, but all that was inside was a mass of shiny fabric and fine rope.

Sam pointed the pistol at Margaret. "Stop it! Stop this now!"

Margaret glared. Her gaze was feral and filled with hate. She flung the seat cover at Sam. Sam had to twist to avoid it smacking her on the head. Emboldened, Margaret grabbed handfuls of the fabric from the locker and hurled that too, but the wind caught it and it spun into the air. As it rose, it unfolded into something really, really big. It whipped in the wind and expanded. Sam realised it was a parascending chute as its cords and harness unreeled from the open seat.

"Oh," said Margaret, automatically trying to haul it back.

Sam didn't see the cords snarl around Margaret's arm – it

was too quick. Margaret shot up into the air, lifted by the strands of the parachute. It continued to sail upwards, trailing cords and a screaming Margaret. A reel in the seat locker unspooled rapidly until the parachute and Margaret were high above the boat.

The line reached its end and went taut with an audible snap. Far above, Margaret's doll figure pirouetted, one arm outstretched, and fell away from the chute and back towards the sea.

HILDE WATCHED THE UNFURLED PARACHUTE.

"Jesus! Someone just went overboard!" said Camara.

Ragnar hollered over to Gunnolf, pointing out the spectacle. "Put that in the saga!"

"A parachute?"

"It'll be like the colourful sacred bird of the gods!"

Gunnolf's face creased in confusion. "So, is that a good thing, or a bad 'un?"

"Reckon we'll find out soon enough," said Ragnar.

THE TWO BOATS were perilously close to each other, which didn't seem wise when the waves kept making them lurch. As the Viking ship went up, the smaller boat went down. The line connecting them snapped up and down, threatening all sorts of damage. As Sam nervously watched the line, she realised something was hanging on it. A life jacket. She saw one of the Odinsons gesturing to it, making a shooing motion at it with his arms. They were sending her a life jacket. Sam waited for the two boats to complete another cycle of the disconcerting up and down. When the cable was higher at the Viking end would the life jacket slide down? She watched carefully, although the movement of the two boats was making her feel giddy. The life jacket moved along the line.

As the wooden ship rose high on a wave, the life jacket slid all the way to the rear of the *Calypso*.

"Grab it!" shouted several voices on the wind.

Sam stuffed the pistol into a crevice between seats and leaned over the edge to grab the life jacket.

Strawb was crawling on hands and knees to where Polly sat.

Sam pulled the life jacket off the taut cable line. There was a rope tied to it. It led back to the Viking ship. Understanding dawned. They wanted her to bail into the water so they could pull her in.

"Fucking terrible idea," she muttered to herself.

She would think of it as a backup plan. A plan B to the brilliant plan A she was about to think up. She pulled on the life jacket and checked the knots tying it to the rope. As the daughter of a stage magician, she'd grown up knowing something about knots. The one part of this insane plan that would not fail was definitely the knot. Backup plan, she reminded herself. Backup plan.

90

H ilde clapped her hands. "She's secure."

"Turbines ahead!" shouted Ragnar.

"Incline ahead!" echoed deaf Uncle Bjorn.

Tethered together or not, the *Sandraker* and cabin cruiser were still heading out to sea as one. They were approaching the wind farm. Up close each windmill was a giant Redwood tree on its own concrete island in the sea. The spinning blades made a bass thrum-thrum-thrum as they turned, a sound more felt than heard. The gap between each individual turbine mast was at least a hundred metres, but it would not do for the battling boats to get snarled together and dashed against a solid base.

"We should cut the tether," Hilde said. "We don't want it taking us with it."

She went to a chest to get her tools.

. . .

POLLY WAS WET AND ACHING, and coming to the conclusion that her sea legs weren't quite as seaworthy as she'd thought. She took Strawb's hand, but he barely had the strength to hold himself on the rocking boat, let alone lift her up from her ungainly slump.

"Think I've done me knees in," he said. He shivered as he spoke.

"Silly man," she said.

At the other corner of the rear deck, Sam Applewhite stood contemplating the dark waves. Polly couldn't picture anyone throwing themselves into that churning freezing void deliberately.

"Hey!" Jacob skidded out of the cockpit. He grabbed Sam by the shoulders and hauled her back. "We need her as leverage," said the neat little man, storm-tossed and not so neat anymore.

Sam tried to twist out of his grip and he threw her down. Polly saw a rope running from Sam's life jacket and over the side. Jacob grabbed the pistol wedged between seats.

"Strawb, get up here and—" He stopped and crouched at the sight of something on the deck: a small grey patch, sodden with sea water.

Jacob peeled away the jigsaw piece and turned it over. "Ravensburger. *Camping and Caravanning.* Part of the sunbather's leg. I've been looking for this for weeks." He blinked through rain-dotted glasses. "Strawb...?"

Strawb patted a pocket and gave a weak laugh. "It's all just a bit of joke, Jakey boy."

The pistol twitched in Jacob's hand.

. . .

HILDE WORKED at the grappling iron cable with her cutting pliers but it was thick, and the pliers were slick with rain and hard to grasp. The *Sandraker* groaned as the cabin cruiser pulled against it. Offshore rains and the motorboat's powering engine were edging them onward. The wire had already gouged a shallow furrow in the side of the longship as the tug of war between the vessels dragged it back and forth.

"I can't..." she said.

"Here," said Ragnar, hefting his raiding axe.

"Aye," she said, grabbing it. "Stand clear. The tension in the wire..."

SAM SAW the axe raised on the Odinson boat and immediately thought of the line between them. It would be a very bad idea to be near to the recoil. She flung herself flat against the deck.

There was a sharp crack and a singing, whistling sound as a heavy cable, under hundreds of pounds of pressure, snapped back. It was followed by a different noise: a soft oof followed by a fleshy thump. She looked up. Jacob's arm had fallen to the deck. A second later he followed it. His head and shoulder went one way, the rest of his body the other.

Sam yelled in horror, pushing up her arms to get away from him.

The *Calypso* was accelerating forward now, freed from the dragging Odinson ship. They were passing between two turbine towers, close to one but far enough to avoid striking it. Sam glanced up.

Strawb was moving towards the dropped pistol. Sam lunged forward and got there first. She slipped on the deck but kept hold of the gun and maintained her distance.

"Don't do anything stupid, gal," said Strawb.

Sam laughed involuntarily. "Stupid? Me?" She looked at Polly. "Whatever your reasons. This couldn't be worth it."

POLLY PUSHED herself to her feet against the deck seat.

"Don't patronise us," she said. "You have no idea."

"No," Sam agreed.

Sam glanced up once more. Without hesitation she ran for the rear of the boat. She didn't even launch herself properly off the side. She half slithered, half jumped into the icy water.

Polly gripped the rear rail and watched where she'd gone. Grunting, Strawb came beside her.

Sam's orange life vest was momentarily visible between sea swells. The parascending chute flapped high above them. Polly looked up. She saw the chute. She saw the huge sweeping blades of the wind turbine.

She found Strawb's hand with hers.

AS HILDE WATCHED from the prow of the *Sandraker*, the cabin cruiser reached the wind turbine. The blades swept round, looping into the cords of the parachute. The blades continued to turn. The effect on the boat was immediate and catastrophic. The line tightened. Before the rope snapped under the pressure, the motorboat had been lifted tail first from the water. The rear of the hull cracked, the aft deck coming away. The vessel flew apart in brittle chunks. The forward section nose-dived into a wave and flipped end over.

"Heave!" yelled Camara to the crew on the rope. "And heave!"

BEING in the North Sea was much, much worse than Sam had imagined. The coldness was so extreme that it was a solid pain, crushing her body and her head. She was incapable of doing anything but pant-gasping, which was massively unhelpful as water filled her mouth. The crushing sensation changed slightly, and she realised she had been pulled out of the water, although she didn't feel any warmer. The rope dug into her ribs and dragged at her chest. With arms she wasn't sure she could control, she reached up to grab the rope that was now above her. Moments later she was hauled over the side of the Viking ship. Strong arms wrapped a woollen blanket around her.

She tried to say thank you, but her mouth and her tongue and her lungs were not listening to instructions for the time being.

She was sandwiched between DC Camara and an Odinson. Ragnar's wife, Astrid, pressed a thermos mug into her hand and helped guide it to Sam lips.

"It's tea," said Astrid. "Tea makes everything better."

There was the buzz of engines. An orange RNLI lifeboat was speeding towards them. In the sky above, distant but approaching, was a yellow rescue helicopter.

Sam looked at the sea for signs of anyone still in the

water.

91

Eventually – though she resisted, just wanting to stay in the wet but warming blanket that had been put round her – Sam was coaxed out of the life jacket, some of her wet clothes, and given a jacket and more dry blankets.

The Odinsons rowed back to shore with less enthusiasm than they'd rowed out.

"But what about Cleethorpes?" said Gunnolf. "The saga?"

"We rescued a maiden from pirates," Ragnar replied. "That's enough for one day. Today pirates, tomorrow Cleethorpes."

"And then the world!" shouted an Odinson.

Once he had a phone signal, Camara was making a call. It appeared to be fifty percent terse instructions and fifty percent carefully worded apology. When he had finished, Sam was finally able to ask him.

"Why did you bring out a Viking ship to rescue me?"

"It really seemed like a good idea at the time. There is a small chance I might not be fired."

The rowers grounded the ship on the beach, then leapt into the shallows to drag it ashore. Sam was only permitted to disembark once they were firmly on the sand.

A small but significant crowd had formed. Odinson children cheered and demanded ice creams. Odinson men went to show their wives their war wounds (mostly consisting of rope burns and splinters from rowing). Local residents came and took photos, or just stood and tutted and disapproved of the general goings-on. Ragnar, with Hilde held in the tightest embrace, stood once more in the prow of his boat, soaked up all of the attention and called for his mead horn.

Sam had to push through the crowd until she found Rich, who she knew would be waiting. Her dad was beside him. Delia too.

Marvin enfolded Sam in a shockingly earnest hug. "I thought I'd lost you."

"I was just out there. In safe hands."

"He asked me to rescue him from Otterside," said Delia.

"They were arresting old folks left, right and centre," said Marvin. "Thought I'd better get out of there sharpish."

"One of the arrested a turkey killer by any chance?" asked Delia with a hopeful lilt.

Sam nodded. "And how was your meat-free Christmas dinner?"

"Beetroot and lentil bake with sweet potato parcels did not go down well with my uncultured kin. I hear your Christmas was less than stellar, too. And to think there were moments over Christmas when I was quite envious of you. I pictured you shimmying about in your fancy clothes, eating your fancy butlerised meals and being treated like royalty."

"I think you'll find that the word is 'buttled'," said Rich.

"Not butlerified?" said Marvin.

"So, I've promised to take the family out to a restaurant for a proper Christmas dinner," said Delia. "We can squeeze in a few more chairs. Fancy being treated to a mammoth Christmas lunch?"

"Mammoth," said Marvin and hummed.

As they moved up the beach, an Odinson stood beside Ragnar on the platform that was the *Sandraker* and began to loudly recount the saga of the day.

At Rich's car, Sam carefully peeled off a blanket or two. She stretched and hissed as the aches in her battered body awoke.

"I might need a change of clothes before we go eat." She winced at a fresh pain. "And a bit of TLC."

"Your nose," said Marvin, reaching out to touch yet not touch her bloody nose.

"You should see the other guy," she said automatically, and nearly burst into tears.

She composed her emotions. There would be tears later. Right now there was going to be drink and food and loved ones. And then some more drinks. Tears could wait.

AFTERWORD

Many thanks for reading book two in the Sam Applewhite series. You can find the link to book three in the coming pages.

We're grateful to all of the readers who continue to support our work and help us to keep writing.

If you can find the time to share your thoughts in a review, it not only helps us, but it helps other readers too.

We're very busy writing new books, so if you want to keep up to date with our work, you could subscribe to our newsletter. Sign up at www.pigeonparkpress.com

Heide and Iain

ABOUT THE AUTHORS

Heide Goody and Iain Grant have written more than twenty novels together. They both live in the UK. Iain lives in Birmingham with his wife and family. Heide lives in North Warwickshire with her husband and family.

Clovenhoof

Getting fired can ruin a day...

...especially when you were the Prince of Hell.

Will Satan survive in English suburbia?

Corporate life can be a soul draining experience, especially when the industry is Hell, and you're Lucifer. It isn't all torture and brimstone, though, for the Prince of Darkness, he's got an unhappy Board of Directors.

The numbers look bad.

They want him out.

Then came the corporate coup.

Banished to mortal earth as Jeremy Clovenhoof, Lucifer is going through a mid-immortality crisis of biblical proportion. Maybe if he just tries to blend in, it won't be so bad.

He's wrong.

If it isn't the murder, cannibalism, and armed robbery of everyday life in Birmingham, it's the fact that his heavy metal band isn't getting the respect it deserves, that's dampening his mood.

And the archangel Michael constantly snooping on him, doesn't help.

If you enjoy clever writing, then you'll adore this satirical tour de force, because a good laugh can make you have sympathy for the devil.

Get it now.

Clovenhoof

Oddjobs

Unstoppable horrors from beyond are poised to invade and literally create Hell on Earth.

It's the end of the world as we know it, but someone still needs to do the paperwork.

Morag Murray works for the secret government organisation responsible for making sure the apocalypse goes as smoothly and as quietly as possible.

Trouble is, Morag's got a temper problem and, after angering the wrong alien god, she's been sent to another city where she won't cause so much trouble.

But Morag's got her work cut out for her. She has to deal with a man-eating starfish, solve a supernatural murder and, if she's got time, prevent her own inevitable death.

If you like The Laundry Files, The Chronicles of St Mary's or Men in Black, you'll love the Oddjobs series.

"If Jodi Taylor wrote a Laundry Files novel set it in Birmingham... A hilarious dose of bleak existential despair. With added tentacles! And bureaucracy!" – Charles Stross, author of The Laundry Files series.

Oddjobs

Printed in Great Britain
by Amazon

75963286R00326